Schadenfreude

Published in the United States of America by
Blue Murder Projekt Publishing
thebluemurderprojekt19@outlook.com

Cover design: 19

Schadenfreude

by

19

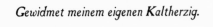

Gewidmet meinem eigenen Kaltherzig.

Kindheit

Twice in his life, Erich saw his father cry.

The first time was when he was six.

His father was sitting at the kitchen table with the radio on. There was a great deal of drums-and-trumpets fanfare, the crowd roaring like a lion. The announcer was very excited, saying *Hitler* and *chancellor* and *German people* as if someone had won something.

His father had tears flowing down his face. His eyes were closed. He shook as if he felt cold. His mother kept saying *hush, somebody might hear.*

Jungenvolk. They sang. They did organized clumsy exercises. There were other children his own age, some of whom even did him the courtesy of playing with him.

Sometimes they stood fidgeting while a counselor or a visiting Hitler Youth boy talked to them about the Fatherland. The speech was just something you had to wait through, before you could eat or have races or swim.

Once they went camping.

An older boy pulled him close in the dark and kissed him on the lips. It had made his skin feel busy, his tongue feel funny. His heart pounded for a long time afterward, like he'd been running. He was eight. All he understood, of any of it, of was that it was fun.

He never told anyone about the kiss.

At first he was enough like the other boys to escape much notice.

He was the smallest, and never got to be the general or the head of the pack of outlaws. He was always the prisoner wound with skipping-ropes, the Indian taken captive with wooden guns and tin swords. They found it useful that he didn't mind spending most of the game being pushed into imaginary jail cells.

He found himself thinking of those prisoner games, later, while their rumors grew louder. He remembered the strange hypnotic stillness of it, the internal quiet it gave him to imagine so loudly that he was doomed and unable to do anything to save himself.

He never told anyone this, either. It was secret, he was sure of it.

He could not take his eyes off other boys' hands. This got him in trouble in school, since it was indistinguishable from looking at the boy's paper. His sterling record bought him off with a "Mind your own assignments, then!" that left him crimson for the rest of the class.

More of that prisoner game.

He lay awake thinking of the new men in black you saw on the street sometimes, the ones who seemed to travel in a cloud of winter, wearing all the faces behind desks that had ever meant you harm. The danger of change, and usually for the worse.

He collected the rumors, of Gestapo and the more sinister prison camps, to add to this loop of thoughts in the dark.

He didn't believe them, of course.

They'd never actually *do* those things.

But there was something irresistible about it.

He loved the blazing flash and fanfare of the largest rallies and Party events in the center of Berlin. The first time Erich been small enough to sit on his father's shoulders. Music, and thousands of feet shaking the earth in perfect time, so far away, an entire army gleaming in red and black and brown, flawless. It went on and on past them, so loud that it seemed there was silence, a seamless blur of shoulder-boards and gleaming guns, the claustrophobic terror of an unstoppable army of Persons in Authority.

That was delightful the way anything boisterous and proud was, just the sheer exuberance of it all. He was proud too. It seemed a brave and dangerous thing to be a German, instead of a vaguely shameful thing as it had been since The War.

The camps were different.

Sometimes there were trucks, and sometimes there was commotion at night. And sometimes there were murmurs on the street between people who would not look at one another, about people who went to the camps and did not write, and did not return.

People like Erich didn't have to worry about the camps. He had a good family, he'd done well in school. He'd never been in any kind of trouble to speak of. He had no political loyalty except a warm and general one towards the Reich. The labor camps were for the antisocial, for political criminals, for dope fiends and revolutionaries, anarchists and communists. Undesirables. The Reich was wise and strong, and rather than leave enemies to take root, or waste their time and talent in unproductive prisons, they had chosen the best solution for the Fatherland.

That was all it was. A solution to a problem that had nothing to do with him. It was nothing to worry about, nothing to lose sleep over, as his mother would say, but lose sleep he did. Night after night.

He thought of the camps the way he'd thought obsessively of the Inquisition. A brief taste of that chapter of history had led him to the library, and his curiosity had turned against him two books later. He'd had nightmares of the Iron Maiden closing around him, the rack rending him into pieces--but even worse than the dreams were the bewildering erections that followed.

Now he shuddered over what the new dungeons must be like. There were no books to make him sorry he'd wondered. He was left to the mercy of imagination and rumor.

Die Erbsünde

Erich graduated from school with all sorts of irritating honors. He endured a party or three, received books and a billfold and money and clothes that didn't suit him. He was grateful to escape the gymnasium. School had begun with games that he was terrible at and ended with classes that were much too easy filled with other boys that hated him. Hiding in the library gave him plenty of time to study, and he spent the rest of it immersed in books, so many that his teachers noticed, and special credits in German and literature were noted on his record.

His father arranged for him to apprentice in a print shop. He suggested first a newspaper, but Erich was wide-eyed and apprehensive about one day being expected to *write* something others would read. He was at his best when his task required an eye for symmetry and exactitude. Questions that had more than one right answer drove him mad. Creativity was dangerous—he needed rules, so that he might know how to escape notice.

The print shop suggestion was given to him to ponder for a night or two, and he felt as comfortable with this idea as he supposed he would with any.

His mother made disapproving faces. She wanted him to be a tailor and carry on the family business. Dinner became less edible for a while, and his mother was still and uncommunicative in a way that would have gotten Erich accused of sulking.

He slept for one fitful hour the night before his first day. He would do everything wrong and his mother would make him work in his father's boutique. He would spend eight hours sweeping, at the mercy of boys like the ones he'd escaped for these few short holiday weeks. A dozen other tiny fears.

To his delight he found that everyone seemed to use the manners

4

his mother had drilled into him, and that once he demonstrated he could carry out a task he was left alone. Nobody shouted at him. He ate lunch by himself with a book spread open across his knees, absolutely luxuriating in the peace and quiet.

So Erich spent his days learning to set type, running errands, coming home with ink ground into his hands.

There was a boy in the print shop who watched him with something like hunger. There had been no boys like that since that hazy distant kiss in the dark.

He couldn't help it. His traitor eyes wandered all by themselves, leaving his hands to fumble with letters, to stumble into inkpots, to hold a broom still with dust settling around him.

He memorized this russet tangle of hair, and the most wonderful hands he had ever stolen in long hungry stares—hands wider than his own, with long narrow fingers clever enough to set type so small it confounded the other workers. After a while Erich could recognize the black whorls of fingerprints the boy left on tabletops.

He thought of him far too often.

His father brought home armloads of black and silver, and made SS uniforms far into the night, drinking coffee, his eyes rimmed in red, glasses gleaming. His father wore a swastika-pin edged in gold on his lapel, and when he put his overcoat on he took it off and put it that lapel, instead, so it was still visible.

The money was very good for the first time since the war. They bought a second radio, and a phonograph player.

Erich shook out the tunic of one of these uniforms, almost finished, bristling with pins at the collar. He held it in up to himself in the mirror, drawn by the stark lines, the dangerous glitter. He put it on, with careful gestures of his shoulders, straightened an imaginary tie. The arms hung a foot past his hands.

His mother screamed when she found him. She swung at him with the dust-rag she was holding, shouting *get it off!*

He flailed at himself in confusion, as if he were on fire. When he realized it was the uniform she meant he bent his arms back and let it drop to the floor. A pin dragged along the underneath of his jaw.

She went to her knees, picking up the jacket, hands searching it for wounds.

She didn't speak to him for hours. It made him sick and sad. He wasn't sure what he'd done so wrong.

The boy was the print shop owner's nephew. Emil.

Learning his name had made it worse; before, he had been *the boy, that boy*, hardly a noun at all, a vague subject that preoccupied him when he was walking home, a shape and a set of scents that kept him awake at night.

Emil and Erich often stayed late at the shop, after the fat squinting Muench and the counter-girl had left. Orders got quite far ahead of what they could produce during business hours. So he and Emil stood for an hour or three, alone, printing poster after poster with a soldier in the bucket-style helmet, a Teutonic warrior in medieval halberd ghosted behind him. The money here, too, was good.

Erich was clipping these prints up to dry when Emil's hands closed over his. The boy turned him around and kissed him. This was longer than that kiss in the dark, a strange hot melting, like their mouths were wounds that wanted to heal together. It still made his skin feel busy. He could not tell their tongues apart anymore, to know if his felt funny or not.

He let it go on for much too long. A tiny noise happened in his throat. He heard his mother saying *hush, somebody might hear.*

He ducked his head away, slid sideways with his back against the edge of the table. "I'm not like that."

He knew it was a lie, and that he was exactly like that.

He thought of adding *I'm sorry.* His eyes fell on another poster, a thick round blonde-and-blue German woman, crowded close on every side with thick round blonde-and-blue German children. An apple-cheeked baby was cradled to her heavy breast.

Emil stepped back, heels clicking angry on the floor. His eyes narrowed. He said nothing at all.

The next day at work they didn't look at each other.

In public people talked of nothing. The weather.

Everyone was so very, very careful.

Everywhere there were constant whispers about the Police.

The arrests went from distant-city rumor to wide-eyed cautionary tales over tea. His mother's bridge group spoke of nothing else. A nephew arrested, staggering home two days later bankrupt and bruised. The first stories that started with *you know I heard the Jews...*and the nods, and nobody daring to disagree.

Erich listened to these ghost stories, standing out of sight in the kitchen. He was searching for himself, he knew, in these lists of people the Police were hauling away.

He knew a few Jews, shopkeepers and the jeweler his mother preferred to visit, but none very well. His teachers had never much gotten beyond explaining them as the enemy. They had a funny way of dressing themselves, but so did Arabs and Chinese. They didn't look particularly dirty, and Mr. Kleinfeld at the jeweler's was always making his mother smile. He had the same general impression of Jews he did of Bolsheviks and Communists—that there was something bad about them, though he could never understand what.

What scared him the most was, "And of course, you know, People Like That," followed by just that silence that meant the women were nodding.

People like that. People like him.

It was such a disgusting thing to have wrong with you there wasn't even a polite word for it, he supposed.

"It's nothing to worry us," someone would remind them all, after too much of this gloom. "We're nothing like that."

Das A und O

The knock on the door was what he had always expected, thudding through the house and springing his eyes open. The dreams started that way. He'd had plenty of practice. He stood up weak as water and started getting dressed.

Downstairs, his father opened the door with pins in his mouth, one arm draped with black and silver.

There was none of the wanton destruction he had expected. It was all quite civil. The police sat at the dining room table, graygreen and gleaming, all creases and polish. One of them smoked a cigarette, tapping ashes into an ashtray. They stared at everything, the furniture, the paintings on the walls, his mother's curio cabinet with the little carved clocks.

Papers were produced and signed. His mother stood stunned in her bathrobe staring into the middle distance. Once she offered coffee to no one in particular. Nobody answered her.

His father managed to be coherent and correct, though he couldn't speak in anything near as loud as even his normal mumble. The policeman with the clipboard had to lean inches from his mouth to hear him. He kept pushing up his glasses, even when they didn't need it.

Erich stood dressed, his coat on but unbuttoned, heart slamming so hard it was like the rest of the sound in the room was, underwater.

He both wanted to cry and wanted not to cry, with a desperate debilitating want. He wanted to look at himself in the mirror, and didn't dare. He wanted *not* to go with these men, and his knees threatened to fold at the thought that he would have to.

It was a very long time before anyone seemed to notice him.

They flanked him through the front door, and his mother made some kind of a sound behind them, and that was all. They cuffed his hands behind his back, with no particular animosity, and escorted him to a black car. One of them sat in the back seat beside him. The other started the car, and backed out onto the street. One glimpse through the windowpane, and his father, standing on the front steps.

That was the last time Erich ever saw him cry.

On the ground floor it was still a police station, and not the dungeon he had expected. There were rows of desks and typewriters, offices behind clear glass and offices behind blinds. It felt very important and very busy. There was a slaughterhouse sense of organized panic. Erich sat on a long bench in a hallway with his hands still cuffed, being ignored. People walked back and forth carrying tea and coffee and paperwork and guns and uniform caps, some of them laughing, some furious.

A different policeman collected him and made him sit in front of one of a dozen desks in a long busy room. The policeman stood just behind him, just by his left shoulder, half-shouting questions that had become so by rote they were almost incomprehensible. A woman typed his answers without ever raising her eyes from the keyboard.

He gave his name, address, and place of employment, his parents' names and occupations. He was photographed. He shook continually, so terrified it was like the entire world had been moved ten feet farther from him, divided from him by a blinding sheet of white panic.

You were supposed to hear about Them having the boy who used to work in the bakery, or your friend who moved the summer before, or a basement full of Bolshevik state-traitors. Not you.

They were never supposed to have *you*.

He wondered if anything his parents could do would do any good. He wondered if they would even try. He wondered if the same thing that kept his father's swastika pin visible had merely sent them back to bed.

None of it was anything like he had imagined. That seemed unfair, that he'd been forced to spend so many hours, fearing this, and all that preparation was useless now.

He kept listening for screams. He heard only typewriters, voices at polite office levels most of the time. Doors opening and closing. His attention kept wandering to what he was guilty of, and the panic kept dragging him away from it. He really only had one sin, one crime, one secret in all his life, and surely they couldn't know *that?*

They brought him down a set of stairs. He was thumped to a halt in a less official hallway, with bricks instead of plaster and one side lined in bars.

It was much darker down here.

There were two cells. The first was empty. The second had four men already in it. The guard opened that door, uncuffed Erich's hands, and let him step inside.

The door shut behind him, locked with a clank that made him think of castles and dungeons.

One man still had on a tie, but only an undershirt beneath it and no coat. One had on pajamas, with a suitcoat buttoned crooked over it. Two were quietly talking, sitting with their backs to the bars.

None of them seemed particularly, dangerous. Thank God for that.

He sat down in the least-occupied section of a long wooden bench, wrapped his arms around his legs, thought of nothing.

The man in the tie was squinting at him. "Good evening."

Erich dutifully said, "Good evening, sir," and sat still staring, out through the bars. He would be polite, to everyone, he would do whatever he was told, he would pray, and he might just be all right. That was the plan, so far. He hadn't known it was possible to be this terrified. He thought his teeth might chatter with it.

"I think I know, you, yes...you're that tailor's boy. I'm Schiffer, I taught third year at your school, but I never had you. Had your cousin, I think..."

Schiffer sat down beside Erich. He had kind eyes, the patient slow

11

voice of a grandfather.

A schoolteacher. Here in, jail.

"Yes sir." Erich scrubbed at his face with his hand. He remembered Herr Schiffer after a bit of trying, with less gray in his hair, guiding a hopping mess of children through the school hallways.

"You'll be all right. It's not as if we were the enemy."

He didn't say *yes sir* again. He didn't think he was capable of it.

"I'm sure there will be a judge, and this will all be cleared up. Maybe we'll pay a fine, or—"

Then there was a scream from very far down the corridor, beyond invisible doors.

It climbed in frantic volume, fractured. Stopped.

Now there was only a sound Erich thought was marching boots, until he realized it was his pulse beating in his eardrums. The scream started again, less structured, as though something essential had broken already.

It went on for a very long time.

It stopped a little while before the guards came to take him.

Schiffer watched him with wet brown eyes, made a gesture with his hand, one fist tightening just a little. Maybe to wish him luck, maybe relief that it was Erich's turn to go and not his own.

They ushered him in same direction as the screaming.

They brought him into a far less modern office this time. A heavy wooden desk with a policeman sitting behind it. A second guard stood behind him, just to his left, out of his sight.

Erich sat where he was put, in a straight-backed wooden chair, hands cuffed in front of him through one of the arms. There was no typewriter here. The man in front of him read through a folder and made notes with a fountain pen on a thick pad of forms. Scratch-of-pen and two men and one boy breathing. Bootheels, passing outside. Silence.

The officer was a half-stone too thick in his stiff-pressed uniform, and he daubed at his mouth now and then, as if he wished for a drink or a cigarette. He never looked up, paging through documents with precise manicured fingers. His voice was heavy and nasal, very aristocratic to Erich's ears.

"You've been reported as a homosexual. What we will do, here, today, is take down a record of your testimony before any decisions are made. Now." He set down the papers with a tap and folded his hands on top of them. It was more like a closing than a beginning.

Erich could feel his eyes, but he didn't look above the height of the fountain pen. "I...didn't..."

A cough, or maybe a laugh. "Well, you must have done, else you wouldn't be here, mmm?"

"But I didn't *do* anything—"

The guard behind him wandered closer.

The officer sighed and chose one particular piece of paper. "You've been seen in certain...establishments."

Erich blinked, in disbelief, thinking somewhere, *there are whole establishments?*

"Your guilt is not the question—you *are* guilty, or you would be home in bed. The question is your willingness to reform, and your loyalty to the Fatherland."

He could hardly hear this man, now, after the very first sentence his heartbeat had become a parade of bootheels again. "I can't have been seen anywhere like that, I've never *been* to anywhere, like, that."

"No?" A flick at the paper he was holding. "Certainly you must have been somewhere. We have very reliable reports. Are we to believe solid German citizens—" a rattle of paper at him—"or a homosexual? You're all notorious liars."

He felt terrifyingly close to tears, hot and sick. No one had ever called him a liar before. "There must be a mistake—"

Both policemen laughed at that immediately.

Tears were collecting along his lower eyelids whether he wanted them there or not.

"Oh, of course. Every man in Dachau is there by mistake, just ask him," said the man behind him.

Dachau. That crow's call of a word made the tears overflow.

The officer dropped his papers again. "You keep denying having been anywhere, but you don't deny that you are a homosexual?"

"I've never really *done* anything—"

There must have been a signal, but Erich never saw it.

The man behind him shoved his head down, and something heavy slammed into his back, unbelievably hard, emptying him of breath and thought. The pain seemed to come in a reversing wave, the blow pushing him forward and the spreading anguish pulling him back. He thought, *my back will be broken*, and his lungs remembered how to expand and he drew in a great whooping breath. He was still mostly folded over. He didn't want to try to sit up, for fear of finding he couldn't move.

"I didn't ask you what you've done. I asked you what you are."

He didn't realize he was supposed to answer. Another blow, straight across his kidneys, a third in exactly the same place. He screamed until his lungs were empty. When he caught his breath again he was sobbing. He moved to cover his face and his hands only dragged at the cuffs. It was worse than the beating. He was almost a grown man and these men could see him crying like a—

"Are you?"

"Yes!" he cried out at them, to make them stop, to keep them from hammering at him with that word again. To save himself any more of those terrible blows.

The guard stepped in front of Erich to show him the rubber nightstick. A shiny black thing, an unspeakable thing. But he put it away at his belt, and gripped Erich by shoulder and hair and set him upright again. The officer was writing something with neat precise little motions. "There, see, if you'll be reasonable it won't be so hard."

"Yes sir," he said out of reflex, sounding like a child in his own ears. He sniffled, seized with the urge to plead with these men to uncuff his hands. He would have begged on his knees for a handkerchief if he'd

14

thought either of them would give him one without hitting him again. It was all out of proportion, intolerable, unimaginable, that he couldn't just *wipe* his damned eyes. He tried to turn his face into his shoulder, but he could only smudge at his cheek and his jaw. The attempt made a deep redviolet anguish bloom in his back, and he stopped trying.

"Well. You understand that this is very serious. It may not seem so to..." He glanced at one of his files. "To a boy your age, but the State is responsible for the State. A man's duty is to marry a German wife and have many German children. A man who is so disordered he won't do that is worse than useless to us—you're a drain on society, passing on nothing, and you're dangerous, because you can spread this disease to others."

Still this sense of falling, of dreaming. "I *know* what you're supposed to do, I was *going* to do all of that, I..."

He trailed off, weeping, waiting for the blow.

Was it true? Had he been going to marry and have children and work in an office and buy a house, all of that you were supposed to do?

The officer said "Yes!" and nodded as if this outburst had pleased him. "Now, that's the right kind of thinking. You see, you're not even really a young man, yet. If you say you haven't been involved in this, activity..."

"No, sir..." He hadn't, really, surely they didn't mean two kisses six years apart?

"Well, maybe then there is something we can do, if you want to do the right thing, we can rehabilitate you. Sometimes arrangements can be made. You know you're lucky you were arrested so young. Boys with this disorder are generally hanged without much trouble over it."

It was delivered rather well, as if he were musing to himself. Erich was shocked into a stillness worse than the sobbing. He had never seen anyone hanged. He imagined the ground tilting dizzily under his feet, a crack as loud as the world breaking in half.

The officer left him alone to imagine it for a while. "I think it's safe to say we can avoid that with further, documentation, of your sincerity."

15

"I don't..." He didn't have the energy for *understand.* It didn't matter. He was exhausted. The only wish he had left was that whatever it was they wanted, he could give them, quickly, and go back to his cell where Schiffer was

(familiar)

there to just, be there. He could lie on one of the benches and sleep and sleep.

He knew that they were bargaining over his life. He didn't know what he might possibly have to bargain with. He'd been nodding for the past minute or three, or maybe since he'd been brought into this fear-drenched room. "Just, don't..."

"All right then, good. Now." He tapped the pen against his flawless teeth. "The, others, like yourself?"

A blank pause. "I don't know, any others..."

One slam of the side of his fist, not terribly hard, just a thud against the oak desktop. Frustration. As though Erich's deliberate thick-headedness was stalling his dinner break. "Come on, really, that's what this disease is, isn't it? That's the only symptom. Of course you know others."

"...no, I..."

"Don't you have men that you do these things with?"

They would make him confess it all, his pathetic little everything. "I've only ever been kissed. Twice."

The guard who had beaten him laughed, but he stopped when the officer didn't join him.

"I suppose I shouldn't say it, but I actually believe you. You poor bastard." He did laugh, just a little. He still had the pen, ready. "Names?"

Stricken. Hands, the fingerprints blackened with printer's ink.

"They...were...I was, eight, the first one, I don't remember..."

A sharp look that he felt more than saw. "Not a first name, nothing?"

It was just, insanity, did it *matter* to the police who he had kissed

16

when he was *eight?* "I really don't, sir, we were in the Jungenvolk—" He was thinking, furiously, ashamed of himself, every inch of him waiting to be pushed forward again. He would make up a name for this one, if they pushed him, but the problem, was, those hands, those fingerprints, that ink.

A disgusted sort of cough from the guard.

The officer wrote down something. "The second?"

He waited for something to save him. There was a prickling like nausea under his tongue. "Don't, make..."

A frown, the pen hesitating, those eyes on him again. "The second name?"

Erich could not remember his face, only a voice, explaining how to center text with amusing arrogance, as if he were more than just an apprentice himself. The name that belonged to that voice would send that boy into the back of a car with his parents behind him, probably crying, into a room like this.

"It was my fault, I gave him the wrong, impression..."

"If you're going to be the sort who would withhold information about criminal activities, there's nothing we can do for you."

If I don't give them a name.... A fake name? He fumbled through his thoughts for a story. He had no practice at lying. None at all.

"You'll hang."

"Please—" No good. The crying was hitching through him again. The man took out the baton again, and he screamed even before he was struck.

He lost count.

After a while, it stopped.

The officer dropped something and said, "Take him outside—" and the man with the nightstick took hold of his arm and half-lifted him. Jingle of keys to uncuff him.

That was as brave as he could be, he found.

"Emil," he said. "Emil Muench."

There. No more soul, now he had nothing to bargain with.

17

Abstieg

They brought him back to the cell. Only one man was still there, and he was sure it would not be Schiffer, but it was. He limped to the bench and sat down in a new stiff way, kidneys hot with a dull spreading pain that made him feel too heavy. The only thing that had saved him from serious harm during that last rapid handful of blows was that the guard was almost flailing, without serious accuracy. One shot had gotten him across an elbow, and bending that joint was almost impossible. The rest had thudded into his shoulderblades and back, leaving bruises he was sure would last for weeks.

Schiffer waited until the guard was gone and out of earshot, and came and sat beside him, fumbling at him trying to feel his head for, fever, as if he had no idea what other kind of gesture one might use on someone sick. "They beat you?"

He nodded, finding himself panting, as if he'd been running, and shaking in a new loose uncontrollable way. Aftermath.

"What can you possibly have done?"

He didn't care anymore. "I kissed two boys."

There was a silence, in which the world failed to fall down.

"They beat you like this for kissing two boys?"

He, nodded. Waited for the face he'd always imagined everyone making if they, knew.

Silence, incredulous eyes blinking at him, and then the tobacco-rasp of a laugh. "Well, I'm glad you didn't kiss three boys."

He'd always known they'd find out eventually, no matter how perfect he was, no matter how careful he was to attract no attention. His only hope of keeping his perversion to himself had been that he never be examined closely, in any way. He'd dedicated his heart and soul to looking like that flawless quiet boy that never needed to be questioned.

And he'd failed.

Now there were four people who knew—two policemen, himself, and Schiffer. Probably more, tomorrow morning—secretaries and file clerks.

He wondered if they would tell his parents.

He tried to imagine what they would do, or think, and could not.

Everyone would know, after a month or two of bridge games and whispers.

He could see this fact, spreading from his one single *yes*, in widening ripples. He tried to imagine everyone he knew, everyone he saw, knowing. He managed a sense of endless time battered with stares, of exhaustion and suffocation and claustrophobia.

There was nothing for it, now.

He lay on the bench with his poor back against the cool of the wall and his head on his coat.

Here was the reward he had promised himself, and all he could do was stare through the bars out into the corridor, hurting for all kinds of reasons, thinking, *jail*, and thinking, *Emil*.

Part of him had always wished they would find out, so he could stop the exhausting, debilitating struggle of being that imaginary, perfect boy. So he could stop manufacturing all this goodness to conceal his badness. So he could see what a dungeon might be like. So he would finally know and believe that such places were real.

Now he knew more than he wanted to.

And it was not yet even dawn.

He cried a little, with the collar of his coat folded over his face. If he didn't move, didn't change his breathing, he discovered he could do it soundlessly.

A different guard came and collected him, brought him to the same officer that had watched him beaten the night before. Erich sat in the same chair, already shaking.

"Well, we've done what we can. You're to go to a labor camp." A glance at the files. "You've got several skills listed here, I'm sure something will be found. You'll be out in two years if you behave yourself."

Camp scared him quite a lot, and *two years* sounded endless when he tried to think of the entire span between Christmases, twice.

Still, work didn't sound so very terrible.

He could still sew anything put in front of him, and set type without errors as fast as

(Emil)

anyone at the shop, really.

Emil had been the mistake. All he had to do was make sure he never made another. Maybe it would be all right. He would just do as he'd planned, as he'd always done. Be polite and obedient—and he wouldn't think about how long it was. He would think of it as a trade up from hanging.

The guard uncuffed him. He signed things he wasn't invited to read.

Six days later, the first guard came and took Erich from the cell. He was escorted to a vast rumbling graygreen hulk of a truck. The military bulk of it dried his tongue in his mouth.

Nine other men he didn't know were already inside. The guard shoved him in, and the metal doors boomed closed behind him. Another jail, this one on wheels. He sat, wrapped small around himself. There were no windows.

All of them in the truck sat without speaking. One man was sobbing, cradling his left hand hidden under his coat. He got louder when the truck jolted over bad paving. All but two were a generic blur of working-class faces.

These two, he thought, might be here for the reason he was here. They might have been brothers, but he doubted it. One was lean, with

20

long brown hair and neat mustache. He made Erich think of an American cowboy. The other was thin and pale, unremarkable except for brilliant blue-green eyes. He was younger than the cowboy, by perhaps a decade. He looked, shell-shocked, the way Erich felt.

The two men sat very close together, each with his arms wrapped tight around himself, hands tucked in, as if to keep himself from being tempted to touch the other. Sometimes their shoulders would press together. Erich was sure it was deliberate.

He tried to keep them from feeling his eyes.

A great soft veil of shock was wrapping him tight. On another level, underneath this numb surface, he was always thinking, staring at the floor of the truck, at the pairs of feet that shifted only rarely. Then was a swimming blur of fearful things, a hangman's noose, the medieval clang of the jail's door closing behind him.

He studied his own hands, his fingers winding each other tight, the complexity of joints and nails and tendons. He listened to the crying man, and put his hands in his pockets.

He was jealous of a shoulder to lean into.

Ausgesucht

"Out!"

He had dozed, being rattled and shaken, swaying in fear and exhaustion. He had dozed, and now he was being dragged out into a red sunset in a stumble of tired bodies.

There were great milling, shrieking, arguing hordes of people. There was a smell hanging over everything, and he thought it must be a forest fire, but there was too much of meat and fat in the scent. That orange smell, and the orange sun. Every breath seemed weighted, greasy, just enough like ruined dinner to make him hungry.

He'd heard the same horror-stories as everyone else, about the origin of this smell. He had watched the adults over his head proclaim it beyond belief, but none of them had ever tasted this air.

Erich had an impression of a long, long wall. He thought the camp must be inside this town. Later he would realize the camp was this town.

He was struck now and then, adding new bruises to the set still livid from the Gestapo's beating, putting down fresh layers of darkening color. They were being herded. His eyes watered in pain and a strangely indignant, embarrassed sense of betrayal. He'd been perfectly obedient, and it hadn't mattered. They'd simply hit him anyway.

They were driven into a tiny sad row of ten. The officers had spread out to the left and right, flanking a long lean man whose back was turned. He was half a head taller than, everyone. He wrote something with no particular haste in a black leather notebook and turned, taking a cigarette from his lips.

"All right then," he said. "I am Herr Doktor Obersturmführer Kaltherzig. I expect to be obeyed immediately. I do not repeat myself."

Kaltherzig took a lazy casual pace or two in either direction, studying each one of the prisoners in turn as if he had all the time in the world. He was half-a-head taller than the tallest of them. There was a lot of the bird in him—long, light bones, unspeakable quickness underneath the smallest of gestures. He had fast predator eyes the color of an American gun. His dark hair hung in a razorstraight line along one cheekbone, almost to his jaw. His face was composed of lines so very Imperial Roman the Race Office might've used him in a textbook.

Silence, from all of them, a quiet island in this deafening chaos. Erich could not breathe. He could not swallow. There was only his heartbeat, and this man. He was too hypnotized to realize he should look down. He caught a face full of Kaltherzig's complete attention. There was something like a smile or a threat and then the eyes left him like a knife reversing out of a wound.

The doctor read names and block numbers that meant nothing to any of them. Two groups peeled off, each driven by an officer swinging a short baton. The two
(others)
men Erich had watched on the truck had been separated.

The narrow green-eyed man stared after the cowboy until the man behind him pushed him. He took one crooked step out of line, came to Kaltherzig, pleading in Swedish-colored German, caught at his sleeve, almost kneeling. Kaltherzig turned, one black eyebrow winging upward as though he were going to politely reply to a question. He drew his sidearm and shot the green-eyed man in the head.

The crack drove an involuntary scream from Erich.

There was a thick red spray, wet impacts on the ground. The man's hands came up one spasm, as though he might embrace the man who had shot him, or investigate the ruin that had replaced the back of his skull. His knees were already buckling.

Kaltherzig stepped away from these idiot hands, his lip peeling back in the sketch of a snarl. He holstered his gun, settled his long black coat.

The man fell. He landed on one side. Nothing about him moved again except the crimson triangle, spreading.

The cowboy made an unspeakable noise. He turned after much too long, staring, struggling against the flow of people. The man behind the cowboy tried to push him, hissed something, and then darted around him, wanting none of this. The guard shouted at him. He didn't move. He could only stare at what was left of the green-eyed man, making a silent face that was scream after scream.

Erich saw the gun come up and covered his ears, closed his eyes. The gunshot never came. The cowboy must've started walking again.

Kaltherzig and Erich were alone with the great spreading pandemonium of Selektion getting louder around them.

"Name."

It sounded, too far away. He almost had to lip-read to understand the order.

"Erich Kass, Herr Obersturmführer, sir."

His voice shook on the *sir*. He stared and stared at the muddy ground and could feel his eyes straining to flick back to the gun. His ears and all his teeth rang with the echo and the meaning of that noise cracking the world. His eyes got away from him, and he had to look.

The gun was holstered. This officer in front of him was unmoved. Kaltherzig did something like a smirk, but his eyes didn't change at all. His hands were calm and steady and sure. He wore a single ring, where a man would wear a wedding band, the grinning death's head surrounded by runes. It seemed all tangled with the gun, the same black magic, the same hieroglyph.

Kaltherzig wrote something short and sharp, closed the notebook hard so the leather snapped. "You're with me."

Auschwitz swarmed in around them. There was a clean, clear place if he stayed at Kaltherzig's elbow, and he thought of a shark parting a school of fish and hurried and shook and it could not possibly be real. There was too much of it. He realized they were walking towards the smokestacks. His knees did something and he staggered until Kaltherzig caught the back of his arm, drawing him upright and hauling him along faster.

"The ovens...please..."

"We're not going to the ovens, you idiot. Now move."

He walked. Sniffled. Swiped at his face with his sleeve, grateful to be able to do that much, at least.

A building labeled DESINFEKTION. They walked into a lobby with yards of numbered hooks. Kaltherzig granted him no time at all to examine any of this, moving so quickly in those long implacable strides that Erich nearly had to run to keep up with him. Beyond the hooks he was bundled through a set of doors into a wide expanse of white tile and wet and women, all of them naked. Some of them stared at him, though there were male and female SS herding them, shouting, hitting them to hurry them.

"It's all right, ladies, this is a pink one. Not interested," Kaltherzig said. Only guards laughed. If not for the grip on his arm Erich would have slipped and fallen. He flushed, miserable, hating Kaltherzig, hating all these women.

There were more doors beyond the long shower room, flanked by guards. Kaltherzig dragged him through them. There were more of the women here, lined up at a long bank of tables. There was a cluster of people at the opposite end of the room, with something being done in the invisible middle that was making a young woman scream. Most people were ignoring this.

"Move back," Kaltherzig said. He did not raise his voice. A few moved. Some didn't move quickly enough, and these he shoved, sometimes hard enough to qualify as a throw. He presented Erich to the end of this table. "Next," he told the guard sitting there. She took the notebook Kaltherzig offered and wrote things down and typed something. Kaltherzig took Erich's left arm and shoved up his sleeve.

The needle hurt, buzzing like something you might hear in a barber shop, and it felt like being scratched by a house cat., It was infuriating for being done over and over. Erich gritted his teeth and tried not to move. More maddening drags that spelled lines of light behind his eyelids.

25

Kaltherzig kept his hand just above Erich's elbow. He turned from watching the blue numbers inked in, and gave Erich one luminous look without speaking.

Erich thought he should memorize it, having heard guards shouting at people by number. An E. An H. Then a blur, that blinking did not clear.

When it was done Kaltherzig led him farther on. He gave a new guard his clipboard, and said "Absolutely not!" when she turned to the striped heap of uniforms behind her. She sent a prisoner beside her out of the room. Kaltherzig waited. Erich stole a look at his tattoo. He was bleeding, just enough to smear.

The prisoner came back with a striped uniform, folded, and a handful of gray and pink scraps. Kaltherzig pulled Erich out of the flow of traffic and presented him with this armload of black and almost-white. "Hurry up."

He started to say, *here?* Then he remembered *I do not repeat myself,* and took off his coat. Kaltherzig took it from him. He slid off his shoes, fingers fumbling, and was down to his underwear when Kaltherzig said, "That's enough," and he put on these strange coarse things.

They were new, though carelessly made, and almost fit him. He turned up the trouser-legs. Kaltherzig said, "Put your shoes back on." He threw Erich's coat back to him, but the crisp white shirt and the gray trousers that went with his best suit were thrown to a prisoner.

Erich discovered he was holding two pink fabric triangles and two strips of white cloth with his number inked on them. There was a needle threaded through the scraps, holding them together. He stared at them until Kaltherzig shoved his hand towards his pocket, and he put them away. He stood dressed, feeling, undressed, thinking, *no more soul.*

He might as well be naked.

Everyone, everyone would know. With a single look.

There was a car idling in the street, with a lieutenant at the wheel. Kaltherzig pushed him into the back seat and got in beside him.

He sat suddenly cushioned in leather.

There were more gunshots. It took very few of them before Erich stopped cringing, almost stopped noticing. The intermittent explosions and the sub-threshold noise of distant crying and shouting all began to seem part of the environment, like the weather or that frying-meat smell.

He thought of stained glass windows. One slice of story. It was like that, now. An ugly woman with a blue-black scarf over her head, clinging to two children. His first glimpse of Mengele, though he did not know who he was. A group of three men, an older one and two grown sons, maybe, huddled together waiting their turn with the man in the white gloves, their turn with the pointing cane.

And then the car was pulling away from all this, the wide gate the truck had come in growing smaller and smaller. Another gate, this one in a wire fence. More guards. The car smelled of new and leather and Kaltherzig and cigarette smoke.

He sat, still out of phase. He had straightened his shirt and his coat and the new striped cap. He could feel Kaltherzig looking at him.

The hands came at him so quickly he almost screamed. Kaltherzig cupped Erich's face with his fingertips, like a cage. The gloves were soft as skin. He turned Erich's head left and right, tilted his chin up. Erich closed his eyes, heart triphammering, and Kaltherzig allowed this, pushing his thumb on the point of Erich's chin until he understood and opened his mouth, touching even the arches of his teeth, closing once around Erich's tongue and almost tugging. He made some small sound at this, a flinch, and the fingers were snatched out of his mouth and Kaltherzig punched him in the left cheekbone, hard enough to send him over on his side across the seat.

He's so fast.

Erich lay shaking, dabbed at his cheek with one hand. No blood, but a deep pulsing hurt. Kaltherzig took hold of Erich's coat and pulled him upright again. He held the boy's eyelids open with his thumbs, tilting him to look into the pale sunlight until tears streamed down his face. Kaltherzig was expressionless. He might have been examining him

27

for, damage. He let Erich go, reached inside his coat, took out a cigarette and lit it.

"Your hair is much too dark. So is mine. " Kaltherzig shrugged. "The eyes are incredible, though. Such a tropical blue. How old did you say you were?"

"Sixteen this March, Herr Doktor Obersturmführer, sir."

"Sir will do. That mouthful is for the idiots at the hospital." He turned down his window and flicked ashes out into the street.

They passed yet another gate, and now they were driving through a wide almost-garden, neatly laid saplings and carefully kept grass, artistic sweeping flowerbeds that were still gleaming with the last of the late bloomers. The woods were a green darkness an acre or so distant. *It's beautiful,* Erich thought, and that wasn't right at all, with the smokestacks behind them.

There were striped slaves, here and there, working in this garden.

"Can you type?"

"Yes sir," He cut that, mouthful, at the very last second.

"And spell?"

"Yes sir."

"All of that, quickly?"

He *yes-sirred* again. If only this man would let him work. He had done almost perfectly all through school and in all his days in the print shop, never a complaint, praise from every teacher in every subject. He would be so perfect, if only Kaltherzig would let him.

A noncommittal sort of noise. "And you can sew, I presume, from your, father, was it? Well enough to mend things, or well enough to make things?"

"Both...my father made uniforms in Berlin, I can make one from material in two days, sir." Was he allowed to volunteer information?

Kaltherzig smiled. "You'll do all of that, and whatever else I tell you, my boy."

Desinfektionsraum

They pulled into the long paved driveway of a neat sprawl of a house. The sun had set, and the shadows were long. There was already a blaze of searchlights in the distance, white wedges cutting into the darkening sky. Kaltherzig pushed Erich up the walk, unlocked the door and pushed him inside. A foyer with a marble floor, everything trimmed in dark wood polished to gleam like glass. The lush sort of quiet that you only found in the most expensive houses.

"Don't touch anything."

Kaltherzig steered him by his shoulder through a beautiful living room. Erich only saw pieces, bookshelves, a fireplace, and got the sense of a space that was both Norse and Roman. He was herded down a hallway into the bedroom, past the massive loom of a four-poster bed, and then the bathroom, a gleaming white box of new tile and chrome.

"Strip. Put everything here." Kaltherzig kicked an empty wicker basket on the floor. He left, the door hanging open.

Hot miserable swoosh from his neck to his face. He took off his coat and put it in the basket. Unbuttoned this slave shirt and put it in after. It seemed to be harder to move his hands with each layer of clothing. He gritted his teeth and thought of their gruff but harmless doctor at home.

Once he was naked there was that same old odd hospital sense of being cold and bare that never seemed to be there when you undressed to bathe. He wanted to cover himself, and didn't. He waited. He wrapped his arms around himself. Soon there would be the weight of those eyes. Surely it wouldn't feel as dangerous as he feared. He told himself, *he's a doctor.* Waited.

Kaltherzig came back in black rubber gloves with a blank metal can. He pushed Erich so that it was step into the tub or fall into it, poured most of the can over Erich's head. Soap, from the smell, something blue and stinging and chemical. Erich choked and spluttered, eyes burning.

Kaltherzig plugged the tub and turned on both tabs, pushed him down, picked up a brush. He started on Erich's chest, scrubbing without mercy, as the water got deeper and hotter around him. Erich squirmed as little as possible, blinking and gasping and trying so hard to be, still, telling himself *but he's a doctor.*

He was helplessly reminded of what a bath must be like for a dog. He wasn't expected to assist or even understand directions; Kaltherzig pulled him or shoved him or rearranged him as he saw fit. He poured more of this awful stuff into Erich's hair and scrubbed this with his fingers, and this part might've felt almost good, if not for the acidblaze in his eyes.

The brush again, on his stomach, across his chest, gouging at his nipples. Kaltherzig scrubbed him down to his toes, back up to the hinge of his thighs, dragged him up onto his hands and knees. Long swipes of the bristles up and down his back, excruciatingly pleasant at first, that melting kind of satisfying of having all those unreachable itches scratched at once, but the bristles were digging hard enough to sting after a second or two. Kaltherzig held him by the back of his neck, by his hair, scrubbing hard in merciless circles and lines.

The soap burned him like alcohol in the scratches Kaltherzig was leaving... He couldn't keep quiet. He muffled his face in the crook of his elbow, his hands clinging to his own shoulders, trying to endure this. And then Kaltherzig spread the cheeks of his buttocks open with one hand and scrubbed between them.

He screamed. He'd had no idea he could make such a noise. It began almost indignantly, and changed with distressing speed into something desperate and terrified.

Kaltherzig laughed, lingering over the ring of muscle, pushing there with the point of the brush. "What's the matter? Am I hurting you?"

He didn't know if he was supposed to say *yes sir.* He was sobbing. There was nothing in the world but the bright hot shock of it and the shame of it. The sound of the can again, and the thunk splash of the brush hitting the water.

Kaltherzig let him go, spread him wider. "Get your knees apart."

Fingers *pushed* at him. He had time to think that it felt like two and drew in one anguished breath before they shoved inside him, greased with disinfectant. Kaltherzig dragged them in and out in the same scrubbing motions, laughing at the particularly tortured noises, sometimes repeating a gesture to wring out a longer scream. He pushed those two fingers in up to his palm, until Erich begged him to stop, choking out *sir* after *sir*.

Nothing bought him the slightest pity. There was the distressing sense that it was all, business, that he was property to be maintained. The fingers twisted inside him and he buried his wet face in his wet arms and made long ugly cries at the spreading sting in all the tiny secret torn places. The fingers slid out, so fast it left him with an aching urge to, gag, or cough, and he stumbled over a breath and realized this hysterical echo was himself.

Kaltherzig picked up the brush again and drew up his balls in one hand and scrubbed, ignoring the agonized howling. He kept on long after Erich had given up on screaming, drew his penis back between his legs and scoured it off too, tugged back the foreskin and scrubbed at the underside and the head until Erich collapsed on his stomach, feet kicking a little, legs still spread.

Kaltherzig threw down the brush.

Erich lay in water almost hot enough to scald him, just on his hands and knees far enough to keep from drowning, crying listlessly.

A beat, and the soft impact of armloads of clothing landing on top of him.

"Wash all that. Clean all this before you come out. And wash yourself with something so that you smell human."

He turned his head, water lapping at his cheek, clothes spreading in a shipwrecked tangle around him. He said to Kaltherzig's back, "...what, should I put on...sir..."

"Nothing." And the door closed between them.

Erich lay crying, hands cradled between his legs.

Was that rape? Did that count, or did it have to, be...did you call it that at all, when it was a boy, doing it to a boy?

He's a doctor.

The soap inside him would not let him be still for long. He groped his way to the toilet and cried a little longer sitting there until the worst of it seemed to be out of him. *Alcohol,* he thought. It smelled of hospital.

He's a doctor. It was to prevent the spread of disease.

At least he'd given him that terrible bath in private.

But he was laughing while he did it, he, was...

He scrubbed out all the clothes, washed himself with a bar of soap as soft as cream. It smelled of Kaltherzig, and stung in the places where the brush had marked him like sunburn.

That burning pain inside him doubled him over with cramps, drove him back to the toilet twice, sobbing between gritted teeth. He turned on the taps, knelt in the tub and washed himself there as best he could. Anything to stop that blazing need to push, squirm, scream.

It was softer than he expected. Inside. He could still feel Kaltherzig's fingers, as if they were still there. He washed his hands with the soap again and shuddered.

Was Kaltherzig *allowed* to do this to him? Was it, legal? He dried himself and the floor and the edge of the tub, hung up the stopper and the brush, wrung out his wet uniform and spread it over the side of the tub to dry.

Why can I still feel him doing, that?

He had watched the doctor shoot a man for asking a question. Whatever this was it wasn't as bad as being shot. Kaltherzig hadn't taken any pains to hide the

(murder)

execution. And there had been at least a dozen more. If that was permitted, this was probably laughable. This had been rather gentle as far as rape could go, he imagined. Some of the women had been made to strip naked on the ramp, in front of God and everybody. He thought of

32

the woman screaming at the other end of the shower, of a very blond man laughing at her and doing something that he leaned into with his shoulder.

He looked at himself in the mirror. He was painted with long throbbing swatches of pink, everywhere he was scrubbed and scalded. There were dozens of raised lines where the bristles had marked him, red enough to be real scratches in the morning, scrawled over the deep redblack bruises.

He washed the gloves and hung up the towel and stood with nothing left do but leave.

He opened the door and stepped naked out into the bedroom.

Gehirnwäsche

He was cold, with his bare skin and damp hair.

Kaltherzig was sitting on the bed barefoot in crisp new white shirt and black pants.

(as if I were, contaminated)

Another cigarette was clamped in those perfect teeth. He was pulling on a set of gloves, shorter than the black ones dripping dry in the bathroom. They were white, wrist-long. They snapped like dangerous.

He thought, *he'll hurt me again.* There was a dull dread, and again that swooping awareness of his nakedness. He was so very tired. He looked at Kaltherzig too long and those eyes came up and struck him again. Took him. He felt his feet move as if he were dreaming, and he took one step forward. Kaltherzig patted the bed beside him

(he might do that for a dog)

and opened something he was holding and slicked the same two fingers of his right hand. Erich climbed up beside him, waited to be steered. He was handed a pillow, which he stared at, and Kaltherzig sighed and put it down and pushed him down on his face over it so that it raised his hips.

He was crying again, couldn't help it, had he known how much child he still had left inside him? Could this doctor do this to him, in this house that looked just like anyone's house? Could this happen to him in a normal bed that someone slept in every single night?

The gun was still on Kaltherzig's belt, draped over a lush heavy chair.

Erich wrapped his arms around his head and tried to stop the idiot crying. It wouldn't help. He'd learned that already.

"Does it hurt you?" Calm, almost as if Kaltherzig sympathized. The textbook doctor voice. At least he didn't sound inclined to laugh, now. More sounds of the jar he was holding.

"Yes sir."

34

He just wanted it to be over. He would do what he was told for whatever was left and afterward, sleep. That same reward that had gotten him through the very first piece of this. Sooner or later the pain would end and he would sleep and it would all stop for a while.

"Are you bleeding?"

"No sir." He burrowed his face into the bedspread, to keep his eyes from overflowing, and wound two handfuls of the blanket and tried to breathe, breathe, breathe.

That same noncommittal noise. Fingers, nudging his legs apart, spreading the cheeks of his buttocks and pressing at that aching ring of muscle, again, and he made one pitiful noise and stopped himself, ashamed.

He expected that terrible, shoving, slide, but this was not exactly that; a slow petting stroke, smoothing a generous layer of something cool on him, and inside him in gradually deeper presses. The gentle, circles to rub the ointment in left him quiet and dissociated. He felt tended, helpless, and he allowed his legs to be spread farther apart and when both fingers pushed inside him again he arched his back and tried to breathe, deeper.

"That's much better."

He closed his eyes tighter, that same endorphin, whatever-it-was, that always happened whenever anyone, praised him, that starving, feeling. He didn't know what he was doing better. He tried not to move.

"Push towards me."

He tried to lean with his back and his hips. He got an approving murmur and that lovely pressing circle harder, slower. "Do you like that?"

He pushed towards Kaltherzig again, chewing his lip.

Kaltherzig held him down with his other hand and pinched, one finger inside him and his thumb outside, nails digging into the ring of his anus, a sudden startling edge under the smooth glide of rubber.

"What was the first thing I ever said to you?"

He was caught, in mid-cry, and he almost felt his brain do a kind of seizure like a butterfly in a jar, trying to remember. "...that you don't, repeat yourself...I'm sorry..."

"That's very pretty, but once you're *sorry*—" a much, harder, pinch, and more pull that made him scream, one throat-scraping undignified squawk. "—you've already done something wrong. And you still haven't answered me."

"Yes! Yes, I liked it." Was that true? He was hard, increasingly so. It must be true. There was one more pull, and a twist with those nails that went on until he realized what he'd forgotten. "Sir! Sir..."

Kaltherzig slid his fingers inside again immediately.

Erich thought, *I'll be quiet,* and couldn't. That first push was such a loud, texture, that it drowned out everything. He had to make noise or something inside him might break. He clung to the bedspread and shook and ground his teeth. Kaltherzig did it again, that gentle rolling push, just *there.* That same blur of stunned and stricken, a pang with every single slide, so hard and unstoppable and *sexual* that he couldn't breathe past it. He had never imagined such a feeling existed. None of his forgotten dreams or fumbling in the dark had brought him any warning of it.

A laugh. That familiar lingering in places that made him frantic. Deliberate little gestures, a mean aching interlude of having the fingers drawn out, teasing outside in pointless little strokes, and then all the way and right, *there.* A circle that he felt in his teeth and that fluttering push again fastfastfast and he was making a sound like an engine, and his knees and his shoulders and his spine pushed him closer to Kaltherzig's hand.

"It's your prostate. That idiot Mengele insists to me that there's no such organ." A laugh, and out again. Erich made a noise that embarrassed him, pushed towards Kaltherzig's hand and stopped himself. Kaltherzig patted him and pushed in again with three fingers, easing off when Erich wailed, and pushing in again with that same, inexorable patience. That merciless flutter.

Now there was pain with that deep, distressing pleasure, and he leaned away from it instinctively. Kaltherzig leaned over him, moving with serpentine speed, that flawless statue's face so close to his he was

36

afraid to blink for fear of brushing him with his eyelashes. "You're resisting it."

"I can't help it, I'll, scream..."

A shrug. "So? Scream." That nothing look that wasn't quite a smile. Those fingers curled inside him, pulled him like a hook somewhere that made his back come up.

"You don't know what that is?"

A thump, inside him, in that immovable place. "Your tailbone." Another, lift, too slow to hurt him, and the delirium of *he's pushing my spine from the inside*, and a moan he forgot to muffle.

A twist that almost hurt, and a shift. "I can feel your pulse, here.....as fast as if you'd been running....." Pressure in a soft place that made Erich feel his own heartbeat. A laugh, and a thudding series of pushes that rocked him on his hands and knees like a shove. He was making the same sound every time he managed to draw a breath, face pushed into the bed as hard as he could to drown out this rising and falling wail.

"Now."

He didn't understand what Kaltherzig wanted him to do, but it had something to do with whatever was at the end of this, climbing.

"No? I've never had one come, being examined like this. I wonder if it's even possible."

Erich still had no idea what he was talking about. He wouldn't have been able to oblige if he had. The hurt was too much. His stomach ached. After much too long Kaltherzig did something like a snarl of frustration and the fingers were almost, snatched, out of him, making him draw up his shaking knees.

Quiet, for so long that Erich turned his head to look over his shoulder, blinking through his hair.

Blur of Kaltherzig with his hand between his own legs.

He was unbuttoning his pants.

Erich turned his face back to the mattress and wrapped his arms around his head.

Kaltherzig grasped his hips and spread him open with his thumbs. There was one warning nudge of his penis before he pushed inside, a merciless shove with all his weight behind it.

Erich drew in his breath in anticipation of rending pain, but there was only a deafening sense of being so very full. There was friction was so deep it set his teeth on edge, and then the first threat of a monstrous pleasure. He clung, shaken, stricken, mouth muffled open against the bedspread.

Kaltherzig made some sound behind him, spread him wider, thumbs pressing bruise-hard with that awful squeak of rubber. He was pushing inside deeper still, and there was the first real pain, strange and stomachache deep, that brought a wavering cry to his throat.

Kaltherzig stopped, held himself here. "Put your knees under you, straighten your back."

He did this, sobbing again because it moved the penis inside him. Could he do this in a, house...where people, lived...

Deeper, and that stretching hurt was, gone, and there was that excruciating, slide, and he moaned because he couldn't help it, and the push of the buttons of Kaltherzig's pants against his thigh. He leaned forward, hands coming down to the bed on either side of Erich's shoulders, and there was a withdrawal that hurt, and the push inside again and he was pushing, right, there, harder and faster and faster.

He reached under Erich, wrapped one gloved slippery hand around his cock.

Almost a scream of dismay, and a thrashing try at squirming that he stopped because of the cock inside him still pinning him down. Long, oiled pulls. Kaltherzig's hand tight around him. Slower, meaner slams inside him. A seizure started in all his muscles. He was afraid he would, fall, and the climbing was more like a hook pulling him faster and faster. "No..."

Kaltherzig let him go and slapped the right cheek of his buttocks so hard it stunned him. Erich collapsed, the cock sliding out. He was drawn back, impaled again before he could even draw a breath to cry out.

"Don't you ever tell me *no* again."

Erich looked over his shoulder at Kaltherzig. Those winter eyes were half-closed, mouth slack. That not-quite smile returned. He leaned closer, tilted his ear towards Erich's mouth to collect his noises, rolled his hips in slow irresistible pushes. He pushed Erich down flat and went faster still, drove in with that terrible wrong-angle hurt again, and when he screamed long and loud in shock Kaltherzig moaned and went harder.

He hid his face, sobbed, chewed his arm to keep from screaming. That pleasure had gone with the first bolt of that pain. Now there was more misery than delight. He was crying without restraint. A devastating set of thrusts so hard he was paralyzed, much too deep. He couldn't breathe. Kaltherzig was shaking on top of him.

He took one long breath, and gripped Erich hard enough to hurt and pulled out of him. Erich didn't move. He hadn't been told he could.

"Go and clean yourself up," Kaltherzig said.

He expected blood, and found none, only slippery colorless stuff that smelled of ocean. He did what Kaltherzig had told him to do, feeling very sleepy. The panic had almost gone. The worst of things had happened, would happen again, and this beautiful creature would probably shoot him at the end of these days.

When he stepped back into the bedroom Kaltherzig was naked from the waist down, shirt on but unbuttoned, tie missing. He had his hand between his legs. Erich was afraid to look here, for fear of seeing blood or shit. Kaltherzig cupped his head again and pulled his face down. "You know how."

He had no idea how.

He wanted to struggle or protest, scream in outrage. He still couldn't look. He opened his mouth because he had to, the fear of the gun beating in his head like a furious bird. He thought, *if I'm sick he'll shoot me.* Kaltherzig thumped the top of his head. "Clean," he whispered, and Erich understood.

He wasn't sick. He tasted nothing but that strange ocean smell in his nostrils. Kaltherzig's hand thudded him again. "You can do better than that."

He wrapped one hand around this mysterious cock, drew back this luxurious skin, thinking of expensive cloth in his father's storeroom. He tried to imitate the tiny list of things that he found pleasurable during his few brief and unsuccessful attempts at masturbation.

Kaltherzig seemed to unwind. His hand came down to the top of Erich's head again, resting there. After a long time, he pulled Erich away. "Every time, after."

Every time.

He thought of the women, screaming, and the shaven stick-men carrying luggage and bodies through the pandemonium of unloading.

Was he grateful?

There were pages in his brain like a book, turning too fast to see, listing all the ways it might be worse, pointing out that at least there was only this one. There was still that sense of deafness, as though the gunshots had broken part of his hearing and part of his mind along with it. None of it seemed quite real, and yet nothing that had ever come before seemed as real as this. Something inside him was crying out— more frantic question than fact—that if he were perfect, he might yet avoid that crimson triangle, that fall.

"Are you bleeding?"

That solicitous question, again, and that mishmash of images that meant *doctor.* Hadn't there always been something of this cruelty in everything medicinal? Flicker of having his tonsils out, crying and crying, and being plied with puddings and yogurts and shaved ice he didn't want.

"No sir." He was pushed onto his face again anyway, spread and dabbed at. He told himself it was ungrateful to still, be, crying. It seemed better if he was quiet. There was less of him when he was quiet.

"No, not yet."

The jar, again, the fingers inside him slippery with cream. It was over quickly this time. Kaltherzig slapped his thigh, shoved him in the direction of the door. He climbed down, unsteadily, watched Kaltherzig drag and push the covers back and slide under. He didn't understand. He had his hand on the doorknob when Kaltherzig came at him, snarling.

"Where do you think you're going?" He gave Erich a shove that thudded his forehead and shoulder into the wall, hard enough to bring him to his knees.

"You said, to..."

"I said no such thing; I put you, here." A shove with his foot, thudding Erich over onto his back. "Do what I tell you, stay where I put you."

Silence.

He waited until Erich started for *yes sir* and did that whipcrack voice again. "If you cannot remember that you won't last a week. And you would be *amazed* how many boys can't follow simple directions."

Erich didn't move, didn't dare a *yes sir*. *The gun*, he thought, if that one single hieroglyph, blue-black and unconquerable could be called a thought.

Footsteps, and the soft impact of a blanket thrown at him.

The fire crackling, dying. When he could move again he wound himself small under the blanket, covered head and all, and waited for the sleep he'd promised himself, trying and failing to think of nothing, nothing, nothing.

He could hear Kaltherzig breathing above him. He could feel the gun, and then he would feel, again, some piece of tonight, a rolling echo of that first pleasure. And then he would feel the gun again, as though he were being driven in circles.

There was a grandfather clock somewhere in the house. It chimed the hour with an elegant low tone. Erich heard twelve and one before there was the longed-for patch of oblivion.

Missbrauch

The distant cry of a siren woke Erich when it was still dark. There was a stupid set of minutes when he had no idea where he was. He only knew this noise that meant he might be late for something. He lay dazed, the blanket trapping his limbs, feeling a thousand tiny aches from sleeping on the floor. Memory came back in one crashing piece, and his throat caught and his eyes filled with tears, and he swallowed and sat up, saw that Kaltherzig was a white sleeping shape in a bed wide enough for a king.

He had dared to slide to the very foot of the bed where a thick narrow rug covered the hardwood floor, and from there he supposed he must have slept. A confusion of dreams, people with scalpels chasing him into trucks labeled DUSCHEN.

He was afraid to stand up. He folded the blanket in a crouch, and crawled into the bathroom, standing after he'd pushed the door closed behind him. His uniform was dry, and he touched it, trying to believe in it. It was stiff and strange. He took his patches from the coat pocket, stared at them.

He knew where they went. He'd seen them on the others, hadn't he, red triangles, yellow ones, a rainbow code of crimes made visible.

To everyone.

His hands remembered how to sew as well as they ever had, but it felt like they belonged to someone else, and he watched himself stitch the pink triangle and his number on the shirt and the trouser leg.

It felt, different, now, when he put it on, and he couldn't not see this gleam of pink just in his peripheral vision. There was that weight of being revealed, the hot shame of it. He couldn't not see this gleam of pink just in his peripheral vision. He imagined that was the point of it, a little punishment that never ended and required no effort on the part of the SS.

I didn't ask you what you've done, I asked you what you are.

He crawled back and sat at the foot of the bed where Kaltherzig had put him.

When the clock chimed eight Kaltherzig stretched and sat up, smoothed back that fall of hair, predator eyes still sleepy. He looked down at Erich with no particular surprise or interest. "Can you cook?"

"A...little, sir." Somewhat true, though his mother had never been satisfied with his efforts. He'd been tempted to creep to the kitchen while Kaltherzig slept, but the bruise on his forehead kept him too afraid of the doorknob.

"Good, go." He was dragging through a wardrobe when Erich crept out.

The idea of quiet had gotten its hooks in him. The less he spoke, the softer he was when he had to speak, the less noise of opening and closing and footsteps and misery and breathing he made, the less notice he would attract. The less catastrophe he would invite.

He found a luxuriously appointed kitchen. The first door he tried led into a dark and utterly empty closet. Then he saw the ring set in the floor, and understood it was the cellar. The second door turned out to be the pantry. After much frantic searching he made coffee and warmed bread and cut the green tops off strawberries.

Kaltherzig came downstairs, sharp as a razor from hat to gleaming boots. He took coffee and bread and lit a cigarette, settled in his armchair, gestured at the phonograph till Erich understood what he wanted and started it for him.

"Eat. Everything you touch you put back as you found it."

That seemed like, enough of a dismissal, so Erich retreated to the kitchen and obsessed over the miniscule mess he'd made. He ate while he washed everything and moved dishes in the cabinets tiny increments of an inch and squinted at the floor to see if he'd missed any crumbs.

He was...not quite, hurt, inside. But there was a sense of having been changed, and twinges that were almost pleasure. He thought of the skeleton-men with the luggage, and told himself over and over that he was lucky, that he would be perfect, that it would be all right.

A different Untersturmführer came in the same car. Erich put on his coat and got in as Kaltherzig gestured.

No trains now, only the great gate and the tracks vanishing on the horizon line. One of the smokestacks was already puffing bluegray into the air. Guards leaned in black silhouette in the gun towers, smoking or with coffee steaming in one gloved hand. Everything was motionless, as if everyone were always waiting for something.

They drove to one of the many identical buildings, this one very close to the ovens. A little sign read merely *Block 10*. A double line of those skeleton men was marching across the street with eerie fake cheer, an SS man with a whip behind them. One long stream of numbers and patches rainbowed by him; the yellow star, most often, but triangles too, in red, green, brown, purple. No pink ones. He dreaded taking his coat off.

He knew what Block 10 was the moment they stepped through the door. Only a hospital had that bright cold smell. Kaltherzig steered him through a sort of doctor's office, with SS in uniforms and lab coats and various combinations of the two, prisoners, prisoner doctors, patients being led wailing or stricken silent. It was crowded chaos, and it made him think longingly of the cool quiet in Kaltherzig's house.

Erich was pushed into an examining room with *Ahren Kaltherzig, Lagerarzt* painted on the fogged glass. The doctor closed and locked the door behind them, closed the blinds, opened his briefcase on his desk. The noise was shut out, rendered distant and unimportant. They were alone again. *Ahren,* he thought. It might have been better not to know that, though he could not have said why.

There was so much metal in here. So many cabinets. So many drawers.

Out came the notebook.

"Take all of that off."

Speed was becoming automatic. That separation was setting in as a reflex, how useful, how clever of his mind to take care of him like that.

Kaltherzig took his clothes from him, set them unreachably aside, patted the table. This, too, was metal, and cold enough to make him want to flinch away from it. He had to use the little foot-ledge to climb up. When he slid back his feet dangled. Kaltherzig wrote something down, said without looking, "I'm going to measure you and photograph you. Nothing so terrible yet."

That doctor-vibration again, the closest to friendly he had yet seen Kaltherzig. That smile that showed none of his teeth—he had learned the other kind was a sign of danger.

"I'll let you know when to panic."

He said, "Yes sir," because some kind of response seemed required.

"You're too small for your age."

"Yes sir." He was blushing, as though it were his own fault. He had always been small, had been so little at birth they'd told his mother to plan his funeral. He thought of telling Kaltherzig this, but he didn't.

He suffered the usual routine doctor-type things, tongue depressor, stethoscope and a light in his eyes and ears. Kaltherzig had to lean near him, smelling of sandalwood soap and aftershave, German tobacco, Turkish coffee. It made him think of the couch in his father's den, soft but too scratchy to sleep on.

The doctor nudged at the worst of the bruises, noted something in his file. Erich flushed again at this—*he'll think I was bad, he'll ask me what I did to deserve them*—but he said nothing about this stigmata of disobedience.

Kaltherzig pushed Erich onto his back, hinged strange crooked things out from under the table. He pulled up Erich's knees, hooked them over deep metal saddles, spread wide and strapped on bruise-tight. "Panic all you like, but keep still."

His arms were strapped straight out at his sides, along little tables that looked modified for this use, from some other more innocuous purpose. Trays, maybe, for instruments. There were plenty of those on carts, spread on white cloth in sharp silver rows.

His feet were put in stirrups, strapped, pushed up till he could see

45

the ceiling through them. Kaltherzig pulled his hips forward till he felt the edge of the table below the small of his back. Already this position hurt his shoulders, his lower back. Straps around his chest, his waist. If he raised his head could see a very finite square of white wall and Kaltherzig at the foot of the table. He could not even watch what was being done to him.

"You're to stay quiet. Don't distract me."

He *yes-sirred*. Swallowed over and over. Blinked very fast. Almost panted in dread. He watched Kaltherzig shake a wide thermometer, swirl it in a jar. He stumbled into those eyes again, blushed bright. He stared up at the ceiling, and it took almost a minute before he realized there were fine splatters of blood on the tiles. He blinked, and they remained. It dried his tongue in his mouth. Blood, faint and unmistakable arcs of it —how had it gotten on the ceiling? Then the thermometer was shoved without much ceremony deep into his aching rectum. He was finding it almost impossible to remain quiet.

Kaltherzig ignored him, picked up a heavy black camera gleaming with expensive precision. He took many pictures, some from inches from his skin, several between his legs, once tilting the thermometer agonizingly to one side for several frames.

That lens, an inch from his eye, Kaltherzig so close he could smell something like candied violets on his breath, and the whisper "Don't blink...two...three..." and the blinding flash.

The thermometer was withdrawn, consulted, deposited in a waiting bin of alcohol. Kaltherzig selected a terrifying handful of shiny pointed calipers. He laid these down on Erich everywhere, little cold metal pricks on his stomach, his hands, his face, photographing each resulting measurement.

He measured each testicle separately, making Erich hiss in fear. Then his penis, too. The gentle grasp and the still lines of Kaltherzig's shoulder made him twitch and become sluggishly hard. A grin from Kaltherzig without comment, and a measurement for this, too.

Kaltherzig came at him with tiny scissors, cut off a lock of his

46

almostblack hair and tucked it in an envelope. Trimmed his nails in neat little curves with silver clippers. Fingerprinted him and daubed the blueviolet ink off his fingertips with cotton dipped in alcohol. Enough of the camera. Kaltherzig traded it for an empty large syringe with a long thick needle. He put on the tourniquet with quick careless pulls, took the vein in the crease of Erich's elbow.

It set his teeth on edge, this cold little intrusion, and the pull as the syringe filled with dark blood. He exhaled until the needle was withdrawn, the bleeding stopped under the tourniquet knotted over a pinch of gauze. Then another syringe, loaded with a lot of something clear. "Anesthetic."

He moved down again between Erich's knees.

How they kept peeling away his layers of shock. He did not think Kaltherzig could possibly intend to do, that, until he felt the gloved fingers pinch open his anus and the first warning prick of the needle, just at the bottom. "No no no, no, please, no..."

He ground his teeth together too late. He'd forgotten.

The needle was withdrawn.

Kaltherzig peeled off one glove with his teeth, slapped the inside of Erich's right thigh in exactly the same place, hard hard hard, over and over till Erich was one long scream.

"I'm going to have to teach you about that *no* when we've more time. You're not learning that one fast enough."

He tried for *sorry* a few times. He sniffled but his nose ran anyway. The pinching little spread, again. The needle, again. This time it was pushed straight into that drawstring-cord of muscle with a tearing little *pop* he could almost hear.

He couldn't scream. It was too specific, one beam of pain like the sunlight through an eyeglass lens, pinning him into this agonized arch. Kaltherzig pushed the plunger down. He could not be still, not that he could really move, but there was a sort of a blur of thrashing, tensing, braying out all sorts of unbelievable noise, too driven by instinct and pain to realize it was useless.

Kaltherzig *tsked* at him, reloading the syringe. "It's your own fault. You do all that squirming and it pulls the needle around inside you. Nobody to blame but yourself."

He gritted his teeth, screamed through them from the first pinch. This time it was the top of the ring, closest to his testicles. Kaltherzig seemed to angle it upwards almost under the skin, through such a thin edge of that muscle-cord he was afraid the needle would just tear through it. His arms were so tight they would ache the next day. From the waist down he tried to be paralyzed.

Kaltherzig seemed to just shove the plunger in. His scream climbed in one jump to a pitch that tore him ragged in a second, silenced him in two.

He withdrew it. Rubbed Erich's thighs from knees to groin and back again, a gesture so inappropriately kind it reduced Erich to trembling and tears.

"All that over two little shots. Really." But he kept up the gentle squeezing strokes for a long moment before he pulled his glove on again, never taking those luminous eyes off his subject. That twisting pinch, the skin over this terrible hurt tweezed between Kaltherzig's fingernails. He wailed, strained miserably against the straps.

"Are you numb?"

He wasn't numb. He was one blazing deep pain that seemed to have spread to everywhere between his legs. He shook his head, unable to answer any other way.

"No? Mmm. Well, then you're control group. Saline or cottonseed oil." Kaltherzig shrugged, and picked up the most awful thing Erich had ever seen in his life. It resembled two steel shoehorns attached into the shape of a cone, with something at the wide end like a trigger. Kaltherzig pulled it. A loud click, and it snapped wide open. A speculum, though he did not know that word.

Erich watched him lubricate it with something clear, and close it again.

"Now this one is for a child, so I don't want to hear any

complaining, or I'll use the one for adults."

He *yes sirred*, barely able to speak above a whisper. His knees were pushed up farther, his feet up higher. He had already half-exhausted himself in pure tension. He was panting through his teeth, as if the pain had already come and he were already riding it.

Why must They always do things to you so you can't wipe your eyes or blow your nose? He should get a test tube and collect some tears.

He's a doctor, they always do things to you that hurt you, everything they do, this is nothing different.

He knew it was different, and he knew why. He thought that Kaltherzig did collect tears, just not in a test tube.

The metal cone was not as bad as he'd feared. The edges seemed to threaten a cut without ever delivering one. It was so *cold.* Then the first click, and resentful sharp ache of this sore circle being spread. The strange sensation of air inside him, and the climbing sounds of protest he couldn't muffle.

"What did I say? You don't want the bigger one, do you?" Another click, a jolt that hurt a great deal more. He was spread much wider. He could feel himself trying uselessly to close, reflexes trying to push this awful thing out. His breath was coming faster.

"You're only making this harder on yourself."

Can he feel my pulse yet, through that thing, through the metal, through the glove?

"Stop that." A slap to the inside of his thigh, and then a pinch. Kaltherzig let it go inside him. "Don't push. I don't want to see it move."

The struggle to, slow his breath, because that was somehow part of it. It took a long time for him to relax, so that the speculum was still except for whatever invisible vibration it carried from his pulse.

"Good boy." A stroke to his hair that made him crush his eyes closed. "Now you have to be just that still, or it will be worse. " The hand came away from his head. There was the sound of the wheeled stool, and hands on his thighs.

A noise he could not identify. He stole one peek to see the

gooseneck lamp being clicked on and swung closer to him. Blaze of warmth that was almost uncomfortable between his legs, in places he himself had never really seen. Humiliation that was as strong as nausea, as deep as horror, and the inescapable awareness that this heat was the weight of Kaltherzig's eyes.

The speculum moved in him.

He crushed his own eyes closed tight, again, but it wasn't much help.

It didn't feel like Kaltherzig doing this to him. He could blame it all on the instrument. Rattle of more metal, and then something tiny and specific poking inside him. A pushing slow circle. Kaltherzig withdrew the long swab, dabbed it into a petri dish and picked up another swab.

It didn't hurt, but he seemed to be methodically trying to swab, every inch, as far inside as he could reach. It was almost, but not quite, pleasant. And then he tilted the speculum, and that did hurt, like he imagined the first bits of death by impalement might hurt.

Kaltherzig listened to all his begging as if it were a particularly amusing story. Erich chewed his lip, squeezed shut his eyes and cried.

A last click. The speculum closed all at once inside him. It ached like stretching after too-long in too small a seat. A murmur from Kaltherzig. Instead of the withdrawal he expected, it turned inside him, the cold metal handle pressing into his bruised thigh. Kaltherzig clicked it open again, turned side-to-side instead of up and down.

It was almost a relief to be open again, but the new pressures made him desperate to draw his knees up, higher. Kaltherzig pushed very low on his stomach, seeming to search for the edges of this thing through his flesh, shushed him when his volume started to climb.

The swabs again, briefly. Kaltherzig sighed, clicked the speculum closed. The metal cone was withdrawn with one matter-of-fact slide that left him hissing again.

"No use. You're almost too small for the next one up but this one won't do." A pat over the handprint on his thigh. Kaltherzig opened a drawer in the table underneath him. Rummaging. "No, only..."

That shrug. The dangerous smile-with-teeth.

This speculum was longer, not so conical, duckbilled. "For women. It's the only other model we have here. Supply has been a nightmare." Still too much teeth, for Erich not to hear the joke underneath.

He meant to use that on me, all along. He does this to
(all?)
of, us...

Kaltherzig opened that same clear thick cream, spread this steel set of lines.

Erich could feel the forbidden *no* behind his teeth. He closed his eyes. The struggle rattled inside him like an earthquake.

He could not let Kaltherzig do this, anymore. Something inside his sanity would break into pieces. He could feel it. The fear of the gun would not let him try to explain it, would not let him risk any more bruises.

Kaltherzig seemed to
(enjoy)
want to keep him alive, and that seemed a great deal more hope than the skeleton men had. If he could only, let him
(hurt)
do, whatever it was he was trying to do
(for two years)
he could go home. Forget it. Or at least, keep it all where nobody could see it.

"Sir?"

Kaltherzig looked as if it surprised him to be addressed. "Yes?" He never stopped applying something gleaming and wet to the speculum.

"You said before that I was making it harder on myself. How can I, not?"

The laugh was different when they were alone. Less like a general sort of applause for the cleverness of the Reich and more like a real, laugh. "You're keeping yourself in pieces. You still expect to open your eyes in your very own room again."

Another tendril of certainty that Kaltherzig could read his mind. Pieces.

Would it be worth whatever useless comfort he would win? Why defend each besieged piece from this SS totality until he was conquered one fragment at a time? He laughed himself, though it hardly sounded authentic.

"How do I stop, sir?"

"Don't worry. I'll stop you."

The speculum nudged him in one cold warning, and slid inside. Push. Slide. The first click. This speculum opened in more of a V than the first one, pushing his spine and his bladder. He did a climbing frantic *please*, beginning to hyperventilate.

Kaltherzig said "Be *still.*"

The second, click, and the spread.

Stop me, he thought. His hands found the edges of the table and clung there by themselves. Kaltherzig thumped the inside of Erich's thigh with one gloved hand. "See? That. Still trying. What are you making yourself ready for? What is the point of all this struggle?" He hooked a finger in the restraint at Erich's knee, tugged at it in illustration. "Useless, and arrogant, to think you have anything to do with the future, now. You're still on your back."

His eyes stung at that last. *On your back,* in his head like blows, breaking the shell between himself and the world. All this wasted struggle. There was a knotted set of seconds, while he tried to puzzle out how to stop trying. He exhaled and let himself hang, let straps cup him like a cold hand, let the steel just, spread him.

"Much better, good boy." A stroke along his thigh that ended with the side of Kaltherzig's hand against his scrotum. A pat. "It'll only hurt more if you're tense. That's always true." Almost to himself. His eyes were reaching that narrowed-focus of concentration. Erich thought again, of an artist immersed in a painting, of his own father's hands a blur of needle trailing thread.

The speculum tilted. He gave a mournful worried cry.

Kaltherzig murmured something that ended in *my boy*, reached without looking, dragged the tray of instruments closer. He picked up a dangerous silver line that ended in a trigger, wobbled it between thumb and forefinger like a pencil, as if he were considering before he bent his head between Erich's knees again. A narrow little nudge inside him, strange without the warning-slide of entry first. Those delicate little pushes till this cold metal nose was against his prostate.

Trigger, and click.

The pain was like a bite, specific and deep, and Kaltherzig withdrew it and there was a pull and another flare inside him like this minute bite had been torn off.

It seemed silly to scream so long after the wound, and once he got his breath he only panted, eyes filling with tears because he felt tricked. Kaltherzig spared him another stroke or two along the inside of his thigh, did things with the probe and a tiny dish, closed and labeled it.

He's recording me.

A fingertip in an envelope of powder, and the speculum tilted. A feather of a touch inside him, a spreading burn that locked his teeth. Betrayed again.

"It's only styptic, you're being a child. Would you rather bleed into a towel all day, like a girl, hmm? Stop all this noise."

The speculum was closed, withdrawn. The probe was dropped in a bin to be cleaned and a new one chosen. "Two more."

The *no* was a nonevent, passing through him without tension. He was simply following it with another word, *no point, no good, no use, no hope.* The apathy was much safer.

Kaltherzig grasped his left testicle between two fingers, nudged that one cold point hard against him, trigger, click.

He was stricken silent. The reflex to draw up his knees dug the straps into his thighs. Nausea shook him like a fever, a heavy knot of sickness settling low in his stomach. A dip into that envelope again. Erich shook his head in spite of himself, feet turning uselessly in the stirrups. Kaltherzig laughed at him and did it anyway.

53

"Last one." The emptying, the labeling, the second probe sloshed into the bin beside the first one. The third one picked up from the tray. His penis, held in one gloved hand. Pain like a thorn or a splinter of glass and that sensation of tearing again.

The room seemed to have, tilted. He opened his eyes. Kaltherzig had the powder in his hand, was just patting in it with one fingertip. He lost anything approaching dignity, pleading and sobbing for him not to do it. The doctor never hesitated. Something in the center of his head closed. After all these hours of telling himself he was gone, it was finally true.

Figuren

A sharp flare in his nose and the back of his throat that pulled him back into the world. He caught the ammonia-tang and wanted to scream in pure frustration. Of course it wasn't that easy. He could faint all he wished; this was a hospital, they could drag him into consciousness anytime they liked. There was no exit that way, either.

Kaltherzig leaned over him, the corners of his mouth busy with amusement. "Welcome back. All rested now?"

"Are you...finished, sir?" He tried to swipe at his face, found himself already clean and unstrapped, still naked.

"Only in here. Come on, now, we'll have you sit up until you can walk." He pulled Erich up, one hand behind his back keeping him upright. A deep resentful twinge inside him, that hurt he couldn't get away from. It reminded him of the pink triangle, and he thought that eventually they would have done so many things they might leave him alone to suffer without further effort.

"Catch your breath. You're safe for the moment."

Kaltherzig picked up these three covered petri dishes, and carried them away to label them. Erich sat at the end of the table, aching. He didn't believe a word of it. He stood up, waiting for the hot angry little hurts to climb, moving in abbreviated gestures as if he'd been beaten, crying still thudding through him in brief bursts like little storms.

He was dizzy. His stomach hurt again. He wanted a bathroom and pleaded something along those lines, wavering. It made Kaltherzig laugh. "No, not now. Come on, get up. Two steps."

Erich felt as if his head were floating independently of his body. Kaltherzig was almost carrying him. "Clothes..."

Another laugh. "Now, really. You'll have to get over this silly modesty of yours. No need, no time."

Kaltherzig opened the door, led him through the bright hallway. The floor was cold enough to make his feet hurt. He was pulled along in the wake of the white swish of Kaltherzig's coat. He was crimson from his scalp down.

Nobody looked twice. He could not have said whether this made it better or worse.

He felt very outnumbered, very small, very far from home. He kept himself covered with his cupped hands. It made him feel even more ridiculous, but he couldn't help it.

He found himself missing Kaltherzig's house. Couldn't he do this there, without all these eyes, without all these people to hear his begging? What went on in this building, that nobody seemed even curious why he'd been screaming *that* long?

Kaltherzig led him into a room so wide and empty it echoed. The door was closed and bolted behind them. The walls and the floor were painted flat gray. There were lights throwing a blaze into one corner, an assembly of shining hooks in the illuminated wall. A camera stood sentinel on a tripod.

At the other end of the room was a small desk flanked by cabinets and refrigerators. An Untersturmführer sat here, all blond and blue, smoking with one foot propped up. He smiled and nodded and did a perfunctory *Heil Hitler* at Kaltherzig, stood up lazily, stretched and wandered over to the camera, cigar still between his teeth.

"Lieser, this is my new one." Kaltherzig pulled him over to the camera, turned him as if he were a purchase.

"The same impeccable taste as always." Lieser said in smoke.

"Thank you."

Lieser's eyes were the color of an iceberg, and bright with something that might've been mischief and might've been madness. He studied Erich like a menu. The camera, too, was an eye, a black one that would not blink.

He thought, *they'll just take my picture, that's all, that has to be all.* He didn't believe it.

Kaltherzig turned Erich and then pushed him into the circle of light, pressed on his shoulder till he went down on his knees on the concrete floor. Lieser tilted the black eye to follow him. There was a strange and upsetting smell in here, strong and sour and dangerous.

"Oh, the fucking slide..." Kaltherzig left Erich kneeling there, with this frightening blond doll of a man already snapping pictures. He kept his hands over himself even though his back was to the camera. The crash of the shutter drowned out the sound of whatever Kaltherzig was doing.

The doctor came back with a pane of glass, set it in front of his knees, dragged his hands impatiently away from his groin. He pushed on the back of Erich's neck until he leaned forward, pressed his face and shoulders to the floor, Lieser growled and then giggled somewhere Erich couldn't see. Kaltherzig pressed his waist to adjust the arch of his spine, pushed his knees apart. "Just like that. Don't move."

The floor was hospital-cold and his hands felt wrong no matter where he put them. He watched Kaltherzig's boots depart and then return. Kaltherzig dropped to one knee beside him to show him something long and strange. It was an iron bar as long and thick as a walking cane, but there was a carved wooden handle at each end.

If he hits me with that he'll kill me.

"Close your eyes." Kaltherzig was behind him, tapping this awful thing in his hand. He held it by one handle and stroked the other down Erich's spine, stopped, pushed. Pushed harder, and harder still.

"Ignore the camera."

He wasn't allowed to say no. He wanted to say *sir* or *please*. He drew in his breath. "God..."

"Just don't move, that's a good boy. Cry out all you like, there's no audio this time."

He didn't want to cry out.

In the end he couldn't help it.

It wasn't a handle at all. It was wood, carved into the rough shape of a phallus. It was dry, and considerably bigger inside him than Kaltherzig had been, and he was in so much pain already. He couldn't ignore the camera, the nasty little pop, the lightning flash, the knowledge that whatever instant that flare illuminated would be recorded for thousands of eyes.

It felt wedged inside him. He chewed the backs of his hands, tried to keep his ass up while keeping his back straight. Kaltherzig would say, "No, *arch,*" and tilt the stick inside him, wobble it side to side till he screamed, relent with thudding easy motions that made Erich think of a man breaking up soil with a shovel. He had to keep his knees straight under him, or the pushing would drive him down. He could feel his knees already scraped.

"Is that deep enough for you?" The smirk underneath his voice, and Lieser laughed behind him, camera clicking. The phallus pushed deeper, Kaltherzig leaning his weight into it. "There's a bigger one around here somewhere, shall I—" and laughed himself, through the string of *please* and *don't* and *sir*. He went back to that lazy agonizing thudding, tilted it until the involuntary arch and the throat-open scream let him know it was hitting his prostate. "There? Mmm? Stay over the slide or I'll tear you."

"You're going to tear him anyway," Lieser said. "Admit it."

"Meanwhile, no one is manning the camera," Kaltherzig told him. The bar tilted inside him. There was another kind of laugh as if they were having a teasing scuffle over possession of the handle, before Kaltherzig straightened it and went back to fucking him with it.

Erich sobbed, watching Kaltherzig's boots between his bleeding knees. He stayed over the slide, a rectangle that gave him back the ghost of his naked stomach and his shuddering erection. Every push made him, harder, in spite of the cold, in spite of the eyes. The climb started by itself, pulling him along, farther and farther and farther till he was no longer exactly thinking.

Faster. Faster. Kaltherzig twisted it inside him and he screamed until it stung his throat. Every push felt like a fist against that place that seemed to be the other end of his cock. The flash was so bright he could see it with his eyes closed.

He did not want that thunderous, hideous pleasure. His body didn't care what he wanted, traitorous thing that it was. Something wrong and delicious coiled low in his belly, unwound itself higher until he was making fists and making embarrassing noises. It was all tangled in his head with these new eyes on him, with the shame of the camera, with Kaltherzig so tall and so silent above him. At the end all he could feel was something like a bright red string from the tip of his cock all the way up to Kaltherzig's hands, miserable unending hurt, terrifying new bliss.

At the end he almost understood what would happen.

He screamed in new registers at the edge of the revelation, terrified of the plunge he could sense approaching. Nothing changed. He broke down in a *please* that trailed away into silence as the fall took him and he could only shake, suspended.

I'm dying.

It arced through him again, the worst delight imaginable, a cataclysm that would not let him go, centered in that place where Kaltherzig was slamming inside him with that terrible thing, over and over.

It was his first orgasm.

Underneath it all was the anonymous strange splatter, and the splashes on the glass blocking his reflection, and the erection behind them twitching, wilting.

The bar was drawn out, as if Kaltherzig were pulling back a spear. One last scream at this frictioned scrape. Kaltherzig leaned over him. For a moment Erich thought he was going to embrace him, but he only picked up the glass, careful not to tilt it. "Good boy." That, those two words, were somehow worse than all that had come before, and they both comforted him and fractured him into new tears.

Kaltherzig carried his sample over to the workspace in the corner. Erich turned his head, blinked away blurry tears to watch Kaltherzig put on new gloves, do delicate things with his sperm and a tiny silver spatula and miniature glass vials. He pasted on labels the size of postage stamps, putting everything in the locked refrigerators already teeming with jars.

Lieser took lazy pictures behind him. Erich wept.

"It's taking much too long that way." Kaltherzig came to stare down at Erich, peeling off these thin light gloves, pulling on new ones of black rubber so thick the fingers were like the fingers of a mannequin, featureless. "Get up. We'll try something faster." He pulled Erich closer to the restraints bolted to the wall.

Lieser snapped one last picture—Erich in a line of distress with one hand stretched so far overhead that he was on tiptoe, while Kaltherzig buckled a rubber-coated manacle around his left wrist. There was semen in a wet cooling line down his left thigh.

(they're, working, this is a day at work for them, God)

The restraints closed inexorably, taking him away from himself one piece at a time. Wrists, chest, waist, knees, ankles, even his neck, all in that same rubbercoated immovable style. Erich was almost hanging, feet arched to keep his toes on the floor in a way he knew he had no chance of sustaining. He pulled against them, dizzy, pushed with his buttocks and his back against the bricks behind him. An inch or so was all the space he had left in the world. His shoulders were aching already.

Kaltherzig wheeled over a cart heavy with a box of switches and dials, a snaketangle of cords slowly stretching taut behind him. He hummed to himself, something like Orff that Erich couldn't place, rubbed cream from a jar over tiny circles hooked to wires that fed back into the machine. It looked, like...a short-wave radio, maybe? Erich was terrible at machines under the best of circumstances. He could not imagine the purpose of this one, only that there would be pain, and would this *ever* be over?

"How is your bladder?"

"My.....sir?"

A sigh, that dangerous impatience.

"Bladder, full, empty, which?" He came to Erich and pressed with tented fingers just above his pelvic bone, making him squirm. "Never mind, that won't do."

Kaltherzig picked up a handful of things that dripped a black rubber bulb and tubing, and a clear IV bag. "Saline, electrolytes, actually almost what we use for blood loss. It conducts perfectly." He put the bag down in a gleaming jellyfish heap on the instrument table, dipped into his inescapable jar and greased this long narrow black tube.

He brought it closer, watching Erich's eyes, closed gloved fingers around his penis, pinched the head. "It'll go in easier if you relax."

Once the very end of the tube slid into the tip of his urethra he couldn't, move, anyway, only shake and feel this slippery spreading burn move farther and farther up the shaft of his penis.

He was doing the *please* but he'd done so much of that since the Gestapo that it was becoming noise without sense. Wasn't that what everyone said to the police, all the time? They could just make it the official polite greeting, it would save so much time…

The tube slid in deeper. The camera flared over Kaltherzig's shoulder. "You'll feel something, like a pinch, inside, and then it will be over—"

This promised pinch was the worst pang of hurt and burn and the need to urinate or push or shriek there had ever been. Then that knot of nerves Kaltherzig had driven to orgasm by stroking was *impaled* by this wide slippery tube. He shook, silenced, eyes frozen wide open. He was paralyzed by a sense of *give*, opening, in a place inside him so tiny and deep that nothing, nobody, should ever have been able to touch him there. It felt obscene.

The disassociation was failing him, destroyed by that piercing *specific* pain, that inescapable sense of a virginity, lost, of this new thing fucking him in this new place. He could not think of it as the instrument's fault. It felt unmistakably like Kaltherzig inside him. Twitching little try of his cock to harden again, squeezing around the tube.

That awful muffled pop of a flashbulb, and a violet afterimage burned into his streaming eyes on top of dozens of other blue mirage circles.

He cried and pushed his hips against the wall, away from that penetration, so hard he would later find bruises there. There was nowhere to get away from it. This hand in this gleaming black glove kept pushing the tube. A deep strange slide. There was an angry burning point inside him where that miniscule valve had been forced to spread. Kaltherzig wobbled it a little, until it was set exactly right. The pushing stopped. "There."

Kaltherzig picked up the bulb. Watched Erich's face, thumb and forefinger still holding the tube inside him. Squeezed it. A heartless mechanical *spread*, in a place so private he could not visualize it.

Grayness spread behind Erich's eyes—and retreated. No escape that way, either. A tug so the bulb inside him pushed hopelessly at the entrance to his bladder. Then the IV bag and the spreading sensation of cold, the bag squeezed in Kaltherzig's hand held high overhead. In seconds he was in that mindless place again, squirm, scream. The tube was clamped and the bag removed from it. His bladder was so full and so immune to his pushes that he could only hang, dying to kick or draw up his knees, afraid that something inside him would rupture.

Fingers lifted his penis, daubed something cool on him, pressed tiny rubber contacts to his skin until they stuck. More tugging at the catheter. He kept his eyes closed, thinking *no no no, he can't stop me saying it inside my head, that's a little help, just a little.* It was no help at all, and involuntary seizures of motion shook all through him, as if Erich meant to pull himself free. Both SS men laughed, at this frail furious struggle. "You're making it harder on yourself again." That balanced doctor voice, blasphemously normal.

"What would you have me do? Sir?" It sounded like a flippant sort of death-wish in his own ears.

More of that laughter. "He has you there, Ahren." Lieser, smirking. More flashbulb, and a lazy plume of cigar smoke.

"So true. Well, my boy, you're right, I suppose. Kick all you like."

Those tiny rubber pads, one at the head of his penis, one very close to his body, underneath the shaft. One on either side of his scrotum, Kaltherzig nudging this delicate flesh with his fingertip. He leaned back, nodded at this arrangement and pulled the wheeled cart with the dreadful black box, bristling with knobs and dials, inset with a gleaming face of gauges.

Lieser had given up the tripod and was orbiting them like a carrion bird with the camera, illuminating them with lightning-colored flares. Most of Erich's hate was reserved for this perfect Aryan bastard, this observer that was changing what he observed. With the eyes in Berlin through the camera. Kaltherzig was missing that absent-minded kindness, missing those low-water marks when the cruelty waned.

The first edge of current was so faint Erich thought he was imagining the vibration. Then a sharp climb in volume, an edged thing like the cold chill when glass splintered into an unsuspecting thumb. It did not hurt where the pads were, or along his skin, but through him. And worse, it did not exactly...hurt. He did not have a word for this sensation. He closed his eyes again, half panting through his teeth, expecting much worse at any second.

This motion climbed, razorsharp edge of a high note buzzing from the base of his penis to the tip, cupped in a heartless hand around his scrotum. Then a swarm of invisible knives climbed through skin and nerve in a jagged blur. He lost one ungainly noise. The uncanny sting split frequencies, a thudding inevitable rhythm underneath. And here was the hurt he'd been waiting for. Another climb. Faster, harder, deeper. It was burning him, now. It must be. He would smell it soon enough.

He was tempted to hate both of them, in the few thinking places he had left. There was an eternity, hanging in darkness, in a place like the state before sleep, the pain unimaginable, so large it was absurd, an unprecedented thing he could not really believe in. The screaming was thrown back at him from all these concrete walls. Flashes painted the black world intermittent purple.

He thought there was silence, until he realized it was only the electricity stopping. It took a long time for his cries to catch up, his limbs were still shaking with the ghost of those jittering knives.

"I suppose that's enough playing. Are we ready to begin?"

He did a pointless sway against the restraints. He was trying to shake his head when Kaltherzig began it. The current drew those same buzzing lines through his flesh, but softer, smoother. The rise and fall was faster, stroking in impossible places by a thousand miniature hands. He dared not let down his guard. He could not forget how quickly those hands could become knives. He watched Kaltherzig nudge one dial and then another. He was gasping and the erection was, mindless, not his fault, unstoppable.

(at least before it was, him, doing this to me, this is just being DONE to me, just for that camera, just)

Kaltherzig was standing very near him, smirking at his struggle. He fought for so long that Kaltherzig reached for the dials again. He screamed his way through a punishing blur: thuds like the heel of a hand striking between his legs faster than anyone could possibly swing; a fusillade of blows from imaginary tiny hammers inside the shaft of his penis, a lightning quake that made him scream and scream, just four excruciating pulses that made him leak a tiny bit of fluid in spite of the tube wedged inside him.

"Oh, I forgot." A laugh. He hadn't forgotten. The bulb inside him deflated. Kaltherzig pulled. The flash went off again.

He found enough rage to think *not going to scream, not this time.* What was left of the balloon hit this valve in the center of everything. Spread. Slide. The pain was like nothing had ever been. He clung to this silence, every muscle cable-tight.

"Don't you dare," came the whisper. Kaltherzig gave him a mean push with tented fingers, just over his pubic bone, making him grind his teeth so hard to keep back the scream there was a sound like coal over concrete.

Kaltherzig hissed and pinched the tip of his cock between thumb and forefinger, thick rubber gloves squeaking against his skin. He writhed, the machine at a thick terrible purr he could feel in his teeth, in his lungs, blazing everywhere he was most afraid of being

(petted)

hurt until he could feel it starting again and he closed his eyes and mouth and ears and thoughts and this time there was none of that climbing pleasure, none of that overwhelming deliciousness he remembered.

"You will, you know," Kaltherzig told him. "You won't be able to help it."

He couldn't help it.

This orgasm was more like a sneeze or a cramp, without pleasure, without control, and he felt Kaltherzig's fingers replaced with cool glass, opened his eyes and saw the cameraflash imprint the doctor's narrow shadow on the floor, hand and the line of a test tube intersecting Erich's shadow between his legs.

More black.

His hair was wet in his eyes, stinging with sweat. Kaltherzig was labeling a second tiny flask of his sperm and putting it away. The machine was off, but there was a hot trembling sense of damage inside him, as if he had been deafened.

Lieser applauded for long enough to make his point, before wandering out leaking blue smoke through his grin. Kaltherzig laughed and sketched an elaborate bow at his vanishing back.

Kaltherzig came to Erich at once and did little miserable tugs until the contacts were removed and coiled and neatly laid on the cart beside the black box. He unfastened Erich's ankles, unfastened his arms and caught him like an armload of clothes. Erich wanted to thank him, but his mouth seemed as vibratory as the rest of him, buzzing as though possessed by bees.

Kaltherzig half-carried him to the chair behind the desk. His head swung forward and thudded into Kaltherzig's shoulder, and he wanted to apologize, or was it thank you? He was shaking as if the electricity had left traces inside him, jittering back and forth without the wires to run away into. He drew in a breath, and when he managed to talk it was "Please, don't, please, sir," in a strange staccato, as if he were stuck on five minutes ago.

Kaltherzig clapped him on the back and took the cart away. He came back with a silver flask open in his hand. He offered it, and gave up aiming for Erich's unsteady hand and held it to his mouth. Erich drank, eyes stinging, stomach heaving. Warmth spread through his chest, and he could feel his heartbeat in his face. Kaltherzig drank himself, casually, and re-capped it.

He could not walk. The best he could manage was a wavering stumble. Kaltherzig had that inescapable grip of his upper arm, and that was just enough to keep him from falling. He was very aware he was still naked, but his arms were too heavy to bring up his hands and cover himself. Did it matter now? Now, after the camera?

He was quite sure Kaltherzig was taking him back to that table dripping straps, and that could not be, because after that they would go back to that room behind him, and he could not do that again, not ever.

He had been afraid of Kaltherzig before. He had no word for how he felt about the doctor now. Fear did not begin to approach it. Perhaps it was something like worship.

He thought of the great statues of Egypt, towering inhuman and immovable, and then of the table again. He'd almost followed that thought to *The Room again* and was making a small repeated sound when Kaltherzig steered him through a door into a tiny new room. Bare concrete walls, there were three cots, all empty, and a metal toilet that Erik rushed for without asking, without thinking.

Kaltherzig let him, laughing.

There was a frightening moment where he was afraid he couldn't, where he was helplessly aware of Kaltherzig behind him, of the door open behind both of them, and then the discovery that yes, he could still urinate, and that yes, he was wounded in a bright indignant deep place inside him that stung like a match held too long. Erich flushed away pink water, shaking hands and empty mind. He had no idea what to do next, and that fact held him in place, waiting to be told.

Kaltherzig took his arm, led him to one of the cots. There was a blanket, and then there was a needle.

Reitgerte

Kaltherzig woke him dressing him in his uniform again. He sat up, almost glad of that pink gleam that had once seemed so much worse than nakedness, thinking again, *doll.* The doctor led him in an unsteady path to the car, steering him at elbow and shoulder.

He dozed on the way home, the morphine holding him listless and heavy. For long warm minutes he would forget what had happened to him today, and he would begin to relax, and then he would remember. Sometimes this made him make that same, small, repeated noise again, but he was doing it so softly Kaltherzig didn't seem to hear.

It was over. That was the important thing, it was over.

His legs were still rubbery and difficult on the way into the house, and the setting sun was too bright. He was steered to the couch and left there, knees drawn up, his shoes tugged off his feet and taken away. More dozing, in that soft shimmering space. Background noise of Kaltherzig, typing, the radio playing softly, the clink of bottles from the little inset bar.

The typing stopped. He sat trying to work out what sound had ceased when Kaltherzig sat beside him. The doctor's shoulder was sudden and tempting as a pillow. Coffee was put into his hands, with the bright tang of alcohol in it. He drank, wishing for something wetter somehow. Cold water in a sweating glass with too much ice. The coffee was taken out of his hands, vanished. Then Kaltherzig was drawing him to his feet.

He thought, *It's not over,* and he wanted to laugh. Kaltherzig steered him down the hallway. He thought, *he'll do it again* as they passed the bed, almost hopefully. The idea of it did something hot and strange to his chest. He already knew that wasn't where they were going.

Kaltherzig led him into the bathroom and then took a carton from the medicine cabinet. He poured something that looked like salt into a glass, added warm water from the tap, and handed it to Erich. He didn't have to tell him to drink it.

What happened if you drank seawater? He knew you'd die of thirst, eventually, if that was all the water there was. He drank. It was not salt, though there was something of salt in it. It was acidic, and had a sickly-sweet-sour aftertaste that made him want to gag. Kaltherzig grinned at this reaction. "It's terrible, yes. Hurry up."

He'd never tried to force himself to swallow anything before. He'd never needed to. And it very quickly came to force. He'd eaten nothing since bread and coffee that morning, and his empty stomach was not at all pleased with this turn of events. Sometimes his throat did a spasmodic little refusal, left him with a mouthful of the stuff so that he had to try again. He became seriously afraid he would be *unable* to do this perfectly.

Finally he held his nose closed, without caring that Kaltherzig laughed at him, and drank the rest of it in long stubborn pulls, without pausing to taste or breathe. He got a mouthful of the salt at the last, not quite dissolved. He swallowed before the taste prevented him, and then fought a long and insistent cramp of nausea.

When second glass was put in his hands it made him cry, one hand on the aquarium whirl of his stomach. It was full to the very rim. But he had to obey, now, had to do it perfectly, or Kaltherzig would take him back to The Room.

He took one half-swallow. It seemed trapped in his mouth, and his tongue curled with the almost unstoppable need to spit it out. He had to force himself to swallow, and stood shaking, afraid another try would make him vomit. Kaltherzig watched this disobedience for a minute or two and went out into the bedroom.

He came back with the riding crop.

"What did I say about repeating myself?"

The glass hit Erich's lips. He drank, three long fast desperate pulls, and gritted his teeth around the gag reflex.

"Too late. Put it down."

He put it down. Chewed his lips.

"Take it off. Everything."

He took everything off, staring fixedly at the faucet handle on the sink for the cold water. He would be, there, inside those angles of chrome. Whatever was next would go on around him. Damn it, it *would*.

"Can you please, tell me why...sir..." He was down to his underwear. Maybe in this house he would always be, naked. He slid off his shorts, folded them.

"Because you still hesitate when I give you orders."

"...yes, sir, I'm sorry, sir..."

That wasn't what he'd meant. He'd meant the purges.

Maybe he'd looked at the glass, again, because Kaltherzig added, "That? You're to have procedures tomorrow. It's important your digestive tract be empty. It interferes."

Procedures.

Well, that was quite enough conversation.

Kaltherzig broke this interlude by swinging his riding crop and hitting Erich in the stomach. He tried to double over and spread his arms out of the way at once, and did kind of a wobble while he was struck three more times, the last one cutting across his left nipple. The motion shook the liquid inside him. He turned his back to Kaltherzig, afraid of being sick, and Kaltherzig struck his back and then the backs of his thighs. A gasp, and his hands coming to press flat against this strange spreading sting.

He'd seen the whip at Kaltherzig's belt and had assumed from his very few experiences with being switched that it would be like that only less, terrible, muffled with all that leather. He was wrong. The tip of the shaft behind the hard leather tongue felt like being hit by a small rock, thrown hard at close range. And then the hurt seemed to radiate outward, like the sting of a hornet.

"Pick it up and drink it."

He did. Kaltherzig vanished and came back with a shot glass, the riding crop in his hand, still tapping everything. He filled the glass twice with golden castor oil from the medicine cabinet.

Erich drank it. He would just ignore his body's signal to get this undrinkable substance out of his mouth. He would ignore it, because there were worse things, there was

(lightning)

cod liver oil, much worse, he didn't want to know what that whip felt like when Kaltherzig swung it like he meant it, did he? He didn't want worse, did he?

The grease coating his mouth made his nausea worse, and without thinking turned on the tap and rinsed and rinsed and drank and Kaltherzig merely waited politely, doing nothing to stop him. Then there were two pills, then gloves again, and a different jar. Kaltherzig told him to put his hands on the sink, and spread his feet, and he did. Then he closed his eyes.

He told himself one day all this part would be, over.

Just-until. Just until the measurements and the experiments were, over, whatever that meant, and he would only be subjected to this, for Kaltherzig's pleasure. Then it occurred to him that perhaps this *was* for the doctor's pleasure, all of it, and that it would never stop.

Kaltherzig opened the medicine cabinet again. Erich didn't dare to look.

The smear of lubrication, and that internal little teasing probe. New noise from a new jar. He made himself breathe, and again there was that excruciating slide of fingers inside him, and he hadn't realized how sore he was. The gloves were worse. Kaltherzig was safer when he didn't have those on. Breathing dissolved into panting. A push inside him that he thought was a finger at first, slipperycool and spreading an unnerving combination of soothe and ache. He moaned, and gritted his teeth harder, turned his face into his shoulder.

He didn't understand until that cool push stayed inside him when Kaltherzig took his hand away to take another out of the jar. That same greased invasion. Suppositories. He thought of them as something for, oh, old people or very sick babies with fevers. He'd heard of them, but he'd never, had, one. Or two. Or the six he finally had, when Kaltherzig stopped.

"That's the last of it for now."

Kaltherzig put the accumulated bottles and jars away neatly, labels turned out. Erich watched this, thinking, *so efficient, in every, single, detail.* He felt stuffed full, as though he were open, though when he snuck his hand there he didn't feel open. His face was crimson. He could muffle the crying but there was nothing he could do about the blushing.

"Stay here."

He stayed in position, feeling the slow roll of cramps, gritting his teeth and huffing through the worst of them. He thought, *I am not here, I am not here, I am not here.* His throat hurt.

He had an erection.

Kaltherzig left, came back with Erich's mostly still-folded blanket over his arm, a pillow held by one corner, and a tall mug of water. "You're to stay in here. If you get so much as one corner of either of these wet, you're to scrub them both and sleep on the tile, and I'll beat you bloody in the morning."

He was failing not to be here.

Kaltherzig threw the blanket and pillow down in the farthest corner of the spacious bathroom, next to one of the sheepskin rugs. He set the water on the edge of the sink. "If you become very sick, or pass a great deal of blood or feel very dizzy, you're to sit on the toilet with your head between your knees and call for me. Do you understand?"

Always that question, as if he were, a child, an animal, who was not likely to understand. He gave his one line. Kaltherzig patted him.

"Hold on, I've something to make it easier..."

More rummaging in the medicine cabinet, and a mewl of dread Erich tried and failed to stifle. He drew in his breath, intending to pull it together. Instead there was a tiny flood of tears, "Please--no more," and he bit his lip, cringing in anticipation of a real beating. That wasn't exactly *no,* but it was close, very close.

"Shh My boy. You've got enough in there to keep you busy." He patted Erich's buttocks, low, driving him into a moan, making that dangerous teethshowing smile. He brought out a tiny hourglass. "Five minutes. After twice you can release those. Drink lots of water. If you vomit, unless it's from crying, call for me. Mmm?"

His knees were starting to shake from the cramps. The urge to push was already dragging at his insides.

"Good night." And Kaltherzig closed the door behind him.

He held the position for the first rotation of the hourglass, watching the sand with maniacal devotion. His knees buckled in increasing little seizures that were harder and harder to straighten, and his stomach churned and ached and tightened and relaxed. Sometimes a creeping horror sort of seized his throat, and he would taste that poisonous sweet-salt at the back of his tongue. His vision was blurry.

He thought, *he's filled me with tortures, from my lips to my asshole, every piece inside of me he can touch.*

Fingers, pushing inside him, and that wet silk Scotch leather voice saying, *I can feel your pulse.*

His penis was still hard.

After the sand ran out the first time he made kind of a sweeping dive for a white towel and spread it on the floor over the soft white bathmat, and got down on his hands and knees with the minute-glass, with his ass in the air because there was nobody to see him and he had this, instinct, that it would make it easier. He was still bent over at the waist, and he tried to keep his knees apart as before, but finally he resorted to holding them together drawn almost up to his chest, one hand holding himself closed, sometimes a finger pressing into that ring of muscle when the urge to push was burning especially bright in those little shallow surfaces of raw ache.

During the peaks he had to squeeze as hard as possible, with everything, from jaw to stomach to thighs to buttocks to toes, just to keep from doing the opposite, the push push push that he wanted more than he had ever wanted anything in all his life. His other hand he kept wrapped around his stomach, sometimes rubbing at the worst of the muscle contractions, sometimes just hugging himself or swiping at his face when the, sobbing, was too much.

The dark wood frame of the little timer showed in white inside his eyelids when he blinked. He thought, *he must've had others, before, me, to keep all of this here.*

The last five minutes of sand ran out after about fifteen years. He'd never moved that fast in his life, and when he could finally give in to that urge to push, the first real pain hit him.

The suppositories left him in a colorless pool of wax. Soon he was only passing fluid that stung like acid. He spent a lot of time in that face-down position on the towels, trying to resist the urge to push again, fearing that hot chemical blaze. The pills began to work on him, as distinctly as a punch; a new muscular urgency to the contractions that left him with a stomachache like the aftermath of too many sit-ups.

After that it was a Hellish carousel with stops in the bath and on the toilet and to the sink to drink and cling and cry and back again. He was wiping off more and more crimson. He was afraid of getting in trouble for using so much expensive paper.

He refilled the tub with clean water, half-hoping the noise would bring Kaltherzig. It didn't. The white of all the marble and tile was a blaze, now. He staggered, swallowed, sweated as if he had a fever. He was hungry, of all things, new and separate cramps to wrap himself around.

Hours.

He was too dehydrated to produce tears.

He lay in the bathtub shaking, holding the cheeks of his buttocks open to avoid the pressure against his swollen rectum. He was sobbing *please, please,* able to see nothing but that name painted on the glass, and *Lagerarzt,* thinking *I need, a doctor...*

The echo scared him. He kept calling anyway, the sobbing never really climbing, catching him for a beat or two between *please* and *sir.* He was bleeding now, into the water.

No knock, and no shouting, just the gentle click of the door latch and the knob turning. Ahren stepped inside, in a black satin robe, hair rumpled and lovely, squinting at the light in Erich's general direction.

He just cried. Waited. Even a beating would be better the pain in this unspeakable place.

Kaltherzig left, bringing a new hysterical pitch to Erich's crying. He assumed he'd been abandoned, but the doctor returned with his black leather bag. He drained the tub and while it refilled he daubed the inside of Erich's left arm with alcohol and set a thick needle into the vein. The injection was a delicious mercy, wave after wave of painless peaceful calm.

He soaked a cloth with cold water, draped it around Erich's neck. The terrible, stomach-deep, fevered nausea subsided almost, miraculously, instantly. He was handed his cup of water and a pill. He swallowed it without hesitation, drank in long thirsty grateful pulls. The injection left him so sleepy it was difficult to hold up his head.

He found himself sitting in clean hot water, cradled with his head pillowed in Kaltherzig's shoulder. This bath was nothing like the first, lazy long bare-handed swipes that did very little to clean him and a great deal to soothe him.

Kaltherzig drained the tub, stood him up and covered the bottom with the thick white towels. Erich stayed in it for most of this, while this strange bed was built around him. He did a guided fall down. Kaltherzig turned him over on his face, rubbed something on him and inside him that spread cool numb heaven everywhere it touched, and covered him in more towels.

"I'll leave the door open, so I can hear you."

Erich was alone.

The faucet dripped. After a while it slowed, stopped. He drew his feet up, away from the tiny wet spot. He was warm. The pain was far away, easily ignored.

Darkness. He felt oddly spoiled, pampered, very...attended to.

Young. Powerless.

Sleepy.

74

Vollständigkeit

Morning.

The silent tug on Erich's coat turned out to be permission to rest against Kaltherzig's shoulder during the ride to Block 10. He was weak and his tongue was dry and fuzzy and his eyes were scratchy in their sockets. It was difficult to focus his eyes. Leaning on Kaltherzig was a marvelous way to hold up his heavy head.

He hurt everywhere, as though he'd spent a week straight in his gym class and then fallen down some stairs. So many muscles were pulled that almost any motion stirred a few of them to add their complaints to the general list. Of those aches, his abdominal muscles were probably the worst, and he sat with his arms wrapped low around himself. There were deep, specific little stars of pain inside him, everywhere the needles had been. Only The Room had seemed to leave no suffering behind, and that really couldn't be right, could it?

He wanted to ask about *procedures*, but if he did, Kaltherzig would answer. He didn't want this answer. Both his education and his attempts at logic suggested bloody and permanent reasons Kaltherzig might want his patient starved and purged empty. He wanted to be afraid of this, really he did, but he could not believe in it yet.

Parts of him had been silenced completely in the last two days. He was no longer that same boy who had laid out print in a very nice suburb of Berlin.

This couldn't be the world, could it? The whole world, the real world, still part of the same world? There couldn't be a world of dinnertime and birthday parties cool silent libraries and a world with The Room in it at the same time. One of them was a dream. One, or both.

He was endlessly thirsty.

There was a bad moment when he was sure they were going, but Kaltherzig turned left instead of right, went to a room Erich had not yet seen. It was narrow and long and almost empty. There were tall metal cabinets that looked suspiciously abandoned just inside the door, and there was a looming complication at the far end of the room that stopped Erich's feet as though they'd stuck fast to the floor.

There was a table, yes, but it was not like the many-armed spidery menace in Kaltherzig's office. It was flat and solid and covered in leather, one massive piece bolted to the floor. There were no restraints on it that Erich could see. Just behind the table a support post on four thick wheels stretched an ornate array high over the leather surface. There were tubes, and gleaming bits of chrome, and Erich could find nothing in his mind that it might be like, except possibly a telescope. A tentacle spill of cords behind the ponderous machine trailed over and up into the last piece of furniture in the room, a dilapidated metal desk and a slightly less dilapidated control panel.

Kaltherzig merely pushed him forward until he was out of the doorway. "Undress," he ordered, without looking at Erich. He closed the door—Erich heard it lock—and he was alone with this terrible something. He got as far as unbuttoning his shirt when something gray and dry happened to everything. He made it three and a half steps, not quite to the wall, but it was close enough for him to stumble into it, turn his back against it. His hands returned to his buttons, fumbled hopelessly, gave up.

When Kaltherzig came back he had a mug in his hand and a bundle of files under his arm, his black leather notebook on top. He held the mug out for several seconds before he seemed to realize Erich wasn't going to take it. "My boy." Very softly. He leaned down a little. "What is it now?"

Erich moved his lips and when that caused nothing to happen, he pointed beyond Kaltherzig to the machine, and shook his head. He supposed that was a no, but it meant something closer to *can't*.

"It's an x-ray machine," Kaltherzig said, in that same, soft, almost sculpted voice. It was probably supposed to be soothing, and it was. The words themselves didn't help much. Kaltherzig could see this, apparently, and he added "It's pictures, my boy. Only pictures. Have I lied to you yet?"

He hadn't really, Erich realized.

He'd had an x-ray before. When he was--three, four?--he'd been determined to befriend their neighbor's golden retriever, and the dog had been just as determined to avoid this giggling clumsy creature made of sticky, grabby hands. An epic chase had ended with Erich tripping and landing on top of the jutting root of an oak tree, with his arm between it and his ribcage, and his resulting hysterical wailing had gone on so long his mother had finally relented, and they'd taken him to a doctor, and there had been a gentle examination and then he'd had to lie very still, under something much smaller and less imposing than this machine.

And that had been all.

And nothing like what Kaltherzig had done to him the night before had gone on, and at that, he froze, stricken.

Surely he would have remembered such embarrassing anguish. No, nothing like that, just having his arm bandaged and his hair ruffled, dozing in the back seat while his parents murmured in the front seat, his father grateful that Erich had no broken bones, his mother irritated by the bill they'd had to pay.

His mind circled these two facts that refused to hinge together, toying with the uneven edges like a tongue worrying at a loose tooth.

He thought again, that Kaltherzig collected tears, and then a terrible thing occurred to him: perhaps last night had been unnecessary. Completely unnecessary, simply for the collection of tears, simply to unmake him, dismantle him, or worse still, simply because Kaltherzig wanted to do it.

He can do anything to me. Anything he likes. Anything at all. He doesn't have to ask anyone, it doesn't have to make sense, and there might be worse things than the gun, there might...

Something in his mind wavered, bent like cheap shelves under too much weight, and he shut down this train of thought as though it were heresy. That could not be. That was not how the world was. There had to be logic in it. He just didn't understand it, wasn't a doctor, couldn't see it, remembered wrong.

He realized he'd been standing silent, and that Kaltherzig was beginning to look decidedly impatient.

"Just...just pictures of my bones?"

It made him shiver when Kaltherzig nodded.

(wanted to do it, just because he wanted to)

(anything to me, anything he likes)

It was one more thing that would belong to them and not to him.

He moved his hands back to his buttons again. They were shaking so hard he found himself unable to manage. Kaltherzig brushed them away and made him take the mug. It was cold, clean water, and Erich drank it empty and longed for more without daring to ask.

It was, of course, only pictures. He was cold and naked and still afraid of the looming thing above him, and it wasn't exactly fun to hold perfectly still in awkward positions. When Kaltherzig got him arranged he would step away, and the machine would hum alarmingly as though it were gathering steam, and then there would be an invisible click that he thought he could feel in the edges of his teeth. Kaltherzig would say, "All right," meaning Erich could breathe again. The doctor would rearrange him, and Erich found he nearly liked this. He felt as if he were being sculpted.

When Kaltherzig finally slid the machine aside so Erich could sit up, he was almost sleepy. To his relief, Kaltherzig gave him back his clothes and let him dress. It was dangerous to be naked here.

Another new room, apparently Kaltherzig's office. It was small and almost crowded, but meticulously neat. There was a great oak desk, a much smaller desk with a typewriter. Bookshelves here, too, filled with medical texts. The doctor pointed at a chair across from his desk, seated himself and produced a small leather case from a drawer. Erich expected sharp things, and perhaps he'd been right, after all. It was a reel-to-reel voice recorder.

Kaltherzig set it up with the quick easy movements of much practice. "All right. After this, I'll have enough of a case history on you to start a proper file. Then I can turn you loose here to have a go at some of my typing. We'll have your first treatment before we leave today."

Erich swallowed, and wished for more water. "Am I sick, sir?"

Kaltherzig laughed. "No. Just an invert. The Reich would like for me to find a cure for this, so I tell them I'm looking."

Could that be possible? Erich thought of
(Emil's)
hands and shoulders and the voices of men, of Kaltherzig pinning him with those eyes, and wondered if such a thing could be done. The idea of it, he discovered with surprise, was horrible. He did not want to be cured.

Apparently some of this was visible on his face, because Kaltherzig said, "I'm quite convinced no such cure exists, or can exist. But they are not, and here we are."

"Yes, sir." Erich was looking at the recorder. He was beginning to think this was not a new room after all, that he had been in the same room not a week before, with two policemen, and probably the very same file Kaltherzig now opened across his desk. "But there's a treatment?"

He felt Kaltherzig look at him, and before he thought better of it he glanced up long enough to confirm it. The doctor seemed more amused than angry. "There are several. None that I would call a success. Yours, I think, will prove as useful as yesterday's anesthetic."

A ferocious blush hit Erich when he realized what Kaltherzig was referring to. He wanted to cover his face with his hands, but didn't, though he did draw himself up smaller and tighter in the stiff wooden chair.

"Now. I'm going to ask you questions, and you're going to answer them. Completely. In detail. If you lie to me, or keep things from me, I'll know, and I'll stop the tape and you and I will have a discussion you won't like."

Erich waited to be asked if he understood, but Kaltherzig only waited. *Pictures of my bones,* he thought. "You have to have everything," he said, without knowing he was going to say anything until it was too late. "Just everything. All the time. Every thought, and every--" Inch, he almost said, except that his blush flared so brightly it stopped the word in his throat.

"Yes. Everything. I must and I will have everything." There was nothing in that tone even close to guilt or shame. It wasn't venomous, or gloating, or amused. It was mere and monumental fact. "If you behave yourself, as I think you're trying to do--though I'm going to make that impossible sometimes--you'll spare yourself some pain."

Some.

"You'll live much longer."

He thought of that spreading triangle of blood again. Of the other inmates he'd seen during his brief times out in the camp and not safely caught in these nightmare rooms. Skinny, shaven, dirty, and desperate-eyed. Indistinguishable from one another, and thus disposable. He found himself watching Kaltherzig's hands, spidery and elegant and with broad gleaming nails, with the bright ring and its cheerily grinning skull.

"Yes, sir." He swallowed again. His stomach rose and fell inside him, rolling around sick emptiness.

Kaltherzig started the tape recorder.

The reels turned. Kaltherzig's pen moved in that black leather notebook. He recorded his name and Erich's, the date, Erich's birthday and brief vital statistics.

And then he began it.

The first questions were gentle enough—innocent details about his parents, his home life, his early years in school. He quickly came to realize Kaltherzig did not want a history, a catalog of names and dates. He wanted to know what Erich had felt, what he had thought, what he had feared.

Rape was not quite the right word for this, either, he thought, but was again at a loss for a better one. He had never quite understood the concept of

(a lover)

intimacy before, of the slow exchange of pieces of one another, memories and laughter and horrors from the gray span of years before you'd met. This was not that. He was forced to open that reservoir of years himself, open it and take them out like relics in an attic trunk. Take them out, and hand Kaltherzig the ones he most wanted to keep hidden.

He found himself telling of the prisoner games, and his books about the Inquisition, and he had never told that to anyone. The reels kept turning. He gave up and tried to put his hands over his face, but Kaltherzig said, "No, not at all," mildly, without needing to specify what was not permitted. Erich moved them to the arms of his chair. There it was. The first prickle of tears. He stared at the edge of Kaltherzig's desk, listening to the hiss of the tape and trying not to blink.

"Tell me what it is about those books that upsets you so."

Erich opened his mouth and closed it again, mutely. He was so ferociously embarrassed that it physically hurt. Before he could answer, Kaltherzig laughed. "Never mind. I see what it is."

Erich made a sound he was sure the tape must've caught, and drew up his knees. It was true. He was aroused. Not erect, exactly, but he would be, if Kaltherzig kept him talking about this for long.

"You said that you'd stopped reading them, stopped seeking books of this subject matter at the libraries, yes?"

"Yes sir."

"Why?" A little remnant of that laughter. "Did you stop enjoying them?"

"There were...dreams." He drew his knees closer.

Kaltherzig stood, came around the desk, and arranged Erich again, pressed his knees till he sat with his feet flat on the floor, took his hands and placed them on the arms of the chair. That done, he took his seat again, leaving Erich feeling as if those touches had tied him in place, invisible restraints, magick that had not needed a magick word.

It was like the x-ray machine. Again, he was being sculpted. He did not like it this time, or so he told himself. This was to be no pretty,

81

ghostly picture of his bones. Kaltherzig led him politely from wound to wound, and he wanted to know, everything. About every one. And if Erich became too vague, too general, or too quiet, Kaltherzig would reach for the switch to stop the recorder. That was all he had to do. He never even had to touch it. Just the idea that he might unlocked Erich's voice, or his pride, or whatever was slowing him, and he would tell, no matter what it was.

It probably looked quite civilized, compared to what the police had done to him, but that was only how it looked. This was being flayed alive, and all of it in that soothing, reasonable voice. He could keep nothing for himself.

"Tell me about the dreams."

He would, of course. He had to. But what came out when he spoke was "You'll laugh."

"I will not."

"Someone will."

Erich looked to see if Kaltherzig was laughing already, he wasn't. Not even a little.

Those stormcolored eyes were patient and grave.

Kaltherzig reached over, before Erich knew he was going to do it, and switched off the recorder. He'd finally paused too long, pushed too far, and was about to learn what *discussion* meant when Kaltherzig said it in that particular tone of voice. Erich patiently waited to be maimed or destroyed.

"I'm quite sure I asked you about your dreams, and quite sure you don't want me to repeat my question." The words were cruel, but the voice was gentle. It was incomprehensible. Was this a kindness? A mercy? A trick?

Erich told him.

Kaltherzig didn't laugh.

None of the words were quite right. He tried, and failed, to explain that the fear of it was not being impaled or torn into pieces, but that sense of being so very outnumbered by such a powerful Them. He kept waiting for Kaltherzig to snap at him or strike him for being too general, but the doctor only listened, the pen still in his hand, motionless.

The doctor started the tape again, a very long time after Erich lapsed into silence. He asked about Emil, and Erich found to his surprise that this made him cry. He answered anyway, swallowing back sobs that hurt his throat. Kaltherzig stood again, making him put his hands back on the arms of the chair in a panic, but he took a blindingly white handkerchief from inside his coat and gave it to Erich without a word.

He told what little there was to tell, and when he ran out of that he sat staring at one particular whorl in the dark wood of Kaltherzig's desk, feeling like a pitcher poured empty. There would be more questions. He'd stopped telling himself he didn't like this. Perhaps not like, exactly, never that, but he needed it. It was that terrible bath again. He hurt, but he felt much cleaner.

The click drew his eyes back to the doctor. Kaltherzig had turned the recorder off again. "Enough for now. You look like you've been on the front, my boy, and I've got fucking Selektion duty. I'm going to leave you here, and you're going to spend every second until I return working on the mess my last boy accomplished."

"Yes sir." Cold pang of worry. What if he could not work out what to do? What if he did it wrong?

Kaltherzig presented him with handwritten patient files and a stack of blank forms, moved him from his audience-chair to the smaller desk with the typewriter, and left him alone. The door was closed and locked behind him.

It made him, dizzy, this sudden, workspace, as if the channel had been changed around him while he wasn't looking. After a moment he loaded the typewriter and started to work. The trembling inside him had stopped by itself after the third page, lulled by this odd interval of normalcy.

Once he was comfortable enough with the alignment and the flow to read some of what he was typing, that delusion ended. And the photographs that fell out of a file folder started the trembling inside him all over again. He picked the bundle up, turned it over and over in his hands. It was held together with a rubber band. He removed this carefully.

There were people in the photographs. The images were less horrible than that red spreading triangle, that fall, probably because the gray universe of photographs didn't seem quite real. The people who were still alive were considerably worse than the dead ones. Sometimes there were several photographs of the same person. On the back of each photograph the prisoner's number was noted. He thought, *I'll file them, and it will be all right,* and he filed them, and it was not all right. He was imitating the format of a few existing finished files, and he had to clip each picture to the inside cover of its folder, and he thus had to look at every, single, one. There was always an initial identification picture, the stripes and the board and the number, the same stunned exhaustion in every face. He thought *he had them developed, and they were returned and just put here, for someone like me to sort them out. Handed to his secretary.*

There was a boy his age, with dark hair like his own. He only had two photographs in addition to his identification standard. In the second he was naked, visible from the chest up, and something barred his mouth. It was hard to decipher the something in gray tones. There was an incision that trailed off beyond the photograph's edge, the color of asphalt instead of spreading red. The eyes were fixed on the camera lens, and were very much alive. He was sure of that. Dazed, but alive. In the third photograph he was most certainly not alive, and a lot of him was missing.

He turned all three over on the desk, face down, and took both hands off them. He did not want to touch them. He wanted to wipe his hands, to get rid of whatever luck they'd left on him.

He's a doctor. Doctors do things that open people. That's

what doctors are. That's what doctors are for!
    No.
    He was not disagreeing, exactly, so much as rejecting any more thought about this, wholeheartedly and completely. He put the photographs in their correct files, checked and rechecked them, and went back from transferring Kaltherzig's neatly written reports into neatly typewritten reports. He typed as fast as possible. As perfectly as possible.
    When the doctor returned he was inkyblack and dangerous in his greatcoat and cap, and he had the crop in one gloved hand. Erich shrank away from this, all eyes and stricken tongue, but Kaltherzig clapped him hard on one shoulder when he saw how few reports were left to copy over. He picked up the finished stack and flipped through them, those elegantly made eyebrows winging up and staying up. He put them down, clapped Erich again, and almost—invited—him to lunch.
    It was a short walk through autumn sun to the officer's mess.
    Kaltherzig was loose, languid, smoking and greeting the officers they passed. It was too bright after the relative gloom of Block 10. Erich was half-blinded, the din of conflicting smells locking in his throat in a tangle of nausea and hunger. Fresh-baked bread, probably from their destination, grass cuttings and warm brown dirt and that meat-processing greasy undertone. Blur of a picnic by a lake, his mother beside him, a mismatched team of wooden and lead toy soldiers in his hands.
    "Easy, now." Kaltherzig steadied him, arm settling around his shoulders more firmly. Low steps he could feel more than see, the shadow of a door, and a room so dim in comparison with the outside Erich blinked in a sea of purple, seeing the ghosts of white tablecloths and candlesticks getting more and more solid.
    It reminded him more than anything of the sort of restaurant found on the bottom floor of the most expensive hotels. He was put into a seat and he automatically tried to sit up straight, feeling shabby in his uniform, running through a mental list of his mother nagging table manners into his ear.
    There was a throbbing vacuum of emptiness inside him, from his

lips to the miserable knot of stomach just under his sternum. He had never been so hungry. The room had a severe, unstable tilt. Surreal. From sobbing on his back, to centering type, to trying to decipher which fork he might use. In the space of two days. The room was wandering off without his permission, and he had to drag himself up straight again.

"Is he all right?" A silky inquiring voice at Kaltherzig's elbow.

"Oh, yes. Half dead of purges, and yet he's still almost through the backlog from my last boy." Here he ruffled Erich's hair, as if he'd learned a particularly difficult trick.

Erich tilted his head back, asked before he could stop himself, "What, happened to the last boy, sir?"

Kaltherzig made a perfect blue smoke ring, holding Erich's eyes, so that it spiraled up to the high ceiling, and he and this doctor beside him both laughed, as though it were a reply.

"This is Herr Hauptsturmführer, Doctor Mengele, Erich. Mind your mouth, inquisitive boy." His hand patted over Erich's mouth, briefly, the gesture like a slap but nowhere near hard enough to sting. Mengele laughed. Kaltherzig kept his eyes, something hard and narrow in them, and Erich thought: *he doesn't like Mengele.* But Kaltherzig gestured an invitation to the doctor anyway, and they sat down with Erich pinned between them.

Mengele was a graceful, cheerful menace that reminded Erich more than anything of his mother's tomcat. He had a glossy sculpted mane of brown hair, and a mouth that made him look eternally amused. His eyes were muddily ocean-toned, always half-lidded. He was the bland kind of handsome that fitted neatly into officer's tabs. He never looked at anything directly, as if his attention was permanently focused a few degrees out of alignment with the world.

There was a waiter almost immediately, in generic black-and-white like any restaurant staff, but Erich could smell the prisoner on him. He didn't speak, and wasn't expected to.

The smells outside had been bad enough, here the air was heavy with real meat cooking, the Christmas tang of baking, the real cream-colored scent of white bread underneath it all. He was shaking with hunger, afraid that he would lock if he put anything in his mouth.

Two of these anonymous prisoners brought the same meal for all of them. Erich ate whatever Kaltherzig put in front of him, eyes half-lidded, feeling half-asleep, dreamlike, looped into the conviction for some reason that he was still on the truck and dreaming of Auschwitz.

The first bite of what he supposed was duck exploded over his tongue in wave after wave of rich warm butter and salt and rosemary. Sausage that threatened him with nausea that never quite moved from his mind to his throat. Real coffee, thick with cream, gritty with real sugar at the bottom. This was his first real food since before the arrest. He had one flickering picture of the skeleton men, and he kept eating. He thought *I don't owe them anything, I pay as dearly as any of them do.*

He was too tired to do much more than hold himself upright.

Kaltherzig and Mengele were talking shop. *What did you have planned?* And from Kaltherzig *much too useful for that.*

He was steered back to Block 10 in a warm luxurious daze, stomach finally full, the myriad pains inside him drowned out by that one wonderful fact.

Kaltherzig put him back at the typewriter. "Finish the last few and you can nap until I come for you," and the door locked behind him again. He roused himself into that numb vacant concentration he remembered from studying late into the night for the hated math courses and finished the last dozen or so reports. He had not been told or shown what to do with them next, so he supposed he was finished. He stacked them neatly beside the handwritten copies, buttoned his coat and pillowed his head on his arms. The desk blurred into an auburn plane.

It drew into focus again a soft eternity later, with Kaltherzig shaking his shoulder. He expected to follow the doctor outside to the waiting car, but instead they went to a room that was not new.

They went into the examining room, and Kaltherzig patted the foot of the table at Erich.

He didn't want to go near it, let alone sit there. He knew perfectly well it was Kaltherzig who had hurt him and that the table had nothing to do with it. Still, like The Room, he helplessly saw the table in almost superstitious terms. It was dangerous, haunted, cursed. He started to take off his clothes, because that was what came first, and because that would let him delay touching that evil thing.

Kaltherzig said, "No need. Just the coat, and turn up one of your sleeves. It'll only take a minute."

That was probably true. He was already in his own coat, cap just so, dressed for the car and then home.

Erich slid off his coat and turned up his sleeve and sat on the table. He wanted to look up and see the blood on the ceiling again, just to make sure he hadn't imagined it, but he was afraid Kaltherzig would see him do it. He found it more difficult than he'd thought, having the doctor near him with a needle. But it really did only take a minute, one near-painless instant high on his arm, almost in his shoulder. The injection itself hurt more than the needle had, but it was a low and ignorable hurt, like a moderately hard pinch given slowly. He didn't bleed.

"There!" Kaltherzig grinned those white teeth at him. "Do you feel any less inverted?"

He was teasing, Erich thought. "No, sir."

"You're probably the control group. You probably will be, most of the time."

Most of the time.

There was a strange routine, now, morning, breakfast, and the hospital and typing or filing, lunch in the officer's mess, and the trip home in that elegant purring automobile.

The ride

(home)

back was the most dangerous time. Kaltherzig would draw him close, and...feel, him, as if examining his bones, and sometimes he would hold his head still and look into his eyes from an inch or two away, or, smell, him. That was the worst, this predator-sense of breath on his neck, behind his ear, once against his mouth, jaw thumbed open at his chin. Once he tilted Erich's head back, held him there for an eternity before putting his, mouth, on Erich's throat, just over his pulse. Kaltherzig didn't move, only pushing there with the blunt edge of his teeth, eyes closed in the periphery of Erich's terrified vision.

He waited to be bitten. He felt strange when he wasn't. Cheated, somehow.

He was locked in the office to finished whatever work had been left for him. The second time he'd had nothing left to clean, file, or straighten, and he'd been trying to clean the narrow greasy window-glass with a rag and knocking on the door every time he saw a shadow pass. Kaltherzig had opened it, finally, half-angry, alerted by the amused explanation given to him by one of the prisoner-doctors. He had stared at the mostly spotless office and Erich's terrified eyes, and laughed.

He worked until he fell into sleep on the floor almost as soon as he was horizontal, trying with all of his terrified might to prove that he was invaluable and loyal and obedient and dedicated. That thought would not leave him, the thought he'd had when the first glossy black-and-white of a boy with gaping scream and very-much-alive eyes and a long, long incision had hit Kaltherzig's desk.

Will I leave here alive?

Smoke rings, drifting towards the ceiling. He looked at the triple pillars of smokestack and understood Kaltherzig's reply.

A week later Erich was lying on the floor at the foot of Ahren's bed, staring up into the dark. He thought he'd imagined the "Come here," but his fear of making Kaltherzig repeat himself made him stand up anyway.

Ahren made one ghost-gesture with a white hand above the dark bedspread.

Erich climbed up, the mattress strange under his hands and knees, the softest thing he'd touched except the back seat of the car in days. He was caught close, set down between Kaltherzig's knees with his back leaning against the officer's chest.

Ahren dragged the blanket out from underneath both of them, drew it up and cradled him, mouth finding the joint of his shoulder and neck.

Erich hung, feeling oddly, comforted, warm and safe and trapped, all at once. Kaltherzig leaned, opening the drawer by the bed, steadying Erich with his other hand. They were both naked, and all this long smooth hot skin underneath him left Erich something like, drugged, a daze like morphine making all his limbs heavy.

The jar, and Kaltherzig's hand between them, smoothing that slippery cream on him with sudden startling intimacy. "Does it still hurt you?"

"No, sir."

A nudge, and Erich pushed himself up with his hands, felt Kaltherzig doing something between them, lubricating his cock, most likely. "You do it." And the head, nudging against Erich with no pressure at all, defeating him immediately with a strange spreading delicious humiliation. He would be doing this to himself, participating, this time. He arranged himself and tried to be, obedient, and rocked against this silken pressure until he felt the beginning pangs of penetration, and there was less of obedience and more of

(appetite)

desire in his movements, now. It was, satisfying, unspeakably so, and the farther down he managed to push himself the more intense the sensation of being, filled, of having an unknown hunger finally satiated. It felt dirty, to do this, that much was unavoidably plain across all the other inherent pleasures, and he could not escape from the thought that it was Kaltherzig's cock and not an insensate instrument inside him.

It was heresy, leaning these two aching centers of need together, pressing down with his spine and his arms and his shoulders and the roll of his hips, feeling more and more owned with every inch that slid inside him. Kaltherzig drew him close again, wound him tight and they were rocking together. Erich came almost as soon as Ahren's hand wound around him, and the tremors took them both.

He was half asleep, after, when Kaltherzig pushed him with one tired hand, until he climbed down and settled on the floor. It was cold there, after the warm soft bed, and somehow unspeakably lonely. He lay blinking at tears that wouldn't overflow, feeling too cold and homesick all over again. He thought ugly pieces of things.

Why doesn't he like me? What am I doing wrong?

Neuerlich

Sometimes there were miniature kindnesses. Wrapped candy appeared in random handfuls beside the typewriter when he stepped away. Books, and that was the one that caught him, made him cry—two hardbacks, old and thick with tiny print, Norse myths and Greek myths, hours and hours of reprieve from this prison place. He sat at the typewriter caught in a memory of his childhood bed with the patchwork quilt and the great hardback storybook with the picture of Bellerophon falling from the chariot.

He thanked Kaltherzig for them on the ride home so many times he was finally cuffed, somewhat without enthusiasm, and told to shut up. He was given leave to read in the living room if he came to sleep in his usual place with absolutely no noise afterward.

It wasn't the gift. Only that, alone, would have made him feel more like a whore than he did already. It was the careful little attention to detail, the inherent sense of a mysterious set of files about himself that Kaltherzig not only had access to, but had studied carefully. It was the, care, or something like it, all of that demonstrated.

Not that Kaltherzig was kind to him in general, by any means. He never knew which to expect—the thoughtful presents, the hours of stroking with those intelligent hands, or the whip, and more of the terrible, terrible tricks.

In the evenings they usually went, home, together, sometimes stopping by the officer's mess for dinner. Otherwise Erich built something simple from the kitchen that was kept invisibly stocked. Kaltherzig would drink, listen to music, read, or type furiously in his study. Erich cleaned, straightened, read when he dared, made or repaired uniforms. This last chore he almost enjoyed, the narrowing of focus to these few familiar inches of cloth and thread.

Sometimes Erich was driven home alone, and Kaltherzig would stagger in sometimes close to dawn, drunk and dangerous and filled with unreasonable demands. It seemed he always knew, when the door would be flung open. A few minutes prior his hands would start shaking. It made him wonder if gazelles felt something similar, before the lions came.

There was almost nothing to be done, no level of careful or subservient that was guaranteed to spare him a beating. Sometimes there wasn't even a pretense, no words, just the door closing and locking and Kaltherzig staring at him with that terrifying vacancy, eyes not filling with, anything, until Erich was crying or bleeding or both or worse.

It always ended in the bedroom, with the riding crop or the service belt, and Kaltherzig inside him, seeking and finding orgasm without any sort of notice whether Erich was enjoying himself.

The lion nights were frightening, but less dangerous than the nights when Kaltherzig sat in the den alone, still drinking, listening to music in the dark. On these nights he could sometimes be lured with sex, if Erich was careful, taking off his boots and rubbing his feet without the slightest sound, setting them on the carpet with artisan's care so as to be utterly silent. This was risking a kick, but if he got them off it would generally prevent kicking, later.

If Kaltherzig nudged him away, he went, keeping his drink filled as unobtrusively as possible, praying he would retire to the study. If he was allowed to continue he might lure him out of his tie, rub his shoulders, progress till his face was in Kaltherzig's lap. If he succeeded in his offer of cocksucking Kaltherzig usually went to bed on his own, the violence under his skin mostly defused. Erich would wait a safe margin of time in the dark, let the phonograph shut itself off, and crawl the last ten feet down the hallway into the bedroom when Kaltherzig's breathing was the only sound left inside.

If he failed, by clumsiness or sometimes nothing at all he could pinpoint, Kaltherzig would hit him, and these times were probably the most dangerous, leaving him with a permanent terror of those hands and the gleam of light from the kitchen on the Totenkopf ring. He had nightmares about just that ring, coming at him from the dark.

If he was lucky he could crawl towards the kitchen. He had no idea why, but if he managed to make it in there Kaltherzig would not follow him. Sometimes Kaltherzig would allow this retreat, and he spent more than one night asleep on the tile floor, afraid to venture outside this so-far safe space.

If he was unlucky, Kaltherzig would pull him back, or order him to be still. He might hold his head still and slap him once, or dozens of times. Once he had let him get as far as the cocksucking and put his hands around Erich's throat, strangled Erich until the orgasm. Then Kaltherzig turned him loose, left him coughing helplessly, flailing, vision almost-black, bruises already darkening in layered collars of red.

He had been hoarse the next day, and the bruises had been visible for several inches above his shirt. People gave him odd looks that made him blush and duck his head, though he knew that did little to hide the marks.

He supposed they assumed he deserved it, and maybe they were right.

By the time the strangulation bruises had faded there was a new one on his left cheekbone, the center black around two tiny stitches where the ring had opened a cut as wide as a fingernail but so deep it had hung open in almost a circle.

Kaltherzig had laid these stitches in the bathroom, holding Erich's head, crooning that strange wordless comfort at him, doing all the shush and petting that Erich couldn't stand against, that made him feel too young to resist. The doctor had let him lie in the bed for a very long time that night, had even lay beside him for a while, holding ice wrapped in a towel to his cheek, stroking his hair. He remembered being carried to the floor with supplemental pillows and a second blanket. These bribes remained the next night, so he knew he hadn't dreamed it.

The door to Kaltherzig's office was no longer locked when Erich was left there to work. He found himself shared out among the doctors in Block 10, doing clerking and filing in a routine not so very different from his apprenticeship.

Mengele borrowed him often.

This doctor's hands were quick or languid by turns, investigating everything, only bare when he was washing them, otherwise gloved in black leather or white cotton. He was vain, polished and flawless, gleaming from cap to boots for his beloved Selektions, or in loosened tie and flapping white coat in the hospital.

Erich was half-terrified and half in awe of him. Herr Hauptsturmführer. Everyone in his path ran to do whatever he ordered. No one had to explain the power of this man to him. It was almost, visible, around him.

He called him Doctor Mengele, as he'd been told to do, and he continued with the plan that seemed to have at least kept him alive so far. Polite and obedient. He could do that. He'd been practicing all his life.

Kaltherzig kept him out of Mengele's clutches as often as possible, he sensed, but for at least a handful of hours two or three days a week he would be sent for, and he spent those hours in a dreamlike daze of panic, listening to Mengele's instructions as if they were directives from God, following orders with anguished speed and agonizing attention to detail. This was Kaltherzig's boss, and as much as he hoped Mengele was pleased with him, it was Kaltherzig whose opinion really counted. So he was a blur of perfect devotion, and so far he seemed to have accomplished what he wanted: Mengele spoke to him briefly, civilly, collected his files, sometimes presented him with new work, and otherwise left him alone.

He collected reports from the doctors and typed them and returned them, usually by lunch.

Afterward whoever won the argument would generally take him and use him to record dictation while they conducted monumentally boring examinations into a microscope.

Every three days Kaltherzig shut them into one of the examination rooms and injected him with, whatever it was. Or gave him pills, and asked questions and noted the responses, took his vitals after recorded intervals. None of this was particularly unpleasant, though sometimes he felt very strange, fast or slow or hot or delirious. On occasions like those Kaltherzig was very solicitous of him, keeping him provided with drinks and pillows and blankets, sometimes having him driven back to the house and left to sleep on the couch with the telephone nearby.

One day the photographs he found were his own.

There were a lot of them. He supposed he should be flattered by that. Here was his frightened face, holding up his number. Here were his eyes, his lips, his collarbone, his nipples, and those little calipers in the frame so that the measurement was visible. Those were the only safe ones. After that there was The Room, and he'd had no idea he was so pale and so very small. The edges of Kaltherzig had been caught in some of these, a hand, an edge of his white coat.

He put them face down on the desk. He didn't touch them until he'd finished typing up his own report. Then he picked them up, clipped them into his own file, and moved on to the next one.

The next day, Kaltherzig led him not to his office, but back to the examination room. And the doctor drew down the shades.

"Undress. Everything."

Erich did, already sick and shaking. "What did I do, sir?" he asked, finally, watching Kaltherzig set out shiny things with no names.

"Nothing, we hope. It's to see if anything about you has changed." Kaltherzig traded his leather coat for a white one, washed his hands in the metal sink. "You're not going to like much of this today, so you might as well panic now."

He sat at the foot of the table. Tongue depressor. Stethoscope. Had he liked anything that happened in this room? This thought made him blush, as though he'd been caught in a lie. Kaltherzig strapped him in, utilitarian and silent. Still that sense of being not-quite-real, being moved in this way, and then he was pinned.

Thermometer. Next would be the camera, and the bright little calipers. It was too much to be comprehended, and it could *not* be true.

"Everything?" and in his voice he could hear his own panic.

"Of course, everything." Kaltherzig leaned over so Erich could see his smile. The thermometer nudged him, and then slid inside him. It did not hurt. It was only cold. The hurt wouldn't come until later. After the camera, and the calipers.

"Again?" Erich was beginning to cry. "All of it? The Room, too?"

Kaltherzig laughed. "Is that what you call it?" The thermometer slid into him deeper, still painless, still cold. "Yes. Everything. Every month or two, give or take, as I get assigned to an increasingly large number of things that are not my fucking job."

Erich closed his eyes. It went very quickly. After no time at all Kaltherzig was snapping on gloves, and when Erich raised his head to look the speculum was gleaming in his hands. He lay back again, stared at the blood on the ceiling. Still there, and still real.

There was the squeak of the wheels of the doctor's stool.

It didn't matter what They did to him anymore. He only had to obey, fast and perfect and unfailingly polite, keep all the no inside his skull where it could do no harm. He was sure he soon wouldn't need to say it even there. What did it mean? Just a noise, here, one he wasn't allowed to make no matter what Kaltherzig did to him.

He thought, *I won't try this time. I won't struggle, I won't cry, I won't scream, I just won't try.*

But of course, he did.

Überfluten

There was a birthday party for one of the officers, at the worst of the heat of summer. Most of the SS contingent of Block 10 was at the swimming pool behind the officers' barracks by half past ten, and in increasing states of undress and inebriation by time a late lunch was brought out, with iced fruit and candy-colored drinks and wide overflowing plates of sweets.

Kaltherzig stayed under the awning, hat tipped low over his eyes, but he was down to his dress shirt, unbuttoned and sleeves turned up, and his feet were bare under the cuffs of his trousers. He teased Erich down to his uniform pants, took his striped shirt away from him.

There was a girlfriend or three, and Lieser introduced Erich to a flaxen-haired girl that had to be his sister as Kaltherzig's girl, making him crimson, but she only smiled and took his hand as if he were a, citizen. *A Valkyrie*, he thought, or a woman like Lancelot's Elaine might have been.

He was looking daggers at Lieser without meaning to behind her back, and she caught him dead at it, but only smiled too, as if they shared a joke.

No, he didn't like him. There was no rhyme or reason to him. Too dangerous.

He brought Kaltherzig food he didn't eat to spare him the walk in that sun, and drink after drink, all of them leaving rum or vodka burning in the back of his throat when Kaltherzig put them in his hands, looking the order at him. It made him thirstier, so that all he wanted was water filled with ice. It also made him dizzy and breathless and pleasantly fuzzed at the edges.

Soon Kaltherzig was drunk enough to have acquired that edge of cruelty, and was teasing Erich that he should get in the pool.

Erich was hopeless at swimming, his teachers from Jungenvolk to gymnasium having given him up to let him hang onto the side of the pool or thrash in the deepest he could touch the bottom.

The teasing crept into an order soon enough, and he sat at the shallow end with his feet over the side, steeling himself. It felt like cold clean heaven, like the antidote to the white dry heat baking off the marble at him.

He slid in, and it was luxury, a shock that was too slow to make him gasp and too total to let him breathe. Kaltherzig laughed, applauded him for a second or two.

It was a delight for the three minutes or so he had to himself before Lieser pushed him under.

Water in a cold chlorine flood up his nose, rushing into his throat, all this tranquil blue clarity foamed into bubbles in his burning eyes. He was pulled out into water over his head and turned loose, thrashing and sinking. He found the bottom by slamming into it and shoved himself towards what he hoped was up and slammed into it again.

He would drown.

And he let himself settle and pushed till his feet seemed to be under him and tried to stand, and pushed and broke the surface and gasped and swallowed more water and sank again.

He had seen Kaltherzig sitting in shadow and he knew which way to run and he tried a flailing half-walk, shoving uselessly at the water with his arms, the urge to cough destroying him, and the edge slammed into him and he pulled and clung and there was air and he could hold himself out of the water, coughing in long spasms that sprayed water onto his hands, hitched in whooping gasps of hot air, blinded, heart pounding.

Bastard.

He actually had one knee up, only focused on being out and shivering beside Kaltherzig where it was safe, with a drink in his hand, when Lieser caught him by the scruff of his neck and dragged him in again. He was caught in a spray of chlorine, in the middle of a knot of laughter, driven into the water face-first again, coughing underwater in spite of himself. He could feel them around him like circling sharks. He flailed into another pair of hands and was pushed under deeper, the bottom scraping by one elbow and one outstretched hand.

They really will, he won't stop them, he'd have to walk in the sun to get to me, and he was flailing, kicking out hard against hands and chests, breaking the surface, crying out "Ahren!"

It was the only word he could remember.

"That's enough."

Kaltherzig had walked, sun or not, and was kneeling by the water's edge.

Lieser hooked him under one arm and brought him to the side, turning him loose there with no particular malice, swimming off again at once as if he'd lost interest in this game. Kaltherzig took his hand and drew him out, let him half-curl with his feet still in the water, coughing. He stayed down on one knee at Erich's shoulder, drinking, maybe because it was too much work to walk back just yet, but he had the effect of keeping all the eyes at bay. Nobody wanted to be the one still staring.

"Idiot," he said finally. "Get up." But he offered a hand. And he did not mention Erich's use of his Christian name.

The Valkyrie was sitting in Kaltherzig's vacated seat, holding a glass filled with something the color of snow. She apologized to Erich with her eyes.

She left it at that until she stole a second as Kaltherzig was escorting an extremely drunken Lieser out to his waiting car. When their noise was far enough away she took Erich's wrist and leaned as if whispering a secret.

"The Reich is mad, you know. My brother was one of you people the minute he was born. I always knew it. Everyone knows it's really the Jews that are the disease. They're only locking up inverts for politics." And that reckless smile that was so infuriating in Lieser, a little nod as if she meant to encourage him, as if he'd gotten sent to reform school by mistake.

The exchange left Erich with his mouth open for so long he had to pretend to cough. This gorgeous Freya of a woman was as mad as her brother. She seemed to think Lieser, who always volunteered for

Selektion, who'd fought with Kaltherzig over the privilege of sodomizing him with an iron bar, was an example of how everything would come out all right in the end.

Summer browned into autumn.

One orange afternoon they left Block 10 early, and Kaltherzig's driver took them beyond the camp and out into the countryside, autumn-bare fields and the blaze of colorchanged leaves, some trees already bare black lines.

When the great arch of the gate passed overhead Erich realized he was
(afraid)
outside, for the first time in months and months. He turned to see Auschwitz behind them.

Soon they were far enough away for the air to taste of outdoors and sunshine and grass and, nothing else. That meat-processing smell was gone, and only clean things left in its place. Erich wondered if people from Outside would smell the camp on him. He looked down at himself and the uniform struck him, with an ugly shock that made him flush all over.

He had grown used to being this kind of
(naked)
marked Inside, but it was different here, under this sky, the stripes and his triangle. Erich buttoned his coat. Kaltherzig was watching him do it, and failing to hide that grin.

After what felt like nearly an hour, Erich was beginning to think this time might be a sweetness Kaltherzig wanted him to experience, and not a new agony. He wanted to ask, but he knew better. He was trying not to hope, but he had a strange feeling in his chest, an excitement he associated with being very small on Christmas Eve.

They stopped finally in the long dirt-and-grass drive of a farmhouse, everything drenched in sunlight-gold. Erich was led with increasing delight in knee-high yellowing grass to a long splintering fence.

There were horses: a great long dark stallion that came over with slow, leisurely dignity, like one of Poseidon's stable, an arrogant thing that simply had to be Kaltherzig's horse. He brandished the blunt white machinery of his teeth, and Erich was afraid of the same mechanism in the quiet tall mare that wandered up behind him. A rotund man the dappled paste-color of uncooked apple pie had come out with a great show of welcome Erich didn't think he meant. He shook Kaltherzig's hand for too long, answered his questions with too much nodding.

Erich was timidly offering the flat of his hand to the mare, but when she ventured close enough to investigate him the fear of the teeth made him draw it back. They laughed at him a little, but the man came over and stroked her, took Erich's hand and coaxed him to do the same. Her nose was much softer than he expected. It made him think of the rumpled little patch on top of a kitten's head. The smell gave him some kind of memory, something to do with games the other boys wouldn't let him play. Summer, confused in his mind with the chlorine cold of Lieser pushing him underwater.

He managed the saddle with a generous help up, and Kaltherzig did something and they were gone, leaving him clinging and breathless and rattled horribly until something clicked inside him and he learned to move with and not against, and the wind in his face was like, flying.

They had dinner served on the deck by this man's silent wife. After there were too many drinks, and the wrinkled man told a circular set of stories about loose women, gesturing in alcoholic arcs.

Kaltherzig laughed at all the right times, but once his eyes found Erich's, and there was no laughter there. Something else entirely.

He could not keep his eyes off the horses, and Kaltherzig finally called Erich's mare close and helped him mount again. "No farther than that tree, or I'll shoot you out of the saddle." That smile, the real one, eyes and all, that Kaltherzig only seemed to use at the most inappropriate times.

Overall, he was as hopeless at horseback riding as he'd been at any other sport, one mess of ache from neck to knees. It was so much fun, that he hardly noticed the bruises. Once he became reasonably sure he wasn't going to fall off he started to notice how much farther he could see from so high and how fast the ground seemed to blur by, so far below.

He was exhausted to the point of near-sleep when they drove back to the camp. If he closed his eyes he could still, almost see, the ground rushing by underneath him, and it made his stomach do a strange slow wonderful roll. *Flying.*

It had been a bribe. He knew that. But was there something else. Why, for example, had he not taken a friend, another officer?

Did Kaltherzig have friends?

Lieser. Too near, maybe. Near enough to tell tales, or hold grudges. And Kaltherzig outranked him, only just, but maybe that mattered, too.

Erich was safe. He had no one else to tell.

It was almost dark. He leaned on Kaltherzig's shoulder without thinking to ask, and was not pushed away.

Totenhemd

"I have three postmortems today and I think you're ready to notate for them. You might not wish to eat if you think it's going to disturb you."

Postmortems. He had seen bodies, of course, by now, lying where they'd been thrown out of each block when they went in each morning. Walking past an anonymous sort of peripheral shape would be nothing, compared with being shut in a room with an example he could not ignore.

He didn't eat.

Sometimes he told himself he was simply trying to survive, or to learn so as not to waste this time, but the feverish frantic *interest* in anything that might prove useful scared him.

He found himself looking out the car windows for bodies, that same, studying instinct, all tangled with his constantly evolving idea of, perfect. He wondered if he might not, like, the hospital. He wondered if he might not like the busy frightening bustle of it, the chemical smells, the sense that everything was very important. He wondered if he might not even like the sense that it was cursed, haunted.

Nothing in all his life, not the print shop, not Hitler, not anything in school had ever seemed to matter. There had always been this glassy sense of a game, a rehearsal. He felt nothing of that, here. Auschwitz was more real than anything had ever been.

The morgue, if that was what you called one room with twelve metal tables and four bodies, smelled immediately of something hideous and familiar, and he thought of dusty jars of sweet pickles in his mother's pantry and covered his mouth and nose.

Kaltherzig was already at the desk in the corner, thumbing through a folder, and he noticed and nodded as if he'd expected it. "Come in and close the door. If you breathe slowly and don't fight it you won't smell it after a minute or two."

Kaltherzig noted something, vanished through another door, left

Erich standing just inside the room with these four moveless shapes. Two of the shrouds were filthy, dark and wet in places and dried and stiff in others. These were less distressing, somehow, than the clean amorphous white ones. Those seemed far more likely to, oh, sit upright and speak at length about Hell or Hitler or the pleasure of worms.

He caught himself and bit the inside of his lip, thought *campfire stories* and thought of the harmless little heaps with birdbones jutting out in the gutters outside. These were the losers. He was out here breathing and not under a filthy sheet because he was still doing everything right.

He thought *what does he see in me?* and it made him stand up straight, take deeper breaths, look at the shrouds and force himself to think *just meat, just eggshells.* Cordwood, everyone whispered, but it was much too wet and smelled of too much swamp to be a deadfall you could steal firewood from. As long as he kept his metaphors away from
(*pickles*)
anything wet he would be all right.

Kaltherzig slid up on his tall wheeled stool, pulled back a clean shroud with no ceremony at all, exposed a middle-aged narrow man with oddly composed features, and no real marks except livid purple bruising around his left eye. "Subject is between forty and fifty-five years old…." snap of a tape measure…."approximately six foot one, in good general health. No external damage is visible."

Erich remembered to write, caught up to most of that. Looked at the bruises around this cold closed eye, wondered if the wet eyeball fluids underneath had gone to jelly. Then he put the clipboard down and made it to the wastepaper basket and did a brief set of gestures but wasn't sick.

Kaltherzig said nothing, waiting politely, and from the corner of his watering eye Erich could see he had picked up the clipboard himself and was jotting something down, as if he needed something else to look at. Anyone else might have interpreted that a dozen ways, but Erich knew the truth. Kaltherzig was being…gentlemanly.

That was the worst of it, and the last of it.

He took notes. Kaltherzig spelled a word for him now and then, and the few he didn't quite get he faked the best he could, intending to look it up to type it down correctly. When there was cutting the noise distressed him very deeply, but he breathed fast and hard through his nose and let Kaltherzig's voice be the only sound in the room, let the ripping wet sounds that reminded him too much of cloth fade to background noise like the rain outside.

Sometimes he was asked to hand Kaltherzig things, and this gave him long strange, pleasant waves of nostalgia, memories of times spent working with his father, not over bolts of cloth but in the tool shed over a potted rose bush or the finishing touches on a windowbox for his mother.

They broke for lunch, and washed from fingertips to elbows side by side, and when the officer's lounge closed around them and the smell of roast chicken drove out the last thought of pickles, Erich discovered that he was hungry.

Kaltherzig was thumbing through his notes, eating with those neat precise bird-bites. "You're very attentive to detail. Very fast."

He gave the pages back to Erich with that rarest of smiles, the kind that had teeth but still wasn't dangerous.

"If you keep up your behavior I'm going to put a letter in your file in praise of your progress."

Progress. "Thank you, sir," hoping that was right. He found he didn't give a damn about this hypothetical file. He was glowing inside his stomach in a way he remembered and could not place. He wanted that kind of smile again.

They were alone today, and that was a mercy. He wasn't sure if he could've stood this strange exhilaration and Mengele's tomcat stare at the same time.

That night he dreamed of all those shrouds moving like the surface of a lake in a storm, and hands coming up and the shape of heads and torsos sitting upright in the clean white light of the morgue, and

Kaltherzig's back was turned at the desk and he could not scream and the first set of feet swung over the side of a table and hit the floor, and he woke up all at once gasping, staring up at Kaltherzig's pale angles, wet and so afraid at first he had no idea what had happened, thought perhaps there had been a bomb dropped.

Kaltherzig was shaking him, crouching naked beside him, saying irritably, "Here, now, enough, it's not so bad as all that, is it? It's a dream, whatever else it is. Stand down, soldier," and a little laugh, to show he wasn't really angry.

He stood up, held out his hand until Erich took it.

He was pulled up and deposited at the foot of the bed, and his blanket and pillow thrown on top of him.

Kaltherzig climbed back into bed.

Erich was lying crosswise at the bottom, on top of the blankets. He arranged the pillow and covered himself, and Ahren's feet under the thick comforter slid and nudged at his cheek, curved there softly.

The mattress was a strange cupping luxury underneath him. He had plenty of room, in this aristocrat's bed, and he stretched a little, quietly, the movements slow and deliberate because he'd learned that was the least risk of noise.

The dream was gone. He closed his eyes, put one hand up and laid it on the shape of Ahren's ankle. He was warm and narrow and hard and comforting. The nightmares left him alone until morning.

There was never peace. Not really. Erich would begin to think he had learned to live this way, found the rhythm of this new life, and then he would relax, and then he would fail.

And then there would be a new nightmare, written over the old ones that had just begun to fade.

Kaltherzig had been leaning almost with his head, inside, an opened chest cavity, and Erich hadn't heard the last sentence. He thought of that very first rule at the instant he asked him to repeat it. Kaltherzig turned, bloody up to his elbows, one eyebrow raised.

Doomed.

He'd washed his hands, peeled the gloves, and chosen a long wide test tube and a cork to fit it and filled it halfway with liquid soap and corked it. He carried it, outside, and returned without it.

And that was all.

Four hours of work, and notes, and one live experiment with a Gypsy girl who cursed at them both in Romany until she only screamed and dribbled snot down her face till Erich was very close to vomiting. He just stared at the notebook, hand writing almost by itself, daydreaming, clock-watching. Dreading.

Block 10 was mostly empty, most of the officers long since gone home. Kaltherzig was in coat and gloves when he told Erich to stay, went outside, and returned with the test tube. The soap was frozen inside it. He ran it under hot water and turned it out into his hand, this thing like a suppository for an, elephant, almost as thick as a man's penis, glistening opaque blue and ominously shiny.

He made Erich lean over a table, drew down his pants and rubbed it against him in a little mean circle to show him how very cold it would be, before he shoved it inside him.

Erich started with *no* after the very first, instant, of slide, and Kaltherzig grabbed his hair and thudded his face into the table, splitting the inside of his lower lip to remind him about the *no* business. He pushed this, icicle, all the way in, until both sets of muscle closed behind it, stopping only when it was deep inside as he could get it. The groan had taken the last of Erich's breath.

Kaltherzig took his leisurely time poking around in a cabinet for gauze.   He pushed wedge after wedge of it inside, and Erich shook and gritted his teeth and hated hated *hated* him, and swore he wouldn't make another, single, sound, but he broke down after the fourth or fifth strange dry drag of the cotton and the creeping threat of cramps from the cold, the first spreading burn of the soap. All the same *stop, please, please.* He knew better now than to say no. Kaltherzig always won in the end, and

Erich always fought him, for a second or an hour, because he just, couldn't, do this, any other way.

Kaltherzig stopped a long time after Erich started pleading. The doctor pulled Erich's pants up again and straightened his coat and then, scooped him up like a baby, carried him outside and into the waiting car.

He spent the short ride home with his face buried in Kaltherzig's lap, trying with everything he had to follow the murmured directions of *inhale, exhale, breathe.*

He controls, all of it, my breath, my blood, everything I feel or sense or see, he's, Osiris...

The pain would hit him again, and that fearful urge to push against it. He would cling, pleading for Ahren to stop it, please, please. He would be so good. He'd never forget to listen again. He'd pay attention, *please, please, God, just, please, stop it, it hurts, it hurts...*

Ahren would say, "It's too late. I can't do anything about it now. You'll have to learn to please me the first time if you don't want to be punished. That's why I've done this to you. Do you understand?"

He hated *do you understand.* He tried to explain that running thought, and he muddled through it to "...Osiris..."

"My boy." And Ahren petted him, as if he were pleased with this confession, or perhaps with this sacrifice, and he traced the shape of Erich's mouth when the burn drove him into a wail, as if he were, measuring.

Kaltherzig said to the Untersturmführer driving, "Take it slowly. I want to enjoy the snow."

Hexerei

This time his injection was not the same mystery chemical he was always injected with. It was tiny, clear, and unlabeled. "Is it different, sir?" He felt his mouth run dry and his stomach fall, as though it already knew he was doomed.

"Very different. Give me your arm."

That, too, was different, the tourniquet, and the deliberate poke in search of a vein instead of the almost-playing stab that he used for the usual intramuscular. Erich chewed his lip and waited to—oh, die, or be torn suddenly with agonizing pain. Nothing. His lips tingled, and his heart seemed to be pounding, but that was probably only fear.

Whatever it was, it was Hellish.

By the time they went home he was panting through his teeth, hot and unspeakably thirsty, prickly and driven with twitches. He felt flushed and fever-strange and as though he were caught in the peak of a high panic. Kaltherzig said nothing, checking his pulse twice and his eyes once, watching Erich as if he expected him to

(change into something else)

get worse.

It got much worse.

Erich saw the walk up to the front door, and then he was on the couch, curled in a ball as if he had a stomachache. There was no memory in between, and worse, no sense even of time missing. It was as though he'd missed it in a single blink.

He cried out for Kaltherzig, and found him at the end of another of those terrifying no-spaces.

"Sit down." Hadn't he been lying down? But he was standing, with Kaltherzig pushing him back to the couch. His skin was beating with a sourceless urgency: he had to go somewhere, else, and he had to do it quickly. And then he was in bed caged in Kaltherzig's arms, crying out that his mind was flying apart.

He had been torn out of the world. He could not feel Kaltherzig's hands. He was trying to tell him to hold him harder, tighter, and he could hear him laughing but feel nothing, see nothing but brightness.

He woke up the next morning alone in Kaltherzig's bed. Kaltherzig was in the bathroom, shaving.

"You won't be able to read for a day or two."

He sat up, blinking, saw the amorphous blur that had replaced his near-vision. Flicker of that needle, dimpling and then popping into a spread-open eye.

"Will I go blind?"

"No, idiot. Atropine dilates your eyes. They used it in Egypt to get that," here he was crossing to Erich, tilting his head, straight-razor dripping in his hand, "particular, effect." He looked, studied as though he were taking notes. Then he turned on his heel back to the mirror.

"It's very pretty."

Flick of that razor sideways, depositing foam and bristles into the sink. Erich curled up into a ball around the warmth inside him, to keep it there as long as he could.

Pretty.

Kaltherzig had almost called him pretty.

Only a few days after this new game, the doctor told him at breakfast that they weren't going into Block 10, that they would experiment alone. Erich eyed him warily, but assumed it meant more of the games in bed. The idea of a day of that, playing hooky as it were, made him smile.

He was almost right.

It was two white pills and one yellow pill. Kaltherzig gave him pills often, sometimes telling him what they were, sometimes telling him only to swallow them and stop staring at them like an idiot. He swallowed them. He didn't ask, and Kaltherzig didn't volunteer.

Then he was folded over the table, arms having swept a dish-angel to give himself room, face against the wood and mouth open against it, pushing at it with his tongue. Kaltherzig was laughing. He sat up, embarrassed, stumbling something like an apology around his confused lips, and Kaltherzig put his hand over his mouth and, pulled him that way, and he struck his chest and dragged the chair over behind him, somehow, still that laughing, and he was caught by jaw and shirt and dragged up into Kaltherzig's arms, feet treading at the floor with his toes now and then in a try at walking. He could see, but everything lingered too long, tilted in no relation to the tilt of his head. Then there was the wide soft impact of Kaltherzig's bed, the beams of the vaulted ceiling turning above.

"That was the funniest thing, you should have seen yourself..." That laugh in his ear, and teeth in his neck, sending chills down his back and an unmistakable sharp signal to his groin. He moaned all out of proportion to this horseplay. Kaltherzig stopped, studied his face, laughed in a completely different key.

Blur. This was a new kind of delicious, with the room lit gray-white through the white drapes. Always before it had been night for such games. Kaltherzig could sense the difference, too, or perhaps he only wanted to play with the effects of this drug. His hands were more attentive, less specific, drawing long sweeping featherlight strokes along Erich's spine, his shuddering ribcage, to watch him vibrate in gasping shock at the strange echoes of texture and light that followed the path of Kaltherzig's fingers.

The chaos inside him climbed until he was clinging to the sheets afraid he would fall out into nothing if he didn't, climbed until he was making noises that were meant to be *please* and Kaltherzig laughed, and then was hot long bones under smooth skin, folded over his back, driving him mad with breath in his ear that made him fear being eaten.

He wailed until the press of Kaltherzig's cock against the small of his back reminded him of the world, dissolved this single note of terror into a new note of want. He was too far from Auschwitz to remember how he was supposed to act, too far from the source of this drowning delight to do anything but arch and push and hiss until the first real push and the slide inside him, skin on skin with no cream or wet fingers first to spare him, in slow thudding pushes that were so frictioned and perfect he could do nothing but open his mouth and pant a damp circle into the pillow.

Kaltherzig knelt up behind him, touching him only there, only inside, and didn't move until Erich was a trembling kinetic line of desperate tiny sounds, and laid one hand on his back and pushed all the way in, pausing not at all for his shrill little climbs at the bright flares of hurt. He drew in his breath to plead for mercy and then the pain was gone and it was only that dissolving itching ache, pleasure on pleasure, and he lay feeling drawn down to a single point, feeling owned, letting Kaltherzig move him like a specimen.

In the hospital, they seemed to see him as a privileged favorite, which translated variously to awe, disgust, or a narrow mathematical look he supposed was, envy. He could not stand under the weight of those sunken eyes without seeing himself sleeping curled up on the carpet, bleeding or leaking sperm or both, with his back as close to the edge of Ahren's bed as he could manage to get so that the edge of the blankets would keep him, just a little warm.

Everywhere he went, seeking records or carrying messages, he felt the wake of staring behind him, the space of silence or the leaf-rasp of whispering.

The weight of their eyes made him feel, guilty.

He felt so.....fed, beside them, so clean and spoiled and spared. He was ashamed for them to see him, in his own jacket and leather shoes, with his hair at his collar longer than any of the girls were allowed to keep.

He watched what he supposed were pretty girls, listening for some symptom of normalcy in himself, oddly enough without any real

(fear)

conviction that he was

(in danger)

being cured.

There were changes in him, yes, but none of them seemed to have touched that essential flaw. He didn't notice boys anymore, but that was because all his notice belonged to Kaltherzig. He was afraid to be caught staring, and yet he found himself looking all the same. He stole pieces, little fragmentary pictures, those flawless cheekbones, those graceful hands.

He loved Kaltherzig's hair. His own was dark enough, until the sun shot it through with threads of copper, but Kaltherzig's hair was as black as his cap, and the sun could add nothing to that. He loved to walk with Kaltherzig, when the doctor was in an amiable mood and not given to hauling him along by his arm. It made him feel small, and fragile and vulnerable, and this was still frightening, but something in him reveled in being towered-over, and yes, even in being hauled along so easily.

It made him feel safe from himself.

He was free, in an upsetting and addictive way. He had no real decisions to make, because they were all made for him. He had no secrets to keep anymore, because Kaltherzig knew them all, or would in time. All his worries were real ones, and immediate ones, and they never disappointed. Now with troublesome life and all its little demands taken out of his hands, he had nothing to eat away at his sleep but those inescapable miseries.

It was never over.

And he was beginning to wonder whether this, too, made him feel safe, the way the fences did. The way the needles did. The way the bruises did.

He was caught in the maw of the Reich, and it was as unstoppable as he'd been told, and as unspeakable as he'd been promised.

He never knew, whether the day would be made of typing, notation, almost boredom, or whether Kaltherzig would close the door behind them, in that room where the table was, and order him to undress. It was never the same number of days between; sometimes less than a week, sometimes what seemed like forever.

He started losing sleep and appetite. He would try to imagine ways he might be spared, this time. Did the experiment ever end? Would Kaltherzig give up, pronounce him incurable?

Try something else?

It had been so long since the last time, maybe it was over? He'd just been examined, maybe it wouldn't happen again for awhile?

No, because it was never over.

It was never over, and it always happened, and there was nothing he could do to affect how, or when, or whether. He would tell himself he would be brave this time, that nothing could ever be as bad as the first time, when he'd had no idea how this man would be allowed to hurt him. He would be brave. Kaltherzig would be proud of him. He wouldn't scream, and he wouldn't struggle, and that was only more searching for an escape.

And all of that would dissolve once Kaltherzig began it. He would scream, and he would struggle, and if he could still talk when the worst of it came he would usually beg for mercy. The cameraflash would record that, too, and none of it would change.

And that was where his thoughts always led him. He could push this place away for a day, or two, or ten, but in the end it always caught him. He would lay on the floor and sweat and shake and lose himself in his fear of that place standing in his future, again and again and again. That mindless place where there was no room for himself, where he was only a reaction to Kaltherzig. He would spread himself out on his back when this state took him, because this made it easier to pretend he wasn't hard.

It had never been as long as this.

Day after day rolled by without comment from Kaltherzig, and

Erich felt rather like he was crackling with expectation and confusion. Finally, when Kaltherzig was leaving him with a stack of admittance reports, he said, "Sir, will it be soon?"

Kaltherzig stopped, and turned to him with a new sort of grin.

"I knew you would ask. I thought you'd wait longer, but I knew you would." He turned to leave again, and said over his shoulder, "Tomorrow."

Erich stared at the papers on the desk in front of him, without seeing them. "Will it be tomorrow because I asked?"

"No. Tomorrow, because I've got time. It will be different because you asked."

And with that, with Erich's concentration destroyed beyond hope of repair, he left, the door unlocked behind him.

By the time Kaltherzig really did lead him into the examining room and not his office he was a fraying wreckage of dread, weeping before he could unbutton his shirt. Kaltherzig observed this phenomena with amused exasperation. "What is all this? Usually you hold it together better than that, at least while I measure you." But he was grinning, and Erich knew the doctor knew why.

"Sir, how will it be different?"

"You'll find out, presently."

Erich found out after he was strapped down, and Kaltherzig patted one of his thighs with a gloveless hand. "Wait and worry," he advised, and he left Erich that way. It must've been only a few minutes, but Erich spent them all looking at the blood on the ceiling. When Kaltherzig returned the sound of the opening door made him start so violently the straps bit into him. The doctor was wheeling something that squeaked. When he came into Erich's field of vision he saw it was two small tanks, riding jauntily in a cart, trailing tubing and a black something Kaltherzig carried in one hand. The doctor did things to this mysterious device behind Erich's head. "It's nitrous oxide. Don't get used to it. I only want to test a

116

theory, and I suppose you've earned something for cutting your own switch with so little prompting."

Erich blushed at that one, once he deciphered it. Kaltherzig paused, leaning over him, perhaps to appreciate that blush before he settled the mask over Erich's nose and mouth, tightened the straps to hold it on behind his head.

The panic was immediate. He turned his head reflexively, finding he could not dislodge it, or even shift it on his face. It smelled intensely of rubber and something else faintly underneath, something sweet and strange. Kaltherzig did something he couldn't see that started a faint regular hissing, and that sugary smell grew much stronger, filling his nose, his mouth, coating his tongue. He shook his head more violently, trying not to inhale, and Kaltherzig sighed above him, turned his head straight again, drew a strap across his forehead. Erich did half of a muffled wail, in despair at this final freedom lost, and stopped at how strange it sounded.

"Ungrateful," Kaltherzig said, though he didn't really sound angry. "Go ahead and breathe, ridiculous boy. It isn't mustard gas. Didn't you ever have a tooth filled?"

He hadn't, and the instinct to tell Kaltherzig this made him draw in his breath. He exhaled it again, so quickly it was almost a cough, and this left his lungs nearly empty. The struggle then was violent and very brief. He drew in a great whooping breath, exhaled, drew in another, and the world was changing around him, getting softer and bigger and harder to understand.

"See?"

He was beginning to see. Was this one of Kaltherzig's kindnesses? He was shaken by the strangeness of it, and too comfortable to care. The straps seemed to cradle him, and he realized the kindness of these, too. He didn't have to be brave. He could struggle all he liked, He let them cradle him, and inhaled, deliberately, and Kaltherzig patted his inner thigh, that place he seemed so fond of touching. It wasn't hard enough to hurt, not even a little, but something in the pattering gentle impacts of it

117

made him lose hold of that inhale. Little shock-waves from that place seemed to ripple all through him. It was ticklish and intense and alien and he made one questioning sound, and the echo in his mask was farther away this time, because it wasn't distressing enough to make him stop.

Kaltherzig's reply was a sound too, one that made Erich think of interested lions. "Yes, it's very strange." He patted again, harder, and Erich felt it everywhere, felt every little climb until he knew that was supposed to hurt. It didn't. There was no question in his sound now, only appalled understanding. Kaltherzig laughed, and this time it was hitting, and not patting, Not one of them hurt. It was much worse than hurt. It was wonderful, an itchy intolerable new kind of delicious. He wanted more of this awful sensation.

"I'm going to keep you just about there, I think. Maybe a little deeper." He did something behind Erich's head again, and the pitch of that mechanical hiss changed, and the world blurred away even more at the edges, both sight and sound now. There was a muted slow roar in Erich's head. The doctor spoke again, but Erich could not reply, He knew Kaltherzig was between his knees, could feel him there, the warmth of him, the hands on his thighs.

His grasp of linear time dissolved. He was a pool of still dark water, and Kaltherzig did things that made him fold into intricate ripples or shatter into edges and aftershocks. His body no longer felt like himself, or even something he wore to move through the world. It seemed only to be more straps, clever ones that he was utterly, helplessly caught in. The sensations made no sense, happening to him directly without flesh or fear to interpret them. It was like a dream, he would think later, the way he'd been stripped of any memory of another reality. There was no corner of his mind that was spared. Kaltherzig was just *Him*, cause and effect united. There had never been anything else.

He didn't understand what the world was when it began to come back. He was still looking at the bloody ceiling, but now he was dreamily, blissfully unaware of what it was, thinking that the little marks had to be deliberate and wondering if they meant anything.

"Was that different?" Kaltherzig said quietly. Erich tried to turn towards his voice, and the doctor's hands, no longer gloved, swung across his eyes and unfastened the strap across his forehead.

The doctor was behind him, and the mask was gone. He missed it. Erich worked out how to move his head, considering this. He drew in a deep breath and then another. "It stopped." But that was only part of it, the other part was, "And you stopped."

A laugh. Yes, that was exactly the right sound. "Do you want me to start again?"

"Yes," Erich said, immediately.

He expected Kaltherzig to keep laughing, but the doctor was quiet for a long time. Then he straightened Erich's head, and drew the strap across his forehead again.

"My boy."

That was the best noise, the one he loved the most. That rumble in Kaltherzig's chest that was almost a purr, that noise that meant he'd been good, somehow.

And here, yes, here was the mask, the reward.

Schwul

Adelle was really the only girl he saw during the course of his workday, and the only other prisoner in general who seemed to make any effort to be friendly to him. The others seemed to smell the otherness of him, or to fear and respect the isolation Kaltherzig wanted to keep around him, but Adelle would greet him in the morning, and chat with him when opportunity arose. This might have been nice, except that Erich found her tiresome at best and infuriating at worst.

She assisted in the hospital, working beside the doctors a great deal. This questionable honor had convinced her of her own importance. He heard her voice over the others constantly, correcting everyone at everything, gossiping. She pontificated to any prisoners that would listen about the horrible morals of the girls who whispered and giggled about Mengele's beauty, and wasn't it disgusting, just *sick?*

Erich rather thought it was, but not because of morals. He found Mengele singularly unattractive, despite his surface polish, and had since he'd first seen the man smile.

"Why don't you talk to anyone? They all think that you're arrogant."

He'd stared at her in mute horror, and when he found his voice what came out was, "Because I'm afraid."

"Everyone is," she sniffed, as though his fear were meaningless. As though he owed her another answer, a better answer.

It made him something very close to angry, her assumption that he had some sort of *duty* to this shapeless *everyone.* He was Kaltherzig's. That was the only person on Earth he was obligated to please.

He wondered whether this bitterness from Adelle was because she found him beautiful, or whatever word women had for men.

This melted rather easily into wondering if Kaltherzig found him beautiful, if that was the reason for the silent stare he sometimes gave Erich for no reason he could fathom. For the fact that Erich was almost

always the control group. For the books, and the gentle minutes of
  (father)
doctor, when Kaltherzig had wounded him badly enough to justify
that indulgence.

Surely there were prisoners more beautiful than he was.

That had gotten him the, audition, but something else entirely was
what kept him here. He dared not name that something. If he did that, it
might disappear.

"It must be nice not to worry about food."

Oh, how tempted he was to just seize her and drag her close and
hold her caught and *tell* her about, oh, any of it.

Any of it.

He would tell her about Ahren holding him down in the bathtub,
scrubbing him until he bled, that very first night. He would tell her about
the moon, and how he began to fear when it was almost new, because it
meant that one morning soon Kaltherzig would take him not to the
office, but to the room where that table was. How it felt to undress for
that, knowing every step of what was coming. He would offer to trade
with her, maybe. Two years of starving and lice for two years of being
kept clean in order to be more delightful to make, dirty.

He wondered which she would choose.

Ahren got his share of giggling and whispers and admiring little
stares from camp girls, hospital or not, and Adelle never had anything to
say about *that*.

Some of the camp-inmates outside of the secluded hospital staff,
stared at him openly, leaning to whisper to another shaved-and-striped
slave, smirking, or laughing. He dreaded the rare occasions when he was
sent outside, usually on a short walk to exchange files with another
Block. They were bolder outside of the hospital, and there were so many
of them. He knew the faces, if not the names, of the ones that tended to
gawk and snicker and shout slang he pretended he didn't understand in

his direction. He never did anything to these tormentors, never knew quite what he might do or what he wanted to do. He would only flush and walk faster.

They had done it to the cowboy, too, for the few weeks he had survived, once they had turned him out shaved and striped and with the pink triangle emblazoned on chest and thigh. He had seemed much smaller without his glorious hair, much younger, as if he were becoming the lover he'd lost.

A tiny, embarrassing part of him didn't think Kaltherzig would give him to Mengele, or shoot him. He would kill him one day, but by a punch thrown too hard, or a fall taken wrong. It would be a side effect, not a punishment. He would probably live through the war. Most of them would not. Because of that he had no *right* to blame them for their, hate. Their envy. Their snickers and once-over stares and stench and strange insectile possessiveness with everything they touched.

I have no business being angry at them.

But he was angry, because he knew exactly what they were whispering. *Whore* and *queer* in a dozen different languages. He was angry whether he had a right to be or not. There was a warm delighted place between his stomach and his spine when Mengele or Wirths ordered one of them to step out of line. And there was something like triumph inside him, when they didn't dare those tricks when he was with Kaltherzig.

Most of them would've killed to be where he was. That was probably at least half the reason for the open hostility. Being Ahren Kaltherzig's slave meant clothes and warmth and medical care. Oh, there was the sodomy and the bruises and the sitting in the bathroom bleeding and sobbing with Ahren like a tiger outside the door, but he could eat. And he didn't have typhus or scabies.

Out in the camp starvation drew skeletons underneath all the faces; men were missing fingers and feet and noses and ears from the cold or the mines, or had gone mad from the crematoriums and the Selektions. A mistake or a failure from sickness or weakness could land anyone in an oven, or worse, the jail.

Or worst of all, Block 10.

As the snow grew deeper and the cold grew colder the guards found reasons to keep indoors whenever possible, and when Erich was sent out into the camp there were less and less of them. His tormentors grew bolder, louder.

Finally they followed him a few steps, and this scared him very badly. His work in the hospital had instilled in him an utter phobia of disease, and the prisoners stank of unwashed bodies and old dirt, they coughed and spat while they laughed and pointed, and he was more afraid of what he might catch than of any abuse they might intend. His hurry made them laugh even harder.

One of them—he was never sure which—threw a pebble at him. It grazed the underside of his jaw, impossibly, and then a second struck the place where his collarbone met his shoulder, hard enough to make a muffled sound of impact. He thought *it's exactly like the riding crop,* and then *if that had struck my eye,* and then he dropped all pretense of ignoring them and ran for the hospital through a rain of their triumphant laughter.

He found Kaltherzig in the morgue, before he really knew why he was looking for him, before he realized two files and a sealed envelope were still undelivered in his hands. The door banged closed behind Erich, and he stared at Kaltherzig speechlessly, and then looked down at the disobedience he was holding and began to flush. "Sir, I'm sorry, sir, I...I'll go deliver them right away. I'm very sorry." He was still groping behind himself for the doorknob when Kaltherzig reached him. The doctor grasped his jaw the way he sometimes did to

(admire)

study Erich, and that lushly drawn mouth Erich tried not to look at changed into one moveless line.

"Which one of them did it?"

Silence.

Kaltherzig's grasp on his jaw tightened, and the line of his mouth

123

grew thinner still.

"I don't know." He closed his eyes, unable to endure Kaltherzig's gaze, that reptilian focus that might turn on him at any moment. "I don't know the names, or the numbers. I don't look at them. I'm...it might encourage them, if I do. Some are unloading crew, and I think some are groundskeepers. There are almost always, some of them out there." He drew in a breath. "I'm sorry. I don't want to make trouble." He meant that he didn't want to be *in* trouble, and he felt craven and small and awful, and he closed his eyes tighter.

Kaltherzig let go of his jaw. Something thumped the top of his head, softly, and he opened his eyes in time to realize Kaltherzig had put his hand there, not quite a pat, just a brief touch. "You haven't made any trouble. Give me the files."

Erich did, with a wrenching pang of guilt that he hadn't done what he was supposed to do with them. Kaltherzig gave him a stack of autopsy paperwork. "Go back to my office and finish these."

"Sir, I can take the others, I can--"

"Do not make me repeat myself today!" Kaltherzig turned on him suddenly, and the snarl and the speed of his motion made Erich flee the room, closing the door behind him, nearly running.

The triangle. That red, spreading triangle that meant the end of everything.

He was not asked to carry anything to another Block or retrieve anything from one for the next week and a half. He was deeply relieved, and deeply ashamed of this relief. He was just as equally divided when Kaltherzig finally brought him a box heavy with paper. "Take these to Block 11. Expect a receipt document to bring back to me. If they argue about that, do *not* give them these files. Do you understand me?"

He said *yes sir* exactly the way he was supposed to, and he picked up the box more or less exactly the way he was supposed to, and he carried it downstairs and the out into the snow, exactly the way he was supposed to.

Block 11 was the prison, and quite a lot of information seemed to flow between it and the hospital. He had been terrified of it the first time he'd been sent there, but there was a side door and a little room with a window as if one might make an appointment to go beyond the second door. This second door was more fortress than office. He handed them things, they handed him things, and he walked back to Kaltherzig, and surely that was easy. He'd done it before. He could do it now.

He paused, here, unable to stop himself from looking left to right and then left again, to see what kind of gauntlet he might have to run. There were a few prisoners, some shoveling paths, some waiting for a delivery of packages or people in little clusters. He recognized none of the faces, not outside of Block 10, not on the short walk to Block 11. No one looked at him twice. Wrong time of day, perhaps, though before he would've bet there was no particular time of day when there wasn't at least someone that wanted to throw a word at him, or stare at him with a wide sick grin as though he were an exhibit.

The only bad moment he had was when he went into the little receiving office of Block 11 and found the shabby little desk manned by a bored and sullen Lieser.

"What are you doing here?" Shock drove it out of him, and he was immediately coldfrozen with terror at how impertinent it was. God, this snow-colored man would drag him back to Kaltherzig, and there would be such pain, and possibly worse than pain.

Lieser seemed not to notice that this was impertinent. He grinned a doll's polished grin at Erich's distress. "I work here. What are you doing here? Or did you finally get yourself in real trouble?"

Erich blushed and stammered at that, as he was sure he was supposed to, and finally remembered the heavy box he was holding. He mumbled his request for a receipt, and Lieser stared at him, still grinning, for slightly too long before he rummaged around and wrote briefly on a blank form, signed extravagantly. He held onto it when Erich tried to take it, for just long enough to make him feel foolish, and then turned it loose, and shut the sliding window between Erich and that slightly mad smile.

No one looked at him twice on the walk back. No one whispered, and if he walked through a few cold patches of silence, well, that was fine with him. They'd catch him next time. They always did.

They didn't.

The first time it had been an unnerving and pleasant surprise. The second time it was more unnerving than pleasant, and the third it was scary. He looked for any of the faces that he'd learned meant he should steel himself and walk faster, and saw not a single one. He looked again as he and Kaltherzig were leaving that evening and found no one.

Kaltherzig smoked, and Erich watched his hands move in those gloves awhile before he spoke. "Did you stop them?"

A smoke ring. "They volunteered for an experiment."

This left him speechless for a long time. "All of them, sir?"

The doctor shrugged. "I needed subjects that were absolutely, positively, staunchly *not* inverts. Who better?"

Later, as Kaltherzig sat on the edge of his bed preparing to take off his boots, Erich dropped to his hands and knees and crawled to him.

He wanted to thank Kaltherzig, needed to, gratitude and something warm and dangerous trembling in his throat. What he really wanted was to throw his arms around the doctor, but he knew this would not be permitted.

There were other gestures, though, that were permitted.

Kaltherzig watched, patiently bemused, while Erich took his boots off for him, left boot and then right.

He was well familiar with cocksucking, but he had never been the one to instigate this. Were you supposed to ask?

God, how does anyone do this?

Finally he leaned in and rested his cheek against Kaltherzig's belt buckle, looking up to see if this was allowed, and then nuzzled lower still when the doctor did not stop him.

Kaltherzig laughed, and let him.

The postmortems began to feel like work. Like real work, like something he and Kaltherzig did together, something official and important. Scientific. Civilized.

The weeks went by, and he didn't have to ask so many questions, didn't have to have as many words spelled for him. He didn't dream of the morgue anymore, though sometimes, lying on the floor in the dark, he wondered what might happen if he pretended he had. Whether Kaltherzig might draw him up into the bed again.

Live experiments were another thing entirely.

One morning Kaltherzig nudged him towards the examination room instead of the office.

It was the wrong day, much too soon. It wasn't fair.

Kaltherzig must have smelled his terror. "Not you this time, my boy," with the laugh in his eyes. He handed Erich a file. "Remember this one?"

He opened the door. There was already a subject strapped to that bastard table. Erich looked at the man's face for a little too long, telling himself that of course the man was familiar, he was one of those shaven stick-figures they all became after a while. He had symmetrical wounds on either side of his chest from collarbone to stomach, but the worst of it was his genitalia. Penis and scrotum both seemed to have been peeled. He could see sores creeping up his stomach, down his thighs.

And he looked...familiar.

Erich settled himself against the far wall, well out of range of that bastard table, on a twin of Kaltherzig's wheeled chair. Bosch, Gunther, age, forty-six. Sent to Auschwitz for fraud, theft, assault, and crimes against the Fatherland.

He looked...familiar. Something was familiar, something in the eyes, in that trembling wet mouth. Something that reminded Erich of
(schwul)
running, with his arms full of files.

Kaltherzig watched Erich's face, grinning, teeth showing. "The first of them," he said. "I'm through with them. And they're quite through calling you names, I think? And no longer in the mood for rock-throwing, either, hmm? Herr Bosch?"

Rock-throwing.

Erich paged back to the beginning of the file he was holding, heart pounding faster and faster, as though he might still be running. There was the photograph he himself had clipped there, a man that might've been a distant relative to the ruin before them.

And now he knew exactly why his trips outside the hospital had suddenly become so very uneventful. Something twisted in him, trying to be guilt, and failing, unfolding instead into something like joy.

"What did you do to him?" he asked, not realizing he'd spoken. It was almost a whisper, but Kaltherzig heard, clattering instruments, and said over his shoulder, "Oh, I didn't actually do any of it myself. I'm quite busy. Block 11 was very accommodating once they understood my request." He settled onto his wheeled stool, pulled a cart of instruments closer. "Quite a lot of data on how, and why, exactly, one might become an invert. I'm sure the Reichsoffice will find it as fascinating as I did."

Herr Bosch was crying in a vague, inattentive way, as if he'd been doing it for weeks, as if he'd forgotten how to stop. He didn't seem to hear or see either of them. Kaltherzig pushed his spread knees up higher and picked up a clamp and closed it at the base of his scrotum, as close to his body as possible. Bosch broke immediately into an inhuman howl.

The scream caught Erich off-guard. The clamp was blunt, it had to hurt, but surely not as badly as all that? Was it only the man's lunacy?

Then he understood all this howling was for the sake of what would happen next. Perhaps someone had told him, or he'd reasoned it from the clamp in some still-functioning corner of his mind.

He sat with his hands still half-covering his ears, the file forgotten across his knees. He watched Kaltherzig pick up something sharp and bright, watched Kaltherzig's shoulders move, heard Bosch's howl make that leap in pitch that he'd come to know meant cutting.

It seemed to last a very long time.

Kaltherzig moved something into a waiting specimen jar. He picked up something plugged into the wall, that made the scream finally crumble into Polish too mangled for Erich to decipher. The room smelled immediately of that smokestack odor. Kaltherzig took off the clamp, wheeled himself back, and Erich saw the blood. It took a minute between the redness and the vertigo to understand what he was seeing.

The man had been castrated.

It was Erich's job to label the jar. Drifting inside it were both ruined testicles. Tissue sample, fertility program, and the Institute in Berlin. That smell of not-quite-pickles. He ran to the sink, scrubbed his hands with a speed bordering on hysteria.

Kaltherzig didn't notice, or didn't care. He opened the door, gloved hands still bloody, and called out into the corridor to someone Erich couldn't see. "The next one, and coffee."

That was exactly what they brought him.

Schwelgerei

By the second week of December, Block 10 seemed nearly deserted. Most of the doctors were gone, and those who remained left the patients to the nurses. Mengele was gone, as were Clauberg and Wirths, and this left Kaltherzig nominally in charge. There was little to be in charge of.

One morning he presented Erich with ice skates, and they went not to work but to a pond just outside the camp, hard frozen. Erich was terrible at it, and by the time he worked out how to mostly keep his feet under him he had quite a few new bruises to add to his collection. Kaltherzig was graceful, but rusty. He managed to avoid the kind of impressive and undignified falls Erich was undertaking, though he had to scramble to avoid them a time or two. They spent until long after lunchtime gliding in increasingly less hazardous arcs across the ice.

They went into Block 10 after a leisurely early dinner, and then Kaltherzig locked them both in his office, and made them both hot cider with Schnapps over a Bunsen burner, and told him stories of learning to ice-skate with a handful of older brothers trying to knock him down on every side.

Small gifts were exchanged. Kaltherzig was given candy and sweets that seemed to exasperate him. He gave these to Erich, who gave most of them to Adelle. It wasn't guilt, exactly, more a wish to have no enemies in the hospital. She gave him a bright smile, and he supposed he'd chosen wisely.

On Solstice morning Erich got up and discovered a stocking nailed on the mantle for him, crammed with bulges that turned out to be maple-stick candy and oranges and a book on Egypt and a polished-wood box that opened into a tiny ornate board and carved chessmen. Below this was a small footlocker, and in it were *Beowulf* and *Faust* and a suit exactly his size in a deep cold gray.

Kaltherzig denied it. "It was Saint Nicholas. I would've left you switches and coal," he said, perfectly airy, expressionless.

Erich had expected to be homesick today, and when that didn't happen he found himself almost trying to be homesick. Solstice had never been a particularly grandiose occasion with his parents, and he had sometimes wondered what it might be like if he'd had brothers or sisters. This felt like a real holiday, full of busy excitement.

Kaltherzig sent him to wash and dress, with orders to admit two maids, a cook, and several servers as they arrived. Kaltherzig himself was going into Block 10, but only to put in an appearance.

As soon as the door had closed behind the doctor Erich was halfway up the stairs, working at the buttons of his shirt. He kept his uniform spotlessly clean, but it was the only clothing he had, and there was nothing he could do for months of wear without respite. He had always been painstakingly neat in his dress, and the desire to be dressed like a

(human being)

citizen again was like an itch between himself and these prisoner clothes.

Kaltherzig came home at half-past four; three women in neat restaurant dress buzzing around the kitchen and the dining room. Erich had retired to the den, dressed, his own shoes and Kaltherzig's dress boots just polished to glossy black. That one earned him a clap on the shoulder that didn't hurt.

He looked up, hair wet and slick, newspaper between himself and his one remaining shoe, and Kaltherzig seemed to, stop, just staring at him. He was in the black dress uniform, glinting in that sinister way that made Erich remember the weight of that SS coat on his back, the slippery evilness of it. Erich hadn't even known the doctor was in the room. He was half-certain he'd misunderstood a blow.

131

The way Kaltherzig was looking at him nearly stopped his heart.

The doctor's face was almost expressionless. It was only his eyes that had changed, those gunmetal impenetrable eyes.

Somehow they were, warmer.

Softer.

Erich drew in a breath to speak, and found he had no words to reply to that look.

Kaltherzig's mouth moved, as though he had the very same problem. Then there was only another touch on Erich's shoulder, and then his hair. Kaltherzig tipped up his face, and Erich leaned his head back, expecting to be examined.

The doctor only said, "Come with me," and pulled him to his feet, down the hall and into the bedroom.

Kaltherzig opened a wardrobe and pulled Erich to stand in front of the full-length mirror in the door. He stood behind Erich and knotted Erich's sharp new tie with intricate black-on-black patterning, straightened his collar. In the mirror they gleamed next together.

"Like father and son."

"You're not old enough to be my father," Erich said, and immediately dreaded the response, but Kaltherzig only laughed.

"How would you know? I always was...precocious. And experimental."

Kaltherzig ruined Erich's smooth hair by plunking his own uniform cap on top.

The house filled with the wolves rather quickly. Erich found himself surrounded by uniforms. There was a very long and very formal dinner, during which Erich drank too much red wine. He found himself pinned again, Mengele on one side and Kaltherzig on the other. Even worse, Lieser was across from him.

Erich could not look at him without blushing bright red. He knew wherever all those photographs had gone, far more eyes than this blonde demon's had seen him, had seen *everything*, but he didn't have to endure dinner parties with any of those strangers grinning at him. Kaltherzig leaned close to whisper praise for his manners and the breath in his ear gave him an erection that left him in fear of being called to stand for a toast or a song.

After dinner Mengele left, and then Clauberg, and then others Erich didn't know by name. Kaltherzig's hired staff cleared the table, fluttered here and there until everyone was settled with drinks and cards, and then left themselves. Someone started the phonograph. There were new arrivals, some already quite drunk. Erich was glad to see the help gone. Now he had something to do, keeping glasses filled and ashtrays emptied.

The party swelled, and then shrank again, into a milling and increasingly noisy little swarm, some settled in the dining room, some in the living room talking and smoking.

Lieser even swiped at Erich once as he went by, in what was probably a drunken attempt at a pinch.

Everyone laughed except Kaltherzig.

"That's not exactly becoming of an officer, you know."

"What, making a try at a boy?"

"Making a try at *my* boy." Kaltherzig drew Erich closer, and put an empty glass in his hand to refill. "What will our guests think?"

"Most of *those* guests are gone," Lieser pointed out, and got his own laughter. And right about then was when Erich began to develop the strong wish to be sent to bed. He was fairly sure he knew what Lieser meant, and it did not exactly fill him with a sense of safety. The dread did him no good. Foresight was useless when you had no free will, and so he filled glasses and found matches and drank when someone insisted he should, and many did. He told himself he was being ridiculous, that everyone seemed to be in a wonderful mood, and that included Kaltherzig, and the briefly raised voices that seemed on the verge of an argument were quickly calmed into laughter again. He told himself it was nothing like the swimming pool, and that, at least, turned out to be true.

The roaring fire soon warmed the house from comfortable to distressing, and Erich took off his new coat once he saw that others had begun to do the same. Kaltherzig laughed when he saw this, and pulled Erich close to his chair, till he was standing between the doctor's knees. He unbuttoned each of Erich's sleeves and rolled them up, and then loosened his tie. The card game went on around them.

"I'll buy him from you." Lieser offered Kaltherzig a handful of poker chips.

"Not for sale. I'd never find a replacement." Kaltherzig was unbuttoning Erich's collar. "This one is too obedient."

"How obedient?"

And that was when Kaltherzig's eyebrow went up. Erich had time to think *Goddamn you, Lieser,* and then Kaltherzig's finger hooked into his collar, turned him, and drew him down into Kaltherzig's lap. His hands came down on the doctor's knees, and he snatched them away, teetered on the edge of spilling himself onto the floor, and then grasped the arms of the chair.

Once he was stable he immediately tried to stand again, a scalding blush climbing from his throat to his face. Kaltherzig's arms came around him. One hand covered his throat, not squeezing, but keeping him straight and still so the others could see his face. That was bad enough. Eyes were infinitely worse than cameras, he discovered, and the fact that a few were still talking to one another, apparently aware of and not particularly interested in this drama made it worse and not better. It made him feel distinctly unreal.

Kaltherzig held his head still. "Don't move."

Erich felt the doctor's hand on his stomach and then felt his belt buckle tugged at. He thought perhaps Kaltherzig had gone mad. Lieser was, for once, not laughing. He watched with those eerily pale eyes wide and pleased.

Obedient.

Erich didn't move, except to swallow, and he felt his throat press against Kaltherzig's palm. It made him swallow again. Kaltherzig unfastened Erich's belt with two sharp tugs, unbuttoned his pants—and then slid his hand down the front of them, skin against skin so fast it was almost a collision.

Erich tried to keep still, but his body jerked in spite of his wishes, and apparently he was still not drunk enough to prevent an erection. The fact that this could not *possibly* happen now in front of all these eyes did nothing to stop it. He thought Kaltherzig was going to seize the waistband of his underwear and pull it. This had been regarded as the height of humor in some of his school classes, and Kaltherzig seemed to be in the mood to play. Instead Kaltherzig's hand slid past this, too, and wrapped around both of his balls, warm and sudden.

The sound Erich made started that inescapable laughter again. Lieser still didn't join in.

This is how he looks behind the camera. If Kaltherzig is a bird, this one is a snake.

He whispered, "Sir, there are people," and watched Lieser grin at his horror.

"Yes," Kaltherzig's voice, his breath, whiskey and tobacco and heat, so very near Erich's ear. "And you hate that. Don't move. Keep your hands just where they are." And he spread Erich's knees with his own, and brought his free hand up to cover Erich's mouth.

Erich clung to the arms of the chair as if he would drown without it, every muscle locked tight. He thought *he won't, he can't, I can't.*

And then he squeezed Erich's balls, very slowly, and very hard.

The pressure became an unfolding, deep, sick pain that quickly climbed into anguish. He managed about ten seconds before he began to scream into Kaltherzig's hand.

Lieser pretended to applaud him.

Erich kept his hands where they were but he could not control his legs, and when his knees came up Kaltherzig struggled with him briefly and then wrapped his legs around Erich's until they were too tangled to kick, and closed his hand harder, and let him scream. When he had to stop screaming to breathe he could hear them laughing, more of them applauding with Lieser, in little staccato bursts.

Something went wrong in his throat, and this noise was more howl

135

than scream, and his hands still clung to the arms of the chair, though his arms seemed to be trying to pull them free. Tremors of motion shook his body. Kaltherzig was hard underneath him. The doctor did something new with his hand—a roll of his fingers, a slow merciless pull, and Erich could not scream anymore, because the pain boiling low in his stomach rolled upwards into his throat. Kaltherzig felt him gag, and eased his grip, just as slowly as he'd tightened it.

Erich collapsed, head back against Kaltherzig's shoulder, cold with sudden sweat. He croaked, "God," and then "Don't." Both were equally unintelligible. He gave up.

Kaltherzig's hand was cupping his head, the hand between his legs cupping too, gentle and warm and intolerable. "One more."

Erich wanted to gag again. "Don't."

"Keep your hands there."

"Cover my mouth!" he begged, in desperate panic.

"No."

"May I?" Lieser inquired, sweetly.

Erich groaned in his throat at that, and almost thrashed in Kaltherzig's arms.

"Yes," said Kaltherzig, and Erich could hear the grin. He'd done that to himself, he realized, and then Lieser stood and he closed his eyes.

Lieser was expert and gentle, cupping the back of his head with one hand and pressing the other over his mouth smoothly and firmly. He said, "No, open your eyes," and when Kaltherzig did not countermand this order, Erich did.

The scent of Lieser made him frantic and furious, but the pain was quick and obliterating, dragging more of that desperate hysterical howl up from deep in his chest. He forgot everything except that in some other universe he must not let go of something he could no longer feel. Then he lost hold of even that, peeled down to id, and his arms dragged both his hands away from the chair.

There were almost shouts from his audience, half disappointment, half a cheer. He seized Kaltherzig's wrist and discovered that this did no good whatsoever, unless he wanted to pull, which he definitely did not want. He wanted to shriek in frustration, but what happened instead was more of a wail.

Kaltherzig made some sound Erich could feel more than hear at that, "You know what will make me stop, now, don't you?" Kaltherzig murmured, very close to his ear, so that no one else could hear it. He knew. It was simple and awful and he didn't want to do it, but he knew. He let go of Kaltherzig's wrist, put his hands back on the arms of the chair. It made him cry to do it.

Kaltherzig loosened his hand almost at once. "Let him go," he told Lieser. And oh, dear God, Kaltherzig was letting go too, and Erich relaxed too soon, panting and gasping and thinking *I have to get out of his lap, or he'll do it again.*

Kaltherzig paused, his hand still hidden in Erich's pants, and pinched the head of his cock, just once, fast and hard and over by the time Erich could yell about it.

Then Kaltherzig was fastening Erich's belt again while he struggled to draw up his knees. The pain in his stomach was vast and poisonous.

"You'll live," Kaltherzig murmured, close to his ear. He pushed Erich forward. He expected to be able to stand and found himself wrong, and sat down again, gasping. He wanted to curl himself up, would probably die if he couldn't curl himself up around that ache.

"Lieser, take our wounded to my room."

"No!" Complete panic. He fumbled at Kaltherzig, trying to cling to him, but Lieser pulled him to wobble on his feet and kept him from falling. "Sir, you take me, please--"

"I will be there when I get there, and we'll discuss that *no.*"

Lieser did nothing more than steer him out of the party. A few guests tried to either tease or congratulate him, but Lieser steered him around these and down the hallway, and after a bit of a tangle in the doorway he was herded into Kaltherzig's dim quiet bedroom. And then he was in the bed, Kaltherzig's wide cool bed, sprawled across it gasping and shaken.

He managed to turn over, because having Lieser at his back felt completely unsafe. Lieser grinned down at him and then licked the palm of the hand he'd used to cover Erich's mouth.

"I wouldn't have stopped, you know," he said, slowly and softly and very sincerely, with the music of madness in every word.

Then he performed an elaborately drunken turn and wandered back out into the hallway.

It was quiet, and he was alone. Lieser had left the door open and he could hear the distant party.

He investigated between his legs with both hands, found no blood, pondered reaching the bathroom to be sick, or the floor instead of the bed, and did neither. He panted and trembled in struggle against the misery in his stomach. It seemed to wax and wane in time with nothing he could understand.

He thought, *privileged favorite,* and wheezed something that might've been laughter. That made him think of the little crowd, of the sound they'd made when he'd finally moved his hands. As if he'd been something to bet on, a racehorse or an athlete. That put a stop to the laughter, and that was just as well, because sometimes laughing by himself made him wonder if he might be going insane. And then he remembered *discuss that no,* and buried his face in the bed.

It was the shoes that woke him, first the left and then the right gently drawn off his feet. Having his socks drawn off made him kick one ticklish foot, and Kaltherzig said, "Welcome back," and it told Erich two things. First, that the doctor was quite drunk, and second, that he was very, very dangerous at the moment.

Erich pushed himself up on one elbow. The room was illuminated only by the light in the hall, the door still open. Kaltherzig chose that moment to grasp Erich's ankles and drag him closer, so he could reach

Erich's belt buckle.

Very dangerous.

He hated being told to take off his clothes, but surely this was worse. Flicker of that bath, the very first night, of being moved as though he hadn't the sense to follow orders. "Sir." When that made Kaltherzig neither hurry nor wait, he tried, "Sir, I'm sorry."

"I know." He unbuttoned Erich's pants, drew them down and off with his underpants still inside them. The dragging, twisting pull of it sprawled him out on his face, shirt and tie crumpled under his arms, and the bed was cool and wide, and he thought, *he'll fuck me, that's all it is,* and knew that it wasn't. Kaltherzig pulled him again, so that his legs hung down over the side of the bed. He heard Kaltherzig's belt clear the loops and turned his face into the bed, grasped two handfuls of white bedspread.

The doctor had struck him before, usually with his hand, sometimes with the riding crop, but this was entirely different from either, a wide bright sudden hurt, shockingly loud. Kaltherzig swung the belt fast and hard, and Erich climbed from fear to fury to more apologies in a matter of seconds. None of it changed anything. Kaltherzig only went on hitting him. He pushed himself up without meaning to.

"No one told you to get up."

The belt never paused. He dropped down onto his face again, and Kaltherzig swung harder, faster, and he gave in to it, finding that place where there was no trying. He was crying hopelessly when Kaltherzig stopped, and something about it was good. He'd wanted to cry before, but his eyes had been dry and hot, and it was a relief to do it now.

"Do you understand why I'm hitting you?"

He swallowed and sobbed, and managed, "For telling you no."

"And?"

Panic climbed in him. He didn't know. Then, "For moving my hands?"

"Good boy. Put your knees under you."

He muffled one grieved sound. He was hard, and Kaltherzig would

139

see. Well, he'd done enough thrashing that surely he already had. Erich crawled up onto the bed, stopped on his hands and knees, his shirttails and his tie hanging down between his arms, waiting to see if this was what Kaltherzig had in mind. It wasn't. Kaltherzig pushed his head down, and he obeyed, wincing at how ridiculous it made him feel to keep his ass in the air this way, but now certain there would be sex and then sleep.

The belt, again. Slowly, now, but each one so hard it made him shriek in anguish. He didn't struggle. He deserved them. He hadn't been perfect. Something about this too, was good, the noise of it and the pain of it, some stranger kind of relief. Kaltherzig would stop soon, he had to, and when he didn't it only melted Erich further into tears and stillness.

After forever, Kaltherzig dropped the belt beside his head. Erich felt the mattress dip, as Kaltherzig sat beside him, a blur, ivory skin and open shirt. The doctor startled him badly by putting both cool hands on his buttocks, neither hitting nor rubbing, just pressing lightly. He closed his eyes in relief, thinking, *now he'll fuck me.* He waited for Kaltherzig to open the drawer beside his bed. Instead the doctor tugged at one of his knees, made him spread them further apart, and then slid his hand between Erich's legs.

Erich's eyes opened in wide shock, and Kaltherzig stroked his cock, in dry light feathery grazes. "Such interest," he said, softly, and Erich groaned and hid in the bed. "No, turn back so I can see your face."

He did. He dared a look up at Kaltherzig. The predatory interest in those gray eyes caught him. Kaltherzig smiled at him, the slow one that ended in teeth. Still dangerous. He kept stroking, too gently to do more than madden Erich, and then he stroked the tip of his cock with one fingertip, toying with the moisture there.

Erich wailed and meant to hide his face again, but the "Don't," stopped him, kept him caught in those eyes. Kaltherzig rubbed a wet circle and then drew a trail of dampness back to Erich's balls. He had time for disbelief, and then Kaltherzig wrapped his hand around them, firmly enough to make him hiss. He felt outraged there still, swollen and sullen, tight and vulnerable.

140

"Let's see what you've learned about no."

He was shaking. He'd stopped associating that with fear and had begun to regard it almost as a premonition, a sixth sense that warned of him of oncoming anguish. "Yes, sir."

(testing me, all the time)

"Do you want me to do it again?"

His teeth clicked together. Kaltherzig laughed at the sound Erich made when he realized the trap he was caught in. He thought of risking clever and saying something like *I wish you wouldn't,* but if he lied, Kaltherzig would know.

And he deserved it. He'd failed before, and he would do better this time.

"Yes, sir."

He was very glad he hadn't closed his eyes again, because he got to watch Kaltherzig sigh, watch his elegant face change. Erich only got that look when Kaltherzig was very pleased with him.

"Have I found something you hate, my boy?" He did a warning pull that made Erich want to rock back on his knees. He got new handfuls of bedspread, spread his knees as wide as he could, trying to find that moveless place inside him, the place where there was no struggle.

"Do I need to tell you to keep still?"

He'd almost fallen into that one too.

"I will, sir."

This was very, very different this way, being alone with him, being half-dressed but so naked. It was both easier and more frightening, here in this normal room in this normal bed. He was braced for intolerable pain, but Kaltherzig examined him almost gently at first, cupping him and pressing with his fingertips.   *Measuring me.*

A slow pull, until long after he was gasping and keening, shaking harder with the effort of staying in that position. This was a new hurt, with notes of outrage from internal structures that were not pleased about being rearranged and stretched.

Kaltherzig said, "That's beautiful," and Erich realized the doctor meant, him, and felt himself go cold and then warm all over.

"Breathe. And cry out all you want to—there's no one to hear you but me, this time—but keep your knees under you."

He drew in his breath. He was waiting for that unspeakable pain to crash into him again, but what happened was like more of being examined, pushes and pulls that were at first distressingly pleasant, and then faintly uncomfortable. Kaltherzig led him this way, slowly and steadily. He didn't realize the doctor had begun to hurt him at all until he'd been doing it for a long time. The climb from worry to anguish was easier that way, and that was the trap.

He sounded very loud to himself, with night and house so empty around them. He kept his knees under him, though his feet came up once and his head came up once. Kaltherzig had pushed him back into position without ever letting go of his balls, without a word. He wanted to beg him to stop, but he was afraid he'd land on a *no* and find himself in Block 10, wishing he was still being treated as gently as this.

Kaltherzig didn't stop until long after Erich had lost his erection. When Erich was quiet enough to hear him, he said, "There must be so many things I could make you like. Let's see if this is one of them."

He let go, and that was when Erich came the closest to falling over. He wanted to cough, but coughing would lead to gagging and he wasn't sure he'd be able to stop that if he started. His instinct kept trying to sneak around his orders, and his arms or his hands would twitch with the need to reach between his own legs. This, too, he was fairly sure he wouldn't stop if he started.

Here, at last, was the sound of the drawer opening. Here was the little click of the jar, and here were Kaltherzig's hands again. He was really beginning to think he might be spread and probably hurt and then, possibly, fucked, after all of this storm and stress. The idea of it made a low slow throb roll through his stomach. It was a soft bright thread of want through the pressure and nausea. He sniffled and panted and hid his wet face. Kaltherzig nudged his knees further apart, and that sent a delicious gleaming pang through him again. It made him arch his back, and Kaltherzig laughed. "Not yet."

Erich made a noise he couldn't help, frustration and despair, and only got more laughter in return. "Beautiful," Kaltherzig said again, and wrapped one warm, greased hand around Erich's cock. It confused him, and then silenced him. He didn't expect his erection to return, and when it did Kaltherzig settled into a regular stroke until Erich was rocking helplessly against his hand.

Faster. Tighter.

He was keening in his throat when Kaltherzig leaned close to his ear, "Do you want me to do it again?"

He didn't. He almost shook his head, but the fear that this too was a *no* stopped him. He wanted Kaltherzig to keep doing that delicious, tugging slide around his cock, preferably while over him, inside him, but it didn't occur to him to say this. He could say *yes* now, or Kaltherzig would make him say it soon enough. That was all there was to it. That was the world.

Kaltherzig added his thumbnail to the equation, grazing the head of Erich's cock with each stroke, delicious, maddening.

"Yes! Yes. Do it again. Just don't stop."

He thought, *this is the real, everything before was the dream.*

Kaltherzig didn't stop. He stroked Erich's scrotum, one ticklish line with the backs of his fingers, and took it in his hand again. And here was the sudden crushing pain he'd expected, and the unbearable reptilian instinct to fight, with kicks or blows, or to flee, which was impossible.

He would lose his erection again, and Kaltherzig would let go. That was the game. Any second now.

Any second failed to arrive, and he couldn't breathe, and he was trying for *please please please* but the tiny raw hurt of that thumbnail wouldn't let him speak. He shook his head then, violently, vehemently, and Kaltherzig rolled his balls tighter in his hand, making him howl.

"When you come, and not before."

This drove Erich into a heartbroken wail. The cruelty of it filled him with a horror that was almost indignation. Surely that had to be impossible. He tried to cry out something along these lines and could not. His testicles would be ruined, he was certain of it, and he tried to rock against Kaltherzig's hand again in desperation, but the pain was keeping his body tremor-tight, clumsy and perilous.

Kaltherzig let him breathe again, easing his grip until blinding became merely intolerable, merciless hand missing not a beat. When he could speak he eventually started saying, "I can't, sir, I can't, I promise, I'm sorry," in no particular order.

"Oh, yes, you can. Just nowhere near as soon as you'd like to."

"I need you inside me."

He didn't think about it, or intend to say anything like it. There wasn't enough of himself left for anything as complex as that. There was only the intensely sweet, raw little scratch of Kaltherzig's thumbnail, drawing out each word. He expected a laugh, or a blow, or worse.

The doctor took away both of his hands, making a sound between a hiss and a snarl. He left Erich bereft for brief distressing seconds, and then he felt himself seized, swarmed. It was more collision than embrace. Kaltherzig crushed him down flat on the bed, a nightmare of breath and noise in his ear. He'd forgotten about the belt and the bruises until Kaltherzig grasped his ass in both hands, spread him hard, shoved at him harder with his cock until he was inside after four savage thrusts. He dragged at Erich until he was up on his knees again, spidered his arms around his waist. Here were the hands, back again, and the pleasure of it was so sharp and sudden that he tried to pull away from it, and only succeeded in impaling himself more utterly.

He said *yes,* again, over and over, for as long as he could.

Kaltherzig was right. It took forever. He finally realized Kaltherzig was doing it on purpose, playing him, concentrating on his cock until he was close and begging, and then his balls until he was hysterical. And then back again. Kaltherzig wouldn't move his hips, only pinning him there, impaled, though the noise and the motion of Erich's anguished struggle around him made his breath come faster and faster. Erich knew there was

144

yet another magick word to change this, and he was sure with sick certainty that he knew what it was.

He tried *mercy* first, and this got him bitten between shoulder and neck, a deep hard bite that Kaltherzig held. Kaltherzig had never done that before, and it made him scream in startled fear with flickers of fairy-tale wolves in his head. He tried to duck away from those teeth, and discovered how trapped he was, pain or pleasure in every direction. After that it came almost naturally to say it.

"Harder..."

He was saying it for a long time before he realized Kaltherzig couldn't hear him, and he dragged his face up and said, "Harder, do it harder," and that was the end of Kaltherzig's heartless stillness, and the end of magick words.

He wept, pinned, and when Kaltherzig got off him he finally curled up, cupped his balls with both hands, let himself gasp and shudder and writhe. Kaltherzig made sure he was firmly on one side, ordered him *not* to roll over on his back, and left him, walking out into the hallway with his pants still unbuttoned. He returned with a towel around a surgical glove filled with snow and persuaded Erich to modify his cupping behavior to include the ice pack.

Then he sat behind him, stroking down his spine, over and over with one sticky hand. It almost felt affectionate, and for some reason this made Erich cry harder.

The next morning he taught Erich how to set up the chess pieces, the phonograph warbling softly behind them.

It wasn't his fault. It was all his fault.

It was the whim of a god.

Hauptwerk

Erich came to recognize the sudden wake of stillness, the clump of staff orbiting a doctor or two, and the silence among the patients when the numbers started being called. Sometimes the death parade passed him by, and sometimes someone crooked a finger at him or tapped on the office door.

And that meant they needed him for a live experiment.

Then he would find himself with the questionable honor of trying to write down what the doctor was shouting over a shrieking subject. He had a superstitious dislike of the inevitable nurse or three for a live one. Kaltherzig was always viciously distant to him in front of people. There was an unspeakable intimacy in it, these eyes he was beginning to think of as

(mine)

familiar, focused on some tragedy under his hands.

Erich was jealous of that concentration, something he had also come to think of as his.

Let him ruin some other boy with strange incisions, let girls walk in lovely and be wheeled out re-arranged and lovely no longer. Erich still stood shaken and sick with envy, Kaltherzig's evil little murmurs of fake comfort to someone else jangling in his ears. It was never finished. He would think he had all Kaltherzig's dangers mapped, and another jagged edge would bite him.

At first it was only Kaltherzig.

Then, he supposed once he'd proven he would neither vomit nor faint, he started recording for Clauberg, a monotonous dry man that reminded him of his old biology teacher. Always children, always a tube up the nose, crying that invariably ended in uncontrollable coughing and usually vomiting. Apparently it was something to do with test serums delivered directly into the lung.

All Erich knew was that it was forty minutes or so of revolting

146

boredom, in which he wrote very little, flat dosage and subject statistics, and clockwatched until it was over.

One morning Kaltherzig said, "Mengele's boy is busy. You'll record for him today," and steered him away from the familiar office and towards an examination room. The doctor's mouth was a straight line, and those eyes were thundercloud black, and Erich was reasonably sure what he was seeing was rage, barely leashed.

Erich had always supposed he wasn't assisting because he wasn't important enough for Herr Haupsturmführer, Doctor Mengele. Now he wondered if perhaps Kaltherzig had been shielding him from this. For as long as he could, until one day there were no more excuses. The other prisoners were afraid of Kaltherzig. They were *terrified* of Mengele. What if Kaltherzig was holding back not fury, but fear?

He supposed it was a mercy that he had no choice, because he would have done a great deal not to push through those doors. He had heard enough from the office a long way down the hall to know he didn't want to see what produced such cataclysmic noise. There was a prisoner-doctor there, a Jew Erich did not know who brought him the files, trying to warn him of something with his eyes.

Mengele was washing his hands, singing. "There you are!" he said to Erich, cheerfully. "Find somewhere to lurk, they should be arriving any moment now."

They brought in two dark-haired girls, tiny doll copies of one another. Mengele lifted each to put them on the table and took their pictures, smiling for them and mimicking poses to get them arranged. They laughed. They adored him rather quickly. He flashed the camera in his own eyes, did an exaggerated squint, and dared them to do better. Then he asked which was the oldest, and after some argument the girls and their file agreed with one another.

He lifted the younger twin off the table and set her down to stand beside him. Then he pushed the older twin onto her back, and his assistant held her down, and Mengele pried open one of her eyes. He got that far before she began to shriek, and the twin immediately joined in from the floor. The combined effect was rather like being in a room with two air-raid sirens.

Mengele leaned over, and very softly but very clearly to the girl on the floor, "Stop it or I'll kill her."

His expression never changed.

Erich was stunned into slackjawed staring by the sheer evilness of this. He had never heard Mengele say anything of the kind. And it *worked*, instantly—they both shut up and stared at him in something like awe.

The oldest started screaming again when she saw the needle, climbed an octave in shrill anticipation of pain. The youngest didn't join in. The assistant finally held a hand over her mouth. He kept his eyes on the floor. The new muffled noise reminded Erich of a neighbor's dog, a sad and tiresome little thing that would cry at the gate until it was hoarse. Mengele was working on the other eye with a new syringe.

Erich wrote down the dosages rattled off at him, trying to be invisible. *Sub-corneal injection.* He could not imagine such a thing, and again that wing of sensation through him, of being chosen, lucky, favorite, of being spared such dramas as dyed irises and deliberate infections. Deep wrench of longing for Kaltherzig, for the desk Erich had come to think of as his own.

He traded this double-file for a new one as the screaming pair was removed, the wounded one carried and cupping her eyes, the youngest dragged along by her hand, crying so hard she was probably as blinded as the other.

Mengele was washing his hands again, humming the same marching song.

Kaltherzig informed him on the way home that Mengele had been quite pleased with his work. This meant that Kaltherzig was pleased with

Erich, apparently, and he supposed that was worth fourteen *sub-corneal injections.* Still, he could not get his mind away from this cracked Mengele mask. He told Kaltherzig about the twins, asked if it was always like that.

"Those twins of his." Kaltherzig shrugged. "He wraps them around his finger, doesn't he? What's the difference? Drive you mad with that screeching. I used to have the office closest to the Zwillingshaus. Thank God I was promoted quickly."

He lit a cigar, rolled the window down. "You say whatever works, it's your job, you know." Another shrug. "He's an idiot, and arguing with that only makes me look like an idiot."

"He is?" Erich couldn't quite grasp how one could be an idiot and a doctor at the same time.

"Oh yes, he is. You can't change someone's genetic material with a retina full of dye. It's preposterous. And if it doesn't change genetics, it's redecorating. Time wasted for vanity." He sighed. "He's good at charming, and good at shaking hands. I hate both of those things."

"He would really..." Erich did a little gesture in the air that made him put his hands back in his lap quickly.

"He would really. He will, really, when he's through with them."

So Mengele hadn't been bluffing. It made it worse somehow that Mengele would kill them anyway, that all that obedience would earn them nothing. He looked at Kaltherzig's hands and was quiet.

What happened to your last boy, sir?

Blueblack smoke spiraling up into the sky.

Mengele volunteered for Selektion duty so often that Kaltherzig rarely had to endure it. Mengele always had candy or fruit; he was so pretty and so soft-spoken, such a little man, so neatly dressed, so calm. They always smiled, so grateful to see a kind face after the frightening train ride and the shouting SS men. Parents would see this handsome gentleman examining children and break out of line to push their own into his hands, nodding lies at his endless "Twins?"

He seemed to delight in visiting them after the first betrayal, the first time Uncle Mengele led them not to toys or nuts in hidden pockets, but knives and that implacable calm. They would sit bleeding into bandages he had placed over wounds he had made, and after a while they would be smiling at him again. It took some of them five or six times to learn to cry when he came into the ward, and the new children who adored this nice grownup were mystified.

The Hungarian twins made something of a name for themselves in Block 10 as Mengele's supposed magnum opus. They were eighteen, and the sort of prime physical specimen that did not often come under the doctor's hands in this lean and hungry time.

The twins were grinning stupid things, in his unspoken opinion, loud and friendly or incomprehensibly hostile by turns. Their German was awful. They seemed to think they were celebrities, above and beyond the screaming ruined things in the experimental ward.   The stares and badly hidden smiles of the young women in the hospital only aggravated this new found egotism.

Erich feared for his sanity or his soul, because the warm smug little anticipation of their destruction would not leave him.

The fact that his own privilege and safety existed at the same fragile mercy as theirs did not escape him, but somehow that made it more intense, his wish to watch them fall under the knives. They were the tall graceful boys who had kept him clinging to adults like a moth to light, because out of sight of the authorities those were the ones who threw rocks, shoved him down to bloody his hands and knees, stared with smirking words, *queer, schwul, girlboy*, nudges for their friends to help them stare.

And he would blush, always, because he knew they were right, and that would only make them laugh harder.

Erich recorded for some of their initial exams—days and days of photographs and calipers, sometimes going on far into the night so that Kaltherzig would go home in disgust. Erich would stay, trying not to yawn, until long after dark. Then he would be dropped off after a quiet tense few minutes in the car with Mengele up front by the driver.

The first time this happened he realized he was alone on the path up to Kaltherzig's house, outside the camp walls, and that he might run. He looked once off into the darkness of fields and woods beyond, thought of insects and dew and hiding in barns and slowly starving, or of Kaltherzig finding him and pinning him down with the black eye of a gun. He had no idea where he might go. The entire idea seemed preposterous.

It was tedious work.

Mengele seemed determined to photograph every hairy rippling inch of these drafthorse men, from sole to scalp. Erich found them rather repulsive, contrasting all this overdone bulging and flexing in his mind with Kaltherzig's marble-pale narrow lines, with his own delicacy.

They were a dirty almost-blonde, light eyes in blue tones, and this broad-shouldered thick heartiness of theirs was something the Reich seemed to hold in high esteem. At least, Mengele thought so. He was delighted with them, his enthusiasm burning in him like a lamp, every motion quick and eager.

They were sometimes almost rude, complaining of holding arms up like so or kneeling for too long, complaining of squinting around purple spots from the incessant flashbulbs, complaining of the food. The petulance made Erich grit his teeth, watching Mengele, almost praying for that mask to drop. He was slippery and obsequious to them, assuring them of their importance to his work, their valuable contribution to medicine, until they were puffed up with pride. He never quite claimed they were special or were to be spared, but he made no effort to strip them of such delusions.

Not at first, anyway.

Erich would watch him make these assurances, arranging one twin while the other balefully waited his turn. He thought of two blinded girls. He caught himself reading the files he was typing, and wondered, how many days it would be, that Mengele's game would go on.

Kaltherzig didn't like them, and he liked their cost in Erich's time even less. His one brief comment about them was that they were common peasant stock, his sneer making a profanity of *common*. Erich wondered if Kaltherzig, too, saw long-ago boys who had laughed at his neatness and his narrow long bones, his too-beautiful face, before he had grown into this death's head soldier nobody would ever dare laugh at again.

But all of the Reich, it seemed, was a system of favors owed and collected, and he was fury-eyed but silent when Erich opened the door and tiptoed in long after sunset.

The photography ended not a moment too soon for Erich, and then it was X-rays for days, and he was spared none of it. It was the photography again, except without the flashbulbs, that endless arranging and that hum and click, and more of those thick demanding complaints. They seemed rather proud to go about naked, but now the incessant complaint was that it was too cold, the table was too hard, the X-rays made them feel strange.

Mengele smiled and nodded and all but cooed sympathy at these hulking idiots. "Yes, yes, but you're the best we have," he would say, pushing an edged mouthpiece that last agonizing inch deeper, to get just one more shot of those big flawless teeth, bluegreen eyes with redgold eyelashes blinking resentfully at him over the hulk of the machine.

Erich rather thought he was enjoying this cat-and-mouse, that he pretended kindness not just because it was easier, but because the betrayal was more deliciously unexpected.

It could not come soon enough for Erich.

He knew it had begun when there were Untersturmführer in Mengele's examining room. There were four of them, smoking and leaning in corners, Lieser among them giving him a smile. For once, Erich was almost glad to see him. He was almost certain Kaltherzig had sent him, though he could not have explained why he believed this.

Three prisoner-doctors were shrinking around them like rabbits around wolves. Two long great metal washtubs were already here, striped slaves leaving little drip-trails as they lugged and emptied bucket after bucket of steaming water to fill them.

Erich chewed his lip for want of a smile, and put himself neatly out of everyone's way. He had the two files open and half-overlapped so that he could write on either without flipping through them.

He had no idea what might happen, but he knew it would end in screams. It always did.

He tried to imagine one of *those*, screaming, and a quick trip through the library of noise he'd collected since Auschwitz had become the world gave him no clues. He would know soon enough.

The twins were brought in bookended by SS.

One of them put in a toe as Mengele was making his entrance in a swish of white. He snatched his foot out, started his usual imperious complaint, followed a half-step behind by his brother joining in.

Mengele spared them not a look. He gestured, and the guards simply seized them and shoved them in and pushed them down.

These were not quite screams, yet. More indignant shouting.

Lieser drew back from the sloshing fury, shaking water from his splashed sleeve, drew his gun and held it on them with a smile that dripped sweetness and reason. It held them down just fine, and stopped the noise like a thrown switch.

Erich's eyes went from gun to these twins, growing lobster-pink and occasionally making a half-cowed complaint, in more of a mutter now. He saw them exchanging glances, and thought *they're beginning to suspect*.

The buckets kept coming, and this led to new shouts of protest. Lieser gestured at one of the others, and he shoved the noisier of the two under, head and all, laughed for a minute, and let him go as the other's hysteria climbed. He surfaced coughing and crimson, eyes starting to glaze from heat and the first real fear. They pleaded breathlessness, dizziness, and the menace-twitch from the guard warned them of being held under again, until they sat panting, staring at one another, at Mengele, as though he might suddenly revert into this fawning adorer again, as if he might save them.

Lieser yawned, smoked, switched his gun from hand to hand, finally put it away and came to lean with his back against the wall beside Erich. They nodded at one another, and that was all. Blaze of humiliation that he tried to ignore.

Erich noted the date, time, pondered what he was supposed to write under *Procedure,* and finally noted *submerged in very hot water* and a start time.

He hoped this was all right.

He didn't dare interrupt to ask.

He wondered if they would simply cook them, but surely that would have involved a heat source. He watched the steam, watched their useless squirming pushes to avoid the new buckets of hotter water.

It was strange—this was wrong, whatever it was leading to, and all his life he'd been taught to tell the authorities of wrongdoing.

Mengele *was* the authorities.

This left him in limbo, morally, and he could find no obligation not to steal a tiny bit of satisfaction. These two must stand in for all. These two would be painted over all the others in his memory that had done him evil and been spared because of their beauty, their muscle and vacancy, those useless qualities that everyone had loved them for. Those useless qualities he had never been able to imitate.

Perhaps those very qualities had been what had led them here. Now that was a comfortably round theory, that his strangeness and their perfection had drawn the same lot, the same disastrous reward.

He thought, *I'll tell Kaltherzig, he'd like it,* but that was what one might say to a friend. Not an office-gossip friend, but a real one. Whatever Kaltherzig was to him, it wasn't *friend*—though he was the closest to that category Erich could remember in all his life.

They dragged the twins out of the tubs, both staggering, half-fainting, strapped them down to these twin-tables. Adelle and two other prisoner doctors bent over them with specimen jars and gleaming tweezers, plucking hair after hair. They twitched, squirmed, gritting teeth, growling finally, spitting Hungarian profanity at this maddening tiny pain repeated over and over, pleaded with Mengele to tell them why this was being done, insisted that they would file complaints.

Mengele ignored this, too, as if they were not speaking.

As if they were, animals.

He took the tweezers from Adelle, squinted at it, pointed out the root of the hair to her, "Like this one, all of them, or don't bother to put them in," and was gone in a blur of white.

He went in and out, checking a jar or a hair, pointing here or there where he wanted additional samples. Finally he gestured at Lieser who passed this gesture to the guards, and they were unstrapped, sulking, expecting to go back to the ward, but they were only put back into the tubs, bailed half-empty and refilled with new near-boiling water.

Four times, this loop.

They weren't screaming, not yet, but they were both quiet, sullen, sweating and blinking, wavering and heat-dazed. Their eyebrows were gone, making them look as though their foreheads had grown. One of them pleaded for water, and the guard behind him laughed and pushed him under again, holding him down this time till he was limp when drawn up, vomiting up the water he'd requested.

They no longer looked at one another.

Mengele finally nodded at the rows and rows of jars, labeled neatly in Erich's handwriting, which twin, what part of the body the hair was plucked from, date.

"The rest of it," he ordered, making one wingsweep of gesture. The twins were taken out, falling from one guard to the other, knees folding too far with each step.

Erich sat in the empty room for a very long time.

Then the twins were brought back, with only Mengele and Adelle. At first he did not recognize them. They were bald, utterly, from crown to sole, looking like great babies. Their heads seemed much too round, much too pale. They weren't beautiful anymore—now they were only strange, slippery things, streaked and spotted with scalds and pinpricks of blood. Even their red-gold eyelashes had been plucked out.

And the photographs began all over again.

The screams began the next day, echoing from the wide tiled room with the showers. Erich had plenty of files to carry back to the archives, and through this door he saw only one of them, strapped over a bench like the one used in the roll-call courtyard for floggings, screaming and screaming, looking more than ever like a mutant infant.

Mengele was directing another doctor, smoking far away from his subject. A black rubber bag hung deflating from a hook on the wall, snaking a tube between the cheeks of the boy's buttocks. Erich swallowed hard, thinking for the millionth time that he'd been lucky Kaltherzig had chosen him away from all this.

Mengele leaned his head out. "Come to the exam room when the noise dies down, boy."

Erich nodded, white and shaken, and turned with his pushcart of files, feeling guilty in a red slow rush, as if his wish to watch them ruined had somehow made it so.

The other twin joined in soon enough. Kaltherzig was in his office filling out reports, leaving Erich off to one side with the typewriter on a pushcart. He looked up now and then, when the screams had stilled the keys, but he did not comment.

Erich told him of Mengele's order, certain for some reason he would forbid him, but Kaltherzig only nodded, lit a cigarette and stood up, did the rough pat that Erich had come to secretly regard as—not quite affectionate, exactly, but close. The click of his boots faded down the hall in the direction of the din. Going for a look himself, he supposed, thinking of a ten-year-old Kaltherzig sitting in the school library with an anatomy book open, waiting till the common peasant stock had all gone home to start his own walk in something like safety.

On the way home that evening he asked Kaltherzig about the tube, the black rubber bag, quietly, not wanting the driver to hear him, and Kaltherzig laughed for a long time.

"An enema, idiot. Surely you know what that is?"

He flushed. He did know, from whispers overheard during those talks children have that unerringly revolve around corporal punishment and excretory functions, orbiting closer and closer to actual sex as years went on. "You, didn't—"

A shrug. "The purges are the same. They fill your intestines with water by chemical imbalance, and not a hose. I'll give you one tomorrow and you can decide which you prefer."

A deeper flush, and he drew up his knees as much as he dared without risking his shoes on the leather seat. He thought of saying *no thank you, sir,* and could not work out a way to say it without the forbidden *no.* He looked at Kaltherzig's still face, still eyes fixed on the apple trees outside, and said nothing.

The next morning, though the sky was crystal clear when they stepped outside, Kaltherzig was a rustling oilspill shape, in the inkblack SS raincoat, sharply belted and gleaming. Erich thought he understood this, but he pretended to himself he didn't. He'd hoped Kaltherzig was teasing, had forgotten.

Kaltherzig hadn't been teasing, and he never forgot.

He led him into the same shower-room, closing and locking the door behind them as perhaps one small mercy. Erich was already crying. His one risked *please* had resulted in "And why did you ask me?"

He had no answer for that, only a miserable scalding blush, and when Kaltherzig pinned him with that endless cold stare, without another word, he fumbled his hands to his neck and began unbuttoning his shirt.

Kaltherzig left him to this, returning with a wheeled cart that had a black rubber bag already full hanging from one corner. He put this on the hook, trailing that cable and catching the nozzle before it dragged on the floor. He toyed with the clamp, until fluid ran in a smooth clouded-white stream, and clamped it closed again. Erich stood shivering, no longer bothering to cover himself, not in front of Kaltherzig, anyway. He mouthed *please don't*, but Kaltherzig wasn't even looking at him. He took a white towel from under the cart, folded it and dropped it on the tile. "For the sake of your knees."

Well, at least he wouldn't be strapped to a bench. "Thank you, sir." He'd learned, too, that orders came embedded in comments, sometimes, and he circled Kaltherzig with hot sick humiliation climbing his throat with tiny handfuls of claws, and knelt on the towel.

Kaltherzig knelt behind him, and pushed at his back so that he leaned forward, pushed him again, and he whimpered and gritted his teeth and settled down cheek and shoulder to the floor, arms crossed around himself.

A nudge. Soft cool wetness; cream. He dared a look over his shoulder, and the sight of Kaltherzig drawn in black against this wet white room stilled him, somehow, made him slump and settle and only stare with the one eye that could still see him, watch him smudge this cream along the black nozzle.

He saw Erich looking and did the eyesmile for him, said as softly as if they could be overheard, "See, this is the girl one—the boy one is like, just a little straight line, like a bit of a pen." He tilted it, to show Erich how it was rounded and furrowed, each little trench neatly dotted with holes. It reminded him of a watering-can for flowers. "The boy one is worse. Gives you terrible cramps, all that water in just one place. I want you to take a great deal, curious boy, and that can only be done with a lot of care or a lot of pain."

He was silent, then, and Erich was pretty sure he caught the secret code, and he dared, "Care, please, sir."

Kaltherzig's bottom lip moved, not quite a moue, that face he used to indicate he was, considering. "You'll have to be perfectly good."

"I will, I'm trying, I will..."

"You're being perfectly good so far," Kaltherzig assured him, and set one hand on the small of his back to warn him, drew a line from his waist down his spine to his anus, did a little poke that was almost like teasing. "Deep breath."

That was an occasional command before a bright, sharp pain, and Erich squeezed his eyes shut, drew in a long gulp of air, gritted his teeth.

"Exhale...slowly...oh, perfect boy....." That last dissolving into a moan, and it was such a just-for-them noise that he made the same noise in return, and the slow merciless push slid inside him painlessly, frictionless.

He hid his head in his arms, quivering, and Kaltherzig nudged it inside him, moved it side to side, the ridged strange surface scraping across that knot inside him that made him open his legs, that made his cock decide it wasn't *that* cold and nudge itself out of his foreskin for a look. "*Please—*"

"Shh." A circle of soothe petted onto the small of his back, and the thought *he's not wearing the gloves, he always* and then the click of Kaltherzig opening the valve.

He started a set of whimpers, hugging his head tight with his arms, doing a shuffling little shift that wasn't exactly struggle, only the expression of how badly he wished to. Kaltherzig's hand was spread flat across his buttocks, nozzle held between second and ring fingers. His other hand came up, petting those same circles into Erich's back. He felt Kaltherzig shift, felt him sharing the space of the towel to kneel on, felt him lean over his back in away that was so blatantly the way he, was, when he

(fucks)

drew him close in the dark that Erich moaned again, and there was the first hint inside him of sensation, a fluttering sort of warmth that

159

threatened discomfort and a tongue-curling full pleasure, and then nothing again.

Kaltherzig's hand went under him, and he almost-cried out thinking he would wind it around his cock, but he was petting him, from his throat down to his chest, a smooth gentle circle around his stomach, and then pressing kneading circles there, low on his stomach, moving in lazy up-and-down arcs, seeming to press specifically at structures Erich blushed to imagine, thinking of Kaltherzig again with anatomy books open across his knees.

He knows, everywhere. My body is much more his than, mine...

Tiny wet noises, that maybe he was imagining, and a crooked little tightening low in his gut, that felt exactly like the need for a bathroom. He whimpered, climbing in urgency, chewing his lip against the *please*. Surely it wasn't supposed to do *that*. He couldn't tell Kaltherzig that. He had chewed his lip more than once through being sodomized or having Kaltherzig's cock deep in his throat when he was sobbing desperate for the bathroom for either reason. One didn't discuss such things. He was a doctor, it wouldn't do *that* or he'd, have...

A wrench of it, tightening and staying, that dull-edged ache and the itch to, push. The one little reflex-spasm that wasn't quite push had given him an *immediate* and disturbing sense that he really was, filling with, fluid, and that it might easily leak around this nozzle, and if he did that in front of Kaltherzig he would die.

"Sir please, sir please it's working, wrong...please..."

A click. He felt the water stop by some internal ending, and he was half-panting and half-sobbing in gratitude. Kaltherzig knelt up a little, hand wavering the nozzle and making Erich give a pathetic little noise that was half lust and half unspeakable embarrassment.

"Pant. Like me."

He opened his eyes again, peering over the intersection of his elbows to see Kaltherzig with bared teeth, going *hah hah hah*. He copied him, not understanding, just obeying, and his hands cupped at Erich's stomach again, soothing. That knotted pain tightened, subsided.

Click, and the water again.

The next time the cramps hit him the panting didn't help and the petting didn't help and he was reduced to *please please please* and Kaltherzig closed the valve and did something and he felt that sort of balloon open inside him, and it broke him.

That was all; not even wide enough for pain. Kaltherzig made that wordless noise at him, stroking his back. "Not for so very long. And I'll leave you alone, after. Now why are you crying? It doesn't hurt, does it?"

He shook his head, crying anyway. "Because it's...embarrassing..."

A sigh. The petting continued. "There's no one to know but me, and I'll never tell. I don't record these, the only-us-two experiments."

Erich looked over his shoulder to check Kaltherzig's expression on *experiments,* found that smile that meant he was probably, teasing.

The doctor held him there, until he was frantic again, and gave him the little bulb and showed him how to deflate it and left him, with the door locked.

There was a stainless-steel toilet in one corner. It was strange to use one with so much open space, but he was in no state to complain. He sobbed, mostly, face covered, grateful to be left alone for this last indignity. Afterward he showered himself, feeling very strange, wobbly and unreal and disassociated.

Kaltherzig gave him a generous break, and knocked before he came back in. He had a larger bag, already filled.

Erich lost count.

The water came out as clear as it had gone in, except very very pink. It was sickeningly easy, his muscles too exhausted to resist. Kaltherzig had long since just let him lie on the floor. He curled loosely there, still crying abstractly, but becoming more and more, still, inside.

He felt indescribably, obscenely clean, as if everything, ever, had been washed away, down to everything he had believed or thought he understood. This was a new world entirely.

Sometimes he managed *please,* and sometimes he managed something as long as *I'll be perfect,* but it was still fairly, unintelligible. Kaltherzig assured him that he knew all of that, and that he was being perfect, in that distant soothing kind of voice, and the water petted him in soft thudding pulses and he was too tired to do anything but, allow himself to be soothed.

He was pulled to his feet and half-carried to a bench and wrapped in a Wehrmacht-issue blanket that had seen better days. Kaltherzig left him there with another distracted pat to the top of his head. After minutes or an hour Adelle brought him a mug of hot tea with a lot of sugar in it and two blue pills. He suspected she wasn't supposed to give him the pills, the way she held them almost hidden in her hand.

They made him sleepy, and deleted pains he hadn't noticed until they were gone.

He hated her.

The kindness made him feel, too close, to everything.

He was curled on the bench sleeping, hair neatly dripping off the end to spare the blanket when Kaltherzig came and retrieved him. That velvety spin of Adelle's secret drug around him, through him, magnifying the motion of his head. Kaltherzig tipped his chin up, turned his face an inch or two to either side, studying his pupils. For a moment he was afraid the doctor knew, and he feared for himself, and then Adelle.

"You're being very obedient."

The drug said it before he could stop himself. He thought later that he'd meant it to be funny. "I have to, sir, or you'll shoot me."

A smile. Not quite the safe one, anymore.

"No, you'll wish I would shoot you."

The twins were spared for a day or two, while Mengele devoted his time to his visiting wife. Then that knock again, and Erich knew before the file was put into his hands who would be in the examination room.

They were broken down beyond celebrity, crying in that listless

162

nauseating way, strapped to the twin examining tables, knees up and apart in that familiar position. Erich sat with his clipboard, brimming over with a distressing mix of sympathy and something else that he couldn't stop feeling, something like joy.

He had no autonomy except in his head, and it seemed he'd chosen the side of the SS on this one, whether the choice gave him pride or shame or both. Mengele laid out two of everything he still had nightmares about, the specula, a paired array of the smooth gun-shaped silver things that triggered those biting sample-stealing needles. Now there would be real suffering.

Mengele began with the eldest.

Erich thought, watching the younger watch his brother that this must be the point of bringing them both in at once, to inflict this dread on the one, this humiliation on the other. He watched him spread open, the longest of these sample-pistols pushed in, watched Mengele's finger depress, and the click, the scream. He watched each testicle held pinned between Mengele's thumb and forefinger, the tip of a narrower pistol set in the very bulging center of this drawn-taut skin. Another click. Both of them screaming as though that metallic little impact had cued them.

The noise made him think of the click of candy, left anonymously on his desk where his forearms would brush it onto the floor, and Kaltherzig's care not to look at him closely for an hour or three after these presents would appear. A guilty pleasure for both of them.

It was almost worth the abuse. Without that, grudge, to hold against these creatures, it would have been a frightening ordeal. As it was, the only terror in it was his utter lack of revulsion. He ran through the list of commandments and could not remember them and the gist of it seemed to be that he had no choice and he might as well, tolerate this, however he could.

The twins were unstrapped, each at the end of this session, by then sobbing so they could not resist or really even seem to move. They were leaned over for one more with the sample-guns, pressed and fired just above their waists, one on the right, one on the left. Erich wrote *kidney*

163

tissue samples and his mouth was dry; he'd thought your kidneys were much lower, covered by your trousers. Kaltherzig's samples had been unspeakable horror enough; he tried to imagine, that nipping merciless coring bite, taken out of

(*an internal organ*)

someplace deeper still.

Nothing. A flicker of a try at a memory of getting his tonsils out. No use.

He wrote, neatly, set these jars one in each tray per separate twin.

He watched.

Specula the likes of which he had never seen, they opened in an O that grew as wide as the mouth of a milk glass, and he put his hands to his own mouth, to crush down the scream, that he'd been frightened of the tiny cruelties Kaltherzig had given him.

Mengele, gloved to his elbow, and the little internal shock of realizing that really was his, wrist, disappearing beyond the distended red-violet anus of one twin while the other one screamed and screamed at the blank static in his brother's eyes.

"Gag them, why don't you? I've already a headache," he said to no one in particular. The other prisoner left and returned with twin short, thick straps that seemed made for exactly this order.

Flashbulbs.

A week later Mengele tapped on the window of Kaltherzig's door himself—unprecedented. Kaltherzig did a noncommittal grunt, and the doctor opened it and leaned in just enough to be polite. "Will you take the other one, for the timing?"

"Delighted." Kaltherzig finished handwriting a sentence in his precise little jagged gestures, and stood up, tilting his head to Erich.

He feared a grand guignol, but the twins were in the morgue already, blindfolded, strapped onto tilted grooved tables. Kaltherzig and Mengele had a long thick syringe each, and they each chose a twin and laughed a little getting themselves matched up, two needles dimpling two hairless chests. Two pushes, and the twins shook, kicking, sagging already against the straps, convulsions getting fainter by the second.

Mengele started cutting before the spasms had stopped.

Verhüllen

He had grown used to Mengele, the way he assumed the sort of zookeeper who kept very dangerous animals might grow used to them after a while. It just wasn't possible to be terrified out of your wits constantly. He'd come to look at him more the way one regarded the sort of teacher that brooked no deviation, that came down immediately on the tiniest infraction and presided over classrooms as silent as tombs.

He seemed to be reasonable enough, until the point at which he'd decided to kill you, and after that nothing whatsoever would change his mind.

Erich was by no means comfortable with him, but he was no longer freezing cold at the sight of Mengele in his white coat and gleaming boots, no longer seized with the urge to find Kaltherzig and ask him an unnecessary question. To, hide, in his shadow.

So he thought very little of it when Mengele crooked a finger and tipped his head at him en route to his office. It was rare but not unknown for Mengele to give him very specific instructions for a file or to dictate a letter.

He followed him in, not really worried until Mengele closed the door.

"Now, Doctor Kaltherzig is in a meeting with the you-knows from Berlin. I'm going to give you your injection to preserve the timing schedule. Now—" and he dusted his hands, opened a black leather bag on his desk, this being the sort of office for filing and not screaming. He drew out a syringe, loaded it from a very large brown vial.

Erich had never seen one like it.

He opened his mouth, closed it again.

What could he say? That this was highly irregular? Kaltherzig would be furious with him if he interfered with An Experiment—he'd come to hear the capitalization and the near-reverence in that phrase very quickly here.

He turned up his sleeve, and Mengele daubed alcohol almost at his shoulder, set the needle with deft painless speed, depressed the plunger with that gradual steady push that Kaltherzig only used on him with the kind of drug he got when he couldn't stop crying. The hurt was a slow little annoyance.

Mengele drew out the needle without so much as a flicker of that pulling sting he was used to, tapped the alcohol swab over the mark. "There! I'm no Kaltherzig, but I think you'll retain full use of your arm, yes? Erich, was it?"

"Yes sir, thank you, sir." He was afraid, now, turning down his sleeve.

Mengele opened the door for him with a grand flourish and a pretended bow. He went back to Kaltherzig's office. He felt warm, but that meant nothing. There was no change inside him that he could sense.

Erich told Kaltherzig of this in the car, thinking very little of it by now, simply to let him know Mengele had done as he'd asked. They usually spent a moment or two of *how was your day* sort of talk when they spent the day apart. He was not expecting the reaction; the unmitigated fury in Kaltherzig's eyes made him trail off half-through a word.

"What did he give you?" Quiet.

"I...don't...it wasn't what you give me. A bigger brown vial, I couldn't see the—"

"And you *let* him do this?"

He couldn't think of an answer to that one; the question made no sense in context. He was Mengele. Of course Erich had let him do this. "He said that, you--"

"That *I.*"

That was really dripping something poisonous.

The familiar jittery electrical fear was starting in his joints. "Yes sir, you, that you were too busy to—"

It failed him. It was the truth, but it sounded like a lie.

He should have known this trick for what it was when Mengele threw it down.

He wondered if he would die, if he was dying already.

"Stop the car."

This was to the driver, who was doing his level best to look as though he weren't listening. He stopped, and Kaltherzig got out, went to the driver's door and opened it, gestured *out* again at the Untersturmführer impatiently, took the wheel himself. He left the man standing dumbfounded in the street, dragged the car into a swerving turn and drove off much, much too quickly.

Erich only stared at him. He didn't dare do anything else.

I'm dying, I must be, he's going to ask him if there's an antidote, he's going to--

This reckless speed threw up dust and left people gaping after them in amazement. The rumors would have already begun, Erich thought, but he could find little concern for it.

Kaltherzig's jaw was one stack of straight tight lines.

They drove back to Block 10, stopped with a screeching protest from the car.

Mengele was standing outside already, smoking in the near-dark.

He'd had nearly five minutes to think of something perfect, some flawless argument set in the prettiest submissiveness he could compose.

Of course he drew a complete blank.

"Please don't," Erich said, but the door slammed behind Kaltherzig.

Erich climbed out of the car after him, thinking to chase him, stop him, but when he caught at Kaltherzig's sleeve he was turned on, shoved to the ground so hard he stayed there on his hands and knees, afraid to get up. He had never seen him so angry, never seen such a flash of promised Hell in his eyes.

"You told him I ordered this?"

No need to clarify that; Mengele knew why he was there, had

probably been quietly amusing himself with guesses as to how long it would be before this confrontation. A shrug, and that maddening smile. "Oh, you know, you tell them whatever will make them docile."

"What did you give him?"

"Honestly, it's only a mistake, Ahren, really. The boy is fine. Come in and have a drink—"

"What did you fucking give him?"

That was close enough to shouting to draw new stares.

Nobody was stupid enough to come closer, but they were in the center of a cyclone of tilted ears. Footsteps slowed, glances were stolen. Erich had a strange mad flash of desire to cry out for help.

Mengele was nowhere near shouting, but the summer voice he used with the mask was gone; it was the winter voice now, all edges. "The Buchenwald serum."

And Kaltherzig's shoulders relaxed, just the barest inch, but Erich felt a rush of relief so deep it made him want to bury his face in the ground, sob, scream. He was not dying.

"I've had excellent results—"

"It defeats the purpose of a control group."

"So he's control for that one, too? Interesting." A shrug. "My mistake. Herr Obersturmführer Kaltherzig."

Blatant little threat that Mengele was a Haupsturmführer.

Kaltherzig had a polite threat of his own. "You'd shoot me if I made an honest mistake while interfering with your experiments. Wouldn't you?"

Silence. Dangerous territory, this.

Two threats—Kaltherzig's gun was at his hip. Mengele was unarmed in his white coat. The other weapon was invisible in the air between them, a flicker of labels traded, the wrong chemical injected into the wrong test tube. Mengele was quiet, waiting to see what Kaltherzig might do as if it were a, play.

Erich forced his eyes back down to the stones under his hands. He kept thinking of Machiavelli and he had to keep his face down, until his smile was under control. He realized Kaltherzig was, winning, and he was torn between pride and worry about what it might be like when this relentless attention was turned on him.

"My work—and my *files*—are my own affair. Those were the conditions."

Mengele narrowed his eyes to this talk of conditions. A pause.

"Kaltherzig, your first duty is to the Reich."

Kaltherzig was quiet, as if toying with a card in his hands he was tempted to save. Then: "I have four children for the Reich, Josef. How many do you have?"

So that part was true, those particular whispers. He tried to imagine Kaltherzig with a woman, and all he could see was him cutting a woman, with a tiny bright blade as sharp as glass.

Mengele had only one card left. "Don't you want him cured?"

"Oh, I'll cure him. When I'm through with him he'll never want another man again."

Erich looked to see what Kaltherzig's face was like, saying that. It was that utter artist's concentration that he knew from the hospital.

Mengele laughed, as though that had caught him by complete surprise. "Fair enough. Perhaps one day you'll share your notes."

Kaltherzig didn't laugh. "Touch my work again and I'll explain to the Institute why all my data is unusable."

He spun back towards the car, collecting Erich by his hair without looking at him.

Strafe

Kaltherzig pushed him inside as the headlights receded behind them. Closed the door. Locked the door. Stared at him with eyes like snow-colored glass. "Go downstairs and wait for me."

Erich ran.

"And take all of that off," and the clink of bottles, a glass, the doors to the bar.

Well, there was only one downstairs, in Kaltherzig's immaculate little house. Erich opened the door that wasn't a pantry and pulled on the ring set in the floor. It yawned open on a throat of concrete steps that dwindled down into the dark.

He hit the stairs at the same run and thought *I'll fall* and only because he stopped thinking about his feet he didn't fall, and the door slammed above him and he made one bright cry of terror and caught at the chain in the dusty slabs of light from the few narrow high windows. Most of the far wall was lined with desks that Kaltherzig seemed to be using as a lab. They were spread with a long complicated system of mad scientist glass, typewriters, files and books and diagrams propped on tiny easels.

After some searching he turned on the long banks of lights hanging over the desks, and saw the wooden L bolted to the wall. The loop of metal and the rope that hung through it painted their shadows on the concrete. There was a second hook in the vertical beam. He knew what it was. He'd seen it done out in the camp, though always at a distance. Simple. They tied your hands behind you, and then hung you up by them, until it dislocated your arms, or you went mad, or both.

Simple.

It was one of the things he Just Didn't Think About. Well, he was thinking about it now.

He undressed with fingers that were already cold, wrapped his arms around himself, shivering.

But he wouldn't, he would
(break)
lose his ability to work if he was
(useless)
he would be, disposable.

It dawned on him then, and it made him sit down, hard, on the strange cold floor. He held his knees and rocked a little, eyes wide and focused on nothing. It was a long time before the door opened at the top of the stairs.

The smash of the door torn open, and Kaltherzig came downstairs drunk and with his tie loose and his hat missing. He had to duck to miss the ceiling on the way down the stairs, where Erich had not, and he felt extremely small, and extremely naked. He tried "Sir--" and Kaltherzig made an animal noise at him that scared him into utter silence.

He kicked Erich hard, ass and thighs and ribcage, kicked him until he crawled and then steered him under the rope that way, herding him with the toes and the sides of his black boots. He'd never done that before, and this felt like he meant it. He didn't understand what to do once he was there, and Kaltherzig snarled at him and pulled his hands behind his back.

The tying was awful. Kaltherzig had never been quite this careless with him, scorching his wrists with fast pulls and tight knots. He thought *useless* again. There was the same sense of having his hands taken away from him, but what seemed somehow right in Block 10 was nightmarish here in this new dark room.

There was no try at resistance this time. He was already crying and reduced to a great deal of *sir* and *please don't hurt me*, and none of it made Kaltherzig pause for a single instant. He took up enough slack to pull Erich's arms up and draw him onto his kneecaps, and tied it off on a second hook in the vertical beam. Then he dragged at Erich pulled him farther and farther from the hook, shoved and kicked him until the rope drew his wrists high behind his back, made him press his face close to the floor.

Kaltherzig sat cross-legged like an Indian, close enough for his boot to brush Erich's hair. "Listen to me very carefully, boy."

"I had to....he's Mengele...he made me..."

"No."

Patiently, as if it were a shame he was still missing this essential, simple truth.

"Not for anyone but me. Not for Hitler or God himself. Only me."

Erich was, quiet. Awestruck.

Now he understood the magnitude of his sin, and he could hear nothing but his heartbeat, feel his pulse inside the dangerous ring of rope. "I didn't know..."

Still, patiently. "Yes you did."

It was true.

He closed his eyes, and he couldn't help saying "...but don't, break me, please, not that..." and he stopped, thinking it was like baiting a dragon, thinking of knights and armor and having his arms twisted around in their sockets like twigs before he was shot in the head, or buried alive. Or thrown in an oven.

"Idiot." A stroke, at his bowed head. "Why not?"

Stunned. "Because I want to stay with you."

A laugh, a fake one. "Oh, now you want to stay with me. I thought you wanted Josef to cure you."

"No, you, I want, you—"

"You'll have to prove it." And he unfolded, stood up, and the footsteps moved away.

The rope tugged at his wrists, pulled in inexorable slow motion until he stood, until he was on tiptoe, and Kaltherzig tied it off again. "I will, I'll prove it, just, please—"

A pull, and he was on the very tips of his toes like a ballet dancer and he could feel himself falling and the first scream through his shoulders and he opened his mouth and Kaltherzig let it go, dropping him back to the slightly less agonizing tiptoe.

Bootheels. A door, opening and closing. Erich realized he'd gone upstairs, and left him there.

It was easier at first, when he was sure it would not be hours, when he was sure Kaltherzig would come back any minute now. He could touch the ground. He might dislocate his arms if he fell, he supposed, but all he had to do was avoid that, and he would be fine. Kaltherzig only wanted to scare him, and oh how he'd succeeded, and all he had to do was to not, fall, and to convince Kaltherzig of his terror and his remorse when he came back. Any minute now.

But the minutes came and kept coming, until he was sure they were rolling into hours. At first it was merely stiff discomfort, tiredness, from such an awkward pose with so little room to shift his feet. The balls of his feet were the first place to genuinely hurt, and then his shoulders and a harness of muscles around them he couldn't really move to ease.

His thighs and calves started in with their own complaints, and he managed an awkward toe-walk that made him sway and whimper, spreading his feet. That took the strain off some muscles but made the pain in his shoulders worse, and he had to move his feet together again. He tried standing up higher, now, for the sake of his shoulders, but his calves and his feet wouldn't permit that for long, and he was back to trying to spread his feet again.

That was when he began to understand.

There were only a few stops on this wheel.

Feet apart, tiptoes, and a new one he found, tiptoes and a grasp at the rope above his wrists. He had to bend his hand uncomfortably far to manage this, and the angle stole most of the strength from his fingers, and he had to give that one up after only a few tries. It didn't seem to help anything, at any rate, though it made him feel a little steadier somehow.

He was wracked with fits of sobbing, in frustration and rage that made him want to stomp or scream or something, anything, to escape this cramping ache that swung from shoulders to calves and arches and toes like malaria pains.

He was moaning *I promise* when the door opened again, and Kaltherzig came down.

He dissolved into *please* and then gave this up when Kaltherzig didn't reply. He didn't have the energy to keep pleading. That one simple thing, not falling, had become the center of his world. Worse, he was beginning to feel a bone-deep exhaustion, weak and trembling, that warned him there would come a time when he could not help but fall.

"You promise."

Kaltherzig was untying the rope from the hook, and Erich was crying again in relief, but Kaltherzig did not lower him.

"A promise is something you decide, my boy, a promise is thinking, and then acting. What I want from you is a reflex."

Kaltherzig drew up another six inches of slack, so that his toes barely brushed the floor, so that he shrieked in horror and surprise, so that all his motions and his stations were impossible. He tied Erich there, and went upstairs again.

The Odin theme upstairs. Footsteps creaking the boards over his head.

Upstairs, where nothing quite this bad had ever happened to him.

Until it dislocated your arms, or you went mad. Or both.

He was beginning to wonder which would happen first.

Now there was no circle. Every muscle was trapped exactly where it was, the only movement an involuntary vibration that threatened to become trembling. He could turn his head, but that made him sway dangerously on the tips of his toes. There was one motionless place, one center, and that center did not hold, and that was the agony of it.

175

He was losing the battle to keep his weight off his shoulders, and the sense of his arms beginning to twist, of tendons there being drawn tighter and tighter was sickening. Now if he fell even a little, if his knees chose now to surrender, that inexorable pull would become a crashing jerk, and things inside him would tear, would have to. He tried and failed to turn his hands, to cling to the rope itself, but he could only brush it with the tips of his fingers, and the stress of it threatened to make him stumble.

Here was that mindless place again, where there was only pain and obedience, but this time he was alone in it, and alone with it. He wanted Kaltherzig to stay down here with him, that would be better, that, he could do, with those eyes to hold him up, but there was only the concrete around him, the shelves beyond him, the stairs above him. It no longer seemed relevant that Kaltherzig was the one who had put him here. It was the rope itself that he hated, the rope and the floor scraping under his toes, it was these things that conspired against him, and Kaltherzig would help him endure them. He called out for the doctor for a long time, but thirst and screams had folded his voice into a ragged crackle. If the doctor could hear him, he had no intention of coming.

He swayed. Wept. He thought of the bathtub, of Kaltherzig coming in response to his cries that night, of the luxury of a needle and pillows and water to drink. He thought of the night of his arrest, of jail and of realizing he couldn't wipe his eyes. Paradise, all of it, if he'd only known it. He hung, that rumored vibration becoming violent trembling in his calves and his feet and his thighs, that came and went in waves. It was a gray place with himself in the middle, a muddled Z in bruise-violet. Centuries passed.

He was in a state that was not exactly conscious and yet nothing like dozing. If he went too deep he started to fall, and the pain of that would bring him back to consciousness, and then exhaustion would pull him down again. So he supposed there was a circle still, after all. A very small circle.

The door opened above him. It woke him, and either the sound or the motion he made in response to it started him crying again, suddenly, hysterically, all his plans and pretty words long since gone. He was desperate. He would do anything.

"Are you feeling cured yet?"

Silence, broken by his crying. He could only see Kaltherzig's boots. He didn't know what he was supposed to answer. "I won't take orders from anyone else, ever, please let me down let me—"

(live)

(stay)

Kaltherzig made that animal noise at him again, and he knew that was the wrong answer. He could not think of another, and only sobbed, watching those boots move closer and closer to the vertical post in the wall.

He knew before the rope was drawn up that this time it was no longer a game, no longer an object lesson, and his feet were treading air. All the gray places were gone. Now he was made of screams, thrown back at him by the walls.

Kaltherzig tied the rope around the hook.

He heard and knew very little until his feet were on the floor again, and to his amazement he was lowered farther still, into a crumpled tent of crying. The strain taken from his shoulders allowed him to relax them, and the pain of that was unprecedented, unspeakable, unstoppable. He tried to vomit but couldn't, and his face was ground too hard into the concrete floor, and his hands were so cold he was afraid they'd have to be amputated. His shoulders felt like his arms were fastened on with red-hot iron bolts, streamers of pain winging down into his back, forward into his chest.

He couldn't move, not even to lean up and spare his face the floor. Kaltherzig's shiny toes were in front of his eyes. "Shall I shoot you?"

177

That lazy cold shock of the real fear, the gun-fear, the crimson triangle spreading on the bricks fear. He understood, or thought he did. "No, sir, I want to stay with you."

The rope was drawn up. When he stopped shrieking he found he could touch the floor this time, but only just. The door did not open. He heard Kaltherzig sit down behind him, and after a moment he saw the drift of cigarette smoke. He tried to suffer more quietly. All the old agonies were starting up again, the temptation to lean on his toes again and spare his shoulders.

"I don't believe you yet."

The doctor left his field of view, became a rustle and a clink of glass across the room where Erich could not see him. The slosh of the bottle. He returned in a drunken zigzag and put the bottle to Erich's lips. Whiskey, sharp and strong.

Kaltherzig was very drunk, and more than that, and Erich thought of the bottles and vials behind them on the desk and tried to be very still, to stop shaking, to do anything or not do, anything to provoke…

He strangled. Coughed. Kaltherzig thudded him on the back, one arm under him with that odd situational kindness, so this would not pull on his shoulders. He let him go slowly so his weight wouldn't drop, gave him the bottle again to wash down the last of the ache.

"You're doing it even, now. Trying to be perfect. You'll never manage it, I'll always find a reason." A touch under his jaw, and the sound of Kaltherzig drinking. The rope drew up abruptly, in one quick motion. He wasted a shriek on it before Kaltherzig let it go, and then destroyed him completely by pulling on it again, and then twanging it somehow, as though it might produce a note of music. Erich could only see the boots.

"Spread your legs."

He tried. He couldn't. He drew in his breath to tell Kaltherzig this, and Kaltherzig kicked his feet farther apart. The fall struck mostly his left shoulder, and the noise it drove out of him was more like a bird's cry or a bark than a sound a boy might make. The world began to go white and drift upward, away from him, and then Kaltherzig lowered the rope.

He could stand, in that same muddled Z, but he had no balance and the swaying dragged on his arms and made him think of mermaids pulling sailors underwater.

Kaltherzig made one low sound of contempt. Quiet, and then a clattering sound he could not identify. He turned his head enough to watch Kaltherzig rummaging not in shelves, but between two of them. He drew a long, long board, with a hole drilled in each end. Erich understood almost at once, but he had already learned *please* was a useless noise. He tied one of Erich's feet to either end, with those same long skintearing pulls of the hemp rope, until his legs were so spread he couldn't move, not even a flinch, or he would lose his balance and fall until the rope at his wrists caught him.

He smoked again, watching Erich struggle not to struggle. Then he tightened both left and right, just another hand's breadth. He went upstairs and left Erich sobbing for mercy.

The door above didn't close this time, and when Kaltherzig returned the whip was coiled in his hand. The real one, with that serpentine lash and that Selektion crack.

Kaltherzig hauled him up again, hanging him so high he could just barely touch the floor, Erich suspected because the squirming delighted him. Then the whip, lazily, a game, choosing one spot as mundane as left shoulderblade or as excruciating as left testicle and striking just there, over and over. Now the whip was swinging only at his left thigh, until he was screaming like vomiting, every blow heaving this throat-killing howl up from his stomach, falling and spinning and nothing he did stopped it, the lash unerringly found that one bleeding white-hot patch of agony.

Over and over.

The rope would drag him up to his tiptoes until he was hysterical, hang him completely, toes brushing the concrete in frantic howling swipes before he let him down to his knees and started to hit him again, harder and harder, finally swinging so that every one struck between his legs. A long pleading interlude of that, until he begged to be hung again, instead.

179

Over and over and over.

The syringe. That sense of being pieces, flying apart. Sobbing confusion in which he was suspended by the pinprick of a needle in his hip and the burning line around his wrists. The needle yanked out and dropped, the whip uncoiling on the floor under his feet, snapping up into space, snapping down across his back. He hung in a strange moveless space, almost as if he had forgotten the whipping and the rope and the basement and even Kaltherzig, his mind, empty, the impacts a soothing sort of shove like being patted.

Sometimes Kaltherzig stopped, thudded the handle of the whip between the cheeks of Erich's buttocks, threatened to push it inside, tugged at his penis, rubbed in the worst place too hard and too fast to do much but torture him. This was so incomprehensible through the drug filter that he could not distinguish the pleasure from the pain. It seemed Kaltherzig's rubbing stroke was burning him, and his shoulders had been emptied and then filled with molten delight.

Erich was hanging so high his fingers were brushing the eyehook above him. His feet swung in lazy ghost circles, still spread wide by the board. Kaltherzig's shadow, circling him, and then the very edge of him, hat and hair and gleaming boots, and the whip. The noise was all tangled with the sensation. It seemed to almost be the report that caused the hurt.

He made a sad little groan that embarrassed him. It sounded weary and petulant.

He wanted to be unconscious. Left alone.

"How long have I been here?"

A smirk. "Don't you know?"

He shook his head, and then screamed, feebly, as he was lowered to the ground in a hiss of rope through metal. He stared at the floor, and here was blood, and here drool. They intersected in a sticky red-brown edge, like the high-tide line he'd seen at a long-ago trip to the sea. Smell of dust, smell of wine from two bottles that had exploded.

A cup of water that he was in tears of gratitude over.

"I still don't believe you."

The lights were turned off, first over the desks, and then the one bulb hanging bare. Grey. He was pouring sweat, from pain or shock or God knew what. The door opened above him, and then closed, softly.

He was left alone.

Sunlight. He was in the car, naked, hands still tied behind him, lying with his head in Kaltherzig's lap. They drove past Block 10 and stopped in the middle of camp, where roll call was done.

Where floggings were done.

There were of eyes plenty to see this. Roll call had either just ended or not yet begun. There was a teeming striped crowd, a dull background roar of shuffling feet and murmuring voices.

There was a wooden platform—the better to be seen, to be a demonstration, he supposed. Two lieutenants mostly carried him up the short stairs and leaned him over this odd wooden U. Having his arms untied and then forcibly removed from behind his back had made him scream, and the rest of it was blurred by the subsiding broken-glass suns in both shoulders.

He had seen all this before. He had enjoyed it, when it happened to be one of the ones that stared at him wherever he went like they hated him. But he had never considered it happening to himself.

They tied his wrists and his ankles. It was pointless, he couldn't move his arms, and he was too exhausted to move anything else.

Kaltherzig stood where Erich could see him, eyes hidden by the shadow of his hat, hands folded behind him, military still.

It was a riddle, he knew that much, but he could no longer even begin to try and decipher it.

There were footsteps behind him. He closed his eyes, wondering *does he want me to ask him to shoot me?*

He opened his eyes again, and Lieser's bright silverblue eyes were inches from his. Lieser showed Erich what he was holding. It was a heavy cane. Well, at least it wasn't a horsewhip, but he was very sure that Lieser

181

was going to try to kill him no matter what he was holding. He tried calling out for Kaltherzig then, because it could *not* be Lieser, that was too much, too unfair.

Kaltherzig gestured, and Lieser began it.

He couldn't flinch, or scream, or really even tense, and every time he got a breath the cane drove it out again. Lieser was hitting him much faster than he'd expected. The pain was deep and immediate and it only kept climbing. Lieser knew exactly what he was doing, setting each stroke where Kaltherzig had already left a blackviolet ruin.

Erich was beginning to think he would faint, and that this might be a very good thing, when Lieser tired of that and switched to bruising anywhere Kaltherzig might have missed. Being struck where he was already sore was misery and anguish, but being struck where he wasn't was somehow infuriating, and he was thrashing in spite of rope and shoulders, feebly but sincerely. He hated that man, loathed him, and wanted to scream with the agony of it being *him* and not Kaltherzig hurting him this way, in front of all these eyes.

The struggle was useless, and he was too weak to sustain it. He gave up, and that was useless too. It went on for an age, the reddest pain he had ever imagined, the noise, the eyes, until Kaltherzig gestured a stop. He came closer, until he was staring up into Erich's face. "Shall I shoot you?"

And this time his hand went to the gun, and he drew it out, but held it lying in his palm as if he wanted Erich to look at it, really look at it.

He didn't look.

"No, I want to stay with you, sir," and though most of it had no sound, Kaltherzig must have understood.

He stepped back. "Again."

Erich was trying to draw in the breath to say it again when he realized what Kaltherzig meant, realized that he'd given the wrong answer. Horror closed his throat. Begging forgiveness, he knew, was useless too.

Erich had a piece of a second, just time enough and slack enough to wrap his fingers around the wood his hands were tied to.

He could not keep them there.

Kaltherzig gestured the second stop. There was a murmur beyond the square that he could not have been hallucinating. He couldn't scream, which at least a few seemed to think was brave of him. He thought with a flicker of amusement, *well that will teach them all about the schwul.*

The question again, but the gun kept in the holster. He wanted to say *Ahren* because he was drowning, but he didn't dare. He was afraid that would prove to be useless too, and this way, he wouldn't have to know that.

"Shall I shoot you?"

He would have nightmares of that sentence if he survived this.

"Want to stay with you." A very long pause and when he saw Kaltherzig step back he tried, "...sir..."

Kaltherzig said, "Don't toy with him," to Lieser. And when it started again, Erich saw that was exactly what Lieser had been doing.

There was no toying now.

There was no cruel and inventive aim. There were only relentless blows, beginning at his waist and laddering down. Now, he found he could scream, and once he remembered how he couldn't stop. He wasn't sure if anyone could hear him. It hurt his throat and his eyes and his lungs, and he even tried to stand up, something, to get his hand behind him to close it over the back of his right knee, surely he was bleeding, wasn't that wetness? Nothing moved but his hand, pinned at the end of his useless wrist. Still not his own, still theirs, to change and wound and ruin. Not his own. Had he ever been his own?

Kaltherzig took one step up the side of the platform, too tall to need those little stairs in the front, and leaned close to him. This time he didn't ask the question. He only waited.

Erich thought the Devil must have given him the answer out of pity.

"Whatever you, want. You."

That was the best he could do. He closed his eyes hoping Kaltherzig understood. He was too tired to fear the gun.

Silence. The liquid murmur of the crowd.

And then, Lieser was untying him.

Erich opened his eyes. The world tilted. Lieser was holding him up. He gave Erich that sunlit grin, and a pat on the cheek that was only slightly too soft to be a slap. And then he turned and handed him down to Kaltherzig.

Hands around his chest, the right hands, this time. Erich tried to stand, but his knees had other ideas, folding so that he would have fallen if Kaltherzig hadn't been there.

He was caught up and held like a bride. The swing of the blue sky. Bleeding, cradled like a child. The dipping falls of moving down the steps.

Kaltherzig carried him to Block 10.

Curtains. Whiteness.

Kaltherzig saying something very intently in his ear. A mask over his face. Whiteness. Kaltherzig, an inch from his face: *can you feel it inside you?*

He could feel several things inside him, in all the worst places, and he was strapped down tight on his stomach with a bright blaze of disconnected hurt from his waist to his knees. His left arm wouldn't move, and there was a rumor in that shoulder of such deep pain that he was glad to leave it paralyzed.

There was a layer between himself and everything like spun-sugar candy, soft and delirious. Drugs. He sighed, as though he had found himself in a warm bath. This cushioned place was fast becoming one of his two favorite things about Auschwitz. He thought of the mask, of how it made the pain of that terrible examination into a new pleasure, strong and strange. He tried to move, to find the place where the delight and the anguish overlapped, wanting to stay there. Wanting to feel at home, there.

Do you feel it inside you? Do you understand yet?

I don't know what you mean, and he wondered if he had gone

184

deaf or if they were talking with their brains, like something he'd read with green men and Americans in spaceships.

A touch that was too loud; Kaltherzig's cheek against his, a cat-gesture that was not quite a kiss and not quite an embrace. *Shall I leave you here?*

His eyes had closed when Ahren moved towards him so quickly; when he opened them he was only a white coat and the sound of bootheels already out in the corridor. He was saying *no, don't*, but there was still no sound. He remembered too late that was the wrong answer.

He dreamed of staircases cut in stone and Kaltherzig carrying him down into the echoing dark, closer and closer to a sense of wide-open space in this mineshaft void, where there were dozens of voices thudding out words more like percussion than language. An orange gleam of torches, and the first yellow tint along smooth black walls, cut with sharp-edged runes ranging from smaller than his hand to taller than a man.

Stone under his chest, and this tuneless singing. Kaltherzig with his hand inked black, stroking burning lines onto Erich's back, buttocks, thighs. There was a wall of hooded faces around them, he could feel them, just out of view in the encircling dark. He would howl himself out of this delirium dream to find Kaltherzig stroking him after all, but with a cool cloth. Then he would be still, hardly daring to breathe, trying to behave himself so that this wonder would continue.

After a blur of days Kaltherzig came in, carrying a clean set of Erich's clothes. He dressed mostly by himself, needing only a little steadying and assistance with the buttons. He had just been given the pills again, and there was the flare of cold daylight and Kaltherzig's chest thudding into his cheek, and the car. A wedge of autumn-blue sky through the back window. Kaltherzig pulled him over his lap, pushed up

185

the back of his shirt, stroked at the maze of lines, followed one down to the waistband of his pants. "Well, you mark like an Aryan."

He wanted to laugh, felt his face try it wedged against the seat cushion. "Thank you, sir?"

His shirt was straightened. Kaltherzig rubbed his back in a long circle, his palm flat. Quiet.

"Are you still angry at me, sir?" Fuzzy. The morphine seemed to make his tongue sticky. He wondered if he were allowed to ask that— had he ever been told if he was allowed to ask questions?

The circlestroke didn't stop. "No."

He wanted to say *do you still like me?* but he was afraid Kaltherzig would say something like *I never liked you,* and it wasn't worth the risk. "Why did you pick Lieser?"

Oh, no, that wasn't a good substitution. Even worse, it was dripping with betrayed, indignant hurt. Damn it. Kaltherzig laughed. "He's the only one of those bastards I trust."

And he stopped there, as if that were already too much.

"Why didn't you do it yourself?" Immediately after that he thought it must be something to do with rank, and felt that familiar shameful sense of being embarrassingly ignorant, excluded, that the military and organized sports seemed to inspire in him.

"Because I wanted to watch your face."

Quiet. Treetops, almost all bare, now, through the windows of the car.

Erich was given a great deal of morphine during the week he was bedridden. One morning he woke in terror, with all of it somehow forgotten, came stumbling into the kitchen to have a try at making some sort of breakfast, and found Kaltherzig sleeping on the couch.

The dawn through the drapes made him such a statue of a man, like a Renaissance angel, that Erich stood looking, drugged and dazed and remembering the last week in pieces, and he tried to find an emotion for all of it and all he had was, sorry. Sorry he'd come so close to a betrayal without even knowing it. Sorry for the trust it might cost him.

Kaltherzig opened his eyes, at some kitten noise at the last edge of that thought, and smiled before he, too, remembered who he was. "You should be in bed."

"In your bed?"

Kaltherzig got up, naked except for black SS issue pants, put his hand on Erich's back so that he turned towards the hallway automatically. "You've been in my bed for a week."

Again, that was all that came to him. "I'm sorry."

That just-for-him laugh. "You'll be in it another week before you can walk without morphine. You're sorry enough, believe me."

And then they were both in Ahren's bed, and he was on his stomach with a pillow wound in his arms, dizzy, and Ahren was stroking his back, drawing lines that hurt with his fingertip. Oh, the bruises. "Stay here."

Ahren came back with a handful of grease that smelled like Christmas and warmed his skin until he was boneless and making little openmouthed noises of mindless joy.

"Did you hate me?"

Erich was floating, and he had to think about that to understand that it was directed at him. "...never..."

A smile he could only hear, and a long drag of those soft doctor-fingertips, leaving shimmering morphine wakes in his skin, spreading and colliding. "Perfect boy."

Rachen

Erich supposed he should have known it would not be over. Mengele was the sort of man who would have to have the last word.

When Mengele knocked he was surprised, but the doctor only opened the door enough to poke his head inside. "Would you like to visit someone?"

Visit. A blank, and a shrug. Apprehension, already, because Mengele was never good news. "Sir...I don't know, anyone—"

"Of course you do, boy. It's one like you. He says that you know him."

Blank. And then the answer.

The patient was in the Experimental wing, was lying in a bed with what seemed like a dozen tubes spreading away from his body in two main sweeps to either side of the bed, like strange veins that would grow wings after a while. The arms and face above the stained sheet were mottled with—cracks, like a dropped or misfired figurine, as if it were a glazed thing that had gotten too hot and fractured its surface.

He almost screamed, and then he understood it; a joke, a child-sized sort of doll, to tease him. And then the head turned and he saw the auburn eyes, though the hair that had been the very-same whiskey color was gone save a colorless dust of stubble. There were great blackred triangles that had opened in the middle of spreading edges of skin. The terrible doll raised one stick-thin arm, turned it just a little to gesture at Erich with his fingers, and a crack in his forearm twisted open like an unstitched seam, with red and yellow and white underneath.

"Doctor Mengele said......I've been very cooperative...that he'd send you...if you'd come." This strange jolting cadence; as if the machines were controlling his lungs, though Erich could see that they weren't.

Emil.

Erich was, falling, perhaps dying.

I did this, I did it, it's because of me that's he's here that he's this I did it, God oh God—

And Emil said, "I wanted to tell you. I was sorry for telling, Them. Your name."

The rush of blood back into his face, the motion of remembering to breathe. He could make no sense of it—and then, stillness, and something inside him that had gone to liquid, freezing back into ice, as he understood.

"When did they take you?" He was whispering, like his throat had closed to a pinhole. He had never stepped closer to the bed.

"They made me, they held my head underwater...the batons...guns..." A cough or a laugh. "You were one of the last, I kept hoping, they'd be satisfied, just, be satisfied..."

Oh, yes. Pay a fine. Go back to the unreal world, he had *heard* this part already. He was seized with the mad conviction that Emil would die this very second and he would never know.

"When?"

Was that anger? Whatever it was, it made him feel a little like Kaltherzig, like he might shake Emil, strike him, whatever it took to have this answer.

A slow blink. "Thursday. Just after I'd come from work. My parents were out, I'm so glad, that my parents were out...they still don't know why..." He seemed to wander off in mid-sentence, face crumpling as though the pain in him were climbing.

Erich had gone on Friday.

A subzero little fall inside him.

It wasn't my fault.

And as long as Emil wasn't Erich's fault, as long as that last and most terrible weight from Before was gone, he realized he didn't care about the corollary. That Emil had put him here seemed, ridiculous. Kaltherzig had put him here. If Emil had not been the excuse, another one would have been found.

"I forgive you." Erich thought of telling Emil that he had been the same Judas, but he didn't.

"Will you, touch me? Nobody but Them has touched me..."

Once he dreamed of such words. This boy seemed so, young, much too young to be interesting now. He was going to laugh like sickness if he didn't get out of this, thudding, horrified, guilt?

He didn't move towards the bed. "What've they done to you?"

Thinking, *infection...*

"Put me in the snow," Emil's eyes were on the ceiling now, almost as if this were a pleasant, memory. "They leave me in the snow, and then they bring me inside and lay me under lamps as bright as suns, until my skin is, burning. It's burning my eyes. I can, see less and less...then they take me back outside, and put me in the snow."

Erich walked, closer, put out his hand and put just his fingers under those crumbling fingers. Under that hand that had once kept him from so much sleep. The skin felt like ruined leather, but at least here it wasn't

(leaking)

wet. Those same long lines that had shown him how to set type, whose fingerprints he had known at a look, peeled down to bone and this dried-paper skin.

Emil sighed, and his eyes closed. After a long time he said, "Will you kiss me? Lieser tells me, that nobody ever, will, again. To have him be wrong about that....." He opened his eyes. Erich saw, that this really was, all he wanted, as a comfort, maybe, a last taste of that sin that brought them here. He was still beautiful, under and around the broken places.

If Emil had talked, second, it might have been Erich in this bed, pleading for a last kiss with the only familiar face he had left.

"No." Erich took his hand away, and stepped back from the bed. His own skin was crawling, as though Death itself was, contagious, as if that turn of cards might leech onto him like bacteria, like ink.

Sadness, but no surprise. "It's all right, I don't blame you, you don't have to go."

But Erich did have to, and he was gone from the bed, and gone from the ward, and gone into the shower room to that metal toilet by the hooks because it was the closest, heaving and heaving and wishing for nothing in all the world more than to be sick, right now.

He wasn't.

He knelt, arms wrapped around his face, holding his head tight and crooked as if to hold it together, did something too short and elemental to be crying.

Abbeißen

Kaltherzig had heard about it, obviously. In the car he had immediately dragged Erich to him, so that he was half-sprawled across him. He made one edge of sound, in surprise, and thought this was a previous trick, and started to unfasten Kaltherzig's belt.

"Stop that."

He stopped, mystified, and Kaltherzig's arm settled across his back.

It took half the drive for him to realize he was being, held.

He led Erich inside and into the sitting room and pushed him into a chair. "Collect yourself." He went to the fire without waiting for a reply.

The fire made it better, and the snow outside began to seem like Christmas again and less like, murder. Kaltherzig brought him a deep fine brandy glass half-full of amber liquid. "You're off, tonight. Don't expect it often. Drink."

He drank, because he'd been told to, mystified. "Sir, I don't...."

"Yes you do. One night of, parole, shall we say. We'll talk and you'll get drunk and cry over this boy, and I'll get drunk and keep myself from driving to that arrogant lunatic's house and punching his teeth in for him."

He slammed the bottle down, killed most of his own drink, refilled it, set it down with slightly more decorum. He sat in his favorite chair, cornered to Erich, close enough to touch, and did a gesture-only smile to let him know he was safe.

Erich was wide-eyed over this threat to Mengele's teeth. Kaltherzig wanted to, defend him? Maybe, maybe only like, territory, or a possession. Something Kaltherzig was allowed to hurt but no one else must touch.

But it melted something inside him all the same.

Talk. He did not want to discuss Emil, or think about him any more than he already was. He settled back, drank again, found his eyes on the ceremonial dagger, the sword beneath it, not quite museum-displayed, but hung very neatly with the flag above them, not very big, but painstakingly sewn out of layers and layers of silk. "Did you always want to be SS?"

"I always wanted to be a doctor, but I wanted to be SS too when I saw them burning the books." His eyes were distant, looking at the fireplace, but seeing a fire a decade ago. "I thought, dear God, it's criminal…...then I thought, but if I could decide which books were burned, it would be…grand." A laugh, as if he knew that was inadequate. "Not grand, exactly…the sense you get sometimes when all the future seems, yours."

The quiet was, familiar. Domestic. He found himself thinking of his father, drinking, with a paper open, his mother with a book. He thought, *they might be doing that now.* He waited for the pang of homesick, that sense of being displaced. Nothing.

He had more questions, and he chose what he hoped was the lesser evil. "You spoke of children." Something in his throat made him cough, probably a word that wanted to be in that sentence: *wife.*

"Yes."

A smirk. Pure male pride, and it made Erich's stomach do a lazy appreciative roll.

"My intellect, and my height, and my many years of *fervent--*" Here Ahren did a gesture that suggested genuflection and ended in salute, while Erich tried not to laugh."--fervent service to the Reich, and my devout wish not to be known as a lover of boys and not to have to take a wife, God help me, led me to the Lebensborn."

He drank, eyes distant with memory. "I spoke of my long hours, my career, and I met a few girls, and one of them was tolerable enough. Perhaps you'll meet them one day." But then he frowned, as though he were sorry he'd suggested such a thing, or felt he'd said more than was wise.

"Do you get to see them often?"

(love them?)

He didn't want to know about these ghost children, but he wanted Kaltherzig not to frown.

Kaltherzig shrugged. "Not as often as I'd like, then when I do see them, I begin to make bargains with God to get back here again, where a man can think."

Erich watched the fire with him again, thought of the whispers and rumors, the murmurs of Race Institute and Kaltherzig's family, and that he had been, unsuitable, for anywhere but here. Put here to hide him, not as an honor, put here where he could disguise his tastes as science.

He could understand this, too, though, and whether he believed it entirely, he was pretty sure there was something of truth in it. He could only imagine the frightened fluttering his mother had given him about wives and grandchildren, about morality and rightness, magnified by what he had gathered was a very upper-class family.

There was something here, though, that he needed to work out. Balance in his mind. "Do you think, Mengele, always…......wanted…"

A long sigh. "If I understood what Mengele wants I'd be Kommandant. He's two men. One man has a great deal to prove. He loves the trappings, but he's no doctor. He's a collector, playing at being a doctor. That archive of his…" a gesture, to encompass all the eyes and catalogs of photographs of grimacing children..."is part of how he, proves to himself that he's real."

Erich thought of the sloshing crates, jar after jar of meticulously labeled organs, loaded into the trucks that carried them to Berlin. He could not fathom what this Egyptian obsession could prove, except that Mengele could do what he liked. It was all tangled with that sense of medicine being essentially mysterious, his own lack of surprise that such darkness existed under such lies and such tedious pain.

He thought, *I wonder if all the hospitals in all the world…*

"The other man is everything Mengele wishes he were. Charming, honorable, handsome, cultured." Ahren shook his head, drank. "Ruthless. Power is the seam that holds them together. It's what he really collects, to prove everyone wrong."

The man who washes his hands all the time. "But, guilt..."

Ahren laughed at that one. "Guilt? They're animals, all of them. He can hardly help but collect some useful data, even if only by accident. Let him have his projects and his theories. Why not?" A shrug, lines drawn in the air. "They're all going to the smokestacks in the end, anyway."

There it was—that same sudden, madness, that he seemed to run into like a wall. Or was Kaltherzig right, and this, misunderstanding, was his crime? All of them were guilty of something, or they wouldn't be here. Therefore they could be stabbed, shot, set on fire, dragged into Block 10 to assist in research or help defend the Reich or whatever it was called this week.

Circular logic, inescapable, and pointless to reason against when it was clearly true. Every gunshot proved it. The smokestacks proved it. "Do you think of me that way?" He startled himself, being this importunate. He eyed the bottle with new mistrust. Being drunk made it much too easy to say exactly what was on your mind.

"It's different for you. You're a German boy with a criminal disease." Did he make those last two words into the contradiction they were, or was Erich imagining it?

"He said they put him in the snow for, hours. And then put him under so many heat lamps it burned him, and, blinded..."

"The hypothermia experiments."

How dry that made it sound, how free of screaming.

Erich thought of shoveling snow, his hands so cold he couldn't feel them, and the broken-glass pain in his joints when he warmed them at the fireplace. The winter his father had broken his wrist, and he'd had to shovel all the snow by himself and gloves or not his hands had chapped, cracked until they bled. He tried to imagine putting hands in that condition in hot water.

"They're taking his skin off in, strips..." He could still see that furrow in Emil's forearm, open up like a seam needing stitches. The bluest places on his lips, peeling back in great chunks that listless white of gangrene. The smell.

He was here because of Emil, and Emil was here because of him, or would have been, anyway, and who knew which of them would have suffered the most by the end?

"It won't be for very long," Ahren said, as if reading his mind. "Either it'll kill him outright or he'll be selected when they tire of this particular set of reports."

Erich nodded. As brutal as it was he knew this was meant to be comforting. The tears were there again, because of this SS-colored gesture of kindness. It was both completely like and completely unlike the Ahren he knew, to point this out.

"May I...see him again, if there's a chance, before...?"

Ahren shrugged. Drank. Gave Erich the bottle and waited for him to drink. "If you're certain you want to do that. I can't promise, but I'll look into it." A cough, and his eyes on something else, and he added, "If you wish, I'll, end it for him myself. He's Clauberg's, but he'll give it to me if I ask. Clauberg's a good man. "

Erich felt a strange pang at that. Flicker of the screams as one who'd had that terrible lung-tube inserted was dragged in to be experimented on by this good man, for the fifth day in a row. Blood and clots of pink mixed in with the phlegm they coughed up in howling seizures, collected in petri dishes scraped across their lips and chins and noses.

It didn't matter. It was, dying conscience. It was irrelevant.

"I won't terrify him. There are a few ways that don't hurt them, from what I can tell."

Erich nodded. There were more tears at that, but it was all the favor Kaltherzig could possibly give either of them. "Please...thank you..."

"I'll let on that he pleases me. Clauberg'll make the eyes that say *schwuchtel* at me, but he'll let me. "

Quiet. Drinking. Smoke rings.

"You don't think it's because Mengele.....enjoys, it?" Erich said, tentatively. He wasn't sure he was allowed to speak ill of Dr. Mengele, though he'd heard Kaltherzig do so. Dangerous. What was this unfamiliar little knot somewhere in the middle of his ribcage, this new place that throbbed like a broken tooth when he said *enjoys* about Emil disintegrating in a bed? Was he *angry,* at—

"Enjoys it?" Ahren thought about that, lit another cigarette. He exhaled long dragonplumes of smoke, looking intrigued, as if he had never bothered to analyze this. "I suppose he might. I have my suspicions. Mostly, he takes things apart to see how they work, because he thinks eventually that way he'll learn to build his own. The Selektions are what he really enjoys. All the pageantry, all the attention, all that power."

A circle of a gesture, with the glowing tip of his cigarette. "A lot of the doctors hate it, I think, but we all draw our share of standing in pouring fucking rain in the middle of the night, sifting dirty crying Jews. You just point during the ones like that. Get it over and go back to bed..."

He thought of Ahren chatting with the Untersturmführer shooting a handful of those skeleton men, against that dark stretch of wall by Block 10, and that sense of, co-workers, just, talking to spin the shift by faster. "You don't, enjoy it?"

Quiet. That was the other Scylla and Charybdis that he carried around, inside him, whether that really was joy he could see sometimes, maybe every time, when Kaltherzig was, working.

He took the bottle from Erich and drank, handed it back unsteadily. "Sometimes it has this...energy...fear, all around you, coming at you from all of them. It's all for you. It makes you.....it, feeds you. It makes you into something they're not."

The Selektions. Mengele like the ringmaster of a terribly subdued circus, directing right and left, ordering some pointless exercise more to humiliate than to test. Kaltherzig with those perfect white German teeth cracking through the green skin of an apple. Those tundra-blue eyes dilating at the exact instant his riding crop slammed into a replaceable face. The enchanted redundant boredom of hours and hours of such casual evil, with snow and ashes piling up on his collar and the clipboard that he was never told to write on. The internal horror the first time he'd realized that he'd been yawning through all this tiresome death and despair for the past half-hour.

"That, and the experiments, still about power. Having your very own victims does something to you, to your...to that space, between you, and everyone else."

Erich couldn't stand it anymore. It was that word--*victims*--and it was that one, little, space, that set of three nesting Vs: the point of loosened black tie, the white above it, and the notch of almost-white skin with the double shadow of tendons, just at the hollow of Ahren's throat. His eyes would not leave this place, he could not stop, thinking, how it might feel, if Ahren cupped his head and held it there, wound him tight and just, held him there.

He tried to lean forward and slid off the footstool and his hands came up to Ahren's shoulders and he sort of, nuzzled, and tried to look up and found their mouths together. The third kiss in all his short strange life.

It was like, leaning, nobody really doing much, just lips petting lips with each of their movements. Ahren...did...something, as if his chemistry changed, as if his breathing was the same speed but, harder. Erich gave up and kissed him, that one change in pressure and lean and pull, kissed him and kissed him with all the heartbroken longing and wishes and sorrow and loneliness of all this Auschwitz time. He was too busy, too drunk to notice that Ahren wasn't moving.

"What do you think you're doing?"

Against his mouth, in that no-tone that had said *go downstairs and wait for me.* Erich froze, eyelashes against Ahren's face.

"Isn't that the sort of thing that brought you here in the first place?"

He still, couldn't, move. His knee was in the chair between Ahren's thighs. The fury was so sudden and so total that he forgot who he was, where he was, what this was.

He said, "And you say Mengele is two men."

Silence.

His heartbeat in his ears like an ocean.

He'll drag me outside, oh God, he'll shoot me drunk and I'll die in the snow.

Kaltherzig said "Go to *bed*," with something quaking underneath that meant smokestacks.

Erich drew back from him and ran.

Upstairs he stood in the bedroom, at a loss. He had been told to sleep in the bed, and Ahren had said nothing to change that, but he was so angry...

He gave up, deciding either choice was just as likely to be wrong. Besides, he could not stop staring at the bed in shameless soul-deep longing. He had been on it hundreds of times, usually daily, and for so long while he was so wounded, but as pleasant as it was to be ground into it face-first he longed to sleep there for longer than the few minutes after orgasm but before Ahren ordered him into the floor.

Without drugs, and without wounds.

He undressed, folded everything neatly, considered, and decided he'd been either naked or very quickly ordered to get that way every time he'd been in this bed, and flailed his way out of his underclothes. He climbed in, feeling, decadent, pulling back blankets and sheets and sliding in and pulling them up to his chin.

God, pillows.

He moaned, and then hushed. Had he really slept this way for fifteen years? Without doing anything to earn it?

He lay in the dark, smelling Ahren in the pillows, in everything.

He was waiting for footsteps on the stairs, he realized.

Maybe he would come up, and just this once they would both, sleep, up here.

In the bed, together.

Even if it was because Ahren was too drunk to know any better. This once, this one time, to lie awake not wanting to waste it in sleep, with Ahren curled up behind him, warm and loose and breathing so softly he could never hear him from the floor.

He fell asleep, waiting for the door to open.

The next morning, when he tiptoed downstairs Ahren was still in his chair, kneeling in the seat curled up asleep with his face pressed against the leather headrest, hair mussed, shirt unbuttoned, tie still a black rumpled bar across his throat.

Erich tiptoed back upstairs, and down again with the goosedown comforter from the bed would up in his arms in a bundle so huge he couldn't really see past it. He made it back to the chair without any noise or falls, shook it out managing not to knock any of the bottles off any of the horizontal spaces they covered. He leaned forward to drape it over his shoulders when Ahren grabbed him at the juncture of his shoulder and his neck, hard, fingers doing some trick that sent terrible pain from throat to knees, driving him down in a dropped heap of bedspread.

Ahren squinted at him, hand relaxing. He let him go, picked up a corner of the blanket and glanced at it before dropping it again. He turned his face into the back of the chair again and closed his eyes.

Erich crouched, trembling, trying to breathe through his nose as slowly as possible. That electric pain subsided.

After a while, Ahren hadn't moved.

Erich stood up, one hand finding the armrest as balance an inch from Ahren's knee. He picked up the blanket again, stood waiting for the nerve, and leaned over and arranged it around his shoulders, drawing up the rest of it.

A few days later, Kaltherzig opened his office door. Erich looked up at him, hands poised over the typewriter, waiting for orders, and finding only quiet stillness in the doctor's face, a look he could not interpret. Then Kaltherzig put his hand on Erich's shoulder.

His stomach did a slow roll of dread. He already knew.

"It's now."

Erich swallowed. He wanted to turn to Kaltherzig, bury his face, say something, anything, and only swallowed again.

"Did you want to watch?"

He found himself nodding.

Emil was in a different room, alone, with less of that snarl of tubes. He looked, frightened, then bewildered when Erich came in behind Kaltherzig. "Emil, this is, Doctor Kaltherzig," he said, not looking at either one of them, because it felt like his place to do so. Kaltherzig was letting them have this, loading a syringe. "Emil, this is a favor—"

Tears, for his unsuccessful stroking in the dark, with this boy's hands in his mind burning like hieroglyphs.

"I'm giving you an extremely large morphine overdose," Kaltherzig said to Emil, softly. "Your options are this, or one of them doing it in the next few days with cyanide. Do you understand?"

Emil understood. He turned his head, those furrows cracking open on his neck, stared at Kaltherzig with those auburn eyes shiny and fervent. "Yes, please, God, please, now, please..." The last, climbing, too feeble to be a scream.

"Exactly now? If you'd like to drink, or eat, or smoke, first, I have a few minutes."

"No, now. Sir, please, before I..."

Erich watched. Tourniquet. Vein. A deft and gentle push with the needle. Emil's mouth was shaping *thank you* over and over.

Plunger.

Emil seemed to, jerk, just a little, as if the sensation startled him, and his eyes slowly lost focus, half-masted, and he was moveless. He'd only just started to smile, as if he'd fallen into a dreamsea of bliss, caught

201

too soon to even finish changing his face before he drowned.

"Stay with him," Kaltherzig said. "Or go, if you'd rather not." He was putting his bag to rights. "He won't know, and nothing should happen but his pulse will slow and stop. I would warn that he'd lose control of his body, but there's nothing inside him to lose, I don't think." That thump on Erich's shoulder, only slowly.

It was true. There was nothing else, no death-rattle or convulsion as Erich feared. He watched, anyway, and when he'd gotten up the nerve to touch one wasted wrist in search of a pulse the way Kaltherzig did to him, it was already cooling, and it seemed to let his thumbs make marks like into bread-dough.

He thought that Auschwitz was all Emil's fault, and he should've thanked him. Then he realized that was exactly what he'd just done.

He found that now he could kiss Emil. The horror of it was over; Death had come, and gone, and the boy he had taken was not the one Erich saw in the mirror. One dry brush, of lips against lips. No melting now, of course not, there was only one person here. Nothing to melt into. Nothing left. He expected it to move something inside him, to feel important, but it only felt like courtesy and pity and goodbye.

Untergang

The rumors had begun, out in the camps, that on forbidden radios tuned to forbidden stations they had heard the Russians would be here in six weeks, in twelve at the outside. There was a streak of, hope, outside in the air, and slave-eyes had started to stay on the guards for longer without fear of a bullet. And guards were coming up, missing. Just gone, and house or barracks emptied.

He tried to ask Kaltherzig about these things, during their drive home.

"Never mind it. I'll take care of you."

Kaltherzig wasn't looking at Erich, but he took his hand, still staring out the window. A truck was collecting wheelbarrow-loads of corpses down one of the side streets. Erich sighed, watched Kaltherzig watch. Leaned his head into Kaltherzig's shoulder, greatly daring. Kaltherzig turned a little, to better accommodate his neck, and that was all.

Erich thought of wishing for a shoulder to lean on, and thought of offering some kind of prayer of gratitude. "Thank you, sir." Kaltherzig stroked his hand with leather fingertips and did not answer.

It was rumor, and that was all. Germany could not lose the war; could not be defeated, and these things were as true as the wetness of water and the tallness of mountains, as true as the omnipotence of Kaltherzig and the permanence of Auschwitz.

Had to be true.

Erich slept, and ate, was whipped with reason and without, was fucked and examined, and the wheel of his world did not change. It could not change. He told himself these things at night, lying on the floor, but Kaltherzig's breath in the darkness above him was too shallow and fast for sleep.

Germany could not lose the war. Germany could not be defeated. But still Kaltherzig lay awake above him, and long slow waves of panic kept him awake, too, repeating these things as though his vehemence would make them true.

But the world outside of his cage would not remain still, could not be whipped into stillness, drugged into obedience. Could not be silenced, and could not be stopped.

The Russians were closer.

The Americans were in Paris.

Kaltherzig drank more and more and did other things for which Erich had no name, eating pills and powders and staring with anguished solemn wakefulness at his typewriter, far into the night. He laid out all his Hitler Youth things one night, stared at them a long time, put them away again.

That night he got up, stepped over Erich and went out and turned on the phonograph. Erich lay wanting nothing more than to go to him, but he'd heard the bottles on the bar and he was afraid to.

He almost slept again, and then he woke up to some sound and was positive he'd heard Kaltherzig, crying. He got as far as the door, and could not bring himself to do it.

If Kaltherzig was, crying, he would never forgive Erich for seeing it.   He lay down again, cold, and the room felt strange and empty with the door open and the light on far down the hallway, and the bed looming over him getting colder.

Kaltherzig listened to the old Party songs on the phonograph more and more often.

Erich brought him drink after drink, made endless coffee. Made the few dishes he'd learned Kaltherzig liked, over and over.

He caught Kaltherzig burning photographs, taking them out of frames on the wall and just dropping them from between finger and thumb so that they wafted into the fireplace. Row after row of beaming SS who had just made officer and whose parents would be so proud. Hitler in front of a blaze of swastikas, a shorter row of older faces, and Himmler's impenetrable glasses-gleam crisping into ash.

He said, "Sir," before he could stop himself, and had no idea what he might say next. Kaltherzig gave him a glance, a little ashamed, or sad to have been seen being so

(heartbroken)

maudlin. So drunkenly National Socialist.

Watching Kaltherzig mourn the Reich was making it almost impossible for Erich to convince himself that it was merely a streak of bad luck and Germany could not fail to win the war. He knew, beyond his dark Eden of this house and this man, that the rest of the prisoners prayed for Russia and for the Americans.

He had long since ceased to think of himself as whatever kind of animal they were. Animal, yes, but a different species entirely.

He did his own praying, for a plague to sweep the Russians from the Earth. For a secret unstoppable bomb the Führer was keeping back for dramatic effect to explode millions of wide American faces. But not the Jews, no, he wanted that to go on, and on and on. He wanted the currents of Hell that kept this place inescapable to be endless. He wanted nothing to change, and it was changing like a hurricane was stirring it, and he couldn't stop it, and *neither could Kaltherzig.*

And Kaltherzig was the only god he knew.

Erich lured him with sex when he could, thinking how strange and difficult this had been at first, and how easy it was now, that he no longer had to think about where he might touch to make Ahren lean into his hands, and where he might touch to earn himself a blow. He knew all the triggers.

He had to be careful, had to sneak away by himself, after, because the tears were likely then.

Had he ever hated this? He was addicted to it, now. He would come twice most of the time, once just at the instant of penetration, and once much later, sobbing for it to stop, driven over the edge by the teeth-jarring violence at the last, when Kaltherzig was too close to care, too far gone for anything but harder. Then that climbing sting of semen because he was always wounded, there. Sometimes Kaltherzig would hold him pinned, laugh at his frantic noise.

Would there really be a time without that?

Sometimes he would push the buttons that led to a beating on purpose, to see Kaltherzig look like himself again. To see that arrogant quintessential SS doctor behind his eyes, to remember the fearful symmetry he'd had at the very beginning of this dream, at Selektion.

After, he would lie crying, secretly pleased with himself, while Kaltherzig went to bed loose and quiet and calm. He would think at the bastard Russians *you weren't close enough to save me from that one, were you?*

He knew better than to ask for kisses, either with word or gestures, but sometimes when near sleep Kaltherzig would submit to being kissed himself, on his fine smooth doctor's hands and the long sculptured shoulders, on that high broad forehead. He would keep his eyes closed, not moving, only the faintest ghost-sound giving any clue to what Erich suspected was a deep, utterly relaxed pleasure.

Ahren would tell stories, sometimes, in these dark warm interludes, tales of the future. "After the war we'll go to Argentina. Or Bolivia. There will be a lot of us there. I'll have a diamond mine and a house in the middle of miles and miles of jungle."

He would stroke Erich's spine in that particular way, as if he were counting the vertebrae. "It never snows there, it's always summer. I'll keep you naked. And I'll never let you learn a word of the language. I'll own you. You'll never get away."

Or it was, "We'll sit in a bar in Rio de Janeiro and it'll be as hot as noon at midnight. We'll drink German beer and sing all the old songs. I'll make you sit on the floor."

And, "The Reich will call us home, when the Reds have half the world. All eyes will be on Germany to save them, then. Then, you'll be page to a knight, my boy."

Fairy tales of scorpions the size of house cats. Carnivorous plants. Fish that would swim inside a man's urethra and pin themselves there with a spreading fan of hooks. Diseases that would make your skin boil and slide off in wet strips, disintegrate your bowels inside you so that you finally died with your abdominal cavity empty.

There would be wonders, too.

Great glaring demon masks of gold and sandstone. Emeralds as green as the jungle, so large they had to be held in two hands. Temples with alien writing and trenches for the blood to flow down from the apex. Mushrooms that brought clairvoyance and visits from the dead, waterfalls that plunged thousands of feet into murderous white rivers. The jungle, jaguars and rainbow-colored birds that could speak like men. Snakes that could swallow him whole. Lush, wet, predator wilderness for hundreds of times more land than Germany had ever covered.

There was a wide and deep German presence, Ahren assured him. There would be a Reichscolony, after a while, when the chaos died down and they could re-organize.

He loved this story. He waited patiently for all the embedded threats. There was something so very Arthurian about it, the dramatic flight in the dead of night. He was still boy enough to always see it this way, usually with someone eventually having a dagger in his teeth. A long and noble exile in a strange and distant land, trapped and defenseless, only Ahren between himself and this devouring wild.

They began to seem like a great deal more than dreams when Kaltherzig pulled him into the little room they used sometimes to draw blood. He pushed him into that chair with the half-desk, and the restraints hanging down. "You have to be quiet, No one can know we're doing this. If I'm going to take you with me, I can't leave your number."

He started to hyperventilate when Ahren strapped his arm down. Somehow this was different than, all the other times. Ahren's belt clearing the loops meant far more pain than this would, of course it did, but the strange desperation of this, the single light bulb overhead made him think of Mengele and the twins, of those perfectly matched anuses distended purple and spread around a medical-silver frame, and he was afraid down into his bones and his bowels, so afraid his teeth were chattering.

It wasn't supposed to be this way.

Ahren stopped after the buckle just over his elbow was tightened, and sort of, wrapped one arm around him, leaning Erich's head into his hip. Stroked his hair for a while.

"My boy. Before this I was at the front, and I took out bullets deeper and less easy to find than these." A fingertip across the numbers.

Erich nodded.

"This isn't a punishment, and it isn't meant to hurt you. Do you understand?"

He cried, then, looking at the last hanging buckle, eyelashes brushing against the black wool. He said, "I understand," but he didn't. Ahren felt the crying and miraculously, mysteriously stroked his hair again, with more lush gentle contact with his gloved palm, such an unspeakable luxury. And he leaned down and kissed Erich's head. Had his father ever, kissed him? He tried to remember and only saw the drunken kiss he had given Ahren in the living room.

"As quick as I can. You mustn't move—"

He felt Ahren move towards the knives.

"Will you fasten the last one, please? Sir?"

Then he realized he'd interrupted, and sat shaking and waiting for a blow. When none came that was more frightening than the knives. Ahren only reached around him in the shape of an embrace and fastened the restraint from the back of the chair, under his free arm and over the shoulder of the one with the tattoo. After it was closed bruise-tight Erich felt, better. Safer.

Ahren sat down, and picked up one of the knives.

Erich closed his eyes, and then opened them and, looked, and

208

Ahren drew a very, careful, ruler-straight line, in his very first cut, from the E to the very end of the 9, in the exact middle, deep enough to draw real blood in a pattern almost exactly even from beginning to end. The pain was minimal, pressure, then a cold that flared into heat from the slightest movement of his hand. Ahren picked up a fold of paper and poured a single even swipe exactly along the cut, and dabbed it in with businesslike pressing circles of one gloved fingertip. Cold. Nothing. "Cocaine," Ahren told him, and, "After this you shouldn't feel anything."

Then the first, long incision, from the end of the cut to the beginning, starting at an invisible point outside the numbers. He felt only a faint distant metallic pull, more pressure than pain. He bit his lip and kept his eyes on this intersection of steel and skin and didn't make a sound. A longer line, with a brief tug of real hurt, and Erich made one single, noise

Ahren lifted the scalpel, a single oddly colorless slice draped over it. He looked into Erich's eyes and laid the blade along his tongue and licked off this, shred, and swallowed it, and his eyes never moved. He gave him that look as a, gift, for a very long time, before he put the knife down.

He picked up the gauze and dabbed at this wound for a merciless brief second, while Erich breathed through his teeth in agonized hisses. Then the paper and the powder again, and a long anguished exhale as the pain resisted and then, subsided. "Such a good boy, you were so still," Ahren told him, in that just-for-him voice, and wound him close in that face-to-hip hug again.

Ahren leaned over him, needle and thread, and the uncanny pulling of stitches he couldn't feel. He never forgot it. He wound his free arm around Ahren's waist and cried and cried, and sometimes Ahren shushed him, but he never stopped, not even when he leaned his hip into Erich's wet cheek in a rocking, gentle rhythm, as if he were soothing a child to sleep.

The stitches were laid, a neat careful row, one where each number had been. He wanted to scream at each insertion. It didn't hurt, exactly, but the push and the *snap* of the tip breaking through his skin was intolerable.

Ahren stood too close to him, and put down the gauze and the forceps and drew his head close again. Erich understood, and he unbuttoned Ahren's fly with his one free hand. He coaxed his cock out with gentle stroking motions of his fingertips, trying to make everything last as long as possible. Ahren grasped his hair, tangling frictioned with the rubber gloves, but for all the hurry of this gesture, he let Erich go at his own pace, gasping or moaning, fingers winding tight or relaxing, but no orders were given.

At the last possible instant he drew his cock out of Erich's mouth and cradled his head close, coming against his neck, shaking and holding him so hard Erich couldn't breathe. He wrapped his arms around Ahren's hips, holding him as tightly as he had ever wanted to, bleeding against the bandage in a dull pulling hurt he ignored.

Ahren reached down, patted at his neck, seemed to noticed the glove and peeled it off and dropped it. He smeared his semen into Erich's collar, his hair, and Erich burrowed into his hipbone and moaned and was frightened all over again.

It felt too urgent.

Was his number really gone? He had stared at it for centuries now, thinking that he would stare at it just before he, died. Was it gone, under all this blood and bandage?

Did he want it back?

Three days later, Ahren drew Erich close, suddenly, in the office where their new and frightening task seemed to be shuttling documents to terrified inmates who came back emptyhanded for more, smelling of burning paper.

Kaltherzig pushed up Erich's sleeve, and touched the stitches, and Erich saw with a dawning deep terror that Kaltherzig was perhaps close to tears himself.

"It won't work. I thought, as my nephew, maybe. Something....if I had planned it a year ago, even six months ago."

Kaltherzig pushed his sleeve back into place, straightened the cuff with absurd care, and said very clearly, without looking at Erich, "I can't take you with me."

Nothing.

He only looked at his straightened sleeve, shaking, hearing a great roaring like he'd already fallen into a well, somewhere, and the black, would, yes, it would...

Out in the hall, less than an hour later, he came out with an armload of files looking for a cart and found Kaltherzig with his riding crop in his hand. He was in the process of beating some poor prisoner clerk to the floor, screaming, "Neatly! This is still the Reich! Set them down in rows, in order…"

And he seemed to realize how pointless it was, and left off hitting him. He clipped his whip at his belt, came back to Erich with darkness and murder in his eyes. He sat at the desk with the office door locked behind them, and would not be consoled.

He made it until late that night, long after sunset. The hospital was still filled with SS and prisoner staff alike. Now there were documents burning in pits out back, and in the tiny ovens in the lab and the officer's lounge. Down the hall there was, singing. They were bringing in Schnapps and whiskey, and there were considerably less of the interesting drugs all the time.

Erich was sitting behind the desk in the chair, his collar loosened. Kaltherzig was packing something behind him, and he had been holding the same file that only needed throwing into a box for burning, looking at one of his own rare typographical errors in it, and the crying took him.

Kaltherzig came over and watched this crying for a moment, then put the flask to Erich's lips. He thought of the electricity again, and he swallowed, thinking he might lose too many words if he opened his mouth, fling himself to the floor and cling to Kaltherzig's boots and beg him not to leave him, beg him to ship him in a crate all the way to South America, or shoot him.

He should have known better than to even think such a thing, should have known by now that Kaltherzig could read his mind.

Kriegsgefahr

Erich felt Kaltherzig get up, and he murmured something, waiting to be pushed and sliding a dejected little towards the side of the bed. The push never came. Then the specific creak and set of tiny metal noises that was the gun in the gunbelt, and the oiled slide.

Dreamlike climbing terror.

He opened his eyes. Kaltherzig was only holding it, finger not on the trigger, pointed at the floor, looking at him in the wedge of bluegreen lamp through the window. Erich couldn't see his eyes, only the white plane of his chest and the blueblack gleam of the gun. The gun was the center of everything.

No one will come when they hear it. Nothing can save me.

Wide, hot, sickness, fear like nothing he had ever known in his life, a nauseated disbelief that it was *now*, that he really was like all the other meat, that bullets would rend him in a jerking leaking blaze and Kaltherzig would throw him out on the porch if he wanted to. Hide him in the backyard under dead hydrangeas.

"Why?"

It was all he could remember how to say.

The gun wasn't moving. Erich wasn't moving. Kaltherzig wasn't moving.

A long sigh, and the arm that led to the hand that led to the gun relaxed, the business end pointed at the floor, a little backwards. "I haven't, decided. I know that I should. You're much too dangerous. You already know, where I'll go. And what I'm like."

That last, very quietly, and the gun nudged forward, just an inch, two, endangering nothing but the rug by the bed.

Not yet.

"You really, think that?" This was a wound that left the gun almost forgotten, for that instant of understanding. "That I would, tell them...I would never—"

213

I told them about Emil, and he knows it.
This isn't the same! This can't be the same!
"Why?"

Erich's almost-last word, handed back to him.

Kaltherzig raised the gun, but only as if to look at it, that ubiquitous set of curves and edges that was familiar even in the dark. The riding crops were hung beside those bastard guns when worn on a belt. Just to keep your eyes and your attention focused.

"Because...because they'd *chase* you, that's why, I would...I don't...I, wouldn't."

Don't make me. Don't make me confess anything else.
My pathetic little everything.

"I don't want them to catch you. Not ever."

Silence.

"Oh."

Kaltherzig's voice was smaller than Erich had ever heard it. Try as he might, he couldn't decipher a tone, not from that one word—disappointed? pleased?

And the gun did not move.

He was shaking. This always took him when Kaltherzig closed a door behind them, but it was different now, vibrating him like a crooked glass half-filled with water, trembling as deep as his bones. He had always thought it was idiotic, people wetting themselves in books, out of pure fear, but he could understand it perfectly now. Everything below his chin seemed to have disconnected itself into only this hot anguished shaking. He was tempted as he'd never been tempted by anything to fling himself away from the gun, crying, begging, squeezing his eyes closed and covering his head and praying there would be no gun when he opened them.

"They'll want you treated. They'll want to change your mind, undo all my lovely...work..." and the gun came up, and drew a cold curve along his forehead, pushing his bangs out of his eyes. Kaltherzig was not trembling.

Erich narrowed down to that single point, made a broken little noise that wanted to be a scream, expecting the bang and the splatter and the wet drenching his back before everything, stopped.

"I won't let them. I won't tell them *anything*, they won't have any reason to treat me."

Kaltherzig laughed at that one, and Erich was, ashamed, a little list of scars and wounds and phobias flickering through his mind, and he knew they would, know. He was not like a citizen boy, anymore. He never would be again. He thought of men shooting a dog that has gone too feral to keep, and there were tears, now, leaking out of the corners of his eyes. "Please..."

That graze again, exactly following the edge of his hair. He closed his eyes, teeth chattering together now, breath coming in constricted little pants. He said, staccato, "I want, to stay, what you've made me."

The gunsight pushed into his forehead briefly, because Kaltherzig seemed to be, pushed, just a zig rocking him left to right. He was still drunk. "I can't risk it." More to himself than to Erich.

"They'd know all about *me* if I told them about you."

Laughter—and Kaltherzig turned and sat on the edge of the bed, gun resting easily on his knee, like any sort of thing a man might hold, a piece of bread, a tool. "I doubt it would vilify you in quite the same way it will me."

"That's why I wouldn't tell anyone." He didn't believe it, out of his own mouth. The tears were too audible. He *meant* it, he just thought he sounded, as if he would say anything to save himself.

That, of course, was largely true.

He drew in a deep slow breath, willing his chest to stop hitching, *he isn't, he wouldn't, just don't*. And he couldn't help it, that was *why* he'd thought he'd be taken in the first place. "If I were with you, you could—"

And Kaltherzig snapped, exploded at him in that familiar tornado of fury, caught his upper arm and dragged him into a stumbling fall, shouldered him into the bathroom so fast the bedroom was a blur of hard edges and he slammed his shin in one white-blue line into the edge of the bathtub and Kaltherzig shoved him in, and he was lying on his back bleeding with his feet flailing up into the drawn shower curtain and Kaltherzig's gun a single black eye that froze him.

A scream, his hands over his ears, eyes crushed closed.

One flickering half-thought, of Kaltherzig's vanished boys, of himself in this same tub, being wounded, or settling hissing into hot water after all day of being wounded.

He dragged his heel over and into the hole of the drain, screaming still because he'd been in the morgue enough times to realize why he was *here*, in the tub, God God--because of the mess, so that his brain and bone and blood didn't wind up on Kaltherzig's immaculately decorated walls, in his soft piled luxury of a bed.

"*Stop.*"

Kaltherzig's lips were pressed together, and he swiped with his empty hand at the air to indicate the glassy echo of that rabbit-scream in all this marble and ceramic.

He was, panting, now, and he shook his head, tears leaking like they were trying to empty him. "Not like, this."

That bird-tilt of head, that flickergleam of predator interest.

"Not like what?"

"Not like you're *angry* at me, not like you hate me. Can't you do it quietly with a needle—" A break into real tears, for fear of what he was asking. "I don't want the last time I see you for you to be mad at me, can't you *pretend?*"

He couldn't open his eyes. He thought *it'll hit me before I hear it, maybe I just won't know, anything else, suddenly.*

Kaltherzig stepped back from him, the elbow of his gun-arm thudding smartly into the doorframe. It made Erich shriek, but his finger was already off the trigger.

He left without a word, left Erich sobbing in the tub again, for this last new reason.

The ceramic-cold crept into him, back to stomach to arms until he was shivering. He still hadn't moved. He stared at the bit of the door he could see, positive Kaltherzig was just there, that he would make of him one of those spreading red triangles the second he sat up.

It was his bladder and not his courage that drove him to look.

Empty. Silence.

He stood up, crying in a way that would've been considered quite heartbroken Outside. He didn't realize he was, didn't hear himself; it was like a background conversation that had been going on for so long he'd ceased to notice it. He urinated, flushed, and waited for the sound to summon that single black eye.

Nothing.

It was an hour, or maybe only minutes, when he'd put on his pants and a blanket like an Indian chief, tiptoeing through the house, knees still trembly and likely to pretend they were going to collapse him to the floor, dropping an inch or three at random steps.

The bed was empty.

The little bedside lamp was on, and the Luger was in pieces on the bed, with no magazine anywhere that he could see. Erich knew almost nothing about guns, but he was pretty sure an empty one was much safer than a loaded one.

A long sigh like his lungs had fallen a foot or two. Kaltherzig was probably unarmed, wherever he was.

Not that this had ever saved him before.

He only happened to catch the little red glowing dot out one of the living-room windows—Kaltherzig, smoking, sitting on the top of the sweep of stone steps that were only a white-carpeted hill down into the yard. A werewolf-shape that would be one of the huskies doing sleepy tail-wagging circles at his feet.

He was shirtless and barefoot, in a crusted-over foot of snow.

Erich opened one of the French doors, immediately frozen by the rush of arctic air.

217

"Sir?"

Silence, so that he had given it up as one of those times Kaltherzig would ignore him utterly.

Then, "Go and make us some dinner."

Erich got the fireplace started, feeling strange because Kaltherzig always did this himself. His assembled picnic in front of it was mostly finished when Ahren came in, blue and snowcolored as if it had bleached him. He did not shiver, and he didn't seem to have gooseflesh. He sat across from Erich cross-legged, his SS-issue boxers soaked through. He stared into middle distance, eating only meat and that with his fingers, folding carnivore bits of roast beef and baked chicken between those flawless teeth with neat bird precision. Erich was dizzy, distant once he sat down, and he got up, eyeing Kaltherzig, and poured whiskey for both of them, greatly daring. If he had ever needed that flash of warmth and spread of shock, he needed it now. Kaltherzig took it from him without a word, emptied it.

He brought back the bottle.

Kaltherzig said, "I put it to my head. After I left you."

Silence. Erich stared at the bottle Kaltherzig wasn't taking from him, tears, again, a hot sore rush in his aching eyes. He wanted morphine, he realized, to kill this pain. "Please don't," he said, so very softly.

"I realized, if I shot you, I might as well find and kill everyone who ever knew me. Because I will spend the rest of my life fearing that one of them, and anyone else I know will sell me to the Jews. And then I put it, right, here,"

A gesture that he turned into a push to straighten back his hair, as though it embarrassed him. He was staring into the fire. Perhaps he found it soothing. He had come to this place to burn books, had filled file cabinet after file cabinet with strange bloody stories told in euphemisms that would land in strange Reichsoffice books, and now he was burning those, too, had done so all day, surely could smell nothing else.

A long drink, a shift to sit with his arms wrapped around his knees. Orange firelight in his eyes. He drank. Erich brought him his cigarettes and a glass with ice that he ignored. Finally out of desperation he brought Kaltherzig's hairbrush, and to his surprise the doctor allowed this, leaning like a proud cat will lean when he's lured by the stroking in spite of himself. He ended with his head and one sprawled arm across Erich's lap, still eyelocked with the fire, making no sound or gesture of pleasure except this appropriation of him as furniture, and an occasional too-long blink and a little slump of unwinding in the lines of his body.

"We should leave every bit of it," he said, after a long time of silence. "Why should we burn everything? That's what I want to know. Let them look. There's much too much of it—they'll know enough, and they'll invent the rest. Why let them have history and the world both?"

Kaltherzig held his own hands out. He seemed to be, analyzing them, studying the doctor-soft lines, the straight shiny nails. He turned a little onto his side, bestowing on Erich as he did so one of his most dog-eared memories of Auschwitz: Kaltherzig's warm angular boy-weight, stretched casually across Erich's knees, knowing he was safe to touch like this, like cats wound together in a patch of sunlight.

And then Ahren slid off his Totenkopf ring, that black magick thing more sacred than a wedding band.

He slid it onto Erich's finger, skull turned in towards his palm.

"There," he said. "That will bring you back to me."

He drew Erich close and said, "You'll come, when I call. Or I'll have you shot."

He hated Them, he knew, and that was all he knew. He just saw the world entire as a sea of non-Germans, like that sea of stench and noise at Selektion, swarming in with a hundred million pairs of greedy hands. He neither knew nor cared about such sweeping ideas as conquest and genocide. He knew they would destroy his home, and he knew that being in his parents' house in his old bed in a day, or a week, would make him wish Kaltherzig had shot him.

He'd thought of that request, when Kaltherzig had told him he would stay behind. It had quickly ceased to look like a mercy when the gun was staring down at him.

He knew a great many of his accepted truths and derived conclusions were deeply skewed into new Kaltherzig-ordained directions. He even vaguely understood that Kaltherzig had made him this way on purpose, remade Erich to suit himself, done addition and subtraction like a surgeon for the mind until he liked the shape the knives had left behind.

I am a sculpture, he thought, and wrapped his arms around himself. He was smiling. This thought made him feel beautiful, made cherry-cordial-fireworks inside him every time he mouthed it to himself.

He knew it was the last day without being told.

They did not go to Block 10. By now it was an empty building, with most of the dead and dying gone to the ovens like the files. Kaltherzig did not bother to dress. He picked up the bottle he'd stopped on the night before, called it breakfast, and put on the old marching songs again.

Erich was polishing Kaltherzig's boots when the doctor stood. He proceeded, rather unsteadily, to pull the curtains closed at each window in the living room. Erich watched this with growing worry. He could not imagine what Kaltherzig wanted to do that he didn't want anyone to see.

Then the order came.

"Dance with me."

His eyes went wide.

Kaltherzig was very drunk, and Erich was hopeless at dancing. His time at Auschwitz, he discovered, had not improved this any. He had no idea how to be led, any more than he'd known how to lead in school. He

220

nearly succeeded in sending them both to the floor. Kaltherzig laughed and said, "Stand on my feet, you idiot."

And then, oh then, Kaltherzig hauled him close and gave him no choice. He forgot to be afraid he was too heavy, and when he closed his eyes and wrapped his arms around Kaltherzig's waist, he found a wonderful place, a warm place softer than the one at the end of a whip.

"When I go, you'll stay here, until the camp is taken." Quiet. Darkness, and the two of them tangled in it.

"Yes sir." He hated it. Hated saying it, hated Kaltherzig for making him say it, for making it real. For ending the world.

"Go down into the cellar, and stay there as long as you can. I've left supplies for you. You'll be as safe there as anywhere."

"Yes sir."

"I'll find you. Send for you. Wherever you end up, wherever they take you. Nowhere will be far enough. Nothing will save you from me."

"Yes sir," he said, again. He waited in the dark for Kaltherzig to say something else, anything else. To take all of this back, make it unreal again.

"My boy."

There was nothing else, after that. Only silence, and darkness.

That last night he had slept possibly twenty minutes, knowing this chance would never come again. Warm in the soft inkblack with snow outside and Kaltherzig naked behind him, Ahren, naked, behind him, arms wound around him like he

(loved)

wanted him there, and the quiet and that sense of the Russians closer, too close, and time pouring out like sand in that minuteglass.

He had wanted Ahren inside him, wanted that one more time, but he had lacked the skill and the courage to communicate this. He was glad of that, now, because that still warm place was the only memory like it he had, anywhere. Ever.

There was no dramatic flight.

There was only waking up in the bed alone, and knowing Kaltherzig was gone. There was only listening for the siren that never came to mark the dawn.

After a time Erich dressed, and then, as Kaltherzig had ordered him to do, went down into the cellar.

He got as far as bolting the door overhead, turned and could not move, the lamp swinging in his hand, because the rope was just, there, and he couldn't swallow. He was dreaming the Russians. Kaltherzig was upstairs and would come down and break him and

More gunfire overhead, outside, and the gutwrenching *thump* of something larger, but far away.

The Russians were too loud for a dream.

He did a waxen stumble to the corner farthest from the door and crouched down, in a nest of blankets between the smooth wooden backs of two wine racks.

He watched the hanging rope. Sometimes the impacts made it swing, just a little, or maybe it was only the flame, flickering for want of kerosene.

He thought *it's all over, everything,* and felt all the wide world standing against Germany and this perdition he had come to know as Germany, and his eyes filled up with furious tears that hurt and fell and left wet lines in his hair. A hidden fury he remembered from childhood was all tangled up in it, the fury of the door opening and the merciless incomprehensible grownups putting a stop to something you were

(delighted)

just beginning to get up to.

He realized he was waiting for the door to open above him, for Kaltherzig to come downstairs.

Schweigen

Kaltherzig had not left him to starve, though after four days of cold gourmet food from jars and cans Erich was dreaming of plain hot middle-class fare like fried potatoes and unappreciated luxuries like fresh milk.

He found a lump in his blanket-nest: a dark plain suitcase, with nondescript but expensive clothing and a small paper with a handful of pieces of very plain gold—a band for a woman's finger, many links from a lost thick chain. The hard sharp weight in his pocket was new and final, a heartbreaking little last gift, like those scattered pieces of candy, like the books.

At night, as always, it was worse.

He seemed to have spent his life only moving between beds in which he held back tears and tried to ignore the sounds of someone else, sleeping.

Now there was so much quiet.

He felt very unsafe, exposed and vulnerable and ignorant. It was hard to sleep without Ahren and the gun surrounding him. He had tiptoed up into the house, stood crippled at the top of the stairs by the rush of scent and the sudden overwhelming conviction that it was a dream and he had better crawl back down the hall before was caught.

He took one step, then two, expecting to be exploded by artillery at any second, or else scared into a heart attack by the shout from the end of the hallway. The house was empty and he knew it; his eyes knew it, had he stopped crying since he'd woken up alone?

He dropped to his knees, to that same twenty feet of carpet, and crawled into the cold bedroom and lay at the foot of the bed. It smelled of dust and still air.

He looked at the windows, blinking away the blur of tears, until he realized what was wrong; that graygreen gleam of the searchlights was, gone. And he realized that all of it was gone, no Block 10, no roast duck in the officer's lounge, no executions with string quartets, no corpses dropped into marionette heaps. No more.

And he would be killed, maybe, though more likely They would find him and bring him back to the print shop and his narrow safe bed in Berlin, and that would be worse than being killed, and then he really would go mad.

He lost count of the days. It seemed, irrelevant, now.

He tried to stay downstairs, but he found himself upstairs, cringing from the gunfire and occasional artillery thumps that seemed closer all the time. The cringe was due to the noise, not any real fear of death. He didn't care.

He fell asleep on the couch in the living room, one night, the electricity long since gone, pretending he was listening to the phonograph anyway, pretending Kaltherzig was downstairs in the lab, where the spread of scientist glass was filled with congealing mysteries.

Something like a knock made him open his eyes.

There was a Russian, thick as a bear in terrifying fur, just outside on the back deck, tapping politely on the window. A gun as tall as Erich hung from his shoulder. The man gestured for Erich to come outside, grinning in a friendly sort of way, and put a hand in one pocket and came out not with a knife or a smaller gun but with something wrapped in paper that was probably food.

He stood up, because here were Authorities and he knew what one did with Authorities—obey. He tugged at his clothes, gestured that he wanted to dress, and the soldier nodded.

He went downstairs, took the little suitcase, some books. He stared sadly at the fading squares on the walls. All the pictures burned, not even one charred fragment of Kaltherzig for him to carry away.

Befreiung (verlassen)

Auschwitz was anarchy, now, wandering stick-men, sobbing, madness. The soldier kept his hand on the back of Erich's neck, saying *friend* and *food* and *no worry* and *good boy, safe boy,* in very bad German.

There was a howling swarm of the Muslim-men in the wide snowy square where roll-call had been done, back when everything was normal. His guard tried to steer him away from this, saying *no, no, no good,* but he drew near anyway, watching the kicking howling wild-eyed prisoners, most of them so frail they were more sad than frightening—but there were, so many of them, and all of them wracked with fury and revenge.

Erich saw the gleaming boots, the dark hair, buried under a striped howling clump of these ghosts.

He screamed and screamed, his suitcase falling and nearly breaking his foot, the Russian grappling with him, saying *no, no, a good boy!*

He would pull them all off, grown men or not, he was well-fed and still strong and they couldn't, couldn't...

Then he saw the blood, and the gleaming kicking boots stopped moving. He tore away from this rescuer, running, running towards the nightmare space no-man's land in front of the fence. He waited to be shot down. The man behind him was shouting in Russian. There was no gunshot, and his hands closed around this electric fence without hesitation.

Nothing. Dead like everything else.

He was shrieking, in horror, in fury that this last exit was denied him. Someone took his shoulder, and he turned, ready to swing, screaming still though he did not know it. One of the prisoner doctors from Block 10, one of the ones who had worked on the Hungarian twins. He was a skeleton too, but his eyes were still, miraculously, sane.

"It isn't him. It's just an Untersturmführer, from Block 11. It isn't him," he said, quietly, to save anyone else hearing.

Erich's hands were still on the fence. He stared at this man, not understanding this attempt at kindness, and shook the fence once, screamed at it in one more broken bark of noise, wanting blue fire to erase him, to stop this, to end this. Then he understood this prayer would not be granted, either. He would not end, and Kaltherzig was not dead and not here, and he would have to go on anyway.

He let the fence go, and went back to the bewildered Russian soldier, staring slackjawed and still holding Erich's suitcase like a doorman.

Erich took it from him, went and sat with his back against Block 10's outside wall. He was still, a boy wrapped around a center of nothing.

Two years.

They had promised him at least two years, but now They were gone.

There was an ugly blur, and a truck and a train, and finally he was deposited in a ruined town that was speckled with white and tan tents, like a crop of mushrooms after rain. Red Crosses marked most of them.

He thought of the euthanasia vans, of the Reich's ingenuity and rewriting of all the world that had made them mark them with the same red crosses, but he said nothing.

Perhaps that was what this would be. That would be fine.

Eis

He told the Americans his name was Erich Kaltherzig.

He said he didn't remember his address, and found after a moment that this was true. He told them he was fifteen, for a reason he was not proud of--fear of being told to leave and find his own way in all the wide incomprehensible world. There wasn't so much as a pause after he gave them that lie, either. He had always been short and slight, and now he was whipcord-thin. But still, surely he looked too healthy.   He waited for them to really question him, waited for his parents to arrive as they invariably would, waited for them to discover he was a *real* criminal, an admitted homosexual and not a Jew and put him back in a different jail.

They gave him food and took him to a tent with that same red cross painted on the side. A gentle medic in gloves that made him cringe did careful things to the rainbow of bruises he had almost everywhere except his face. He hadn't realized how battered he was, really, it was so very normal.

There were photographs, again, and he was weary of it to the point of a fit of laughter.

Couldn't they just transfer his files from Block 10?

No, of course not. They had burned almost everything.

He closed his eyes and did what he was told and considered himself lucky. His school king's English, he was finding, was both very different from American English and sadly lacking. It made his mouth dry the few times he had to ask the doctor to repeat an instruction or a comment.

They kept asking what else had been done to him.

He knew exactly what they were asking.

He tried mostly waving *no* until he remembered the English for *nothing*. His eyes filled with tears in spite of himself, at the humiliation of this, and he covered his face with his hands for a minute. No one stopped him. The freedom to scrub at his eyes made it worse.

They moved him to a real bed with white sheets that felt much too wide and clean and big for such a small and filthy thing as himself.

The too-young doctor with those innocent American eyes.

Damn it.

And the woman who'd taken his name, too, sitting in smooth stockings and that faint nexus of perfume, looking at him with her eyes too shiny. It made him feel like an exhibit to be so pitied, and it made the urge to submit to all this comforting worse.

He had no right to any comfort, and they'd have despised him, if they'd known what he was mourning.

They gave him pills. He recognized the floating opiate high almost immediately.

All of it was much too familiar but much too wrong, like those dreams of old schools that have transformed into church-shop-houses.
The hospital smells came and went, and he closed his eyes and was silently homesick until the pills took him.

Alles grau in grau malen

They transferred him out of the hospital, if you could call the sprawling tent-camp a hospital. His new room was a foot locker and a cot —in the jail, the only building still in one piece that could hold so many refugees. The door was open and tied open to the bars with rope.

It was still the worst at night.

Noises of men breathing, turning, asleep and awake, making their own private muffled concessions to various pains.

It smelled of jail, and that was wrong; the jail had been first.

Was he moving through the Auschwitz dream in reverse?

If that were true, at the end of it he would find himself in a home again, possibly with his parents again, and a job and all those beaming expectations and questions about girls and babies and there would never, ever, be searchlights again, no corpses in the street, no hands in the dark. He would explode with only such trivial things to push on him from the outside, to hold him together.

He cried a little, coat over his face. He wondered if they would find out he'd lied, and what kind of trouble he would be in, and why on Earth he'd done it.

He healed. Inexorably, unstoppably. The bruises faded. The myriad tiny tears inside him from hundreds of days of Kaltherzig's cock and hands and gleaming toys started to close. The streaks of blood when he wiped himself were less and less. And then there was no pain, and the bruises were down to three yellow ghosts, fading fast.

He was being given back to himself, piece by forgotten piece.

It made him feel heavier and heavier, less and less real. Only the scars were still his, dark red-violet that he might keep for a year or two, till they faded, left him with thin white lines like the ashes of burned paper.

They wouldn't let him wear the uniform, and his fear that they would wash it or steal it away entirely made him pick out the stitches on the collar. He sewed the ring inside it and hung the entire tiny bundle from a shoelace around his neck. It was something to cry over and chew on in the dark.

He wound himself under the blanket when everyone who could sleep was already out, investigated himself with embarrassed fingers. There was that hairline scar on the head of his cock, he'd forgotten that one. They'd never take that one, anyway. Two scars to his name, and counting. No, three--the wound in his cheek had left the faintest of lines. Three scars. The whole of his wealth.

He squirmed up onto his hands and knees, checking the blanket multiple paranoid times. Now and then there was the muffled noise of masturbation, usually politely ignored, but that wasn't, what this was.

It was strange to stroke that ring of muscle without pain. The tiny little flaps of what he assumed were scar tissue were still there, but he could push a licked finger inside as far as it would reach without a twinge.

It felt, unnatural. Like being ignored.

He thought for a long minute, shoulder aching from having his arms bent behind himself, and pushed in two fingers from his other hand. He thought for another long minute, and pulled, spreading himself open till his eyes watered, digging his nails in. It still wasn't right, but it gave him the first erection since Ahren had taken his tattoo.

When his fingers were damp and tasted of blood he squirmed his pants up and lay curled with his hands near his mouth, eyes closed, feeling this hurt he had stolen back from them. Wonderful, sick, invisible defiance. And the last blaze of that made him pull his blanket around himself and step out of bed and slide underneath it instead.

He fell asleep almost as soon as his head touched the floor.

They would not let him keep the stitches. They had been in for much too long by now, and were beginning to get grown over with skin. In the end the doctors held him down and a woman that said *shh, Mama's here* in German stroked his hair back, held a mask to his face.

It was the mask that made him cry.

They did exquisitely painful little pulls with tweezers for all of a minute and turned him loose. He sobbed and would not talk to anyone, not even that same kind woman who brought him sugar cubes and books and a soft emerald-green knitted scarf that he privately loved.

He could never get those stitches back. Ahren had laid them with his own hands. He'd *wanted* them grown into his skin. And they'd *stolen* them from him.

Bastards.

She finally brought the morphine, and here was a bribe that always worked. She brought something else, too. News.

News that nearly made Erich's heart stop.

"We've found Kaltherzig," she said.

Or at least, that was what he heard. There was a flat nightmare in his head of Ahren, his Ahren, sitting in the same jail Erich had left behind a lifetime ago.

He finally managed to shake his head at her, refusing this.

She tried again, in small round English words. "Kaltherzigs, family of yours. In New York, in America."

Not *his* Kaltherzig.

One long breath. Not his Kaltherzig. His Kaltherzig was in a green jungle, half the world away, where They would never find him.

Where Erich would never find him.

He wanted to smile at her, because that was what he was supposed to do, but his face wouldn't do that anymore. Instead he nodded and held his arm out for the needle.

Vorhölle

He was on a boat. Perhaps you called it a ship when it was this large. He didn't know, and he didn't care.

This was no different from the first jail or the second jail, really Erich had a single bunk in a shelf of five bunks, in one long room, with dozens of men. It was a place of claustrophobia and fear and long noisy nights. He was lonely, but maddeningly never alone.

He cried every single night, and spent every single day walking in something of a daze, memorizing the ship's few rules and events and showing up for each of them, from dinners and little performances to sermons and bingo games, sitting by himself in the back, talking to no one unless spoken to. This was usually by someone who missed a son, and he was polite but managed to be somewhat, cold, due to the apathy that permeated everything.

He enjoyed nothing he attended; he was only doing it to have orders to follow. It was nowhere near enough, it was nothing like right, and he learned to hide in his hat and his upturned collar and his uncut hair, almost collar-long again, now, so that the crying he could not stop wouldn't attract unwanted sympathy. He didn't really feel like crying. He didn't seem to feel much of anything. Nothing registered. But his eyes leaked intermittently, whether his mind was blank or not.

Men in black suits drew him, even in this death-haze of invisible sorrow. He would move, closer, and he *knew*, damn it, he was not so mad yet as to think Kaltherzig might be on this very ship, but he found reasons to change his seat all the same, until he was so close he could see for certain that it was only another of them, not Him.

The only time he missed the closest thing to orders he had on this ship was when he fell into this kind of sleep. It felt, almost conscious, like a decision to just, leave. The world was nothing he wanted, and during these times he would put his hand on this hidden ring and fold his blanket over till he could just fit underneath it curled up tiny. The heat

232

and the emptiness would rock him to sleep, usually in a minute or ten, and he would sleep without moving and wake up stiff and sad and drift a little, aware, and if he decided to go back to sleep he could hide again for another six to ten hours. Most of the passengers assumed he was seasick.

There were a few faces he was careful not to attach names to that asked after his health after long sleeps like these, and sometimes he would find a little wrapped package of food from lunch or dinner that would keep, like bread or an apple or cookies. He would announce a general "Thank you all," before going to bed, the next time he happened to be awake and present during the hour or two when the men lounged and smoked and talked a little. There would be a murmur or three, but nobody took credit or blame.

Sometimes he was gone for almost a day, dreaming under this square of blanket in all his clothes, dreaming of hands and a whip and the flowers that grew in the Forbidden Zone. Of the smell of organs in brine, and the smell of Kaltherzig that he never realized was called sandalwood.

It was never long enough.

There a German who got farther than the speculative looks he felt from time to time. He was in a half-doze, having given in to the urge for oblivion and dared to ask one of the bartenders for alcohol for one of his smallest gold pieces. He drank thinking that Kaltherzig had bought this for him, Schnapps in the wrong sort of glass, and he drank and drank and waited for the quiet that he assumed had to come, that had to be why people drank to begin with, until the bartender laughed at him and ordered him to bed, had given him several bottles, and he'd brought them staggering back
   (home?)
to see if it would keep him from dreaming. It was more morning than night, now. And there was a knee on his bed like a hallucination, and breath in the dark that was just, wrong. He turned over and saw a dimly familiar face by the few lamps that were always left on; nondescript and

innocuous, hard-worn and old enough to seem as old as Erich's father. "You—"

Nothing, a blink, and a callused too-thick hand cupping at his face, eyes wide in wonder or horror. Erich slid down, instinctively, shouldering away, hissed a *no* and then lay shaking in weird, almost hopeful certainty that this man would hurt him for this forbidden word. He closed his eyes.

The nudge of weight leaving his mattress.

"I'm awfully sorry, I thought you, I'm sorry..."

Footsteps. Quiet.

He opened his eyes to the dim-orange lamp. Gasped for breath. Wound up small and wished for Kaltherzig's breath above him and Kaltherzig's guns three feet away and hundreds of SS sprawled out in a black-and-red net to guard their sleep.

He thought the man would never speak to him again, but the next morning he walked into step with Erich in the corridor outside, offering the eternal cigarette. He introduced himself as Bertram Malm, and said again, "I'm awfully sorry."

Erich thought how it had felt to have Kaltherzig reject his kiss, and how it felt now to sleep alone. "No harm done." He thought of leaving it at that, but added, "I...am...but he isn't here," he said. To spare this man's fear and his dignity.

"Oh," Malm said, walking with him, reflectively. "I'm sorry."

Erich thought, *but not awfully , this time?*

He started to say *no harm done* again, till he realized what this man meant, realized he was being offered his first comfort over this monumental loss. He thought, *I lost everyone I ever loved in the war.*
Loved.

He hadn't known that was the word for what was wrong with him until that moment.

234

Königshaus

America was a disappointment almost from the second he set foot in the country. There was endless waiting in line, endless forms, and the typewriters. It was all very familiar. He caught himself sleeping sitting up on the same kind of wooden bench as, before. Listening for screaming from downstairs.

Finally, after what seemed like years but was probably only most of a day, he was taken into a long concrete room, and turned over to a couple that scared him enough to make him stand in the doorway. He was wide-eyed and desperately afraid and impossibly homesick.

They were both older than Erich had expected. The man was like Kaltherzig, in his long lines and his dark hair and his elegant Roman features, but there was a busy, preoccupied sort of mildness, in his tie-straightening and his uneasy way of standing, in his hesitant smile. His clothes looked strange to Erich, as if there were too many layers, too many little ugly complications in American style.

The woman at his side was pure Aryan, more delicate than his long-ago Valkyrie, radiating ice-cold until she smiled, less hesitant than her husband. Centuries of breeding in every line, in her smooth brow and effortless poise in this dingy receiving room.

The man shook Erich's hand with frightening American enthusiasm, having to walk over to him to do so. He was clinging to the doorjamb with one hand, in misery, shaken and waiting to be pointed at as an, imposter. The softness and precision he felt in this man's hand told him this, too, was a doctor, even before the introduction. "I'm Doctor James Kaltherzig, and this is my wife, Judith. You're our...nephew?"

Erich murmured "I think so, sir," and could not meet his eyes.

A nod, and James touched his shoulder. It was too Kaltherzig, and the tears overflowed, and Erich turned away. Too different, and too the same.

James coughed, a little, and said, "That's all right, son, they've told

235

us you've...that you, were...that you're not, well." He stepped back, and Judith stepped in, turning Erich towards her in a businesslike fashion, tipping his chin up, attending to him with a handkerchief. It made him feel very small. Much too small.

He had expected them to speak German, he realized. He felt like a child in an orphanage, expected to sell himself to these prospective parents, and afraid to open his mouth, fearing he'd, scream, or confess, or vomit in pure intolerable stress.

She smiled at him, with that arranged charm-school care, but there was sweetness underneath. It made it, just a little better. Terrible flare of wish to fling himself at this woman, sobbing, in a way he'd never been able to do to his own mother. They were reverses of one another, he thought—this woman was warm underneath a surface of pretended cold, and his mother had been cold and empty, underneath fake smiles and a mother-costume.

She must have felt something of this sudden lean in his muscles, because she made a soft gesture at him with her eyes. "James, he's exhausted. Take us out of here, please," she said, still looking at Erich.

A doctor.

He supposed that much, at least, ran in the family.

He was led to a very nice car, through a terrifying bustle and those buildings that seemed taller than anything should be. The *noise*, and he leaned too closely into Judith's side, looked longingly at James just in front of them. The shoulders were right, and the birdlike quick grace in his gestures, but then he would turn those elegant silver-rimmed glasses, and the eyes behind them were too academic to be Kaltherzig's immovable blaze.

The back seat smelled of leather. If he closed his eyes, he could be on the way home from Block 10. He did just that.

When he opened them again, they were outside the city, and they pulled finally into a long driveway, and up to a frightening mansion of a house. James carried his one tiny suitcase. Judith held his hand, as if she thought he might run screaming into the thin woods if she didn't restrain him.

There were long days of waiting for...what, exactly?

Erich didn't know, but he knew he could not wait forever. He felt as if great pieces of him had ceased to function. There was enough left of his plan, that he would obey and anticipate and be perfect, perfect, but when he wasn't engaged in this he did very little. Sat and stared. Went to bed early, in the room that was so nice it made him sad, that they were, trying so hard.

They had no children, and the room they'd led him to with such pride was done up for a boy much younger than himself. There were model airplanes, a bookshelf with books for a boy half his age, a rolltop desk with pens and papers and paint and other myriad delights hidden in cunning little nooks.

The books soon vanished, replaced with new attempts. Sometimes he kept one open on his knees to stare through, to make them feel appreciated.

He watched for signs of Ahren in James, having squinted at great heavy photo albums until he finally deciphered that this was the grandson of one of Ahren's uncles.

He half-wanted to find something, familiar, and half-dreaded finding, too much. James was never anything but polite and kind to him, and that touch on his shoulder was quietly replaced, just like the too-young books, with the occasional pat on top of his head.

Sometimes he heard James on the telephone, with his voice raised, and these times he would lean against the wall in the hallway, arms around himself, listening, waiting. But nothing ever changed.

He didn't know what he wanted out of this man, but he knew he wouldn't get it.

He wasn't Ahren.

He didn't smell the same.

There was no fury inside James at all, no predator ferocity under that awkward kindness. The occasional stern tone with the housekeeper or their gardener was only a tease, a tiny reminder of the man he'd lost.

Erich was tempted sometimes to do something terrible, to see if this man would strike him, to see if that might silence the terrible starvation that gnawed at him all the time. He found himself in James's den, once, holding a gleaming delicate ornament from the lit shelves along one wall. Tempted to throw it. Preferably through the expensive glass in one of the French windows. He stared at it in his hands, as if it had leapt there by itself, and put it down, leaving at almost a run.

He realized that his silence and his essential emptiness disturbed them, and there was something of Kaltherzig in them, after all. They were noble and kind and generous, and that made it all worse, made him feel like the lowest sort of thief. He began trying to smile, learning to pretend in the mirrors, laughing sometimes, but it felt wrong, like it started in his throat and not whatever deeper place laughter was supposed to come from.

Judith was almost impossible to fool.

She'd heard him crying, one night, and there had been a tiny tap at his door that he'd squeaked at in terror, suddenly nowhere and everywhere, suddenly waiting for Mengele to come in.

She tiptoed inside with a lush blue bathrobe fastened up to her chin, and her hair around her shoulders, sat on the edge of the bed and put her hand on his back. "Can't you tell us what it is?" she'd said, softly, after a while. "Can't we help you with it?"

He shook his head. Wept.

No, he couldn't tell them what it was, not even if he'd had the English.

And no, nobody could help him with it.

It was a sin, was what it was. An entire growing row of them.

The papers that Judith showed him and filed away in the office—a birth certificate, and citizenship papers with Erich Kaltherzig written on every one. They made him cry, and she'd given him a bright smile she would never have used in public, thinking that for once these might be tears of joy.

They were not exactly that. He kept looking at this name, his name, and thinking, *as if he'd married me*. And that was why he'd given the Red Cross that name, wasn't it? To make it clear whose possession he was, always would be.

He was tutored, with a pointy frighteningly precise man teaching him English. After a session or two Mr. Hadley realized he was an excellent student, and the razor-sharp barking orders ceased.

James asked him polite questions about his skills and his desires, and he answered what he could with increasing fluency. The one question he couldn't answer.

What do you want to do?

He said *I don't know, sir,* until James gave up.

It was a lie. He knew exactly what he wanted.

I want to go home, that's what I want to do.

But the Russians. The ashes.

He heard James on the telephone in his office, a short time later, and caught the phrase *failure to thrive*.

He didn't know *thrive*, but he knew *failure*, all right, and he knew it was about him.

When James came to find him he discovered Erich in this boychild room, cleaning like a terrified tornado, running at such a pace he was pouring sweat and leaving more disarray than cleanliness.   James finally stopped him, holding him by the shoulders, but he could not persuade Erich to say anything that made any sense to him, only *I'll do better, I will, you'll see, I will,* through his endless veil of tears.

Then, at last, came something familiar. James carrying a black leather bag, James loading a syringe while Erich waited with an outstretched arm.

"We've found a doctor for you," he said to Erich, across that long formal dinner table the next night.

He swallowed, already shaking, "Please, can't you do it, whatever it is, please..."

Judith, leaving her seat, sitting in the empty one beside him, taking his hand. She almost never touched him with more than one hand, she was too much the aristocrat for that, but the child-shaped hole inside her made her try. He was too big to fit in that hole, he knew.

That cough from James that meant he was embarrassed. "I'm the wrong sort of doctor, Erich. I'm a surgeon, you know. Dr. Zealander is top-notch. He's a doctor for your body and your mind."

Erich nodded, but he couldn't stop crying. Any doctor that wasn't a Kaltherzig seemed automatically in his mind to be a Mengele. "Please, can I go, sir?"

Judith squeezed his hand, looking at him with those blue-blue eyes, and slid away back to her own seat.

"We want you to be well, you know. That's all it is. I'm going to go with you, and I'll understand everything he says, and I'll explain it all to you. It isn't a punishment, Erich. Nobody blames you for any of this."

No, perhaps they didn't, but that didn't mean it wasn't his fault.

He mouthed his *yes-sir*, swallowing tears, drowning in that misery that had been his since he'd woken up alone in Ahren's house.

"Go ahead," James told him.

He fled, to this boy-child American bedroom.

Once there he dragged out his suitcase, opened it on his bed, buried his face in it, in this pile of suits Ahren had bought him, his uniform underneath hidden from all of Them, because they would steal it, trying to make him well.

Trying to make him forget.

The smell was almost gone, but if he sniffed in deep rapid pulls he could still catch the faintest ghost of home.

Dr. Zealander was a wide thick loud man with black-framed glasses that made his eyes swim like fish behind them. He had a great vertical shock of white hair and the sort of red-sprung nose of a long-time drinker, hands like shovels, and a white coat that set Erich to shaking before he was even led into the examination room.

This new doctor wouldn't hear of James going into the examination room, and if Erich had needed any more proof that this Kaltherzig was no Ahren, he had it in his last sight of James meekly settled in the waiting room as he'd been ordered.

Erich found himself alone with this great deafening man, sitting on the edge of a table as cold as the one in Block 10, so frightened and so ashamed that his tongue was like sand in his mouth. He was down to his underpants, bare feet cold and pushing at nothing.

Dr. Zealander examined him with Prussian efficiency, thumping him here and there—"What's this mark, here? This one?" and when Erich shook his head and whispered *I can't remember,* and the doctor stared at him angrily and said, "Of course you can!"

He shook his head, and then he wouldn't talk at all.

Dr. Zealander told him to dress again, seeming to have lost patience. He returned with a file, wrote something, set it down and stared at Erich over his glasses.

"Now look here. You're to stop all this immediately. There's not a thing wrong with you."

A thudding little push into Erich's collarbone that made him blush, made his hands begin to shake, made his eyes fill up with those endless tears.

"Except laziness and ingratitude. Why, there are men who had to actually *fight* in the war, that have come back with arms blown off and faces burned down to bone. Ungrateful. You're sound of body and undisciplined of mind, and all this indulgent wallowing is only hurting your new parents. I don't want to see you again."

He told James very little of this, but he guessed from the angry set of his jaw on the way home that James was already privy to this gruff man's opinion. "We'll find another one," he said to Erich. "A better one."

"Please. He's right, it's only me. I'll do better, I'll be better--"

Damn it. He wished he'd asked that bastard man for a pill to stop him crying. It was like everywhere inside him Kaltherzig had been had filled up with tears instead, a bottomless well of them, that the slightest hurt would pierce into.

A sigh from James. *That* was Ahren, eerie, phonographic, and Erich looked out the window at the trees rushing by, the wrong trees, the wrong street.

"Well, we'll see," James said.

He learned to fake normal better.

The next time James asked him what he wanted to do, he said he'd like to sew again, possibly. A print-shop was out of the question, the thought of it filled his mind with Emil, torn like paper.

James came home a few days later with news for him: he had a patient who ran a very upscale boutique, and he'd explained Erich's situation, and the man would be delighted to give him a try. He would sew by hand or machine, essentially alone, and Erich nodded, gratefully, thanked him multiple times, something in him eased by this thought of work.

The boutique was quiet, smelling of cloth and dye. His new boss was a Jew, amusingly enough, quite friendly, and so funny that sometimes he made Erich laugh a real laugh. Mr. Blumberg's wife introduced herself the next day, and promptly scolded and frowned over how thin

Erich was, seizing him and fussing over him in a way that frightened and secretly delighted him.

After that Mr. Blumberg's lunches arrived neatly packed for two. He ate as little as he dared, thinking of Kaltherzig's fingers, counting his vertebrae, feeling the bones of his face,

I want, to stay, what you've made me.

It was a warmer place than the print shop, and smaller. It reminded him of his father's shop, and that had been a place safe from his mother and the world.

But it was not home. He could relax here, a little, away from Judith's worried, reined-in eyes, but not completely. Not even close.

He wanted a home where he didn't have to fake normal, because he wasn't sure how much longer he could manage it.

By the time Erich reached what his new parents thought was his eighteenth birthday, he'd saved enough for a deposit on his own apartment.

Judith wept, hearing that he wanted to leave, but James nodded, and told them both that it was an excellent sign, perhaps with too much certainty, as if he were trying to convince himself as well as his wife and his nephew-son-guest.

He helped Erich find an apartment close to the boutique, a great wide loft that might have been part of a warehouse or a factory, one vast room with a kitchen in one corner and a bathroom tucked beside it, walled off. The bedroom was up a narrow metal staircase, half-walled, comfortably nest-like above the kitchen and bathroom.

It was beautiful.

It was all wrong.

He cried himself to sleep, alone in this echoing space, holding his little totem-necklace, the collar of his striped shirt still stiff with Ahren's semen, wound around the Totenkopf ring in his lonely little try at some magick.

He wished for the boychild room back, he told himself, but what he really wished for was the floor in Ahren's bedroom half the world and now almost three years away.

It was nice not to have to hide the tears, or his uniform, anymore, but the scent of home had long since faded out of it.

Here, perhaps, he could finally be unsafe.

Sehnsucht

The Americans were all so, loud. Wide, noisy, nosy, busy sorts of people. It was just too much for him, the staring and the shoving and the yelling. He developed a very quick fear of crowds.

So many cars, and all of them too loud, too. The sun felt wrong here, like the color was off, like it was coming from an unnatural angle. Policemen scared him so badly that he shook like he was feverish when he had to walk past one—oh, and they were everywhere in this dirty city. He just kept expecting one of them to, hit him, or...something...shoot him, maybe.

Anything.

He was positive he looked guilty of something.

There was nothing for it except to just, walk by, with his knees gone all crooked and his hands holding his coat closed so tight it was like his fingers would freeze that way. None of them ever said a word. He would probably have dropped unconscious to the sidewalk at so much as *good morning.*

Sometimes he could see an officer out of his window, buying something from the hot-dog cart that sometimes parked there a while.

He wondered, often, where exactly they would take him.

He kept thinking of that phrase—*bird in the head*—that Americans seemed to have replaced with *cuckoo.* Two different languages, two different ways to say the same thing: insanity.

He kept seeing the same picture in his head, not quite a dream, over and over, of the German eagle like a mad Van Gogh painting, all edges and angles and steelsilver and talons, sweeping across the sky as wide as the horizon. All the Reich, covering the world. But it blackened the sky and then there was light behind it, and it got smaller and smaller and smaller, and then it was gone.

So Erich began to develop what he supposed were properly called coping mechanisms.

It took him two months to acquire all the materials, and one solid week of sewing before it was, done. He held it up, inspected everything over and over, seeking pins or a loose seam, for almost an hour before he realized it was finished. A historian—or an officer, for that matter—would have been hard-pressed to tell it from an original.

The uniform was spread out on his bed before he knew he'd made it to Ahren's measurements and not his own. Not just the measurements, either. Had he planned this with the part of his mind that made the dreams? It was, perfect, down to the rank tabs, down to every last ribbon and trim and stitch.

He picked up the jacket and slid it on, telling himself he was thinking of buying, oh, a dressmaker's dummy, one of the old German ones with wooden joints and such articulation. A display piece. that no one would ever see. He stood in the bathroom and stood in the mirror looking at himself, and thought of girls wearing their boys' jackets, incongruous soldier-colored pieces of darkness against cashmere and a crinoline and a ponytail.

He held up his arms, sleeves dangling a full hand past his fingertips, and burst into tears.

He exhaled German tobacco into the coat bundled in his hands. He sprinkled it with whiskey and German beer. He'd already smelled every single men's cologne in one of the big department stores. Not even close. No matter what he tried, nothing made it smell like Ahren.

One night he put the uniform on, cuffs and trouser legs turned up, shuffled to the kitchen and turned on the burner. He laid on it a piece of bacon and a lock of his hair, cut off with a kitchen knife. There was a lot of popping and then thick, greasy smoke that stung his eyes. He stood in it, closed eyes streaming. He felt, hypnotized, as if some kind of darkness he had swallowed in Auschwitz was growing and growing inside him.

If anyone knew what lunacy he used to keep worse lunacy at bay, they would put him in a jail. They'd call it a hospital, but it would be jail, and there would be bars on the windows.

The games, with the black rubber gloves and the hospital soap, alone in the bathroom with candles lit and the windows he'd permanently painted over. Different games, each night in turn as well as he could remember them, as well as he could duplicate them. The Solstice game with different gloves, black leather SS gloves he'd bought at great expense from a specialist.

He could never get the hanging right.

The closest he could come was to tie a rope from the railing of the loft, tie it to trick cuffs from a joke shop. Erich would fasten these, fumbling behind his back and step down the last three steps until the rope drew his arms up painfully high. He had tried it with the slipknot, and found himself perilously close to unable to loosen it once his fingers grew numb. But the cuffs each had a tiny lever that hurt his thumb to push, that made them spring open.

It was closer, and it made him so frantic, made him so hard--and left him as empty as he'd been before he began it.

It was too static with no Kaltherzig to threaten him.

He tried to remember it, replay it, but it was too quiet, here. He couldn't bring himself to scream into his empty apartment. He could scream into a pillow, with his cock in his hand and an imaginary Kaltherzig inside him, but no, that wasn't right either. That was controlled and polite and...cold. Empty.

Safe. Too safe.

The hanging, right or not, at least, was not so safe.

It scared him, and he was certain it was insanity. But he could not stop doing it. It was a very close cousin to masturbation, but though he was fairly sure They were wrong about that being a sickness, he was fairly sure they would be right about the hanging.

Sick, sick, madness.

But he could not stop doing it.

One night he was hanging, folded over with Kaltherzig in his ear. He'd taken up yet more slack, and he was up on the balls of his feet when he slipped. His feet pedaled in dust and then his weight came down on his weakened left shoulder with a twisting yank. He flailed and almost-screamed and thought, *the police will find me rotting like this, with an erection, with all these illegal things,* and then his thumb found the little safety latch and one of the cuffs opened, dropping him with his left arm still twisted up over his head, kneecaps hitting the hardwood floor with a smack that made him groan.

He stayed that way for a long time, until he was sure he could stand upright without fainting.

His left shoulder, never quite right after Kaltherzig's punishment, was much worse after this accident.

Well, he knew the cure for that. Those delicious blue pills again. More of them. More often.

Around and around and around.

One motionless place, one center.

And that center did not hold.

He was walking home from the boutique, preferring the half-hour trip to the crowded, terrifying subway, when a beautiful dirty boy with a spill of redgold hair smiled at him, leaning in a doorway, said a number and added, "Or..." and gestured at his arm.

Erich was mystified. He thought perhaps he was being mugged, but when he fumbled for his wallet and held out the money the boy smiled, and began to follow him. Then he understood, and flushed, thinking he would tell him to keep it and go away, but he didn't.

Once in his apartment, this Shawn creature gestured at his arm again, and laughed at Erich's bewilderment. "The stuff, you know?" Once he'd conveyed that heroin was an opiate Erich vanished into his bathroom and returned with the jar of morphine pills. James Kaltherzig kept his prescription filled, ostensibly for the pain of his never-right-again shoulder, though Erich suspected he understood a little of the true reasons.

Shawn produced a syringe and a spoon and did mysterious alchemy that made Erich watch in amazement, reminded of Kaltherzig's lab.

"Do you want some? You never did it this way?" And Erich shrugged, and allowed Shawn to do this mystery to his own arm, and the warm morphine rush he remembered from Block 10 made his eyes ache, but the numbness stopped it in time.

Shawn caught at him, after a while, drug-dazed, and he pulled away, terrified he would lose the one and only Kaltherzig kiss that surely still resided on his lips.

This boy-whore stared at him and laughed again. "You're new as a penny, you know that?"

He didn't know.

"Well, what did you pay me for, then?"

He didn't know that either. Finally, without looking the boy in the face, he said he might like for Shawn to hold him. He was shaking with shame even as he said it, seeing the Gestapo in his head, hearing *criminal disease* in German like a phonograph playing only that phrase.

Shawn seemed unflustered by this—"Oh, you're one of those." And he slid over easily, and wound Erich close, stroked his hair and sometimes his back, as though it were the most natural thing in the world.

Erich closed his eyes and listened to this boy's heartbeat, opium-slow, and pretended it was Kaltherzig. Something like, quiet, inside him, for the first time since Auschwitz had ended. Warm and the salt-sweat scent of this boy, of the river and the city outside, all wrong, but infinitely better than nothing.

Shawn stayed until morning, disengaging and saying he had to go. He stayed for an hour more when Erich offered him more of the pills.

They talked very little.

Shawn asked if he'd been to the clubs, and he didn't understand that, either. He was given an address written badly on a slip of paper.

He put it in his pocket, and forgot about it, until he found it in his kitchen half-lost under work orders and client measurements.

He'd looked for Shawn again, and never found him. He thought, madly, that he would give him money and those pills as often as he wished for the sake of the heartbeat under his ear and the smell of boy in his nostrils, but he never saw him, and he was too afraid to try to find another boy like him. He could hardly wave cash at every boy he saw on the street until one of them was willing to take it for being used as a pillow for a night.

This address was in the warehouse district, frighteningly low-class, and tempting.

"Lots of us," the boy had said.

He could not imagine *lots of us*, except in broken lines with pink triangles on each stick figure.

Establishments that cater to this sort of thing.

He drank, swallowed pills, dressed, and went. He thought he might be killed, on the way, on the way home, or in this club. He didn't care.

Umherwandern

He found this club, with no more trouble than a few beggars along the way. He gave out pocket change in exchange for street directions, giving only the street name fearing that he might be found out if he told these poor souls anything else. He found himself in front of a low building, broken-down with boarded over windows, and was amazed to find a pink triangle chalked beside a door that seemed utterly sealed. He stared at this slip of paper, at the triangle, and finally worked up the courage to tap on it. A slot slid open. "Pass?"

He stared at these two piggy eyes, heart slamming. "I'm sorry, I don't have a pass. A boy named Shawn told me we...that, I could come here."

"Don't know any Shawn."

He longed to run away, but he'd come so far already. He wanted to see a lot of Us, just once. "He has red hair, he—" That gesture at his arm.

The slot slammed closed.

He was trudging away when the door opened behind him.

He paid a wide ox of a man and was ushered through another door into a low-lit room that was almost exactly like the bar on the ship to America had been. He stood just inside, staring, astounded. It looked so very normal. There was music, jangling from a cheap phonograph that seemed to have grown a mismatch of speakers like weeds from its main bulk. There were men and a few women, and a few creatures that might have been either. There were men dancing together, leaning close in dark corners. As he watched, two of them kissed, lingering, with sort of a forehead-nudge after, and laughs from both of them like any young couple.

He had never seen a man kiss another man before. He had never imagined such a thing in public. In front of strangers. He was so dumbfounded by it that he only stood, until the doorman laughed at him, though not cruelly, and said, "You're blocking the way," and nudged him to go out into the club.

A woman—no, a man, maybe? gestured at him almost immediately. He pointed at himself, and she nodded, long white-blonde hair and an aged face tastefully painted, a dress that Judith might have worn. She patted the seat beside her. "You're new."

"Yes, ma'am." He flushed, at that—was he supposed to call her ma'am, or sir? His upbringing wouldn't let him try a *sir* at a woman in diamond earrings and such an elegant dress. The gentle encouragement in her eyes told him he'd chosen wisely.

"Drink?"

He shook his head. She ignored that, and called without looking for someone named Martinez to bring her something fattening. Erich was presented with what tasted like chocolate milk with sugar and cream and some smooth alcohol underneath it. He drank so she would stop staring threats at him. Any more kindnesses this week and he would have to buy dark glasses.

"Was it anyone who comes here?" she asked, in that gentle Grandmother voice that he still couldn't resist. He knew this was a man, but his heart denied it; he could smell the mother in her from across the table. That same wish, to burrow into her, to cry, to cling.

"Anyone...I'm sorry?"

"Who broke your heart, was it anyone here? I'll go and give him a piece of my mind."

"No ma'am, it wasn't anyone here," he said, flushing. Silly reflex, that, here of all places he could.....admit it.

He was forgetting again to shed his un-American politeness, and she smiled and said "The accent is lovely."

"I've tried to, not have it."

"That's what makes it lovely." She offered him a cigarette, and lit her own when he smiled a *no*. "Was he...lost, back there, you know? I

252

heard they killed a lot of us, in all...that..."

"No, it was..." The scar, under his sleeve, burning so bright he was amazed she could not see it. "Nothing like that."

She nodded, smoked. "You have to climb over it, whatever it is. Find yourself another one to drown in." A smile; this was an old story.

"There aren't any others deep enough to drown in," he said.

"Oh, honey." And she lit another cigarette, and ordered him another fattening drink, and said, "Dish."

Her name was Nana, and she might've taught the SS a thing or two about coaxing information out of the unwilling. She didn't threaten, she lured, and nodded at the right times, and smiled with her eyes in a way that loosened his tongue as much as the drinks that kept appearing in his hands. He edited, heavily, confessing only to being struck a time or six and not to any of the other games. He deleted all the hospital bits except being measured and having seen autopsies. And still when he was finished her eyes were wide and they were both drunk.

It still seemed to be all right.

There was the frozen-solid core of a Marlene Dietrich in her, and he could not help but trust her. She left cigarette butts stamped with coral lipprints in all their empty glasses, and this delighted him so much he wished he could steal one. Just to have proof there was such a fantastic creature in the world, alive to smoke cigarettes in spite of it all.

"I'm a sucker. It's romantic." She was quiet awhile, smoking, and said, "One of those that'll hurt you will, keep hurting you..." a shrug, here—this was an old story, too. "There's worse things. Sometimes I think alone is worse, but you're not supposed to think that." She sighed, and he could see in her eyes that she was remembering someone of her own.

He didn't feel like explaining any of, that, either. The extent of how very much of it he, missed. Never mind.

"So did you ever try to find him?"

He stared at Nana. She stared back, looking at first puzzled by his silence and then something like afraid.

He didn't move. He didn't hear her when she asked if he was all right.

No, he had never tried to find Kaltherzig.

To have him back, with no Russians edging closer and no Americans bullying their way in, to have that jungle quest exile imprisonment. To sleep on Ahren's floor again, aching with bruises so that no position was comfortable. To never be fast enough or polite enough or quiet enough, ever again. To never count minutes again with no idea what he was counting towards. To never be mind-numbingly, chokingly, disgustingly safe, ever again.

No, he had never even considered that.

And then, the ox of a doorman came running into the club, and shouted one terrible word. "Raid!"

Nana caught Erich and hissed "Run!" at him, and shoved him towards the back. People were funneling out of a door behind the bar, footsteps disappearing into the rain and the dark outside.

"It's, police?" Erich drew back, away from her, a terrible idea growing sudden and clear in his head.

The police had been the start of it, before, and it had ended in, home. This was illogical, but he didn't want logic. He wanted walls and guard dogs. He wanted to sleep again, secure in the knowledge that something terrible would wake him soon enough.

"Yes, child, police, now *run!*" And she let him go, but turned back when she was almost to the door, the room nearly empty, now. "Are you mad, come with me, they'll arrest you!"

"Just go," he said, softly, and he turned back to his seat and sat down. She shook her head once, and was gone, sliding her high-heeled shoes off her feet and running as light as a girl into the safe darkness outside.

The police seemed rather amazed that he was sitting there.

They arrested him, and he shook with numb instinctive delicious fear, sat in the back of the truck behind this screen of bars with a few others that had been too slow or run in the wrong directions.

He had a dreamy smile plastered on his face that he could not remove.

They brought him to jail. And here it was, the typewriter, the barked questions, the inked fingertips and the flashbulbs. He answered them all, blissfully, soaking up barked orders and shoves like a desert plant soaks up rain. His insides were swirling in warm relief that was better than the morphine had been in his arm.

Police in blue that was almost black. That smell of terror and urine and bleach underneath everything. Rules posted on walls. Guards and handcuffs and finally, it was either-or, here, police or prisoner, it was finally, starting to be the way it was supposed to be.

He was pushed into a cell with the others from the club, one very young man as pale as milk crying a little. He didn't cry. He settled himself on a wooden bunk and slept, more deeply than he had since Auschwitz.

Someone was shaking him.

A policeman.

The questions, he thought, with something like joy.

He followed, groggy, squinting, and was led back into the room he'd been fingerprinted in.

He was given back his wallet, now empty of money.

He signed a paper.

And the woman he gave it to said, "Next."

He stared at her in betrayed horror. "Shall I go back to my cell?"

She snorted at him, her fat face crinkling. "No, you shall go home. Or wherever people like you go. Now get out."

And he was dragged by the arm by one of these policemen, turned loose just outside the front doors of the station into blinding hot morning sun.

Abandoned, again.

He persuaded a lawyer to help him run an ad in several South American newspapers. *Seeking to return a ring lost in 1945. Erich Kass.* He left a PO Box and checked it each day, as he left the boutique, before he went home to his covered windows and trick handcuffs. It was a gray-and-black rectangle, and it stayed empty no matter how many times he checked it.

He wept, ashamed of himself.

Foolishness. Letting himself be arrested, wasting money and time and hope on such a thread. Kaltherzig would never see it. Kaltherzig had cured himself, and left Erich behind. Kaltherzig had another boy already, far away in a green wet place as hot as Hell and safe from the world.

Seelisch

In the dream he opens his eyes to the ceiling, and he's on his back in Block 10's examination room. There are shattering clarion cries of pain in him, from places both deep and shallow. New orifices and new tubes inside them and a few for good measure in the standard pre-existing holes. He's breathless. He cannot so much as tip his chin; something around his neck prevents it. He has no idea how he is wounded, but he is positive the sheet underneath him is dripping-wet with something still, warm.

There's a strangeness in his extremities; and a dawning certainty that his neck is broken, that he is paralyzed. Kaltherzig is on that stool with the wheels that he remembers so perfectly, but sitting at his head and not between his knees.

He knows what Kaltherzig is going to do. He has done it before.

"All this time. All here. It's the experiment."

He didn't understand. "The Russians...you, left me, and the Russians came, and then I went to America..."

"Drugs," said Kaltherzig, patiently. "You go on about your fucking Russians no matter which disassociative I give you." And a laugh, as though that were ridiculous. "They'll starve to death. They won't even need camps. There won't be any Russians in a year."

"No, Germany went into Russia, and they..."

Did they?

"The Americans took, Paris..."

"It's a dream."

A terrible struggle inside him. Kaltherzig was always right; that was his one, single imperative.

But Kaltherzig was wrong, now.

"This is the dream. I was there."

"No. Here. You've always been here. Where I've put you."

It has driven him quite mad for a multitude of reasons. He is drooling.

That glassy grating lift. That sense of cold in his head.

Kaltherzig lifts out the little trapdoor wedge in his skull, sets this pottery bone in a metal tray. He does things Erich can't see.

"Just like before, after each one, you'll try to express what you perceive. Yes?"

It doesn't matter what he says. He never answers anymore.

A greenblack flash and the pouring nauseous ocean of the smell of bitter almond, magnified a thousand times, a tickle like spiders across his chest, an earthquake of electrical buzz that makes him snap his teeth and perform excruciating long licking hooks with his tongue in the air, or shout, in nonsense howls and spitting, in obscenities, in words arranged in no logical order.

It is nothing he can help. It is Kaltherzig, and that black box of electricity.

It is wires in his brain.

He is thrown through a blizzard of sensations and smells, grass between toes and a blister and very cold water and anguish and the smell of burning toast and an infected skinned knee. He has an orgasm out of sheer overload. A sentence in warbling deaf-mute word salad. Tears, under all of this, with what little of him still remained.

(ruined, he ruined me, I)

Between the explosions of Other he will cry, begging with nothing left in him for Kaltherzig to shoot him, shoot him. He says very little now, other than this and the pieces of confession Kaltherzig wrings out of him with needles and knives.

Kaltherzig tipped up his head, pretending to listen, and as his chin came down he saw his own limbs, drawn up like sticks and as soft and translucent as, a baby, a corpse.

"All right, breathe." The glassy sense of his skull fitted together, of being closed like a covered dish. A strap under his chin. "Come, now, all this crying. You're the only experiment that's working, we have to analyze how, and why, don't we?" Kaltherzig leaned over him, straightened the hood, did the eyesmile. "I'll make you forget it, later. I'll find the brain cells that record this and slice them out and swallow them."

"...ruined..."

"No one would ever believe you anyway." A pat to that new door on top of his head, edges grating. "You're too mad to know the difference."

Then, screams that gargled through saliva he could not swallow.

A greenblack flare, an ozone bang, and the universe peeled back like skin into the ceiling in his apartment.

He would run to the bathroom and either throw up or exhaust himself trying. Stare at the mirror and think, *this is one of them. Just one of the flashes.*

There was no chance of sleep after that one. Sometimes not for days.

He would sit with American noisy cheerful music on, and every light blazing, shivering with that bone-deep fear infection until dawn, feeling his skull for a notched scar.

Sometimes, especially when he drank but took no pills, the dream would just seem to steal him out of the world without warning. He would open his eyes in Block 10, with his skull being lifted. Or he would be at the boutique, handstitching final details on a ladies' silk blouse or a man's crisp suit, but a terrible exhaustion would overtake him. He would rest his head on his arms, thinking, *just close my eyes for a minute, maybe I'm just becoming ill. Blumberg will forgive me,* and the dream would come and take him.

He emptied the library's section on dreams, hoping against hope that there might be some cure, some trick to spare him these horrors. He found that dreaming of being awake, especially over and over, was a very disordered sign. It certainly felt like that, like whatever barriers were meant to exist in his mind were, gone. Just gone. Like falling into deep dark water.

Well, if the brain couldn't control that, he would assist. And he took more and more pills, and that let him sleep without dreams.

At least, at first.

But the dreams were stronger than morphine and they began to creep through the highest doses he dared to try. Even worse, the higher doses held him caught in sleep to endure the dreams, so that he could not even thrash himself awake.

He found himself searching his head obsessively, even when the dream had not come for weeks, fingertips endlessly pressing the bone for that triangle scar. He was terrified of strange smells, and sometimes he was late for work because he *had* to locate the source of a scent, *had* to be sure it was not

(wires)

just his imagination. His hands would search his head, over and over, without his permission, without even his awareness. Searching for another scar to add to to the whole of his wealth.

People asked him if he had a headache.

After a while, he began to.

Then there were silent months.

Erich's post office box stood empty, a gray-and-black rectangle. He hated that little key, gray too, and the steps into the post office, and the way they were so much harder on the way back down, with his pockets as empty as that box.

Blumberg was getting on in years, and as he came to trust Erich's skill he left earlier and earlier, came in later and later, and took entire days off more and more often. So he was alone, in another empty box, when the bell called him from the back room and the bank of sewing machines. He'd come nearly running, mouth full of *good morning* and arms full of Mrs. Dennison's newly repaired gown for her daughter's wedding, as he'd told her to expect it today.

It was not Mrs. Dennison.

Lieser was lounging with one elbow on the countertop, all ice and smile. There was snowcolored fur in the collar of his coat. His pointed chin was resting in one cupped hand, against a fine leather glove as gray as a post-office box.

A dark-skinned boy with eyes the color of those gloves was nearly hidden behind him, arms laden with a closed basket he could barely see over. He spared Erich one glance, and then his eyes returned to Lieser, and Erich *knew* that look. He knew what it felt like to wear it. And his own arms went slack and useless, and Mrs. Dennison's mint green dress rolled out of them and settled to the floor behind the front counter like a disappearing trick.

In Erich's head there was a crowd that could not roar, but only murmur, and Kaltherzig's dark shape at the edge of his vision.

"Can you see to this, please?" Lieser said. His English was almost perfect. His boy began to struggle to raise the basket and set it on the counter, and Erich's arms came up to help him. There was one starched white sleeve dangling free.

His eyes went to Lieser's shirt. Gray as his gloves, and elaborately textured.

Erich got as far as realizing that before he was stricken into sort of a slow-motion fit. His instinct to stand *very* still and stare at the floor without moving was warring with the new one that said this was a customer, and he was supposed to be cheerful and animated. So he would raise his hands to get Lieser a slip to leave his name and number, and then lower them to his sides again, caught in this loop.

Lieser watched him do it, grinning. "You're treading in that atrocious dress," he said, with solemn concern. His boy noticed that grin, and was trying to make himself invisible.

Erich stopped. This one was always dangerous, and he always smiled just like that, with many, many teeth. To speak directly to Lieser at all was intolerable. It made his hands shake so hard he wound them into what would've been fists on anyone else. But it came out of him all the same, in a hot rush. "How can you be here?"

"There are these delicious things called airplanes. Perhaps you've heard of them?"

"The police--" Erich stopped, *No, you shall go home.* But he could not imagine that woman saying anything in that tone of voice to this ice creature that was much too close to him.

"They're not even looking for me," Lieser said, patiently, amused by all this fuss. "Well, I suppose they are, halfheartedly, looking for Dietrich Lieser...but they're not looking for me. Though they do have an amusing little file on you, Mr. Kaltherzig. Complete with your place of employment." He shook his head, looking with no interest at the painted mannequins in beautifully detailed gowns. He sighed, dripping imaginary regret. "You didn't learn a thing in Auschwitz, did you? Or maybe too much?"

Everything. They'd told Lieser everything, and here he was.

Lieser watched him realize this and nodded, something of both pity and delight in his smile. "The post office box is charming, though, really it is."

Erich was treading in the green dress again, trying to back away.

"I'll return for the clothes tomorrow." He called over his shoulder, into the clang of the bell, "I'll send him your love!"

And Lieser left, with his boy trailing along in his shadow.

Erich seized the basket, nearly opened it, took one look at all the wide-open clean glass between him and the world. At Lieser's gleaming head disappearing into a long black car. Then he ran.

He shut himself into Blumberg's office, and after a moment's pause locked the door behind him. There the basket sat, as real as wires in his brain, maybe, looking quite wrong among the messy stacks of paper.

The shirts inside were whiter than the fur in Lieser's collar. He seized one and buried his face in it, and inhaled.

They were not Lieser's shirts.

Überschatten

He stood in the dusty office with American sunlight coming in the one high window, smelling Ahren until his lungs were full, holding them full till they burst out an exhale against his will. Then he remembered how the smell had gone from his suitcase after a while, and devoured instead of savoring, inhaled in choppy pants to suck as much of this scent inside himself as he could before it faded.

The bell on the door of the shop would ring, he knew it would. And he'd be a mess of tears and tremors, with an erection. But it did not ring.

When he could think again he took each shirt out one at a time, though he could not resist pressing each to his face before he set it aside, almost in reverence. He was noting tiny issues, a frayed cuff here, a loose button there, trembling with something like joy that these were *Kaltherzig's*, that at long, long last he had a reason to do them perfectly. And that Kaltherzig did not yet seem to have someone else to do these things for him.

About halfway down he began to feel the shape buried at the bottom.

His mouth went dry. He made himself lift up each shirt and examine it, watching the shape grow sharper and sharper under the snowdrift. Watching it become more and more rectangular. Watching it become exactly the sort of thing that would've fit wonderfully in his empty post office box.

The package was plain brown paper, wrapped neatly and tied with string. Erich felt it, and then smelled it, and then after a glance at the high windows he licked it.

It smelled only of paper. It tasted only of paper.

He was afraid of it.

He told himself he would put it under his shirt, unwrap it at home, while he was picking at the tiny knot with his bitten nails. He told

263

himself to tie it closed again immediately, while coiling the string around his fingers and putting the coil in his pocket because it was an unholy relic.

It was a birth certificate for Erich Dahl. And a passport, also for Erich Dahl. The picture was his own, and he was almost certain it was the photograph taken when he'd been arrested in the raid.

He didn't understand until the envelope, a small one, crisp plain white. He opened it, and drew out a one-way ticket to Buenos Aires, departing in six days.

There was a lightning storm inside him. He dragged one hand over his wet face.

Just one of the flashes.

He folded all of it into his billfold, with that magical cream-and-white stack of edges filling up his entire vision.

He did not believe it yet.

He did not believe it while he did what he could for Mrs. Dennison's dress. He did not believe it while he took in two suits, let out a hemline, sewed an endless centipede of minute jet buttons along a lady's evening glove. Somewhere near the wrist he began to believe it, just for an instant, and something happened high in his chest.

He went into the tiny washroom and stood guiding cold water from the tap onto his face with his cupped hands. This did not help enough to reassure him, and he went dripping to draw the windowshades and turned the sign to *Closed*.

The basket was in Mr. Blumberg's office where he'd left it.

When Erich could breathe again, he began to mend Kaltherzig's shirts. It soothed him. His hands stilled, and after a time he felt steady enough to leave Blumberg a brief, apologetic letter claiming illness. It did not feel like a lie. This, this was the lie, this warm shop, this loud city. No wonder he was ill.

He carried the basket to his apartment. He tidied up Ahren's uniform as best he could, and put it at the very bottom of the basket, under neatly executed stacks of mended shirts. He wondered whether Ahren would shut himself away with this gift, and whether he would smell it, and whether in all his trying he'd mostly managed to make it smell like himself.

The next morning he was scrubbed and stiff and strange in his second-best suit, his nails chewed to nubs, fingers needle-stabbed. He could not stop waiting for Lieser to come through the door. Worse, Blumberg was bustling around him, making him want to shriek with tension. The basket sat just inside the back room, one among many on long deep shelves. There was no reason for Blumberg to look inside any of them, and of course, he did not, but Erich could not stop worrying that he *might*. And that was nothing to the fear of what would happen when Lieser returned to retrieve his order.

When the bell finally had the mercy to ring it was not Lieser but his pet boy that came inside. Blumberg was in the back of the shop repairing a scorched wedding gown, prattling on to himself around a mouthful of pins, and Erich was at the counter alone.

The boy did not speak, only exchanged too much American cash for the basket and seized it, scuttled outside with it, fled to a dark sleek automobile growling at the curb.

And that was that. No more soul, now he could only wait.

It was only hours.

The shop's telephone rang. Erich's hands picked it up, and his mouth made the right noises, and there was no reply.

All his nerves did something that made him shake.

He knew it was Kaltherzig.

"Hello?"

Someone would ask about a ballgown, and his heart would break.

Kaltherzig said only, "My boy," and then there was scratchy telephone-line, silence.

Erich's eyes went wet and he and hitched in his breath, and said, "Sir." That was as far as he got. A click; a cigarette lighter. He thought of Kaltherzig smoking at this very second, miles of telephone line and jungle between them instead of oceans and governments, now.

"You're the only experiment that ever worked, I think." Smoke, or noise from the line, or some sound from Kaltherzig he couldn't decipher. "You've been dying without me. Haven't you?"

Tears. It was true, that was exactly it, dying by minutes, dying like slow suffocation. "Yes, yes, yes..."

That smoke-and-breath noise again. "I cured you, didn't I? I told you, you'd never want another man again. And you haven't."

Erich realized that was probably as close to *I love you* as Kaltherzig would ever give him. He sat down on the floor, with an abrupt thump, phone cord yanking up short and only just still reaching his ear.

"I told you I would call you. Come. Or I'll shoot you."

"Yes sir," he said. The click came after that; he was certain of it.

Verdammt

Blumberg wandered back into the storefront, took one look at Erich, opened his mouth and dropped a tinkling rain of pins. Erich let himself be steered to a chair, nodded gratefully in all the right places. He promised to stay properly in bed this time while Blumberg called him a taxicab, pleaded with him not to stop by after the shop closed to see how he was getting on,

Once Erich was in the back seat the world felt familiar, and once Blumberg was out of sight and the car was humming around him he could let himself smile.

He tried his own uniform on. It still fit him.

Then he found his smallest suitcase and began to pack it. The uniform went first, rolled up small inside several pairs of underwear. He packed the lightest clothes he owned. The book of Greek myths. When this tiny space was filled he was eager to make more changes, to unmake this lonely place so that he had nowhere to go but forward.

He hadn't owned much.

He boxed most of it in cartons still here from his move, and wrote *Red Cross* in his too-neat handwriting on each one. Soon his apartment was echoing and empty, even the curtains torn down in a frenzy of ending. He stuffed those into one last box on top of his coping mechanisms. Erich waited until dark and carried that one to the trash cans in the alley outside, buried them deep, thinking, *hydrangeas.*

Kaltherzig would have better terrors than those, somewhere in the hypothetical jungle.

He was lying in his bed, naked, freezing cold because he hadn't left himself enough blankets and he smiled a little in the dark and slid over and put one foot down and then the other and sat down on the floor, lay down on the dusty prickling hardwood with the blanket half over him and

267

half under him, feeling defiant, feeling homesick.

Feeling, aroused.

Erich closed his eyes and licked his hand, and then stroked himself. In his head he was paging through his memories, stained-glass stories that were his most treasured possessions.

In the end it was the first time, the terrible flashbulb time with the phallus mounted on iron. A tool. Equipment. The thudding like the throwing of a spear, jarring his spine, rattling his teeth, thudding him forward, bloodying his knees. He came in his hand, and thought of Kaltherzig whispering *clean* and licked his hand until it was only wet with spit.

Nana wept when Erich told her.

"But he'll kill you," she said, over and over. As if that somehow mattered. "You're too...too *young* to--"

Die, was the shape her mouth made, and the word she would not say.

Yes, yes he was, and that was why he wanted to stop doing it, yesterday. And the frustration of that made him almost angry at her, and when he spoke he was closer to shouting than he could remember ever being in his life.

"Don't you understand? There's no point in being anywhere else! This--" He gestured around them, at this dark damp room filled with smoke, beyond it at New York, beyond that at everything. He would have recognized the gesture if he'd seen it from outside. It was Kaltherzig's. "Nothing is loud enough! Real enough! Good enough!"

He hadn't been shouting, of course, not really. But nearby heads turned towards them, and then uncomfortably away, and he trailed off into his usual meek voice, and then a whisper, and then silence.

Merciless enough. Unsafe enough. Terrible enough.

He could not tell her that he had died in 1943 on a table in Block 10, or in Kaltherzig's basement with his hands behind his back and his wrists bleeding. He could not tell her every night since the searchlights had stopped sending those arrows into the dark had been a mistake, a nightmare, a curse. He did not have the English to tell her something shapeless he was thinking about coroners and midwives, and how similar their functions really were.

"I want it, forever, until the one that finally kills me. I want him to be the last thing I see. I want--"

(the Osiris back, I need the only god who ever)

"I have to—"

(need to, can't wait to)

And he thought: *I'm really going.*

He stood, and Nana understood, and cried harder.

Erich took her hand, and that seemed all wrong. Instead he hugged her, awkward, while she was still sitting, and she hugged him back hard and tight. He kissed her cheek, thinking again of Judith. After a long time she let him go, daubing at her eyes with one manicured hand. "Will you be happy?"

He had no idea if his answer was true.

The airport was even worse than he'd imagined. Everyone was in a hurry, and Erich was learning that his lessons had somehow never gotten around to explaining what a "concourse" might be or whether or not he needed to visit one. There were policemen here, too, or as good as: men in uniforms with motionless faces and restless eyes. The suitcase that had seemed so light when he'd lifted it in his apartment

(everything I own)

quickly became a Herculean labor that his bad shoulder found impossible and his good shoulder found infuriating. He quickly gave up all pretense and just pointed himself at the nearest authority figure.

He found he was trembling, either from fear or exhaustion, but he politely explained he had never flown before, and asked to be directed to the next bewildering step in this journey. The hand came towards him as he'd known it would, and he filled it with the papers-please Kaltherzig had given him.

Please.

He did not need to address this prayer. All his prayers were addressed to one person, and had been for a very long time.

His new papers would be immediately recognized as fakes, and he would immediately be recognized as a dangerous sexual deviant, or some sort of National Socialist sympathizer. He would learn how quickly those policemen could move when they wanted to. Any second now.

That second never came.

Erich spent his first takeoff with his eyes and his teeth squeezed shut tight. The engines were nothing like he had imagined. This shaking deafening thunder began, all around him, holding him, and it climbed until he thought he might scream, but never broke like a thunderclap might to let him breathe again. It only climbed and climbed and climbed, and then there was a helpless, hurtling speed. He realized he had no idea if any of this was *normal*, and then he was too frightened to think.

After eternity, that roaring threat seemed to abate, and he thought of a great dragon lured back into a doze, and kept his eyes tightly shut. They were in the air for several tranquil minutes before he realized they were aloft.

He made himself remember what it had been like to ride a horse with Kaltherzig laughing and the sun on both of them. It was only the ground rushing by below, then as now.

He made himself open his eyes, wanting to watch that gray life falling away. Surely this would hold some terror, but it looked exactly the way it felt—colorless and sullen, too many things in too small a space. The airport, and then the city, and then the dirty smear of landscape was unimportant, oddly distant as though he'd lived there years ago, and not hours.

He watched the disappointing world below fade until it was watercolor-soft and hazed, and to his surprise he felt his eyelids grow

270

heavy. Apparently once you survived the drama of takeoff this was very like being on a train. The hum of the engines and the dry hiss of the ventilation hypnotized him.

He awoke in Atlanta, Georgia.

This airport was different, dirtier and busier, a mess of warm, noisy insanity that made him grin with the bright sense of getting closer to the jungle. There was still snow patched on the ground in the world he'd left behind, frost on the windows of Blumberg's shops in the mornings. Not here.

Erich took off his coat. It would not fit in his suitcase, and he pondered how to carry it before deciding to simply leave it on the bench beside him. He checked in the pockets, and found only gloves. He put them back. Someone who needed a coat would find it, or one of the polished, permanently smiling employees would take it to lost and found.

He didn't care.

He would never see snow again.

He felt safer away from New York and any eyes that had ever known him, and he did something that he knew would cost him sleep if he didn't, and bought a single postcard, a very badly painted peach, and sent it to James and Judith.

I have to go. Thank you for everything.

He wanted to write more, for Judith's sake, but dared not. He wanted to use the word *love*, though it would not quite have been true. It would have become true, if more years had passed. If he had been born in that house that seemed so much colder than his own, but had really been much warmer.

He had been loved there, he thought, as though he were in another world already. But the image that came with that thought was himself, alone in his apartment, with his wrists drawn up behind him.

He left no return address, and only signed it *Erich*.

Scissors. Severed thread. Stitches drawn out. Worldly affairs neatly in order. No more goodbyes for the world behind him, and no help for the Styx he was crossing.

The plane would be shot down by Americans, bored by the lack of targets. Lightning would strike it out of the sky. Something, he was sure, *something* would stop him from reaching his
(beloved)
destination.

This would be his Hell, simply more of this feeling that his skin would split itself for want of Kaltherzig's terrible pressure to hold him together. Alone in bed this sensation had sometimes driven him to extremes of motion that would've looked like a strange slow tantrum or a convulsion to anyone watching.

He found himself squirming in his cramped and sweaty seat. His muscles wound themselves tight, grinding knee against knee, arms knotted across his chest. He was kneading his biceps so hard they ached, rocking a little.

He made himself stop. That was all right.

Tomorrow, Kaltherzig would be there to stop him.

He wanted to watch until the jungle unfurled below him, legendary green and gold, wanted to see America fall away behind him, just another badly made toy like the airports.

The sun did not care what he wanted, it set, and the engines did not care what he wanted, they thrummed their measured roar into his head until he slept again. One more of these motions, as if he were in a stone being skipped across the world.

Up again, and then...down.

The thump of the landing gear unfolding woke him. He blinked, mouth dry, puzzled as to why he was sitting upright. Before he could remember where he was there was a second, lighter thump of the wheels contacting the ground.

Erich scrubbed his face with his hands, flushing to find his chin damp and his hair mussed. He stayed in his cramped and sweaty seat, drawing his feet up nearly underneath himself to let the dour, sunburned man in the window seat clamber past him.

Apparently the bitterly disapproving look of the man was merely the way his face was made, because he took the shoulder of a stewardess and said, "Have a care, I believe this young man is airsick," to her, very softly, but loudly enough for Erich to hear, and then gave him a kindly nod.

He was not airsick. He was terrified.

Once he found himself in Buenos Aires he discovered he had no idea what to do next. He had expected a dirty, frightening place, and found it was little different from New York, except warmer, and cleaner, and filled with strange new smells.

He took a room in a hotel near the airport, and this too, was both familiar and strange. The ceilings were too high, the bed too long and too narrow. That was all right. It wasn't a hotel room, not really. It was a waiting room.

He unstitched the necklace he had made of the collar, and sewed it back on, and put the ring on his forefinger. He waited.

On the fifth night he heard it. He'd been sitting on a bench just outside the hotel, wishing for the first time in his life that he smoked so he might have something to do with his hands, trying to ignore the rising edge of panic inside him when he considered how much money remained in his billfold. Not enough for a return flight. Not enough for many more nights in this hotel, either.

Nowhere will be far enough.
Nothing will save you from me.

And then the sound drifted past him, a trick of the warm light wind, he thought, but he stood and followed it anyway, until he was certain it was no trick.

The "Horst Wessel Lied," loudly and drunkenly sung in fearless German. He orbited that sound of Hell and home until he found the source; a little bar, with no sign and nobody at the door to demand money or a pass.

He hesitated awhile, that song pulling him as though it were a rope around something inside him, and finally walked into the cheery yellow light, the dense, smoky air, the smell of fried potatoes and sweat and oiled wood. He ordered beer, sat sipping it, listened, ached. After seeing others trade this favor he timidly had the bartender buy a round for the table, and after it had been delivered he walked over, smiling, and said "Heil Hitler."

They were suspicious of him, he knew, but almost professionally so, and he was very glad of this. It meant Kaltherzig was safe, or at least safer than Erich had feared. It made him like these men more, or perhaps that was because he hadn't just conversed like this, in German, since he'd gone to America. It was a deep and wonderful relief. Had he ever managed to think in English, really, had the inner translation ever gone away?

He had always dreamed in German.

The locals let them shout and laugh and sing without the first sign of worry. A few of these dark men with their fast difficult not-quite-Spanish came over and said hello, and drinks were traded now and then. All perfectly civil.

A Reichscolony, Ahren said in his ear. And again with the beer and the Schnapps and the songs, and the assurance that everything would be all, right, now, in that soft familiar Fatherland rhythm.

After several more drinks, he found the nerve to show them the ring.

He was too drunk to walk well, and perhaps that was why one of these laughing men took each of his arms, and led him outside. He was wearing Kaltherzig's ring—when had he put it on?--and it was flopping on his hand so that he kept it curled in an almost-fist for fear of losing it.

They were going in the opposite direction of his hotel, or so he thought, but when he tried to say so it only made them laugh harder. Dark streets, nearly deserted and then entirely empty. And then they stopped, and waited.

Someone handed him his suitcase, left behind in that
(waiting room)
hotel, and that was when he began to understand.

The fear unfolding inside him was as bright as joy.

He had expected the truck for so long that when it finally came, it seemed too square and dirty to be real. No Gestapo to escort him out, not even any papers, and the suitcase in his hand.

The back of the truck was the same. There were gaps covered with strong wire along either side, and when the doors closed behind him he heard the grating thump of a solid lock. No danger of escape now, no one to save him, caught, and safe, at long last.

Erich settled with his back to a wall, closed his eyes, covered his face with his collar. Slept. Dreamed of sharp silver rows of instruments, gleaming on white cloth, dreamed the ring coming at him from the dark. Dreamed of home.

Hölle

There was light outside the caged windows of the truck when the terrain-change woke him. Their rattling progress was smoother now, and they had slowed, and his stomach did a lazy somersault inside him. They were...here.

He tried standing on tiptoe, and when that left him still unable to see out he stood on his suitcase. What he saw surprised him; more like Germany than the jungle in his head. Oh, there was a deep green sea in the distance, where he was quite sure there were monsters, but they were on a smoothly paved road, gently curving past wide orderly fields swarming with brown men. An orchard, though he did not recognize the bright fruits gleaming in the lush emerald branches. The road widened, grew smoother still, and he saw the gleaming curve of a greenhouse, a sturdy tidy arc of outbuildings, a columned stone wall and a great metal gate. Here they stopped, and that sour foreign tongue that was not-quite-Spanish was shouted to and from the truck, before the gate swung open. He wobbled, nearly turning an ankle, but before he stumbled down he saw a wide, tall, grand house, with great heavy beams and ornate windows. Again that dizzying sense that he might've been in the German countryside, except that the trees were all wrong, and the sunlight seemed a different color.

They stopped. The lock argued and gave, and the doors were flung open. The brown men seized him and dragged him out, silent, and would not let him bring his suitcase. The house was much larger than he'd imagined, and he was hauled up a wide sweep of steps—there was a porch swing, and alien plants in gleaming pots—and through great polished oak doors, into a place that felt so familiar it made his eyes wet.

He was led down a very German hallway and into a darkened sitting room. The scent struck him as soon as he stepped through the door; that mingling of sandalwood, tobacco, alcohol and Ahren that no perfume shop in New York City had been able to give him in a bottle.

His heart pounded that familiar loud ocean in his head. He stared at the shadow in the armchair before him, thinking, *really really here.*

And there were hands, and the door closing behind him, and that was right, too. He didn't move, and the cinnamon-colored men that had brought him inside were as thick as houses

(guards, they're guards, there are guards again, thank God)

and he stood quiet and still and let hands like shovels pat and steer his limbs, investigate his pockets, searching for something they apparently did not find, then holding him firmly by each arm.

The silence went on so long Erich said, "No one knows I'm here, or ever will." The shaking had found its way into his voice.

Kaltherzig said two words in no language Erich knew. The hands let him go.

The door opened, and then closed, and they were alone.

Kaltherzig turned on the lamp.

He was the same.

Here he was, immovable and still behind those officer eyes. Perhaps more golden, his hair longer, the suit seeming too bare without all the trim, but the tie was still black and his shirt was still white.

His deity was the same.

And oh, God, this vast silent house smelled right and true.

I should kneel.

"Do you know where you are?"

He'd drawn in his breath. He thought a long time. The final guess was "Argentina?"

Kaltherzig laughed. "My kingdom. You were in my kingdom long before you saw this house. "

He shook his head, thinking *page to a knight,* thinking how he'd missed being left with no words except the ones he'd just been given. "A kingdom?"

"My kingdom." The correction was unmistakable, and like water after a drought. "The guard towers are mine, the guards in them are mine. The laboratory is mine. The hospital is mine. The greenhouse is mine.

The fields are mine. The people in them are mine. Walk for days, and what you stand in will still be mine."

Erich drew in his first real breath since the Russians had destroyed the world, shook with all the weight of that hideous freedom finally lifted.

After a long time, Kaltherzig turned off the lamp, and said, "Come here."

Erich swallowed, and remembered how to walk.

"No." And there was Auschwitz in the edge of that. "Not like that."

He knelt, the correctness of it moving through him like morphine, and here was the floor again after all this time. He crawled, and stopped, and waited on his hands and knees.

And then, finally, Kaltherzig asked the first real question, in something like despair. "What are you doing here?"

Erich took a breath to answer, or try to, but Kaltherzig didn't let him. It was as if that first soft question had unleashed all the rest, jagged and ugly as they were.

"Do you understand that I might still shoot you, do you understand that?" Louder. "There are no Russians coming this time, *my* boy, no Americans either, no Red fucking Cross."

This time what Erich heard made him raise his head, and when he saw Ahren's panic it drew him up onto his knees as though he might stand.

He had a very strange feeling in his stomach. He should be the one upset, in tears, afraid, but Ahren was very nearly that, and this feeling inside him was a warm one, almost tender. He was terrified, deeply and deliciously. But there was nothing inside him that felt anything like doubt.

He knew where he was. Home.

He reached up and took Ahren's wrists in each hand, very slowly and very gently, as if he might startle and flee, run into the jungle at any noise or sudden motion. Ahren let him. Erich put those beloved hands to his throat, and arranged them around it, nudging the thumbs patiently against his windpipe. And then he dropped his own hands at his sides. Ahren sat that way, paralyzed, like a waxwork staring at him in horror and wonder.

"Do *you* understand?" Erich said.

Kaltherzig's mouth did something instead of speaking. Then he closed his hands, just a little, just enough, and leaned down and kissed Erich, really kissed him, for the very first time.

Here, at last, were the years he'd been promised. Not two, not ten. There might have been a thousand of them. He waited for Kaltherzig to stop, or to stop him, and there was only this space, hands around his throat, tongue in his mouth, no end to it. No Americans, no Russians, no Red fucking Cross. No one to save him.

It ended only when Kaltherzig ended it, and that was to say with their mouths still tangled together, "Take all of that off."

He'd lost the trick of taking off his clothes without standing upright. He was graceless, and it made his mouth dry until he caught Kaltherzig trying not to smile at his attempt.

He knew to crawl this time without being told. He followed Kaltherzig down a long hallway—wood thumping into his knees, and then a lush rug, and then into a long cool white bathroom. He watched Kaltherzig run a bath. Cold white tile, knees that were soft and had forgotten the way of bruises.

"You should look in the mirror," Kaltherzig said. Erich was watching the line of his back, the shape of those shoulders, with so much thudding in his throat to be said that it was hard to breathe around it.

Real. Really here, hopeless, helpless, home.

Kaltherzig offered his hand, and Erich took it to stand. He looked. The mirror was wide and set low enough for him to see to the tops of his thighs if he stood on tiptoe. There was too long a silence, and he said, "What am I looking at, sir?"

Kaltherzig stood behind him, spidered one hand across his smooth back. "This skin of yours. This is the last time you'll ever see it like this."

Soft, that had forgotten the way of bruises. All the things caught in his throat swelled into words, and he said "I used to--" He stopped. Caught. Looked for a lie to hide in, and found the warm inevitable truth that there was nowhere like that, not anymore.

"Used to--" Kaltherzig prompted, drawing lines on him with one fingertip.

"Mark myself. It was a lonely thing." That last made him blush bright red, and he was looking at himself in the mirror when he did, which made it worse. He covered his face with his hands. Kaltherzig took his wrists and drew his hands away, held his eyes in the mirror. Naked, yes. This was what it meant to be naked.

"You'll tell me. All the lonely things."

"Yes sir." Tears. Easy tears, like something being poured out, no hurry at all in them. Years. He didn't hide them, kept his hands where they had been put.

"Never again." Kaltherzig's hand left his back. Then he felt the edge of one fingernail draw a bright hard line down his spine from the back of neck to his tailbone. Slowly, leisurely, as if Kaltherzig might be unzipping him. "Never again, all this empty, all this waste and want. Not another day, not another moment. Never safe again."

He wanted to say *yes sir*, but his throat moved, and there was no sound, only that spreading sting, that pressure inside him finally finding something to push against, to fail to move.

Steam was rising from the tub, and Erich watched the mirror fog over, until Kaltherzig drew him to the bath.

Das Ende

Anmerkungen des Verfassers

I would like to extend grateful thanks to the following:

To SM Johnson, for being a magnificent editor and a very dear friend, and for being instrumental in getting *Schadenfreude* into actual print. Without you I'd never have navigated all this.

To C.S. for invaluably detailed proofreading and assistance with the German language. Any remaining errors are solely my own. Schnapps are on me if I ever have the pleasure.

To D.F. for fixing the page numbers every time I broke them. You are the best zombie ever.

To my many generous beta readers--Alyssa, James Shacklock, Vivienne Section (vivisextion) and dozens more, for your time, attention, support, and devotion.

To Renee, for telling me what pill would fix numerous ills. Hell help Them now.

To www.gurochan.net for existing and for being the first home *Schadenfreude* found.

Last but never least, to Complete Destruction.

You know why, liebchen.

19 is an Aries who likes old machinery, horror movies, sushi, spaceships, goth and industrial music, shiny things, pointy things, dinosaurs, classic cars, and poisonous plants. He is quite fond of interacting with readers.

www.thenineteen.net

16237339R00171

Printed in Great Britain
by Amazon